ALIEN
S·E·X

ALIEN S⊙E⊙X

Edited by Ellen Datlow

19 Tales by the Masters of Science Fiction and Dark Fantasy

DUTTON  NEW YORK

DUTTON
Published by the Penguin Group
Penguin Books USA Inc., 375 Hudson Street,
New York, New York, 10014, U.S.A.
Penguin Books Ltd, 27 Wrights Lane,
London W8 5TZ, England
Penguin Books Australia Ltd, Ringwood,
Victoria, Australia
Penguin Books Canada Ltd, 2801 John Street,
Markham, Ontario, Canada L3R 1B4
Penguin Books (N.Z.) Ltd, 182–190 Wairau Road,
Auckland 10, New Zealand

Penguin Books Ltd, Registered Offices:
Harmondsworth, Middlesex, England

First published by Dutton,
an imprint of Penguin Books USA Inc.

Published simultaneously in Canada
by Fitzhenry and Whiteside, Limited.

BOMC offers recordings and compact discs, cassettes
and records. For information and catalog write to
BOMR, Camp Hill, PA 17012.

Library of Congress Cataloging-in-Publication Data

Alien sex: 19 tales by the masters of science fiction
and dark fantasy / edited by Ellen Datlow. — 1st ed.
p.   cm.
ISBN 0-525-24863-3
1. Short stories, American.   I. Datlow, Ellen.
PS648.S5A43   1990
813'.0876208353—dc20   89-28528
                                  CIP

Printed in the United States of America
Designed by Steven N. Stathakis

"The Jamesburg Incubus" copyright © 1990 by Scott Baker.

"Dancing Chickens" copyright © 1984 by Edward Bryant. First published in Light Years and
Dark, edited by Michael Bishop. By permission of the author.

"Roadside Rescue" copyright © by Pat Cadigan. First published OMNI Publications
International, Ltd. in 1985. By permission of the author.

For my sister,
Lori

I should like to thank the following people, who in various ways, made the publication of *Alien Sex* possible: Bruce McAllister, Lucius Shepard, Ed Bryant, Harlan Ellison, David Hartwell, Merrilee Heifetz, Jeanne Martinet, and particularly, all the contributors.

In addition, *The Science Fiction Encyclopedia*, edited by Peter Nicholls and John Clute, first edition (1979), was used as a source in my Introduction.

CONTENTS

CONTENTS

WILLIAM
⊙ GIBSON ⊙

FOREWORD: STRANGE ATTRACTORS

This far into the twentieth century, writing science fiction or horror about sex is a tricky proposition. A vast and growing number of the planet's human inhabitants have been infected with a sexually transmitted virus of unknown origin, a terminal disease for which there is no known cure. Considered as a background scenario, this situation is so unprecedentedly grim as to send the bulk of science fiction's folk-futurists, myself included, cringing and yelping back to our warp drives and all the rest of it.

Beam us up, Scotty. (Please.)

Chaos theory, the hot new branch of science that reads as though it tumbled intact from the womb of some vast unwritten Phil Dick novel, suggests that the human immune system currently finds itself in the vicinity of a "strange attractor." Which is to say that the biochemical aspect of humanity dedicated to distinguishing *self* from *other* is already on a greased slide known as the "period-doubling route to chaos," wherein things get *weirder and weirder, faster and faster,* until things *change,* quite utterly, signaling the emergence of a new order. Meanwhile—if there can be a meanwhile in chaos theory—we have real-life scientists intent on downloading human consciousness into mechanical "bodies," injecting subcellular automata into bodies of the old-fashioned kind, and all that other stuff that makes it so hard for science-fiction writers to keep up with the present.

Against that kind of global backdrop, how do you go about writing fiction about the alienness of sex?

A look at the history of *horror* fiction may provide a partial answer. Bram Stoker's *Dracula* is a horror story *about* sex, a Victorian shocker centered on dark drives and addictions of the flesh. H. P. Lovecraft, in his cranky neo-Victorian way, went a similar route, though he lacked Stoker's physicality, Stoker's sense of lust, so that all those oozing floppity horrors from the basements of Arkham seem finally to suggest the result of playing around under the bedclothes. Stephen King, retrofitting the horror novel for the age of MTV, cannily targeted the bad thing, the central obscenity, the dark under all our beds, as *death*. Sexual *paranoia* can still do yeoman duty producing narrative traction, but the thought that we ourselves are sexual beings has lost its power to make us shudder and turn pages.

In the post-King era of horror fiction, we find Anne Rice, whose sulkily erotic reading of Stoker finally brings the potent S&M aspect of the vampire text into overt focus, and Clive Barker, whose postmodern splatter-prose often overlays a disturbingly genuine insight into the nature of human sexual dependence. Rice and Barker have both used horror, to some extent, as an exploratory probe, a conscious technique owing more to modern science fiction than to the pre-Freudian nightmares of Stoker or Lovecraft.

Think of the stories assembled in this collection as exploratory probes—detectors of edges, of hidden recesses, of occluded zones, of the constantly shifting boundaries between self and other, of strange attractors and their stranger fields of influence. Because these are things we speak of when we speak of sex, whether in the best of times or the worst.

ALIEN
S⊙E⊙X

INTRODUCTION

Sexuality, human or otherwise, has not traditionally been a major concern in science fiction— possibly because the genre was originally conceived for young adults. However, there was some early pioneering in the field. In 1952 Philip José Farmer explored the theme of interspecies love and sex in "The Lovers" and Theodore Sturgeon examined the nature of sexual roles in *Venus Plus X* (1960). Then, during the late 1960s and the 1970s, more science-fiction writers began to explore the issues of sexuality and relationships, and authors such as James Tiptree, Jr. ("The Women Men Don't See"), Ursula Le Guin (*The Left Hand of Darkness*), Samuel R. Delaney (*Dhalgren*), Norman Spinrad (*Bug Jack Barron*), Brian Aldiss (*Hothouse*), and J. G. Ballard (*Crash*) wrote major works that treated the subject of sexuality seriously and occasionally explicitly. Part of the reason Harlan Ellison's anthologies *Dangerous Visions* and *Again Dangerous Visions* were such breakthrough volumes was their inclusion of stories on previously taboo subjects. There have been three previous SF anthologies on sexual themes: *Strange Bedfellows: Sex and Science Fiction,* edited by Thomas N. Scortia (1972); *Eros in Orbit,* edited by Joseph Elder (1973); *The Shape of Sex to Come,* edited by Douglas Hill (1978), and a collection, Farmer's *Strange Relations* (1960).

Sex in SF generally deals more often with the obsessions of human sexuality and relationships than it does with actual human-alien sex. For example, John Varley's story "Options" created a society in which anyone could choose to alter their sexuality, physically and emotionally, at will. Le Guin's novel *The Left Hand of Darkness*, while concentrating on gender and its relationship to social and sexual roles, incidentally created the perfect sexuality: the inhabitants of the planet Winter are an androgynous species. During their periodic sexually active phase, they can alter their sexual identities to complement the person to whom they are attracted.

When I first had the idea for this anthology, I honestly intended it to be stories specifically about "alien sex," concentrating on the alien as in "other world." But as the book began to take shape, I realized that what the material was *really* about was the relationships between the *human* sexes and about how male and female humans so often see each other as "alien"—in the sense of "belonging to another country or people; foreign; strange; an outsider" (*Webster's New World Dictionary of the American Language,* college edition, 1966). *Alien Sex* offers a template for human relationships.

The stories herein encompass many of the ways the sexes perceive each other and deal (or don't deal) with each other, even when actual, off-world aliens are depicted. Most were written since the 1970s, when feminism changed forever the way men and women (in the United States at least) relate to one another. Since then, relationships between the sexes have continued to be in flux, making for "interesting times," as in the ancient Chinese curse. What do women want? What do men want? Indeed, do we want the same things? Less from design than circumstance, the stories are roughly balanced between male and female writers. While I don't think that on the whole this anthology is particularly downbeat, I do think it gives a rather dark view of male/female relationships. Obviously, *both* sexes feel this way, and perhaps that in itself lends hope to the future of human sexuality.

My greatest problem in putting together the anthology was to find the perfect title—the best in my view, *Strange Bedfellows,* had already been used. I came up with *Dark Desires* but was persuaded that it sounded too much like a Gothic romance. Then I asked various writers for suggestions. The following were offered: *Inter-*

stellarcourse, Love with the Proper Alien, Love Without Feet, Love Is a Many-Headed Thing, Strange Bedthings, In Bed with Darkness, Close Encounters of Another Kind, Looking for Mr. Goodtentacle, Loving the Alien, Bems, Boobs & Bimbos, Fucking Weird, Bedrooms to the Stars, Dangerous Virgins—you get the idea. After much thought, my title of choice was *Off Limits: Sex and the Alien.* Unfortunately, when my agent submitted the anthology, she (and I, I admit) kept calling it the "alien sex" anthology, which led my editor at Dutton to refer to it that way to her colleagues. Everyone loved it and it stuck. Thus, you have the genesis of a very catchy title (after all, you *do* have the book in your hands, don't you) for a thought-provoking book. The stories here may intrigue, horrify, and possibly offend you, but I guarantee they won't bore you.

LEIGH
⊙ KENNEDY ⊙

HER FURRY FACE

Leigh Kennedy was born in Denver, lived in Austin for five years, and now lives in a village in Wiltshire, England. She started selling stories in 1976. Her first novel, The Journal of Nicholas the American, *and her collection,* Faces (Atlantic Monthly Press), *were published in 1986 and 1987, respectively. Her second novel,* Saint Hiroshima (Harcourt, Brace & Jovanovich), *was just recently published.*

"Her Furry Face" is for me the story that got away. In 1982, I had recently been promoted to Fiction Editor at OMNI *and was still a bit timid about publishing stories that might cause offense, so I decided against buying this story. It later made the Nebula ballot, and I've always regretted my decision. And yes, "Her Furry Face" most definitely* will *be considered offensive by some readers.*

Douglas was embarrassed when he saw Annie and Vernon mating.

He'd seen hours of sex between orangutans, but this time was different. He'd never seen *Annie* doing it. He stood in the shade of the pecan tree for a moment, shocked, iced tea glasses sweating in his hand, then he backed around the corner of the brick building. He was confused. The cicadas seemed louder than usual, the sun hotter, and the squeals of pleasure from the apes strange.

He walked back to the front porch and sat down. His mind

still saw the two giant mounds of red-orange fur moving together like one being.

When the two orangs came back around, Douglas thought he saw smugness in Vernon's face. Why not, he thought? I guess I would be smug, too.

Annie flopped down on the grassy front yard and crossed one leg over the other, her abdomen bulging high; she gazed upward into the heavy white sky.

Vernon bounded toward Douglas. He was young and red-chocolate colored. His face was still slim, without the older orang-utan jowls yet.

"Be polite," Douglas warned him.

"Drink tea, please?" Vernon signed rapidly, the fringe on his elbows waving. "Dry as bone."

Douglas handed Vernon one of the glasses of tea, though he'd brought it out for Annie. The handsome nine-year-old downed it in a gulp. "Thank you," he signed. He touched the edge of the porch and withdrew his long fingers. "Could fry egg," he signed, and instead of sitting, swung out hand-over-hand on the ropes between the roof of the schoolhouse and the trees. It was a sparse and dry substitute for the orang's native rain forest.

He's too young and crude for Annie, Douglas thought.

"Annie," Douglas called. "Your tea."

Annie rolled onto one side and lay propped on an elbow, staring at him. She was lovely. Fifteen years old, her fur was glossy and coppery, her small yellow eyes in the fleshy face expressive and intelligent. She started to rise up toward him, but turned toward the road.

The mail jeep was coming down the highway.

In a blurred movement, she set off at a four-point gallop down the half-mile drive toward the mailbox. Vernon swung down from his tree and followed, making a small groan.

Reluctant to go out in the sun, Douglas put down the tea and followed the apes down the drive. By the time he got near them, Annie was sitting with mail sorted between her toes, holding an opened letter in her hands. She looked up with an expression on her face that he'd never seen—it could have been fear, but it wasn't.

She handed the letter to Vernon, who pestered her for it. "Douglas," she signed, "they want to buy my story."

* * *

Therese lay in the bathwater, her knees sticking up high, her hair floating beside her face. Douglas sat on the edge of the tub; as he talked to her he was conscious that he spoke a double language—the one with his lips and the other with his hands.

"As soon as I called Ms. Young, the magazine editor, and told her who Annie was, she got really excited. She asked me why we didn't send a letter explaining it with the story, so I told her that Annie didn't want anyone to know first."

"Did Annie decide that?" Therese sounded skeptical, as she always seemed to when Douglas talked about Annie.

"We talked about it and she wanted it that way." Douglas felt that resistance from Therese. Why she never understood, he didn't know, unless she did it to provoke him. She acted as though she thought an ape was still just an ape, no matter what he or she could do. "Anyway," he said, "she talked about doing a whole publicity thing to the hilt—talk shows, autograph parties. You know. But Dr. Morris thinks it would be better to keep things quiet."

"Why?" Therese sat up; her legs went underwater and she soaped her arms.

"Because she'd be too nervous. Annie, I mean. It might disrupt her education to become a celebrity. Too bad. Even Dr. Morris knows that it would be great for fund-raising. But I guess we'll let the press in some."

Therese began to shampoo her hair. "I brought home that essay that Sandy wrote yesterday. The one I told you about. If she were an orangutan instead of just a deaf kid, she could probably get it published in *Fortune*." Therese smiled.

Douglas stood. He didn't like the way Therese headed for the old argument—no matter what one of Therese's deaf students did, if Annie could do it one-one-hundredth as well, it was more spectacular. Douglas knew it was true, but why Therese was so bitter about it, he didn't understand.

"That's great," he said, trying to sound enthusiastic.

"Will you wash my back?" she asked.

He crouched and absently washed her. "I'll never forget Annie's face when she read that letter."

"Thank you," Therese said. She rinsed. "Do you have any plans for this evening?"

"I've got work to do," he said, leaving the bathroom. "Would you like me to work in the bedroom so you can watch television?"

After a long pause, she said, "No, I'll read."

He hesitated in the doorway. "Why don't you go to sleep early? You look tired."

She shrugged. "Maybe I am."

In the playroom at the school, Douglas watched Annie closely. It was still morning, though late. In the recliner across the room from him, she seemed a little sleepy. Staring out the window, blinking, she marked her place in Pinkwater's *Fat Men from Space* with a long brown finger.

He had been thinking about Therese, who'd been silent and morose that morning. Annie was never morose, though often quiet. He wondered if Annie was quiet today because she sensed that Douglas was not happy. When he'd come to work, she'd given him an extra hug.

He wondered if Annie could have a crush on him, like many schoolgirls have on their teachers. Remembering her mating with Vernon days before, he idly wandered into a fantasy of touching her and gently, gently moving inside her.

The physical reaction to his fantasy embarrassed him. *God, what am I thinking?* He shook himself out of the reverie, averting his gaze for a few moments, until he'd gotten control of himself again.

"Douglas," Annie signed. She walked erect, towering, to him and sat down on the floor at his feet. Her flesh folded onto her lap like dough.

"What?" he asked, wondering suddenly if orangutans were telepathic.

"Why you say my story children's?"

He looked blankly at her.

"Why not send *Harper's*?" she asked, having to spell out the name of the magazine.

He repressed a laugh, knowing it would upset her. "It's . . . it's the kind of story children would like."

"Why?"

He sighed. "The level of writing is . . . *young*. Like you, sweetie." He stroked her head, looking into the small intense eyes. "You'll get more sophisticated as you grow."

8

"I smart as you," she signed. "You understand me always because I talk smart.

Douglas was dumbfounded by her logic.

She tilted her head and waited. When Douglas shrugged, she seemed to assume victory and returned to her recliner.

Dr. Morris came in. "Here we go," she said, handing him the paper and leaving again.

Douglas skimmed the page until he came to an article about the "ape author." He scanned it. It contained one of her flashpoints; this and the fact that she was irritable from being in estrus, made him consider hiding it. But that wouldn't be right.

"Annie," he said softly.

She looked up.

"There's an article about you."

"Me read," she signed, putting her book on the floor. She came and crawled up on the sofa next to him. He watched her eyes as they jerked across every word. He grew edgy. She read on.

Suddenly she took off as if from a diving board. He ran after her as she bolted out the door. The stuffed dog which had always been a favorite toy was being shredded in those powerful hands even before he knew she had it. Annie screamed as she pulled the toy apart, running into the yard.

Terrified by her own aggression, she ran up the tree with stuffing falling like snow behind her.

Douglas watched as the shade filled with foam rubber and fake fur. The tree branches trembled. After a long while, she stopped pummeling the tree and sat quietly.

She spoke to herself with her long ape hand. "Not animal," she said, "not animal."

Douglas suddenly realized that Therese was afraid of the apes.

She watched Annie warily as the four of them strolled along the edge of the school acreage. Douglas knew that Therese didn't appreciate the grace of Annie's muscular gait as he did; the sign language that passed between them was as similar to the Amslan that Therese used for her deaf children as British to Jamaican. Therese couldn't appreciate Annie in creative conversation.

It wasn't good to be afraid of the apes, no matter how educated they were.

He had invited her out, hoping it would please her to be

included in his world here. She had only visited briefly twice
before.

Vernon lagged behind them, snapping pictures now and then
with the expensive but hardy camera modified for his hands.
Vernon took several pictures of Annie and one of Douglas, but only
when Therese had separated from him to peer between the rushes
at the edge of the creek.

"Annie," Douglas called, pointing ahead. "A cardinal. The
red bird."

Annie lumbered forward. She glanced back to see where
Douglas pointed, then stood still, squatting. Douglas walked beside her and they watched the bird.

It flew.

"Gone," Annie signed.

"Wasn't it pretty, though?" Douglas asked.

They ambled on. Annie stopped often to investigate shiny bits
of trash or large bugs. They didn't come this far from the school
much. Vernon whizzed past them, a dark auburn streak of youth-
ful energy.

Remembering Therese, Douglas turned. She sat on a stump
far behind. He was annoyed. He'd told her to wear her jeans and a
straw hat because there would be grass burrs and hot sun. But
there she sat, bareheaded, wearing shorts, miserably rubbing at
her ankles.

He grunted impatiently. Annie looked up at him. "Not you,"
he said, stroking her fur. She patted his butt.

"Go on," Douglas said, turning back. When he came to
Therese, he said, "What's the problem?"

"No problem." She stood, and started forward without looking at him. "I was just resting."

Annie had paused to poke at something on the ground with a
stick. Douglas quickened his step. Even though his students were
smart, they had orangutan appetites. He always worried that they
would eat something that would sicken them. "What is it?" he
called.

"Dead cat," Vernon signed back. He took a picture as Annie
flipped the carcass with her stick.

Therese hurried forward. "Oh, poor kitty . . ." she said,
kneeling.

Annie had seemed too absorbed in poking the cat to notice Therese approach; only a quick eye could follow her leap. Douglas was stunned.

Both screamed. It was over.

Annie clung to Douglas's legs, whimpering.

"Shit!" Therese said. She lay on the ground, rolling from side to side, holding her left arm. Blood dripped from between her fingers.

Douglas pushed Annie back. "That was bad, *very bad*," he said. "Do you hear me?"

Annie sank down on her rump and covered her head. She hadn't gotten a child-scolding for a long time. Vernon stood beside her, shaking his head, signing, "Not wise, baboon-face."

"Stand up," Douglas said to Therese. "I can't help you right now."

Therese was pale, but dry-eyed. Clumsily, she stood and grew even paler. A hunk of flesh hung loosely from above her elbow, meaty and bleeding. "Look."

"Go on. Walk back to the house. We'll come right behind you." He tried to keep his voice calm, holding a warning hand on Annie's shoulder.

Therese moaned, catching her breath. "It hurts," she said, but stumbled on.

"We're coming," Douglas said sternly. "Just walk and— Annie, don't you dare step out of line."

They walked silently, Therese ahead, leaving drops of blood in the dirt. The drops got larger and closer together. Once, Annie dipped her finger into a bloody spot and sniffed her fingertip.

Why can't things just be easy and peaceful, he wondered. Something always happens. *Always.* He should have known better than to bring Therese around Annie. Apes didn't understand that vulnerable quality that Therese was made of. He himself didn't understand it, though at one time he'd probably been attracted to it. No—maybe he'd never really seen it until it was too late. He'd only thought of Therese as "sweet" until their lives were too tangled up to keep clear of it.

Why couldn't she be as tough as Annie? Why did she always take everything so seriously?

They reached the building. Douglas sent Annie and Vernon

to their rooms and guided Therese to the infirmary. He watched as Jim, their all-purpose nurse and veterinary assistant, examined her arm. "I think you should probably have stitches."

He left the room to make arrangements.

Therese looked at Douglas, holding the gauze over her still-bleeding arm. "Why did she bite me?" she asked.

Douglas didn't answer. He couldn't think of how to say it.

"Do you have any idea?" she asked.

"You asked for it, all your wimping around."

"*I* . . ."

Douglas saw the anger rising in her. He didn't want to argue now. He wished he'd never brought her. He'd done it for her, and she ruined it. All ruined.

"Don't start," he said simply, giving her a warning look.

"But, Douglas, I didn't do anything."

"Don't start," he repeated.

"I see now," she said coldly. "Somehow it's my fault again."

Jim returned with his supplies.

"Do you want me to stay?" Douglas asked. He suddenly felt a pang of guilt, realizing that she was actually hurt enough for all this attention.

"No," she said softly.

And her eyes looked far, far from him as he left her.

On the same day that the largest donation ever came to the school, a television news team came out to tape.

Douglas could tell that everyone was excited. Even the chimps that lived on the north half of the school hung on the fence and watched the TV van being unloaded. The reporter decided upon the playroom as the best location for the taping, though she didn't seem to relish sitting on the floor with the giant apes. People went over scripts, strung cords, microphones, set up hot lights, and discussed angles and sound while pointing at the high ceiling's jungle-gym design. All this to talk to a few people and an orangutan.

They brought Annie's desk into the playroom, contrary to Annie's wishes. Douglas explained that it was temporary, that these people would go away after they talked a little. Douglas and Annie stayed outside as long as possible and played Tarzan around the big tree. He tickled her. She grabbed him as he swung from a limb. "Kagoda?" she signed, squeezing him with one arm.

"Kagoda!" he shouted, laughing.

They relaxed on the grass. Douglas was hot. He felt flushed all over. "Douglas," Annie signed, "they read story?"

"Not yet. It isn't published yet."

"Why come talk?" she asked.

"Because you wrote it and sold it and people like to interview famous authors." He groomed her shoulder. "Time to go in," he said, seeing a wave from inside.

Annie picked him up in a big hug and carried him in.

"Here it is!" Douglas called to Therese, and turned on the video-recorder.

First, a long shot of the school from the dusty drive, looking only functional and square, without personality. The reporter's voice said, "Here, just southeast of town, is a special school with unusual young students. The students here have little prospect for employment when they graduate, but millions of dollars each year fund this institution."

A shot of Annie at her typewriter, picking at the keyboard with her long fingers; a sheet of paper is slowly covered with large block letters.

"This is Annie, a fifteen-year-old orangutan, who has been a student with the school for five years. She graduated with honors from another "ape school" in Georgia before coming here. And now Annie has become a writer. Recently, she sold a story to a children's magazine. The editor who bought the story didn't know that Annie was an orangutan until after she had selected the story for publication."

Annie looked at the camera uncertainly.

"Annie can read and write, and understand spoken English, but she cannot speak. She uses a sign language similar to the one the hearing-impaired use." Change in tone from narrative to interrogative. "Annie, how did you start writing?"

Douglas watched himself on the small screen watching Annie sign, "Teacher told me write." He saw himself grin, eyes shift slightly toward the camera, but generally watching Annie. His name and "Orangutan Teacher" appeared on the screen. The scene made him uneasy.

"What made you send in Annie's story for publication?" the reporter asked.

Douglas signed to Annie, she came to him for a hug, and turned a winsome face to the camera. "Our administrator, Dr. Morris, and I both read it. I commented that I thought it was as good as any kid's story, so Dr. Morris said, 'Send it in.' The editor liked it." Annie made a "pee" sign to Douglas.

Then, a shot of Dr. Morris in her office, a chimp on her lap, clapping her brown hands.

"Dr. Morris, your school was established five years ago by grants and government funding. What is your purpose here?"

"Well, in the last few decades, apes—mostly chimpanzees like Rose here—have been taught sign language experimentally. Mainly to prove that apes could indeed use language." Rosie put the tip of her finger through the gold hoop in Dr. Morris's ear. Dr. Morris took her hand away gently. "We were established with the idea of *educating* apes, a comparable education to the primary grades." She looked at the chimp. "Or however far they will advance."

"Your school has two orangutans and six chimpanzees. Are there differences in their learning?" the reporter asked.

Dr. Morris nodded emphatically. "Chimpanzees are very clever, but the orang has a different brain structure, which allows for more abstract reasoning. Chimps learn many things quickly, orangs are slower. But the orangutan has the ability to learn in greater depth."

Shot of Vernon swinging in the ropes in front of the school.

Assuming that Vernon is Annie, the reporter said, "Her teacher felt from the start that Annie was an especially promising student. The basic sentences that she types out on her typewriter are simple but original entertainment."

Another shot of Annie at the typewriter.

"If you think this is just monkey business, you'd better think again. Tolstoy, watch out!"

Depressed by the lightness, brevity, and the stupid "monkey-business" remark, Douglas turned off the television.

He sat for a long time. Whenever Therese had gone to bed, she had left him silently. After a half hour of staring at the blank screen, he rewound his video recorder and ran it soundlessly until Annie's face appeared.

And then froze it. He could almost feel again the softness of her halo of red hair against his chin.

* * *

He couldn't sleep.

Therese had rumpled her way out of the sheet and lay on her side, her back to him. He looked at the shape of her shoulder and back, downward to the dip of the waist, up the curve of her hip. Her buttocks were round ovals, one atop the other. Her skin was sleek and shiny in the filtered streetlight coming through the window. She smelled slightly of shampoo and even more slightly of female.

What he felt for her anyone would call "love," when he thought of her generally. And yet, he found himself helplessly angry with her most of the time. When he thought he could amuse her, it would end with her feelings being hurt for some obscure reason. He heard cruel words come barging out of an otherwise gentle mouth. She took everything seriously; mishaps and misunderstandings occurred beyond his control, beyond his repair.

Under this satiny skin, she was troubled and tense. A lot of sensitivity and fear. He had stopped trying to gain access to what had been the happier parts of her person, not understanding where they had gone. He had stopped wanting to love her, but he didn't *not* want to love her, either. It just didn't seem to matter.

Sometimes, he thought, it would be easier to have someone like Annie for a wife.

Annie.

He loved her furry face. He loved the unconditional joy in her face when she saw him. It was always there. She was bright and warm and unafraid. She didn't read things into what he said, but listened and talked with him. They were so natural together. Annie was so filled with vitality.

Douglas withdrew his hand from Therese, whose skin seemed a bare blister of dissatisfaction.

He lay on the floor of the apes' playroom with the fan blowing across his chest. He held Annie's report on Lawrence's *Sons and Lovers* by diagonal corners to keep it from flapping.

Annie lazily swung from bars criss-crossing the ceiling.

"Paul wasn't happy at work because the boss looked over his shoulder at his handwriting," she had written. "But he was happy again later. His brother died and his mother was sad. Paul got sick.

He was better and visited his friends again. His mother died and his friends didn't tickle him anymore."

Douglas looked over the top of the paper at Annie. True, it was the first time she'd read an "adult" novel, but he'd expected something better than this. He considered asking her if Vernon had written the report for her, but thought better of it.

"Annie," he said, sitting up. "What do you think this book is really about?"

She swung down and landed on the sofa. "About man," she said.

Douglas waited. There was no more. "But what about it? Why this man instead of another? What was special about him?"

Annie rubbed her hands together, answerless.

"What about his mother?"

"She help him," Annie answered in a flurry of dark fingers. "Especially when he paint."

Douglas frowned. He looked at the page again, disappointed.

"What I do?" Annie asked, worried.

He tried to brighten up. "You did just fine. It was a hard book."

"Annie smart," the orang signed. "Annie smart."

Douglas nodded. "I know."

Annie rose, then stood on her legs, looking like a two-story fuzzy building, teetering from side to side. "Annie smart. Writer. Smart," she signed. "Write book. Best-seller."

Douglas made a mistake. He laughed. Not as simple as a human laughing at another, this was an act of aggression. His bared teeth and uncontrolled guff-guff struck out at Annie. He tried to stop.

She made a gulping sound and galloped out of the room.

"Wait, Annie!" He chased after her.

By the time he got outside she was far ahead. He stopped running when his chest hurt and trotted slowly through the weeds toward her. She sat forlornly far away and watched him come.

When he was near, she signed, "hug," three times.

Douglas collapsed, panting, his throat raw. "Annie, I'm sorry," he said. "I didn't mean it." He put his arms around her.

She held on to him.

"I love you, Annie. I love you so much I don't want ever to

hurt you. Ever, ever, ever. I want to be with you all the time. Yes, you're smart and talented and good." He kissed her tough face.

Whether forgotten or forgiven, the hurt of his laughter was gone from her eyes. She held him tighter, making a soft sound in her throat, a sound for him.

They lay together in the crackling yellow weeds, clinging. Douglas felt his love physically growing for her. More passionately than ever before in his life, he wanted to make love to her. He touched her. He felt that she understood what he wanted, that her breath on his neck was anticipation. A consummation as he'd never imagined, the joining of their species in language and body. Not dumb animal-banging but mutual love. . . . He climbed over her and hugged her back.

Annie went rigid when he entered her.

Slowly, she rolled away from him, but he held on to her. "No." A horrible grimace came across her face that raised the hairs on the back of Douglas's neck. "Not you," she said.

She's going to kill me, he thought.

His passion declined; Annie disentangled herself and walked away.

He sat for a moment, stunned at what he'd done, stunned at what had happened, wondering what he would do the rest of his life with the memory of it. Then he zipped up his pants.

Staring at his dinner plate, he thought, it's just the same as if I had been rejected by a woman. I'm not the kind that goes for bestiality. I'm not some farm boy who can't find someplace to put it.

His hands could still remember the matted feel of her fur; tucked in his groin was the memory of being in an alien place. It had made him throw up out in the field that afternoon, and after that he'd come straight home. He hadn't even said good-night to the orangs.

"What's the matter?" Therese asked.

He shrugged.

She half rose out of her chair to kiss him on the temple. "You don't have a fever, do you?"

"No."

"Can I do something to make you feel better?" Her hand slid along his thigh.

He stood up. "Stop it."

She sat still. "Are you in love with another woman?"

Why can't she just leave me alone? "No. I have a lot on my mind. There's a lot going on."

"It never was like this, even when you were working on your thesis."

"Therese," he said, with what he felt was undeserved patience, "just leave me alone. It doesn't help with you at me all the time."

"But I'm scared, I don't know what to do. You act like you don't want me around."

"All you do is criticize me." He stood and took his dishes to the sink.

Slowly, she trailed after him, carrying her plate. "I'm just trying to understand. It's my life, too."

He said nothing and she walked away as if someone had told her not to leave footsteps.

In the bathroom, he stripped and stood under the shower a long time. He imagined that Annie's smell clung to him. He felt that Therese could smell it on him.

What have I done, what have I done . . .

And when he came out of the shower, Therese was gone.

He had considered calling in sick, but he knew that it would be just as miserable to stay around the house and think about Annie, think about Therese, and worse, to think about himself.

He dressed for work, but couldn't eat breakfast. Realizing that his pain showed, he straightened his shoulders, but found them drooping again as he got out of the car at work.

With some fear, he came through the office. The secretary greeted him with rolled eyes. "Someone's given out our number again," she said as the phone buzzed. Another line was on hold. "This morning there was a man standing at the window watching me until Gramps kicked him off the property."

Douglas shook his head in sympathy with her and approached the orang's door. He felt nauseated again.

Vernon sat at the typewriter, most likely composing captions for his photo album. He didn't get up to greet Douglas, but gave him an evaluative stare.

Douglas patted his shoulder. "Working?" he asked.

"Like dog," Vernon said, and resumed typing.

Annie sat outside on the back porch. Douglas opened the door and stood beside her. She looked up at him, but—like Vernon—made no move toward the customary hug. The morning was still cool, the shadow of the building still long in front of them. Douglas sat down.

"Annie," he said softly. "I'm sorry. I'll never do it again. You see, I felt . . ." He stopped. It wasn't any easier than it had been to talk to Oona, or Wendy, or Shelley, or Therese. . . . He realized that he didn't understand her any more than he'd understood them. Why had she rejected him? What was she thinking? What would happen from now on? Would they be friends again?

"Oh, hell," he said. He stood. "It won't happen again."

Annie gazed away into the trees.

He felt strained all over, especially in his throat. He stood by her for a long time.

"I don't want write stories," she signed.

Douglas stared at her. "Why?"

"Don't want." She seemed to shrug.

Douglas wondered what had happened to the confident ape who'd planned to write a best-seller the day before. "Is that because of me?"

She didn't answer.

"I don't understand," he said. "Do you want to write it down for me? Could you explain it that way?"

"No," she signed, "can't explain. Don't want."

He signed. "What *do* you want?"

"Sit tree. Eat bananas, chocolate. Drink brandy." She looked at him seriously. "Sit tree. Day, day, day, week, month, year."

Christ almighty, he thought, she's having a goddamned existential crisis. All the years of education. All the accomplishments. All the hopes of an entire field of primatology. All shot to hell because of a moody ape. It can't just be me. This would have happened sooner or later, but maybe . . . He thought of all the effort he would have to make to repair their relationship. It made him tired.

"Annie, why don't we just ease up a little on your work. You can rest. Today. You can go sit in the tree all of today and I'll bring you a glass of wine."

She shrugged again.

Oh, I've botched it, he thought. What an idiot. He felt a pain coming back, a pain like poison, without a focal point but shooting through his heart and hands, making him dizzy and short of breath.

At least she doesn't hate me, he thought, squatting to touch her hand.

She bared her teeth.

Douglas froze. She slid away from him and headed for the trees.

He sat alone at home and watched the newscast. In a small midwestern town they burned the issues of the magazine with Annie's story in it.

A heavy woman in a windbreaker was interviewed with the bonfire in the background. "I don't want my children reading things that weren't even written by humans. I have human children and this godless ape is not going to tell its stories to them."

A quick interview with Dr. Morris, who looked even more tired and introverted than usual. "The story is a very innocent tale, told by an innocent personality. Annie is not a beast. I really don't think she has any ability for, or intention of, corruption . . ."

He turned the television off. He picked up the phone and dialed one of Therese's friends. "Jan, have you heard from Therese yet?"

"No, sure haven't."

"Well, let me know, okay?"

"Sure."

He thought vaguely about trying to catch her at work, but he left earlier in the morning and came home later in the evening than she did.

Looking at her picture on the wall, he thought of when they had first met, first lived together. There had been a time when he'd loved her so much he'd been bursting with it. Now he felt empty, but curious about where she was. He didn't want her to hate him, but he still didn't know if he could talk to her about what had happened. The idea that she would sit and listen to him didn't seem realistic.

Even Annie wouldn't listen to him anymore.

He was alone. He'd done a big, dumb, terrible thing and

wished he hadn't. It would have been different if Annie had reciprocated, if somehow they could have become lovers. Then it would have been them against the world, a new kind of relationship. The first intelligent interspecial love affair . . .

But Annie didn't seem any different than Therese, after all. Annie was no child. She'd given him all those signals, flirting, then not carrying through. Acting like he'd raped her or something. She didn't really have any more interest in him than Dr. Morris would in Vernon. I couldn't have misunderstood, could I? he wondered.

He was alone. And without Annie's consent, he was just a jerk who'd screwed an ape.

"I made a mistake," he said aloud to Therese's picture. "So let's forget it."

But even he couldn't forget.

"Dr. Morris wants to see you," the secretary said as he came in.

"Okay." He changed course for the administrative office. He whistled. In the past few days, Annie had been cool, but he felt that everything would settle down eventually. He felt better. Wondering what horrors or marvels Dr. Morris had to share with him, he knocked at her door and peered through the glass window. Probably another magazine burning, he thought.

She signaled him to come in. "Hello, Douglas."

Annie, he thought, *something's happened.*

He stood until she motioned him to sit down. She looked at his face several seconds. "This is difficult for me," she said.

She's discovered me, he thought. But he put that aside, figuring it was a paranoia that made him worry. There's no way. No way. I have to calm down or I'll show it.

She held up a photograph.

There it was—a dispassionate and cold document of that one moment in his life. She held it up to him like an accusation. It shocked him as if it hadn't been himself.

Defiance forced him to stare at the picture instead of looking for compassion in Dr. Morris's eyes. He knew exactly where the picture had come from.

Vernon and his new telephoto lens.

He imagined the image of his act rising up in a tray of

chemicals. Slowly, he looked away from it. Dr. Morris could not know how he had changed since that moment. He could make no protest or denial.

"I have no choice," Dr. Morris said flatly. "I'd always thought that even if you weren't good with people, at least you worked well with the apes. Thank God Henry, who does Vernon's dark-room work, has promised not to say anything."

Douglas was rising from the chair. He wanted to tear the picture out of her hands because she still held it up to him. He didn't want to see it. He wanted her to ask him if he had changed, that it would never happen again, that he understood he'd been wrong.

But her eyes were flat and shuttered against him. "We'll send your things," she said.

He paused at his car and saw two big red shapes—one coppery orange, one chocolate red—sitting in the trees. Vernon bellowed out a groan that ended with an alien burbling. It was a wild sound full of the jungle and steaming rain.

Douglas watched Annie scratch herself and look toward chimps walking the land beyond their boundary fence. As she started to turn her gaze in his direction, he ducked into his car.

Angrily driving away, Douglas thought, why should an ape understand me any better than a human?

About "Her Furry Face": I had been interested in chimpanzees after reading Jane Goodall's books, and this carried over to an interest in language-using apes such as Lucy and Koko. My first glimmering of the story was to write something funny and satirical about an orangutan who became a celebrity best-selling author. As with many stories, two ideas collided and made something more complete. I had a character in mind whose roaming lover found everything about her irritating and everyone else wonderful. However, I couldn't quite grip the point of it all. So Douglas became a bridge between the two characters, but in my view the most interesting because of his tragic inability to love in a real way.

LEIGH KENNEDY

RICK
⊙ WILBER ⊙

WAR BRIDE

Rick Wilber's science fiction has appeared in Analog, Asimov's, *and the* Chrysalis *anthology series, as well as several university-supported literary magazines. He is coeditor of* Subtropical Speculations, *an anthology of Florida-themed science fiction (*Pineapple Press*). His mainstream poetry and short stories have appeared in a variety of literary magazines in Great Britain and the United States. He teaches at the University of South Florida and also works at the* Tampa Tribune, *where he edits, writes, and is coordinator of the* Tribune's *short story and poetry supplement,* Fiction Quarterly.*

"War Bride" makes unusual use of the "what if" motif in traditional science fiction.

James packs his bag.

Ahab, Huck, Yossarian, Nick Adams, even Hornblower goes in, along with six toothbrushes, a handful of postcards with various sunsets and palm trees and bathing-suited blondes, and four like-new baseballs. He would like to pack his basketball, but it just won't fit.

He needs them—the books, the cards, the baseballs. He won't be coming back, and he's picked the things that will last the longest and serve him the best.

But no clothes. Whistle made that perfectly clear. No clothes. The Pashi can't stand those Earthie clothes, and James won't need them where he's going. Whistle will take care of James's attire, as she takes care of most everything else.

He does pack his prosthetic lengthener. Whistle has promised him an operation once they reach the home world, and then he won't need the lengthener anymore. But the trip will take weeks, James has been told, so the lengthener comes along.

James stands, his head nearly touching the light fixture in the apartment's living area. James is very tall, nearly seven-foot-three. The Pashi are even taller, and thin, but James is about as big as Earthies get, and Whistle has developed a real fondness for him. That's why Whistle has decided to bring him along, now that the Pashi are leaving.

James looks out the sliding glass doors toward the Gulf of Mexico. The Pashi landing rigs and comm relays are just visible on the horizon line. That's why Whistle bought James this apartment on the seventh floor, Gulf Boulevard, St. Petersburg Beach; so they could see the rigs and towers against the setting sun when Whistle came to play with her American pet.

Whistle is beautiful, in her own damp Pashi way. James knows he is lucky to have been chosen by her, lucky to be able to pack his one small bag with anything he can think of that will last forever on another world. Lucky guy, he tells himself forcefully, trying to make the sentiment stick. Lucky guy.

James has not always felt so lucky, so wanted. For most of his life, James has felt alone. He thinks about his loneliness as he looks out the sliding glass doors. All the years of it. Too tall, too many books or too much basketball, too many stares and too many expectations. Only Tom has found the way through all the incongruities, all the implausibilities to be his friend. In all those twenty-eight years, only Tom has been willing to think of James as a friend instead of a marketable product with a few esoteric quirks.

James tries to staunch his thoughts of Tom. Tom, his good and only friend Tom, will die tomorrow with the rest of them, with everyone, when the Pashi leave.

Whistle has explained it to him. The rest of his race, all the Earthies here who don't have Pashi lovers ready to whisk them away, are going to die tomorrow.

24

It will be about lunchtime in St. Petersburg, and Tom will be having a grouper sandwich and order of fries about then if he can afford it. James tries not to think about that.

Tonight the Pashi leave. The great benevolent Pashi who brought so much to the world, who opened wide the doors to all those cosmic possibilities and the promise of trade with a hundred Pashi worlds strung like pearls through the whole spiral arm of the galaxy.

Of course it couldn't all happen too quickly, the Pashi explained. The Earthies would have to be patient as the details were worked out. And there were certain adjustments that would have to be made to accommodate the Pashi presence on Earth. Economic adjustments. Military adjustments.

Whistle had explained it all to James just last night. She was very sorry about it all. The promises hadn't worked out. If *only* the Bendaii hadn't come quite so soon . . .

But the Bendaii *were* coming. The Pashi comm towers had done their job, detecting the approaching enemy. So now the Pashi had to leave. This small planet, this little place where they had built their advance base, had done its job, and now the Pashi had to leave. There weren't nearly enough Pashi to defend against the Bendaii. To stay would be suicidal. So tonight the landing rigs would send the ships home from their bases around the planet. And tomorrow the Bendaii would arrive.

There is a knock at the door. James thinks it must be Whistle, a good two hours early. Very unlike Whistle to be early.

But it isn't Whistle, it's Tom.

James tries to smile as Tom walks in. His best friend, Tom. High school, state champs, college, final four, two years in the CBA—best of friends, the quick guard with the uncanny passes and the giant with the soft hook.

And then came the Pashi and there was no more play for pay now that there was work to be done for the benevolent Pashi. Tom had found a job waiting tables. James found Whistle.

Tom doesn't say anything at first. He just looks at James and then walks past him into the room where he notices the nearly packed bag.

He looks, reaches into the bag to grab a paperback. Laughs.

"Books and baseballs?" he asks, and turns to look at his best friend. "Your Pashi want to get to know all about our way of life or something?" Tom chooses to ignore the sight of the lengthener, its tip just visible, crowded in with the baseballs.

James doesn't know how to answer this. Whistle has made it very clear that James is to tell no one about the Pashi leaving. If James told, Whistle would know. Whistle always knows. And then James wouldn't get to go himself.

James doesn't want to die tomorrow when the Bendaii destroy the landing rigs and comm towers. Whistle has told James about the Bendaii and the struggle the Pashi have been involved in for generations. The Bendaii, Whistle said, are very thorough. James got the message.

Tom walks away from the bag and over toward the kitchen nook, where he opens the refrigerator door, takes out a bottle of Harp, opens it, and takes one long gulp.

"Ah," he says, "the privileges of prostitution."

James doesn't protest for a change. There have been certain advantages to being the lover of a Pashi diplomat, imported beer in these hard times has been among the least of them. James doesn't even drink the Harp anymore, anyway. He just keeps it here for Tom. James has acquired a taste for the salty, thick ooze the Pashi drink. James can't whistle the tune that names the stuff, he just calls it ooze. Whistle laughs at her pet for that, and then strokes his head for being so cute, and then tells him to get out the lengthener, and then . . .

Tom is talking.

"So what's the bag packed for, Jimmy? Seriously, is your Pashi trying to catch up on some American classics?"

"Some of the books are British," says James.

Tom laughs, drinks.

"Damn, boy, you're taking all of this a little too seriously, aren't you? They're going to leave someday, you know, and you'll get left behind. That'll be that."

He points his Harp at James.

"Listen to old Tommy, now. You've got to keep your head on straight on this one, Jimmy. Don't dive off the deep end on me here, all right? Remember who you are. Remember *what* you are."

"Tom," James says. "Tommy." And he takes one step toward his friend, one step toward him and away from the door and the view of the rigs.

But Tom turns away to open a wood veneer cupboard door and

finds some Mexican peanuts, right there where they sit next to the Brazilian breakfast cereal and the Venezuelan pretzels. Most things are imported these days.

"Listen to me, Jimmy," Tom goes on to say through the crunch of the nuts. "It's tough times right now, and you've found a way to get through them. That's great. I understand. Hell, I even stand up for you when people talk. I understand, I really do." And he takes another drink of the Harp, finishing off the bottle in one long pull.

"But there's a big 'but' here, pal. I've been watching this happen for six months now, and you've gone from making the best of a bad thing to, to"—and he searches for the right word while he fishes another Harp out of the refrigerator—"to, I don't know, something really strange. It's like you really like the big blue webber."

James can't stand to hear the Pashi called that. He admits that there is that bluish tint to their fair skin, and that there is a webbing between the toes and fingers. "But what would you expect of an amphibious race?" he has said to Tom in the past. He has told his friend that he's offended by the nicknames that Earthies use for the Pashi, especially the American Earthies, who have so much to look forward to for having helped the Pashi.

Tom has laughed at that sort of thinking in the past, and knows James will be angry for the names, and so Tom uses them anyway, trying purposefully to shock his friend, the recipient of those high, arcing passes that led to all those stuffs and happy screams and TV time.

James turns away from Tom and walks over to the window that is to the left of the sliding glass doors. It will be sunset in another two hours. Whistle will come then, just before the Sun goes down.

Whistle will come and then the two of them will watch the orange sky and Whistle will talk of home. The Sun will seem to flatten a bit as it enters the water, and then it will quickly sink. If they are lucky, very lucky, they will see a quick bright flash of green. And then it will be gone. And then they will leave, the chauffeured floater taking them out to the rigs where they'll board, lift off, and leave. Whistle said it would only take about an hour. Sunset will be about 8:30. By 10:00 James figures he will be on his way. Gone forever.

James turns from the window and shakes his head.

"You've got to go, Tommy. Whistle will be here soon. You know she doesn't like you."

"I know, I know," says Tom, smiling. He walks over to his best friend, James, and reaches up to touch his shoulder. Tom nods his head a bit, shakes it ruefully, squeezes the broad, hard collarbone, and says, "I just had to come by and say something, all right? I just had to say it. You mean too much to me, you know. You understand? You mean too much to me."

Tom leaves.

James cries, gets over it, gets back to packing; the *Oxford Guide to English Literature,* some magazines, his old Norton Anthology so he'll have "The Waste Land" and "Prufrock" and *The Red Badge* and some Faulkner and some Kerouac and some Barth and some Updike and some time to sit back down and cry a bit more. Hard tears. So alone. So very alone.

He stops that nonsense. He rises and looks down at the bag. Quite full.

If he can only get the air out of the ball, he reasons, he can collapse it and take it along. He knows they've got air where he's going, the Pashi breathe it. He can always build a rim and fix up some sort of net. He can always find ten feet high.

He gets the needle in and ten-year-old air hisses out. He looks at the ball as it whistles out the air from ten years back. Tom's signature is right there where he's looking, right under James's own name and the scrawl that says "Kennedy Hawks, State Champs, 1989."

The ball doesn't flatten the way James hoped it would. Funny, but then he'd never deflated a basketball before. Seems odd, but he hadn't.

He pushes, squeezes, even stands on the ball, but it doesn't seem to help much. The ball clearly won't fit into the bag unless he takes out a lot of the books, and he can't do that.

Finally, he takes the obstinate ball and places it on top of the bag, hoping that Whistle will let him bring it along anyway. Surely when he tells her what it means to him she'll let him bring that one extra thing. Surely.

But, later, she doesn't. She insists, and he leaves it behind, leaves it on the coffee table, partially collapsed, so that it seems to flatten against the glass tabletop the way the Sun did for them as it set. Under the flattened part, hard against the glass, are the two signatures.

The Bendaii arrived the next day. About noon.

I read a piece in *The Nation* about Subic Bay in the Philippines and the problems that have existed there over the years as a result of the U.S. military presence—particularly prostitution and the shocking trade in Filipino brides. Shortly after that I saw a documentary on Douglas MacArthur that detailed the U.S. relationship to the Philippines during World War II.

That led me to wonder how we would react, as a nation and on a more personal level, if some greater power established a military outpost here the way we have done in many places around the world. It's a topic I've found myself writing about in several stories in magazines like *Analog* and *Isaac Asimov's*.

In this particular case, I also wondered how we would react if that greater power abandoned us to the enemy the way we abandoned the Filipinos.

There is a narrow brutality to that sort of imperialist thinking—we seem so willing to sacrifice others for our welfare— how would we handle the reverse of that? How would the great power's arrival corrupt us? And what might be the final outcome of that corruption? "War Bride" tries to speak to these questions.

RICK WILBER

HARLAN
⊙ ELLISON ⊙

HOW'S THE NIGHT LIFE ON CISSALDA?

Forty-five books, a dozen movies, maybe half a hundred teleplays, more Hugo and Nebula awards than anyone else, a couple of Edgars from the Mystery Writers of America, P.E.N. award for journalism, and the only person ever to win four Writers Guild awards for solo work in TV, this Ellison person is universally loved and admired. No one has a bad word about him. We also have lovely view-site properties for sale in the Gobi Altai.

In late 1989, two more accolades: Harlan won the World Fantasy Award for his 1988 collection, Angry Candy, *and the Yearbook of the* Encyclopedia Americana *listed the book as one of only twenty-four short-story collections selected as "Major Works of American Literature" for 1988.*

He advises, "You pronounce Cissalda with a hard c as in, 'Kiss me, you impetuous fool,' not as in 'Sis-boom-bah.' "

When they unscrewed the time capsule, preparatory to helping temponaut Enoch Mirren to disembark, they found him doing a disgusting thing with a disgusting thing.

Every head turned away. The word that sprang to mind first was, "*Feh!*"

HOW'S THE NIGHT LIFE ON CISSALDA?

They wouldn't tell Enoch Mirren's wife he was back. They evaded the question when Enoch Mirren's mother demanded to know the state of her son's health after his having taken the very first journey into another time/universe. The new President was given dissembling answers. No one bothered to call San Clemente. The Chiefs of Staff were kept in the dark. Inquiries from the CIA and the FBI were met with responses in pig Latin and the bureaus were subtly diverted into investigating each other. Walter Cronkite found out, but after all, there are even limits to how tight security can get.

Their gorges buoyant, every one of them, the rescue crew and the medical team and the chrono-experts at TimeSep Central did their best, but found it impossible to pry temponaut Enoch Mirren's penis from the (presumably) warm confines of the disgusting thing's (presumed) sexual orifice.

A cadre of alien morphologists was assigned to make an evaluation: to decide if the disgusting thing was male or female. After a sleepless week they gave up. The head of the group made a good case for his team's failure. "It'd be a damned sight easier to decide if we could get that clown out of her . . . him . . . it . . . that thing!"

They tried cajoling, they tried threatening, they tried rational argument, they tried inductive logic, they tried deductive logic, they tried salary incentives, they tried profit sharing, they tried tickling his risibilities, they tried tickling his feet, they tried punching him, they tried shocking him, they tried arresting him, they tried crowbars, they tried hosing him down with cold water, then hot water, then seltzer water, they tried suction devices, they tried sensory deprivation, they tried doping him into unconsciousness. They tried shackling him to a team of Percherons pulling north and the disgusting thing to a team of Clydesdales pulling south. They gave up after three and a half weeks.

The word somehow leaked out that the capsule had come back from time/universe Earth$_2$ and the Russians rattled swords—suggesting that the decadent American filth had brought back a decimating plague that was even now oozing toward Minsk. (TimeSep Central quarantined anyone even remotely privy to the truth.) The OPEC nations announced that the Americans, in league with Zionist Technocrats, had found a way to siphon off crude oil from the time/universe next to our own, and promptly raised the price of gasoline another forty-one cents a gallon. (TimeSep Central moved Enoch Mirren and the disgusting thing to its supersecret bunker headquarters sunk beneath the Painted Desert.) The Pentagon demanded the results of the debriefing and threatened to cut throats; Congress demanded the results and threatened to cut appropriations. (TimeSep Central bit the bullet—they had no other choice, there had been no debriefing— and they stonewalled: *we cannot relay the requested data at this time.*)

Temponaut Enoch Mirren continued coitusing.

The expert from Johns Hopkins, a tall, gray gentleman who wore three-piece suits, and whose security clearance was so stratospherically high the President called *him* on the red phone, sequestered himself with the temponaut and the disgusting thing for three days. When he emerged, he called in the TimeSep Central officials and said, "Ladies and gentlemen, quite simply put, Enoch Mirren has brought back from Earth$_2$ the most perfect fuck in the universe."

After they had revived one of the women and four of the men, the expert from Johns Hopkins, a serious, pale gentleman who wore wing-tip shoes, continued. "As best I can estimate, this creature—clearly an alien life-form from some other planet in that alternate time/universe—has an erotic capacity that, once engaged, cannot be neutralized. Once having begun to enjoy its, uh, favors . . . a man either cannot or *will not* stop having relations."

"But that's impossible!" said one of the women. "Men simply cannot hold an erection that long." She looked around at several of her male compatriots with disdain.

"Apparently the thing secretes some sort of stimulant, a jelly perhaps, that re-engorges the male member," said the expert from Johns Hopkins.

"But is it male or female?" asked one of the men, an administrative assistant who had let it slip in one of their regular encounter sessions that he was concerned about his own sexual preferences.

"It's both, and neither," said the expert from Johns Hopkins. "It seems equipped to handle anything up to and including chickens or kangaroos with double vaginas." He smiled a thin, controlled smile, saying, "You folks have a problem," and then he presented them with a staggering bill for his services. And then he departed, still smiling.

They were little better off than they had been before.

But the women seemed interested.

Two months later, having fed temponaut Enoch Mirren intravenously when they noticed that his weight had been dropping alarmingly, they found an answer to the problem of separating the man and the sex object. By setting up a random sequence sound wave system, pole to pole, with Mirren and his paramour between, they were able to disrupt the flow of energy in the disgusting thing's metabolism. Mirren opened his eyes, blinked several times, murmured, "Oh, that was *good!*" and they pried him loose.

The disgusting thing instantly rolled into a ball and went to sleep.

They immediately hustled Enoch Mirren into an elevator and dropped with him to the deepest, most tightly secured level of the supersecret underground TimeSep Central complex, where a debriefing interrogation cell waited to claim him. It was 10' × 10' × 20', heavily padded in black Naugahyde, and was honeycombed with sensors and microphones. No lights.

They put him in the cell, let him stew for twelve hours, then fed him, and began the debriefing.

"Mirren, what the hell *is* that disgusting thing?"

The voice came from the ceiling. In the darkness Enoch Mirren belched lightly from the quenelles of red snapper they had served him, and scooted around on the floor where he was sitting, trying to locate the source of the annoyed voice.

"It's a terrific little person from Cissalda," he said.

"Cissalda?" Another voice; a woman's voice.

"A planet in another star-system of that other time/universe," he replied politely. "They call it Cissalda."

"It can talk?" A third voice, more studious.

"Telepathically. Mind-to-mind. When we're making love."

"All right, knock it off, Mirren!" the first voice said.

Enoch Mirren sat in darkness, smiling.

"Then there's life in that other universe, apart from that disgusting thing, is that right?" The third voice.

"Oh, sure," Enoch Mirren said, playing with his toes. He had discovered he was naked.

33

"How's the night life on Cissalda?" asked the woman's voice, not really seriously.

"Well, there's not much activity during the week," he answered, "but Saturday nights are dynamite, I'm told."

"I said *knock it off,* Mirren!"

"Yes, sir."

The third voice, as if reading from a list of prepared questions, asked, "Describe time/universe Earth$_2$ as fully as you can, will you do that, please?"

"I didn't see that much, to be perfectly frank with you, but it's really nice over there. It's warm and very bright, even when the frenzel smelches. Every nolnek there's a vit, when the cosmish isn't drendeling. But *I* found . . ."

"*Hold it, Mirren!*" the first voice screamed.

There was a gentle click, as if the speakers were cut off while the interrogation team talked things over. Enoch scooted around till he found the soft wall, and sat up against it, whistling happily. He whistled "You and the Night and the Music," seguéing smoothly into "Some Day My Prince Will Come." There was another gentle click and one of the voices returned. It was the angry voice that spoke first; the impatient one who was clearly unhappy with the temponaut. His tone was soothing, cajoling, as if he were the Recreation Director of the Outpatient Clinic of the Menninger Foundation.

"Enoch . . . may I call you Enoch . . ." Enoch murmured it was lovely to be called Enoch, and the first voice went on, "We're, uh, having a bit of difficulty understanding you."

"How so?"

"Well, we're taping this conversation . . . uh, you don't *mind* if we tape this, do you, Enoch?"

"Huh-uh."

"Yes, well. We find, on the tape, the following words: 'frenzel,' 'smelches,' 'nolneg' . . ."

"That's nol*nek,*" Enoch Mirren said. "A nol*neg* is quite another matter. In fact, if you were to refer to a nolnek as a nolneg, one of the tilffs would certainly get highly upset and level a renaq . . ."

"*Hold it!*" The hysterical tone was creeping back into the interrogator's voice. "Nolnek, nolneg, what does it matter—"

"Oh, it matters a lot, see, as I was saying—"

"—it doesn't matter at *all*, Mirren, you asshole! We can't understand a word you're saying!"

The woman's voice interrupted. "Lay back, Bert. Let me talk to him." Bert mumbled something vaguely obscene under his breath. If there was anything Enoch hated, it was vagueness.

"Enoch," said the woman's voice, "this is Dr. Arpin. Inez Arpin? Remember me? I was on your training team before you left?"

Enoch thought about it. "Were you the black lady with the glasses and the ink blots?"

"No. I'm the white lady with the rubber gloves and the rectal thermometer."

"Oh, sure, of course. You have very trim ankles."

"Thank you."

Bert's voice exploded through the speaker. "*Jeezus* Kee-*rice,* Inez!"

"Enoch," Dr. Arpin continued, ignoring Bert, "are you speaking in tongues?"

Enoch Mirren was silent for a moment, then said, "Gee, I'm awfully sorry. I guess I've been linked up with the Cissaldan so long, I've absorbed a lot of how it thinks and speaks. I'm really sorry. I'll try to translate."

The studious voice spoke again. "How did you meet the, uh, Cissaldan?"

"Just appeared. I didn't call it or anything. Didn't even see it arrive. One minute it wasn't there, and the next it was."

Dr. Arpin spoke. "But how did it get from its own planet to Earth$_2$? Some kind of spaceship, perhaps?"

"No, it just . . . came. It can move by will. It told me it felt my presence, and just simply hopped across all the way from its home in that other star-system. I think it was true love that brought it. Isn't that nice?"

All three voices tried speaking at once.

"Teleportation!" Dr. Arpin said, wonderingly.

"Mind-to-mind contact, telepathy, across unfathomable light-years of space," the studious voice said, awesomely.

"And what does it want, Mirren?" Bert demanded, forgetting the conciliatory tone. His voice was the loudest.

"Just to make love; it's really a terrific little person."

"So you just hopped in the sack with that disgusting thing, is that right? Didn't even give a thought to decent morals or contamination or your responsibility to us, or the mission, or anything? Just jumped right into the hay with that pukeable pervert?"

"It seemed like a good idea at the time," Enoch said.

"Well, it was a *lousy* idea, whaddaya think about *that*, Mirren? And there'll be repercussions, you can bet on that, too; repercussions! Investigations! Responsibility must be placed!" Bert was shouting again. Dr. Arpin was trying to calm him.

At that moment, Enoch heard an alarm go off somewhere. It came through the speakers in the ceiling quite clearly, and in a moment the speakers were cut off. But in that moment the sound filled the interrogation cell, its ululations signaling dire emergency. Enoch sat in silence, in darkness, naked, humming, waiting for the voices to return. He hoped he'd be allowed to get back to his Cissaldan pretty soon.

But they never came back. Not ever.

The alarm had rung because the disgusting thing had vanished. The alien morphologists who had been monitoring it through the one-way glass of the control booth fronting on the examination stage that formed the escape-proof study chamber, had been turned away only a few seconds, accepting mugs of steaming stimulant-laced coffee from a Tech 3. When they turned back, the examination stage was empty. The disgusting thing was gone.

People began running around in ever-decreasing circles. Some of them disappeared into holes in the walls and made like they weren't there.

Three hours later they found the disgusting thing.

It was making love with Dr. Marilyn Hornback in a broom closet.

TimeSep Central, deep underground, was the primary locus of visitation, because it had taken the Cissaldan a little while to acclimate itself. But even as Bert, Dr. Inez Arpin, the studious type whose name does not matter, and all the others who came under the classification of chrono-experts were trying to unscramble their brains at the bizarre progression of events in TimeSep Central, matters were already out of their hands.

Cissaldans began appearing everywhere.

As though summoned by some silent song of space and time

(which, in fact, was the case), disgusting things began popping into existence all over Earth. Like kernels of corn suddenly erupting into blossoms of popcorn, one moment there would be nothing—or a great deal of what passed for nothing—and the next moment a Cissaldan was there. Invariably right beside a human being. And in the next moment the invariable human being would get this *good* idea that it might be nice to, uh, er, that is, well, sorta *do it* with this creature.

Saffron-robed monks entering the mountain fastness of the Dalai Lama found that venerable fount of cosmic wisdom busily *shtupping* a disgusting thing. A beatific smile creased his wizened countenance.

An international conference of Violently Inclined Filmmakers at the Bel-Air Hotel in Beverly Hills was interrupted when it was noticed that Roman Polanski was under a table making violent love to a thing no one wanted to look at. Sam Peckinpah rushed over to abuse it. That went on, till Peckinpah's disgusting thing materialized and the director fell upon it, moaning.

In the middle of their telecasts, Carmelita Pope, Dinah Shore and Merv Griffin looked away from the cyclopean red eye of the live cameras, spotted disgusting things, exposed themselves and went to it, thereby upping their flagging ratings considerably.

His Glorious Majesty, the Right Honorable President, General Idi Amin Dada, while selecting material for his new cowboy suit (crushed velvet had his temporary nod as being in just the right vein of quiet good taste), witnessed a materialization right beside his adenoid-shaped swimming pool and fell on his back. The disgusting thing hopped on. No one paid any attention.

Truman Capote, popping Quaaludes like M&M's, rolled himself into a puffy little ball as his Cissaldan mounted him. The level of dope in his system, however, was so high that the disgusting thing went mad and strained itself straight up the urethra and hid itself against his prostate. Capote's voice instantly dropped three octaves.

Maidservants to Queen Elizabeth, knocking frantically on the door to her bedchamber, were greeted with silence. Guards instantly forced the door. They turned their heads away from the disgusting sight that greeted them. There was nothing regal, nothing imperial, nothing even remotely majestic about what was taking place there on the floor.

37

When Salvador Dali entered his Cissaldan, his waxed mustaches drooped alarmingly, like molten pocket watches.

Anita Bryant, locked in her bassinet-pink bathroom with her favorite vibrator, found herself suddenly assaulted by a disgusting thing. She fought it off and a second appeared. Then a third. Then a platoon. In moments the sounds of her outraged shrieks could be heard throughout that time-zone, degenerating quickly into a bubbling, citraholic gurgle. It was the big bang theory actualized.

Cissaldans appeared to fourteen hundred assembly line workers in the automobile plant at Toyota City, just outside Yokohama. While the horny-handed sons and daughters of toil were busily getting it on, hundreds of half-assembled car bodies crashed and thundered into an untidy pile forty feet high.

Masters and Johnson had it off with the same one.

Billy Graham was discovered by his wife and members of his congregation having congress with a disgusting thing in a dust bin. He was "knowing" it, however, in the Biblical sense, murmuring, "*I* found it!"

Three fugitive *Reichsmarschalls,* posing as Bolivian sugar cane workers while they plotted the renascence of the Third Reich, were confronted by suddenly materialized Cissaldans in a field near Cochabamba. Though the disgusting things looked disgustingly kosher, the unrepentant Nazis hurled themselves onto the creatures, visualizing pork-fat sandwiches.

William Shatner, because of his deep and profound experience with Third World Aliens, attempted to communicate with the disgusting thing that popped into existence in his dressing room. He began delivering a captainlike lecture on coexistence and the Cissaldan—bored, vanished—to find a more suitable mate. A few minutes later, a less discerning Cissaldan appeared and Shatner, now overcome with this *good* idea, fell on it, dislodging his hairpiece.

Evel Knievel took a running jump at a disgusting thing, overshot, hit the wall, and semi-conscious, dragged himself back to the waiting aperture.

There in that other time/universe, the terrific little persons of Cissalda had spent an eternity making love to one another. But their capacity for passion was enormous, beyond calculation, intense and never-waning. It could be called *fornigalactic.* They had waited millennia for some other race to make itself known to them. But life springs into being only rarely, and their eons were spent in familiar sex with their own kind, and in loneliness. A loneliness monumental to conceive. When Enoch Mirren had come through the fabric of time and space to Earth$_2$, they had sent the most adept of their race to check him out. And the Cissaldan looked upon Enoch Mirren and found him to be *good*.

And so, like a reconnaissance ant sent out from the hill to scout the territory of a sugar cookie, that most talented of disgusting things sent back telepathic word to its kind: *We've got a live one here.*

Now, in mere moments, the flood of teleporting Cissaldans overflowed the Earth: one for every man, woman and child on the planet. Also leftovers for chickens and kangaroos with double vaginas.

The four top members of the Presidium of the Central Committee of the Supreme Soviet of the Communist Party (CPSU) of the Union of Soviet Socialist Republics—Brezhnev, Kosygin, Podgorny and Gromyko—deserted the four hefty ladies who had come as Peoples' Representatives to the National Tractor Operator's Conference from the Ukraine, and began having wild—but socialistic—intercourse with the disgusting things that materialized on their conference table. The four hefty ladies did not care: four Cissaldans had popped into existence for *their* pleasure. It was better than being astride a tractor. Or Brezhnev, Kosygin, Podgorny and Gromyko.

All over the world Mort Sahl and Samuel Beckett and Fidel Castro and H. R. Haldeman and Ti-Grace Atkinson and Lord Snowdon and Jonas Salk and Jorge Luis Borges and Golda Meier and Earl Butts linked up with disgusting things and said no more. A stately and pleasant hush fell across the planet. Barbra Streisand hit the highest note of her career as she was penetrated. Philip Roth had guilt, but did it anyhow. Stevie Wonder fumbled, but got in finally. It was good.

All over the planet Earth it was quiet and it was *good*.

One week later, having established without room for discourse that Naugahyde was neither edible nor appetizing, Enoch Mirren decided he was being brutalized. He had not been fed, been spoken to, been permitted the use of lavatory facilities, or in even the smallest way been noticed since the moment he had heard the alarm go off and the speakers had been silenced. His interrogation cell smelled awful, he had lost considerable weight, he had a dreadful ringing in his ears from the silence and, to make matters terminal, the air was getting thin. "Okay, no more Mister Nice Guy," he said to the silence, and proceeded to effect his escape.

Clearly, easy egress from a 10′ × 10′ × 20′ padded cell sunk half a mile down in the most top-secret installation in America was not possible. If there was a door to the cell, it was so cleverly concealed that hours of careful fingertip examination could not reveal it. There were speaker grilles in the ceiling of the cell, but that was a full twenty feet above him. He was tall, and thin—a lot thinner now—but even if he jumped, it was still a good ten feet out of reach.

He thought about his problem and wryly recalled a short story he had read in an adventure magazine many years before. It had been a cheap pulp magazine, filled with stories hastily written for scandalously penurious rates, and the craftsmanship had been employed accordingly. In the story that now came to Enoch's mind, the first installment of the serial had ended with the mightily-thewed hero trapped at the bottom of a very deep pit floored with poison-tipped stakes, as a horde of coral snakes slithered toward him, brackish water was pumped into the pit and rising rapidly, his left arm was broken, he was without weapon, and a man-eating Sumatran black panther peered over the lip of the pit, watching him closely. Enoch remembered wondering—with supreme confidence in the writer's talents and ingenuity—how he would rescue his hero. The month-long wait till the next issue was on the newsstand was the longest month of Enoch's life. On the day of its release, he had pedaled down to the newsstand on his Schwinn and snagged the first copy of the adventure magazine from the bundle almost before the dealer had snipped the binding wire. He had dashed outside, thrown himself down on the curb and riffled through the magazine till he found the second installment of the cliff-hanging serial. How would the writer, this master of suspense and derring-do, save the beleaguered hero?

Part two began:

"With one mighty leap, Vance Lionmane freed himself from the pit, overcoming the panther and rushing forward to save the lovely Ariadne from the aborigines."

HOW'S THE NIGHT LIFE ON CISSALDA?

Later, comma, after he had escaped from the interrogation cell, Enoch Mirren was to remember that moment, thinking again as he had when but a child, what a rotten lousy cheat that writer had been.

There were no Cissaldans left over. Everywhere Enoch went he found the terrific little persons shacked up with old men, young women, pre- and post-pubescent children, ducks, porpoises, wildebeests, dogs, arctic terns, llamas, young men, old women and, of course, chickens and kangaroos with double vaginas. But no lovemate for Enoch Mirren.

It became clear after several weeks of wandering, waiting for a materialization in his immediate vicinity, that the officials at TimeSep Central had dealt with him more severely than they could have known.

They had broken the rhythm. They had pulled him out of that disgusting thing, and now, because the Cissaldans were telepathically linked and were *all* privy to the knowledge, no Cissaldan would have anything to do with him.

The disgusting things handled rejection very badly.

Enoch Mirren sat on a high cliff a few miles south of Carmel, California. The Peterbilt he had driven across the country in futile search of another human being who was not making love to a Cissaldan, was parked on the shoulder of Route 1, the Pacific Coast Highway, above him. He sat on the cliff with his legs dangling over the Pacific Ocean. The guide book beside him said the waters should be filled with seals at play, with sea otters wrapped in kelp while they floated on their backs cracking clams against their bellies, with whales migrating, because this was January and time for the great creatures to commence their journey. But it was cold, and the wind tore at him, and the sea was empty. Somewhere, elsewhere, no doubt, the seals and the cunning sea otters and the majestic whales were locked in passionate embrace with disgusting things from another time/universe.

Loneliness had driven him to thinking of those terrific little persons as disgusting things. Love and hate are merely obverse faces of the same devalued coin. Aristotle said that. Or Pythagoras. One of that crowd.

The first to know true love, he was the last to know total

loneliness. He wasn't the last human on Earth, but a lot of good it did him. Everybody was busy, and he was alone. And long after they had all died of starvation, he would still be here . . . unless he decided some time in the ugly future to drive the Peterbilt off a cliff somewhere.

But not just yet. Not just now.

He pulled the notebook and pen from his parka pocket, and finished writing the story of what had happened. It was not a long story, and he had written it as an open letter, addressing it to whatever race or species inherited the Earth long after the Cissaldans had wearied of banging corpses and had returned to their own time/universe to wait for new lovers. He suspected that without a reconnaissance ant to lead them here, to establish a telepathic-teleportational link, they would not be able to get back here once they had left.

He only hoped it would not be the cockroaches who rose up through the evolutionary muck to take over the cute little Earth, but he had a feeling that was to be the case. In all his travels across the land, the only creatures that could not get a Cissaldan to make love to them, were the cockroaches. Apparently, even disgusting things had a nausea threshold. Unchecked, the cockroaches were already swarming across the world.

He finished the story, stuffed it in an empty Perrier Water bottle, capped it securely with a stopper and wax, and flung it by its neck as far out as he could into the ocean.

He watched it float in and out with the tide for a while, until a current caught it and took it away. Then he rose, wiped off his hands, and strode back up the slope to the 18-wheeler. He was smiling sadly. It had just occurred to him that his only consolation in bearing the knowledge that he had destroyed the human race, was that for a little while, in the eyes of the best fuck in the universe, *he* had been the best fuck in the universe.

There wasn't a cockroach in the world who could claim the same.

SCOTT
⊙ BAKER ⊙

THE JAMESBURG
INCUBUS

Scott Baker was born in Wheaton, Illinois, the home of Billy Graham, Young Americans for Freedom, and the Christian Anti-Communist Crusade. He has been living and writing in Paris for several years, winning the Prix Apollo for his science fiction novel Symbiote's Crown *(Berkley) in 1982 and the World Fantasy Award in 1981 for his short story "Still Life with Scorpion." His most recent novel,* Webs *(Tor), was published in 1989, and he is currently working on the third volume of* The Ashlu Cycle *(a four-volume shamanism-based fantasy,* not *a* series*), which is set in the same world—city?—as his novelette "Varicose Worms." It's about "African immigrants and magic, pet shops, parks, domestic and wild animals, and possibly a cure for cancer using fancy guppies."*

"The Jamesburg Incubus" is, in structure, typical of a particular kind of Scott Baker story—the really weird ones. I see it as an ode to the sixties—and as his belated rebellion against his conservative hometown.

At forty-three, Laurent St. Jacques (né Lawrence Jackson, he'd changed his name in hope of improving his image after the third and last college at which he'd taught French failed to renew his contract) was tall, willowy, elegant, and thoroughly unattractive, as he himself was only too aware. He liked to think of himself as a rationalist and freethinker and idolized Voltaire, though unlike Voltaire he usually kept his opinions to himself and was thus able to avoid their consequences. His wife, Veronica, was slight, somewhat angular, and aggressively healthy; she was five years younger than he, and Catholic. They both taught at St. Bernadette's School in Jamesburg, California: St. Jacques was responsible for French and Italian while she taught geology and coached the swim team. Their marriage was not particularly happy: she stayed with him because the Church said it was her Christian duty; he stayed with her because, even though she irritated him most of the time, he was comfortable and had long given up hope he could do any better by leaving her.

They had no children, to her disappointment and his satisfaction.

Despite his wife's faith, the name he'd chosen, and the religious context in which St. Jacques underwent his transformation into an incubus (St. Bernadette's School being run by the Sisters of Sanctimony, a splinter group of nuns still awaiting the Church's official recognition of their order), there was nothing in even the slightest way Satanic about what happened.

Some years before, the U.S. Army had secretly and erroneously disposed of a small quantity of radioactive wastes and outmoded neurological toxins in the same abandoned mine shaft where the navy had previously dumped the supposedly harmless byproducts of an unsuccessful experiment in breeding a new strain of wheat rust to be used against the Soviets. The army finished filling in the shaft and the land was sold to a commune of Christian organic farmers, none of whom, of course, was ever told anything about the uses to which their farmland had been put. They, in turn, used it to grow the various grains for their seven-grain, guaranteed all-organic bread. This bread tasted so much better than anyone else's seven-grain bread that it was an immediate commercial success, all of which the farmers attributed to the workings of a munificent God.

By the late eighties the bread was so renowned that a distributor was selling it to health-food stores nationwide—after, to be sure, surreptitiously treating it with various chemical preservatives to make sure it stayed fresh-seeming on the shelves long enough to make its distribution commercially viable.

By itself the bread would have been insufficient to bring about the changes that made Laurent St. Jacques an incubus. An opened loaf, however, had been sitting on his pantry shelf for a week, ever since his wife had taken out a slice to finish up the sandwiches she was making for Mother Isobel, who'd stopped by for tea. (Mother Isobel was the nun who ran both the Sisters of Sanctimony and St. Bernadette's School, as well as the person who'd hired St. Jacques and his wife; she was also, and not at all incidentally, Veronica's older sister.) In any case, during the time the bread had been sitting open on the shelf it had developed a spot of some blue-green mold that looked like, but wasn't, penicillin. St. Jacques saw the mold spot while fixing breakfast for Veronica and himself and, priding himself on his manly and rational lack of squeamishness, merely scraped as much mold as he could off the bread before toasting it, then hid what was left by buttering the toast and smearing it with green apple jelly. Because, though he wasn't squeamish, he knew quite well that his wife was.

As usual, she merely picked at her breakfast, so he ended up eating most of her toast in addition to his own.

Some of the mold, which had already been getting pretty strange as the result of its diet, survived the toasting process with a few minor, but significant, alterations, and then survived the effect of St. Jacques's digestive juices. It took up residence in his body where, without doing him any harm, it flourished and grew and eventually interacted in quite complicated ways with his nervous system.

All of which explains how he came to be an incubus, if not the actual physics and biochemistry of the process.

The first night after the mold he was hosting had completed its work, St. Jacques was looking for a book with which to put himself to sleep when he overheard Veronica discussing Edgar Cayce over the phone with somebody who could only be her sister. Fearing the worst—both women had a tendency to go on periodic New Age astrological, dietetic, and spiritualistic binges despite their outwardly almost excessive practicality—he got down his copy of *The Basic Writings of Sigmund Freud* and took it into the bedroom.

Whenever he found himself being assaulted by the Forces of Unreason, St. Jacques retreated into the works of Freud, Zola, Adam Smith, Ayn Rand, and, of course, Voltaire until the crisis passed.

Which it always did, sooner or later, when Mother Isobel finally realized what should have been obvious from the start: that whatever she was so excited about was in direct contradiction to the teachings of her Church.

St. Jacques had fallen asleep, still reading his Freud, before Veronica joined him. Thus, when he found himself, after a momentary vertigo and a sudden, horrible falling sensation—as though he were falling with ever-increasing speed through the back of his head—reliving the day over again in exact and precise detail, while at the same time remaining totally conscious of the illusory nature of the events he was reexperiencing, he accepted it all as a dream brought on, quite logically, by the interaction of his reading and the psychological reality that reading had so well described. The fact that he was experiencing everything reversed, backward, up to and including not only the words he'd heard and spoken but his very thoughts, while at the same time thinking *about* what he was reexperiencing normally struck him as just another example of the wondrous and baffling—though ultimately rationally explicable—workings of his unconscious mind.

He'd never imagined a dream could feel so real. Every detail, every sound, odor, physical sensation, seemed to be really taking place, even though reversed. Finally, though, after what must have been nine subjective hours, he found himself getting unbearably bored. It was about two in the afternoon and nothing strange, interesting, or in any way dreamlike was going on: he was just sitting behind his desk, fidgeting a little, while he listened to a class of fourteen-year-old girls answer the questions he was posing them about irregular verbs not only backward, but incorrectly. His mind had been wandering when he'd first experienced the class period, and it was embarrassing and even somewhat painful having not only to listen to the girls with their horrible accents and ridiculously wrong answers, but to be going over his remembered self's repetitious and futile erotic daydreams again. At the moment he was having the one in which Marcia—the tall, tanned girl with the long, smooth blonde hair and slightly too-large Roman nose, sitting alone in the back of the classroom where he'd had to put her

46

because she was such a disciplinary problem—caught his eye, smiled mischievously at him while she licked her lips the barest instant with the tip of her tongue, then started to unbutton her school blouse a button at a time while he somehow found an immediate excuse to let everyone else in the class out early, but of course asked her to stay behind—

The last of the other girls was closing the door behind herself and Marcia had her blouse completely off, was reaching languidly back to unhook her bra before St. Jacques realized that not only had the day's progression of events changed completely, but that things were no longer happening in reverse order. And by then Marcia had her bra off and was undoing her green plaid skirt, while he himself was struggling out of his rumpled gray suit—

He'd never imagined a dream could be so real. Marcia's breasts were fuller than he'd imagined them, her belly flat and tanned and muscular, her thighs long and golden and smooth, with just the faintest hint of sun-bleached blonde hair on them . . . but somehow he was having an impossible amount of trouble getting his own clothes off, his rumpled suit and wilted, stinking socks and clumsy shoes clinging to him with a will of their own, while the skin he was uncovering was warty and covered with coarse, curling iron-gray hair, his flesh mottled bruise-purple where it wasn't fish-belly white . . . his legs were impossibly skinny and twisted, like the legs of an octogenarian who'd spent the last forty years in a wheelchair . . . he could smell the sweat and grease on him, the sick old man's stench from the clothes he should have changed days before, the grayish boxer shorts with the ridiculous clocks on them . . . yet Marcia was still looking at him with that incredible, impossible mixture of adoration and provocation as she deliberately tossed her skirt aside and, still wearing her panties, was coming up the aisle to him . . . her small, hard nipples brushing against his chest as she helped him out of the last of his clothing, and then she was kneeling, bending forward . . . but somehow he was wearing those ridiculous boxer shorts again even as he realized that she was about to take him in her mouth, there in front of the empty classroom with her blonde hair sliding silky soft over his thighs as she swayed forward and Mother Isobel's office was just down the hall where she was only seconds away if she started wondering why he'd let the class out early and the door wasn't even locked—

"You didn't lock the door?" The boxer shorts were gone again but she'd pulled back just before her lips touched him, was staring up at him, amazed, angry, and somehow infinitely scornful. "You mean you forgot?"

"Yes, but, don't worry, it's all—"

Only it wasn't all right, because at that very instant Mother Isobel burst into the room wearing a white baseball uniform with a bright red Maltese Cross on the chest and carrying an equally bright red baseball bat with a pair of silly white wings on it just above where she was holding it. She began belaboring him over the head with the bat while chanting at him, "You're fired for cheating on your wife, St. Jacques, you're fired, you're fired!" over and over again.

He woke up with a throbbing headache and the events of the dream still perfectly clear in his mind. The bedside clock said 4:00 A.M. Veronica was still asleep. He got out of bed without waking her, staggered into the hall bathroom to get some aspirin, closed the door and turned on the light. In the mirror on the medicine cabinet he saw he had two large goose eggs on the top of his head and a swelling purplish bruise over his left eye.

He was almost ready to believe Mother Isobel really had been hitting him over the head with that ridiculous winged bat, but then rationality reasserted itself. I must have been thrashing around, hit my head on the headboard, he decided. That would explain the bumps and bruises and the way the dream ended; the rest of it was obviously a normal product of libido, association, and memory.

He'd never had a dream that vivid before. Maybe that's why his unconscious had chosen such a violent way of censoring his dream-scenario, while at the same time reminding him that if he ever divorced his wife, or was unfaithful to her in some way that Mother Isobel found out about, he'd have to deal with her. She wouldn't just hit him over the head, she'd fire him like she'd fired Ted Adelard, the art teacher who'd been working nights in that gay bar in Monterey.

He went into the kitchen and put on some coffee, gulped down the four aspirin he'd gotten out of the medicine cabinet. He needed more sleep, but the memory of Mother Isobel smashing him over the head was too vivid for him to trust his unconscious to program any more dreams for him, so he went into the living room and tried to read. But the headache made concentration impossible and he had to give up.

He went back to the bathroom for more aspirin. Suddenly remembering how old and filthy he'd looked in the dream, and how horrible his skin and legs had been, he took off his pajamas and examined himself naked in the full-length mirror. He didn't look young, but he was more dried out and wrinkled than mottled and flabby, and he wasn't nearly as hairy as in the dream. His legs were still good, a little scrawny around the ankles, maybe, but otherwise almost shapely for a middle-aged man's legs. He walked a lot.

Somewhat satisfied, he took extra care bathing and shaving, then went back to the living room to read and drink coffee until it was time to fix breakfast. But the dream kept coming back to him and destroying his concentration. At last he gave up and got out a batch of tests he hadn't planned to grade before the weekend.

Halfway through his second period Dante class, Mother Isobel announced over the intercom that all third- and fourth-period classes were being cancelled for a special assembly in the chapel. All students and faculty were required to attend. St. Jacques was happy enough to skip his classes, since his lack of sleep was beginning to catch up with him.

On his way across the parking lot he saw Marcia coming toward him, accompanied as usual by June and Terri. June and Terri were both dark and slender with long brown hair and huge dark eyes, a way of staring straight at you that was somewhere between childlike and provocative, and high-cheekboned faces that were from some angles smooth and almost babyish, from others angular and striking; the two were never apart more than a few minutes and the faculty had taken to calling them The Twins.

Marcia didn't see St. Jacques at first, but when she did she shot him a look of such pure loathing and contempt that it astonished him. She said something to the others—he thought he heard the word *goat*—then all three looked at him and snickered loudly.

He must've let his feeling show when he'd been fantasizing about her in class the day before. He told himself it didn't matter, that their derision couldn't mean anything to a mature man like himself, but he knew that ridiculous though it was to let such things bother him, they probably always would.

The front row of pews was reserved for the faculty. St.

Jacques sat in his assigned place, between Veronica and Russell Thomas, the insipidly handsome Christian mystical poet who taught English, and whose poetry and conversation Mother Isobel and Veronica found so edifying. St. Jacques was glad to get off his feet; he'd felt stiff and heavy all day, and the bumps on his head hurt when he stood up and walked around. Thomas returned his greeting; Veronica was reading and just nodded back to him when he said hello.

Mother Isobel made her way determinedly to the front, accompanied by a short, rotund priest St. Jacques didn't recognize. The priest was robed in a surplice and violet stole; his roundness and slight rolling walk set off the nun's rigid carriage and severe figure; if Veronica was slightly angular, her sister was skeletal. Veronica marked her place—St. Jacques saw she was reading something about New Age Christian Calisthenics, undoubtedly in hope of finding ideas she could use for her swim team—and St. Jacques allowed himself to relax. Veronica would remember her sister's every word, so he could doze off and ask her what happened later.

When Mother Isobel and her priest reached the front the lights dimmed, leaving only the podium and the open book on it brightly lit. A typically theatrical touch. St. Jacques straightened in his pew and closed his eyes; he knew from long experience that Mother Isobel would undoubtedly talk for some time before introducing the priest. She never really looked at the people she addressed, though she made a point of staring searchingly at her audience.

Her voice was as harsh and pompous as usual. St. Jacques had just started to drift off when he was brought wide awake by the first titters and suppressed laughter from not only the girls behind him but from some of the other faculty members. He opened his eyes and looked at Mother Isobel, realizing with a shock that she was staring fixedly and purposefully straight at him, and had probably been doing so the whole time.

". . . as the *Malleus Maleficarum*'s authors proved beyond the shadow of a doubt," she was saying. "Unclean spirits known as Incubi can take on the form of any man weak or lustful enough to consent to their urgings. They visit the dreams of young and innocent girls in his shape, to tempt and torment them with the lusts of the flesh and so lead them to perdition. . . ."

One such spirit, she explained grimly, ignoring the giggles and suppressed laughter until they finally died away, had visited the school only the night before, though with God's help she'd driven it away. But the girls at St. Bernadette's had been entrusted not just to her personal care, but to the care of the Holy Mother Church—and Christ's church would not let itself be mocked by Satan and his filthy minions. So she'd called upon Father Sydney to perform an exorcism and rid the school once and for all of the unclean spirit that had sought to invade and pollute it. . . .

Sometime during this rather amazing discourse St. Jacques realized she was talking about *him*. He wanted to see how Marcia was reacting to Mother Isobel's tirade, but he couldn't turn around to look, not with Mother Isobel glaring at him.

Father Sydney had started the exorcism, spraying holy water everywhere. He rushed through a Litany and a Psalm, implored God's grace, went through a Gospel and some prayers, made the sign of the cross a number of times, then began intoning:

"I exorcise thee, most vile spirit, the very embodiment of our enemy, the entire specter, the whole legion, in the name of Jesus Christ, to get out and flee from this assembly of God's creatures.

"He Himself commands thee, who has ordered those cast down from the heights of Heaven to the depths of the Earth. He commands thee, He who commanded the sea, the winds, and the tempests.

"Hear, therefore, and fear, O Satan, enemy of the faith, foe to the human race, producer of death, thief of life, destroyer of justice, root of evils, kindler of vices, seducer of men, betrayer of nations, inciter of envy . . ."

Around "kindler of vices" St. Jacques quit listening. Whatever had happened the night before—and he could no longer deny that *something* had—he categorically refused to believe that Satan, demons, or anything equally ridiculous had been involved. Nothing of the sort had ever existed or ever could exist, and in any case the exorcism certainly wasn't having any effect on *him*.

The only possible explanation, he finally decided, after having gone through and rejected everything else, was telepathy. A sort of organic radio that worked only when the sleeping brain relaxed its normal barriers. It was the logical explanation, too, for all the Inquisition's witch trials and wild reports of demonic possession. How could the Church, with only humbug, ritual, and authority to offer, compete with people who became gods in their sleep, who could create their own pocket realities and draw other people in to share them? It couldn't, obviously, and so the Church had tried to kill off all the earlier telepaths. A sort of selective breeding, removing the telepaths from the gene pool so as to produce a race of telepathic deaf-mutes. He was some sort of sport, a genetic throwback.

Father Sydney was still droning on about how God, the Majesty of Christ, God the Father, Son, and Holy Ghost, aided and abetted by the sacred cross and Holy Apostles Peter and Paul and all the saints united, were going to command the spirit, when it finally struck St. Jacques that what had happened the night before had been *real*. Not the classroom, no, but he'd been *somewhere,* in a private reality that he himself had created. And even though his anxiety had drawn Mother Isobel into that reality and so ruined everything, Marcia and the rest had been ready to do whatever he wanted them to—

And still would. Because, he was instinctively certain, *he* was the one who controlled and shaped the reality he'd created. He was the telepath, the one who could enter people's dreams and reshape them the way he wanted, and no one could stop him. Even Mother Isobel had only been playing the part he'd chosen for her.

No one could ever even prove he was responsible. He would always be lying peacefully asleep in his bed, with Veronica there by his side.

They'd married while she was a sophomore in college and looked a lot like Terri and June looked now, when he'd still been convinced he had a brilliant professorial career ahead of him. She'd been conservative, a devout Catholic, though given to transient mystical and psychic enthusiasms—geomancy, positive thinking, even self-hypnosis—that had made him think her basic ideas were much more malleable than they really were. He'd married her in the confidence that a few years of concentrated exposure to his vastly superior way of thinking would be enough to turn her ideas completely around. But in fact, by the time the third and final college at which he'd taught refused to renew his one-year contract he'd given up trying to impose himself in either his career or marriage, allowed himself to sink unprotesting into what he recognized as Thoreau's prototypical life of quiet desperation. Veronica took care of him, mothered him almost, and though they had nothing in common and she often irritated him, he liked her well enough. She was generous and indulgent and still attractive for her age, though their sex life had dwindled over the years to what they both had come to see as a sort of hygienic minimum. He loved his comfort and security too well to risk losing them; he knew he had too little glamour or enthusiasm to hope that he could find himself someone better by leaving her. She believed in marriage until death; he was too settled, despairing, and lazy to carry on extramarital affairs behind her back, and he had no desire to hurt her pointlessly.

But if he could have his affairs, his perfect fantasy adventures, without leaving her side . . . It was the perfect solution. Or would be, if he could deal with Mother Isobel.

The priest was finishing up:

"Therefore, O impious one, go out. Go out, thou scoundrel, go out with all thy deceits, because God has willed that man be his temple.

"But why dost thou delay longer here?

"Give honor to God, the Father Almighty, to whom every knee is bent.

"Give place to the Lord Jesus Christ"—and here Father Sydney sketched the sign of the cross in the air a final time—"who shed for man his most precious blood."

The exorcism was over. St. Jacques exhaled, realized he'd been holding his breath, that he'd actually been afraid something would happen to him. If telepathy was real, then perhaps the Church's ceremonies could focus a congregation's latent telepathic powers against people like himself. . . . But in any case, the exorcism had done him no harm.

Still, he should get some books, find out as much as he could about incubi. To protect himself from Mother Isobel, if for no other reason.

Mother Isobel announced there'd be a short faculty meeting after lunch, then dismissed the assembly.

As he turned to leave, St. Jacques saw Marcia staring at him from the back of the chapel. He had enough time to seize the expression on her face before she realized he was looking at her: no longer the loathing and contempt she'd affected before her friends, but rather a troubled, confused, almost terrified look.

He ate lunch with Veronica and the poet. Thomas was talking, as usual, about Divine Inspiration. Not just any old Divine Inspiration, but rather that Divine Inspiration (something here about "the force that through the green fuse," which St. Jacques was sure he had stolen) that enabled Russell Thomas to write his paeans of praise and thanksgiving.

St. Jacques detested him, but thought that this once it couldn't hurt to be seen in his company. Unfortunately, Mother Isobel never put in an appearance, so it was a wasted effort.

Thomas's monologue left St. Jacques free to worry about what, he finally realized with a certain surprise, was an ethical question. The vulnerable look on Marcia's face had awakened him to the fact that what he was contemplating was perhaps more a sort of rape than it was the consequenceless, if scandalous, series of *aventures* he'd been contemplating.

Though perhaps it would be better to picture the whole thing as a kind of irresistible seduction. There was no force involved; the Marcia of the night before had been willing; it was only her reawakened self who'd been troubled. And that perhaps more because of the interpretations Mother Isobel had put on her experience than because of anything inherent in the experience itself. Or, at least, in what had happened when it had been just the two of them, before St. Jacques's own fears and self-censorship had brought the avenging nun into the scenario.

He'd done nothing to harm Marcia by involving her in his sexual fantasies: her own unconscious must be serving her up similar fantasies constantly. What he'd done wrong was fail to protect her from her subsequent memory of what happened: he had to find a way to censor what she remembered on awakening so as to ensure that she was no more troubled by her memories of his erotic scenarios than she would have been by the memory of one of her own.

Maybe all he'd have to do would be to tell the girls to forget everything that happened, then let their own unconscious censoring mechanisms do the work for him. The same way hypnotized people could be told to forget they'd even been hypnotized.

The faculty meeting was short and pointless. As it was breaking up, Mother Isobel asked some of the faculty members to stay behind, but there was nothing to indicate that St. Jacques was the one she was interested in. All she did was tell him she wanted to see him in her office after her last class, then dismissed him.

He was thankful she hadn't attacked or ridiculed him in public, furious at himself for his gratitude, since he knew her well enough to know she never did anything for anybody without expecting something back in return.

Sixth period was a study hall. Most of the girls had been excused to work on the Mother-Daughter Fashion Show. St. Jacques divided his time between rereading *The Interpretation of Dreams* and surreptitiously watching Liz, a compact, heavy-breasted but athletic blonde he'd had in class the year before; in a few years she'd probably be getting fat, but for the moment she was supremely sensual.

He'd just reread the passage in which Freud relates how he'd told the "intelligent lady patient" that "You know the stimulus of a dream always lies among the experiences of the preceding day." St. Jacques wanted to make sure he was primed with all the proper stimuli for the night to come.

The bell rang. Liz jumped up, grabbed her books, and ran. St. Jacques watched the play of her buttocks and thighs beneath her slightly too-tight plaid uniform skirt, then picked up his own books and made his way to his seventh-period class.

Seventh period was French I. Terri handed him a note signed by Mother Isobel herself excusing Marcia from class indefinitely for reasons of health. St. Jacques couldn't tell if Terri, June, or any of the others remembered their brief participation in his dream-scenario.

In any case, he did his best to make the class a perfect example of classic enlightened pedagogic method as practiced at St. Bernadette's: he started out asking the girls difficult questions about the *imparfait du subjonctif* that he knew they couldn't answer, was abusively critical of their answers, tried even trickier questions about the *accord du participe passé* that no one volunteered to answer, then sent Terri and June and two other girls to do them on the board. Since none of them proved capable of getting the problems right, he gave the class a spur-of-the-moment quiz, as well as a long homework assignment for the next day. This gave him a good half hour to watch and fantasize about them uninterrupted while pretending to busy himself with other matters.

June was having trouble with the quiz. On impulse, he decided to go easy on the grading this once.

His final class he spent going over the tests he'd graded that morning. None of the girls in the class interested him, though some had attracted him strongly in previous years. As he'd gotten older, his fantasy life had become increasingly detached from any real-world possibilities and involvements and the girls he desired had become younger and younger, so that it was the incoming thirteen- and fourteen-year-olds who excited him most, the seniors far less, the other adults he encountered almost not at all. Knowing his fantasies to be impossible, he'd never felt compelled to realize them, or blame himself for not having done so. A perfect example of his unconscious mind arranging things for his ease and comfort.

Mother Isobel was waiting for him in her office. The *Malleus Maleficarum* and various other leather- and cloth-bound books were stacked on her desk.

A stage setting. She probably hadn't even opened any of the books, just stuck them where they'd look impressive.

"Sit down, Lawrence."

He sat.

"You know what I called you in here to talk about."

"Not really. I—"

"Of course you do. You were in the chapel, even if you slept through the first half of what I said."

"Mother Isobel, I'm not a Catholic, I don't believe—"

"You're always trying to find an *excuse,* Lawrence. Make people believe what you've done isn't really wrong after all, so you can come up smelling like a rose. You've been here more than ten years, and that's been long enough for me to learn how you lie to yourself and everybody else. But you were married in a Catholic church, by a Catholic priest, to a Catholic wife, and this is a Catholic school. So if you really don't know what I'm talking about, why don't you tell me where you got that bruise on your face and those bumps on your head?"

"Please, Mother Isobel . . . I had some kind of nightmare last night, I don't know what exactly, but I must've hit my head thrashing around—"

"Quit lying! You remember as well as I do. There're just three reasons I haven't fired you yet. One, you're Veronica's husband; if I fire you I'll probably have to let her go, and she deserves better than that. Two, the Sisters of Sanctimony haven't yet been given official approval by the Church—we're still in a probationary period—and I'd rather not complicate matters any more than necessary, especially with something as controversial as demonic possession. Three, I think what's wrong with you is more basic spinelessness than out-and-out evil. I watched you carefully during the exorcism, and even though you squirmed a lot—"

"Because of the way you were glaring at me!"

"—still, you didn't seem to be in any real torment. Sinistrari distinguishes between those persons who are visited by incubi and succubi through no fault of their own, and the witches and sorcerers who receive such visitations as the result of pacts signed with demons. My guess is you're one of the first kind. Along for the ride, as it were. I'm assuming you haven't signed any sort of pact—"

"Of course not. I don't even believe in the Devil!"

"Yes or no?"

"No!"

"No real harm was done the girl, so I'll take your word for it, this time. And perhaps it's a point in your favor that you don't believe in the Devil. According to Sinistrari, those who consort with incubi and succubi while believing them to be demons are as guilty of demoniality as those consorting with real demons."

"I don't understand. They aren't supposed to be demons?"

"Sinistrari states that they're actually a lower sort of angels, who themselves sin through their lust for men and women. That's why he considers sexual relations with them as crimes against chastity, but not against the Church."

"I told you I don't believe in any of that."

"And I told you I'd take your word for it this time." She opened one of her desk drawers, brought out a sachet of herbs. "Here." He took it warily. "It won't hurt you. Put it inside your pillow before you go to sleep tonight. And keep it there: if I learn you've removed it I'll have no choice but to assume you're in conscious collusion with the forces of evil. In which case not only will I fire you, but I'll do my best to make sure no one ever hires you again. Have I made myself clear?"

"Perfectly clear. Though I can't believe we're having this conversation."

He sniffed the sachet. It smelled of cinnamon and spices and made his head spin a little, not unpleasantly, when he took a deeper breath.

"What's in it?" Knowing that by asking he was implicitly recognizing her right to force him to keep something in his pillow so long as it was harmless.

"Sweet flag, cubeb seeds, root of aristolochia, ginger . . . herbs and spices. The recipe's in here." She pushed a leather-bound book at him. *The Collected Works of Ludovico Maria Sinistrari* was stamped in flaking gilt on the cover. "You can look it up for yourself if you want."

It was a challenge. St. Jacques declined it, shrugged. "I'll try it for a while. Since you insist. But the whole thing's absurd."

On his way to his car, he saw Russell Thomas sitting in a lawn chair by the pool, talking to some students. Veronica was away with the swim team—they had a meet in San Jose—and the poet was acting as lifeguard.

Thomas was young, blond, tanned, muscular, everything St. Jacques wasn't. He had a rich theatrical voice and the total self-confidence of someone so in love with himself that he can't imagine anyone failing to share his passion. The girls were listening to him in wide-eyed admiration, hanging on his every word: St. Jacques recognized Liz in her white two-piece swimsuit on the far side of the group. He stopped and watched them for a while, registering everything for future reference. Finally, having endured all he could, he left.

On the way home he stopped by a bookstore specializing in mystical and occult books where he'd picked up things for Veronica now and then. The clerk directed him to something called *Demons, Demonologists, and Demoniality: An Encyclopedical Compendium* in three volumes; leafing through it he found a translation of Sinistrari's *De Daemonialitate.* The introduction stated the book was on the Church's prohibited index, which could only mean that Mother Isobel was already lapsing into heresy in her attempts to deal with him. Pleased, he bought the books.

Back at the house he took the sachet out of his briefcase and sniffed it again before tossing it on the kitchen table. It smelled quite nice, actually. He pulled up a chair and stared at it for a while. It didn't seem likely that the herbs and spices could do him any real harm, but he couldn't be sure: the Church had had centuries to devise effective methods for dealing with those it considered its enemies, even if it had worked them out by trial and error. He was tempted to toss the sachet out or empty it and replace its contents, but even if Veronica were loyal enough to refuse to spy on him—something of which he was by no means certain—Mother Isobel would undoubtedly continue dropping by for tea several times a week, and St. Jacques was certain she'd have no trouble convincing Veronica to let her search his bedroom.

In fact, he was pretty sure Veronica would have no real objections to spying on him for her sister. She no longer had any real personal loyalty to him, but only to the institution—and to be sure, the sacrament—of marriage. Mother Isobel would be able to persuade her to see that role and those duties as subservient to a larger, religious responsibility, toward not only God and the Church, but toward her husband's immortal soul.

He went into the bedroom, dug a little hole in the foam rubber inside his pillow and stuck the sachet in, zipped the pillow closed. As an afterthought he opened the bedroom window, to keep the air as fresh as possible.

Veronica wouldn't be back before midnight. He started grading papers, but quit halfway through and showered instead, then shelved most of the books he'd bought in the bookcase by his side of the bed. Veronica would never even notice them, though he'd have to find somewhere else for them before her sister's next visit.

He read awhile, trying to tire himself out so he could get to sleep. Most of what he read disgusted him and he dismissed it as the product of the Inquisitors' diseased imaginations and expectations, but some things stuck in his mind: the supposed irresistibility of demon lovers coupled with women's insatiable desire for them, the fact that incubi were sometimes described as having double or even triple penises, as well as the ability to make even their seemingly more normal members expand and contract, throb, pulse, and spin inside women they seduced, so yielding titillations no mere man could ever hope to rival.

All of which, if true, was certainly something to look forward to. He put the book away and turned off the lights, found himself going over and over the erotic scenarios he'd thought up during the day—endless successions of tangled willing bodies, breasts, and thighs, mouths, buttocks, and vaginas—so nervous with anticipation he couldn't relax. He'd had his erection so long it was painful.

59

The herbs seemed to be stimulating his imagination, not helping him lay it to rest. He tossed and turned, twisted the sheets and covers around him so badly he had to get up and make the bed all over again twice. Finally he switched his pillow with Veronica's but even that didn't do any good.

About 12:30 he heard her come in. He switched the pillows back and pretended to be asleep.

The bedroom door opened but the light stayed off. "Larry?" she whispered. "Larry, are you awake?"

He could hear her breathing, though she was still standing in the doorway on the far side of the room, smell the swimming pool on her clothes and hair. All his senses seemed unnaturally acute, as though the sachet in his pillow had been filling the room with some airborne stimulant. Maybe that was how it was supposed to work: keep him awake all night so he'd never get a chance to dream.

Veronica slipped off her shoes, tiptoed across the wooden floor. He squeezed his eyes completely shut. She stopped by his side of the bed and he could hear the crinkling of whatever she was wearing as she bent down beside him. He felt her breath on his face—clean and sweet-smelling and warm—heard her suck in two, three deep lungfuls of air, felt her let them out again.

Checking up on him, to make sure he'd put the sachet in his pillow.

He wanted to yell at her that neither she nor her sister had any right. Instead, he lay rigidly immobile until he heard her straighten and sneak out of the room, closing the door softly behind her. Then he stretched slightly, unkinking his tensed muscles, and heard her pick up the hall phone and dial.

"Hello . . . Yes. No, nothing's wrong, he put it in his pillow and he's already asleep. You must've made some kind of mistake. He'd never— Of course not, if you say that's what happened I believe you, but it couldn't have been him, you see, not really, maybe some evil spirit *pretending*— Of course I'll make sure he keeps it there. I like the way it smells. So I'll see you tomorrow. Bye."

He heard her go into the kitchen, open the refrigerator, pull out a chair, and sit down. The worst of it was that she'd never do anything to hurt him unless she was convinced it was for his own greater good. Whereas he, with no transcendent goals, morality, or justifications, was perfectly aware that whenever he did anything to wound or hurt her, it was always merely for his own convenience and satisfaction, when it wasn't just selfish indifference.

With the exception of one brief affair with a student at the second college at which he'd taught (and which had hurt Veronica deeply when she found out, though she'd never reproached him for it), he'd never done anything, had always known he'd never do anything. Until now, if he could just lull Mother Isobel's suspicions while keeping the girls sharing his dreams from conscious guilt over their unconscious willingness to participate in his fantasies.

Veronica came in a little later, undressed in the dark, and fell asleep almost immediately. St. Jacques stayed awake, nervous and agitated, but afraid to wake her. When he finally did drift off he found himself falling through the back of his eyes again. He felt a surge of triumph: the sachet hadn't been able to stop him after all!

Only this time what he was reexperiencing in reverse was not the previous day, but the time he'd spent lying in bed feigning sleep, and nothing he could think of seemed to make the process go any faster. So he took control of the dream, willed himself to get out of bed. Time reversed its backward flow, became normal again. The bedside clock said 4:00 A.M.

He imagined Terri and June opening the bedroom door and tiptoeing in, but nothing happened. He fantasized the phone ringing, with Liz calling from a phone booth to tell him she'd snuck away from school and would be there in five minutes, but the phone didn't ring. He told himself a car had just entered the driveway and was coming to a halt outside his window, and still nothing happened.

He was suddenly terrified Mother Isobel had found a way to take control, that she'd burst in in her white satin baseball uniform and smash him over the head or try out some of the tortures he'd been reading about in the books on the Inquisition.

For an instant, he was sure he must have come awake again despite what the clock seemed to say. He glanced down at himself, told himself that if he really were dreaming, he could change his pajamas into anything else he wanted, like his swimming suit.

His pajamas were gone. He was wearing his swimming suit. So he *was* dreaming.

He left the dream-Veronica sleeping soundly and padded out

into the hall. Dreams were symbolic; if he wanted to get in touch with somebody what better way than by telephone? He switched the dial so that each number became a different girl's name, picked up the phone, and dialed Marcia. No answer, not even a busy signal. He tried the others. Nothing.

Closing his eyes, he imagined himself lying in the sun by the swimming pool, but when he opened his eyes again he was back lying on the bed, though he'd seemed to feel the sun on his chest and face for an instant. He imagined himself a three-piece tweed suit over his swimming trunks, then added the shirt, tie, socks, and shoes he'd forgotten, and went out into the hall to get his car keys out of the ashtray where he kept them. The phone was next to the ashtray; he saw that the dial had reverted to normal.

No one was waiting in romantic ambush outside. When he tried to drive off in his car, the whole night landscape around him faded out of existence and he found himself back in bed, wearing his pajamas. The clock said 4:20.

A few more experiments convinced him he couldn't get more than a few hundred yards from his sleeping body, and couldn't alter more than a few things at a time before finding himself back where he'd started from.

Further experiments convinced him he couldn't bring any-body from the previous day into his dream. Except perhaps Veronica, who was still sleeping in the bed, part of the dream decor, but he didn't want to bring her any further into the dream—there were too many chances that whatever happened would get back to Mother Isobel if he didn't hit on the right way to suppress or distort her memories. Feeling silly, he went through the maga-zines in his living room until he found the latest issue of *L'Evene-ment du Jeudi*, leafed through it until he found the picture he remembered, an aspiring Italian starlet swimming nude at a hotel in Cannes.

With a little experimentation he found he could enlarge the picture, extract the girl and make her life-size and more or less three-dimensional, but he couldn't make her look like a real hu-man being, only a big, glossy inflatable doll. When he tried to make the doll move it twitched once or twice, and he found himself back in bed with his pajamas on.

So he needed other people to play the other roles in these dream-scenarios. Maybe that was how all dreams really worked, by telepathic contact between people's sleeping minds. Immersion in a truly collective unconscious for purposes of wish fulfillment. In which case, being a telepath wasn't what made him different, because everybody was a telepath; the difference was that he'd somehow learned to enter that collective state while maintaining his conscious will and lucidity.

If he was correct he could put his last doubts about morality to rest: he wasn't doing anything anyone else wasn't doing; the only difference was that he was able to take conscious control of his participation. So he wasn't just inventing excuses for himself, no matter what Mother Isobel said.

But that still left unanswered the question of how to make contact with the girls' sleeping minds. Perhaps he only had access to the dreams of people he'd already come across in his re-experienced waking time. Which meant that tonight there wouldn't be anyone but Veronica.

He looked at her, sleeping, realized he could use her to find out if he could make the people he brought into his dream world forget what happened, so long as what he did was innocuous enough that it wouldn't give her reason to suspect anything, even if she *did* remember. In any case, he'd probably be safer experimenting with her, for all her loyalty to her sister, than with someone with no reason to dream about him.

He climbed back into bed, closed his eyes, pretended to be asleep again, then made the phone ring. You can wake up now, Veronica, he thought. The phone's ringing.

She took a long time to come awake. She seemed confused and recalcitrant, so he just kept the phone ringing until she got out of bed, stumbled into the hall, and picked it up.

"Hello?" he heard her say. "Hello?"

There's nobody on the other end of the line, he thought. Put the phone back and come to bed.

He opened his eyes, watched her coming back into the room. There was a little light, not much, from the moon, and in it she looked younger, more graceful than usual. Almost the way he remembered from when he first met her at the University of Wisconsin and she'd looked like a slightly older Terri or June, before she'd taken on the solidity and practicality she now shared with her sister.

That's how she sees herself in her dreams, who she really is inside, he realized. He felt an unexpected surge of desire for her, suppressed it: he couldn't risk complicating his experiment too much, at least not this first time.

When she started to climb back into bed, he made the phone ring again. She answered it, found there was no one there, hung up, and was on her way back into the bedroom when he made it ring again.

He went through the whole thing three more times before he was satisfied. The last time he didn't make the phone ring, just suggested *she* could hear it ringing—but then as she went back wearily to pick it up again *he* heard it ringing, too, as loudly and realistically as when he'd made it ring himself, though this time she had to be the one who was sustaining the experience's reality. When she picked it up he suggested she leave it off the hook this time and come back to bed, go to sleep. As soon as she was asleep he told her that she wouldn't wake up again until the alarm went off in the morning and that she wouldn't remember having heard the phone ring when she did.

St. Jacques spent the rest of the dream-time practicing altering himself in front of the bathroom mirror. He added and subtracted tans and mustaches, changed his clothing, haircut, age, race, and features, made himself skinny, fat, and muscular, then tried on Russell Thomas's form, face, and way of moving. Finally, feeling greatly daring, he went back to the living room and picked up the *Evenement du Jeudi* he'd been looking at earlier, and using it as a guide turned himself into the woman in the picture. The change was wholly convincing; in the mirror he looked like the woman and yet as real as his real self had ever looked; he could feel the weight of her breasts on his chest, a strange confusion of sensations where his penis and testicles should have been, but weren't, problems with his equilibrium when he took an involuntary step back.

For some reason it was easier to make complex changes in himself than it was to change the things around him. But having a woman's body was disturbing; he changed himself back to normal just before the alarm woke him.

It was Veronica's turn to make breakfast. As usual, she sipped her tea, picked at her eggs, and left most of her toast untouched, finally offering what was left to him. He waited for her to mention Mother Isobel's accusations or what had happened the night before; when she did neither he finally asked, "Did the phone ring last night? I had this dream in which it kept ringing and ringing—"

She thought a moment, concentrating, then shook her head. "I don't think so. If it did I didn't wake up either."

So he could insert himself into people's dreams without fear of the consequences, either to himself or to them. He could even visit Mother Isobel in her sleep, take her baseball bat away from her and hit her over the head with it, then tell her to forget all about it. Though the information would still be there in her mind, buried on some unconscious level, and would just result in more trouble later. What he really should do was sneak into her dreams and convince her he was the most wonderful man who'd ever lived, a veritable saint who deserved a raise, then let the idea percolate up through her conscious thoughts until she took it for her own.

He drank four more cups of coffee before he left for school, but even so he was dead tired, irritable, and almost unable to function all day, though he kept stopping off in the faculty lounge and knocking down Dixie cup after pink Dixie cup of the horribly bitter coffee they kept simmering there. When lunch came he didn't go to the cafeteria, just curled up on the couch in the lounge and went to sleep. Dreaming, he relived his last hour of waking time—the correspondence between waking and dream time seemed exact—but was unable to in any way influence or change the backward flow of events. He was the only one asleep, all the others were awake and conscious: there was no way he could alter or escape from the collective reality they were maintaining.

But it was hard having to endure the gritty exhaustion of last hour's class all over again. Hard to endure his frustrated lust and fantasies yet another time without being able to do anything about them. Hard, finally, to have to watch himself doing such a ridiculous, insensitive, and insanely boring job of teaching books that, when he'd first started teaching, had fascinated and excited him. He was in the same position as his students now, a spectator rather than a participant, and the combination of boredom, frustration, and acute self-criticism was intolerable. He'd have to do something about it, use at least part of the time he spent reliving class periods in reverse to not only think about his subject, but to study the girls' reactions, think about what they needed, why they always learned so little, because if he couldn't speed things up and turn in a performance he felt better about as spectator/critic, he was going to be unhappier than he was making any of his students.

It was ironic in a way: the very transformation that was going to allow him to satisfy all his forbidden desires would at the same time force him to become a better teacher.

He slept through the period bell, was awakened a moment later by Jim Seabury, the new psychology teacher.

"You're going to be late if you don't hurry."

"Thanks, Jim. I didn't get much sleep last night and—" He realized what he was saying, broke off suddenly, then added with what he hoped was the appropriate sheepish grin, "But if you don't mind, I'd appreciate it if you didn't mention anything about it to anybody. Even Veronica."

"Sure. Hey, did you hear Mother Isobel refused to renew my contract? Said I was atheistic."

"I heard. I'm sorry."

"I'm not. I'll be glad to get out of here. But anyway, you should watch out, make sure you get enough sleep. Most people don't realize how dangerous not getting enough is. You can end up on the funny farm that way."

St. Jacques stared at Seabury, trying to decide if the other had meant anything personal, then remembered belatedly that the psychology teacher had served as a subject in some sort of sleep-deprivation experiments once.

"How come?"

"REM sleep. Dreaming. You've got to get a certain amount of dreaming in every night. Missing a few days won't really do you any harm, but after a while it creeps up on you."

"I haven't quite reached that point. Not yet, anyway. But I've got to get to class. See you later."

"Sure. Bye."

He spent the rest of the afternoon avoiding Mother Isobel while compiling for himself a new set of images and fantasies for the night to come, not sure whether or not his morning memories would be available, since he'd already slept on them once.

Marcia was back in class. She seemed to have reverted to her normal behavior—which is to say, she ignored him as completely as possible—though she was quieter than usual. He, in turn, neither called on her nor paid any overt attention when he saw her whispering and passing notes, but he watched her out of the corner of his eye.

Once, when he was staring unguardedly at June, he realized both she and Terri were staring quietly and intensely back at him. After he jerked his gaze away, though, he realized they had just been pretending to pay attention and that their thoughts had been totally elsewhere.

As he was leaving the school after his next class he glanced over at the swimming pool, saw the girls on the swim team all lined up watching Veronica demonstrate a back flip off the high board. They had a meet that evening; Veronica wouldn't be back till long after he was asleep.

He finished his work early and went to bed around seven. He didn't bother to switch pillows: the spices were once again stimulating his imagination and sharpening his senses—if anything, their effect was more aphrodisiac than tranquilizing—but he knew he was too tired to be kept awake by them.

As soon as he'd finished his plummeting dive through the back of his head he looked at the bedside clock: 7:15. If he let himself return to the beginning of his French I class he'd have five hours and fifteen minutes before his dream progression brought him back to the moment he'd fallen asleep. That would be about 5:45, and he had no idea what would happen then.

He let the backward flow carry him along, his exhaustion decreasing with every hour subtracted from the day. On his way back to school he realized he would never be able to return to a point where he felt refreshed if he took control at 2:00, and that anyway he was staying conscious through the whole sleep period, not really giving way to his dreams despite the fact that he was immersing himself in the collective unconscious and sharing the dreams of others. What if he needed that relaxation of conscious control and the release it brought to stay sane?

But perhaps it was just the contact, the shared wish-fulfillment, that was needed, and the abdication of control was merely a means toward that end. He tried to remember what Jung—who, after all, had been the one who'd concentrated on the collective unconscious—had said about dreams. All he could come up with was an anecdote he'd read somewhere.

Freud and Jung had been at a psychiatric conference where

Freud had been lecturing about phallic symbols. He'd claimed that nothing in a dream was what it seemed, that every apparent meaning cloaked a hidden, latent meaning. He'd stated that things in dreams—such as trains going into tunnels, pencils, swords, umbrellas, or whatever—had no meaning or importance in themselves, but were there to simultaneously mask and reveal what they *really* stood for, which was in every case a phallus.

When question time arrived, however, Jung had demanded what the latent meaning of a phallus was when the phallus itself appeared in the dream, and Freud had been unable to answer him.

Which was all very well, and if St. Jacques's unconscious had presented him with the information it had to mean something, but he couldn't see what. Unless a phallus really *did* stand for itself alone, so that distortion was only a means of getting certain things into awareness. Which would mean that what was important was the fact of getting them there, not the subterfuges one normally used to do so.

Watching Veronica come soaring back up out of the pool onto the diving board, he found himself appreciating her grace and control. She and the rest of the swim team would still be awake, so the scene had to be rigidly exact and immutable, but when he looked at her from this distance she seemed almost as young and graceful as her dream-self of the night before. Perhaps it was because she didn't have to worry about the impression she was making on people, but poised on the diving board in her blue tank suit, completely lost in what she was doing, she seemed paradoxically less aggressively healthy, less solidly muscular, than she did away from her sports.

St. Jacques continued backing away from the swimming pool, lost it around the corner. Inside the main building he backed past the faculty lounge up the stairs to his last class. He was surprised and pleased to find the resolution he'd made during his lunchtime nap had already had some effect, though he'd made no conscious alteration in his teaching methods: he was obviously paying closer attention to his students and their needs, trying harder to get things across to them, being a little more sympathetic when they didn't understand him. What's more, some of the students seemed to have sensed the change and were reacting favorably.

Between classes he dashed backward down to the empty faculty lounge, spat two cups of coffee back into their pink Dixie cups and let the percolator suck them up its spout, then backed out of the lounge to his French I class, feeling more tired than ever. He endured the class in reverse until the moment came when he'd first entered the room and put his books on his desk, then took control of the dream and felt the time-flow flipflop back to normal around him.

None of you will notice anything's different unless I tell you to, he commanded silently. You will all see me here at my desk, giving the same lecture and asking the same questions you remember from before. Nothing will be any different from the way you remember it. Except, he decided to add, the class seems much more interesting, and when you wake up in the morning the only thing you'll remember is that it was a good class and you feel like you've really learned something.

He got up, walked to the door, then paused a moment before going out, watching them. They were all staring intently at the front of the room, more alert and interested-seeming than he could remember ever having seen them. Glancing at the front, he realized he could see himself sitting at his desk, shuffling notes. The product of their collective imagination.

The St. Jacques behind the desk looked up at the class, began talking animatedly. What he was saying was not only more interesting than anything St. Jacques remembered reexperiencing himself saying, it was also clearer and better organized. He was fascinated, almost tempted to stay and watch his improved self teach, but finally tore himself away, went down to the faculty lounge, and made sure it was as empty as he remembered. In the lounge bathroom he first became his younger self, then took on Russell Thomas's appearance, practiced moving around until he was sure he had everything down perfect, then went back upstairs.

No one noticed him enter. He had a hard time tearing himself free of the fascination his double exercised over him, but finally walked over to June and Terri and asked them to come to the faculty lounge with him. He hesitated, then asked Marcia as well.

The fantasy he'd worked out—that had elaborated itself in his head over the last two days—called for Marcia to know what was happening, and to have helped plan it with him (the him in question being, of course, Russell Thomas: the poet's identity an additional safeguard in case something went wrong, as well as a physical self it felt good to wear, and which was undoubtedly more pleasing than his own), then persuaded her two somewhat hesitant but interested friends to participate with her. So Marcia was the one who locked the door to the faculty lounge behind them and turned out the lights, plunging the room into a semiobscurity lit only by the faint reddish glow filtering in through the curtains. And it was Marcia also who took the lead and encouraged her friends, undressing both herself and the bogus poet, making quiet ecstatic love with him on the carpet and couch until the time came when June and Terri too shed their clothes and all three were rolling around in a passionate, sweating tangle of bodies, breasts, thighs, genitalia, and multiple orgasms, in ever more complicated and abandoned linkages, pairings, and daisy chains. St. Jacques was indefatigable, trying things he'd never before even allowed himself to imagine, no longer really sure when something had originated in his own fantasies and when it came from one or more of the girls. . . . He found his physical form changing, so that for a while he was a boy of fourteen, at other times various older men he knew instinctively were the girls' fathers, at yet another time a man who could only be his own father, then, briefly, he was two men, one of them Russell Thomas while the other was his own adolescent self. Meanwhile the girls had been shifting and flowing between various identities, Marcia becoming first Liz and then St. Jacques's mother, while Terri and June had become his two younger sisters, then both of them were Veronica as she'd been when St. Jacques first met her. One of them even became Mother Isobel, and for an instant she stared fiercely and furiously around her, but their combined desires overcame the innate censoring mechanism that had called the nun into their midst, and she grew younger, became the Sister Isobel she'd been when St. Jacques first met her, then younger still, a shy adolescent girl, before she melted back into Veronica and the two Veronicas again began to flicker through the identities of various other girls in his classes before regaining their true forms as Terri and June. . . . All of them, every identity, spasming and melting through orgasm after orgasm, each the ultimate possible release from the tensions of the one before until even that ultimate possible release showed itself in turn to be merely a state of intolerable tension by contrast with the release that followed it.

Finally—perhaps gradually, perhaps abruptly, St. Jacques

wasn't sure—they'd disentangled themselves, were showering and soaping one another clean in the shower stall that had made a sudden appearance in the bathroom, then were toweling one another off and getting out. St. Jacques was himself again, no longer Russell Thomas, but a younger self, seventeen or eighteen years old, with the confidence and grace that Russell Thomas had pretended to and he himself had always lacked.

St. Jacques glanced at his watch as he was putting it back on: 7:15. His dream-time had caught up with the waking-time it was recapitulating. St. Jacques reminded all three girls that they'd have to forget everything as soon as they awakened. Marcia said she would make sure she did, then had to excuse herself and leave, as they'd all known she would.

St. Jacques felt an irresistible urge to return home, taking Terri and June with him. He finished dressing then waited for June and Terri to put their heavy pullovers on over their jeans—all three were dressed casually, for the street now—then put his arms around them and walked them to his car. He felt singingly happy, with a quiet excitement growing in him that he was content just to feel. The girls squeezed into the front seat with him and he drove them back to the house, all three waving to the gate guard as they left.

At the house St. Jacques opened a bottle of champagne—St. Jacques had always liked champagne and both girls had a weakness for it—then sat around the living room sipping it in silence and watching the fire that had sprung to life in the fireplace. When they finished the bottle, they went into the bedroom to make love some more.

They start slowly, romantically, this time, as though the three of them are fitting together, following something innate and inborn rather than dictating their private needs and wants to one another. The spicy smell from the pillow fills the room, fills them all with a floating lightness as it blends into the walls and furniture and turns everything into sunlit forest, soft and cool and green. Then a luminous mist with hints of green and gold in its depths is swirling languidly around them as they make love in the long green grass with the tiny red and yellow wildflowers all around . . . as they rise up together in the glowing air on their long, golden-tipped, ivory-feathered wings, beating their way gently and without haste ever higher, until at last the world is lost entirely beneath them and

71

they swoop and turn with ever greater rapidity and grace, falling and floating, all three intertwined now, through infinite golden clouds, St. Jacques's double phallus jade and ruby, twin coiling serpents of light, there deep in both girls simultaneously as they all three cling to one another, not moving, not needing to move anymore, spinning and turning through the cool foggy luminescence of infinite space, the skies beyond the sky, and St. Jacques knows that this is what the phallus in his dreams had always masked and revealed, this ultimate unmoving union, this joyous fusion of flesh and sky.

"I told you that it was just a venal sin, and he'd come to his senses soon," he hears Terri say to June in a voice that is as much his wife Veronica's as it is Terri's, as much Terri's as it is Veronica's.

"Angels always do. I owe both of you an apology," he hears June say in a voice choked with laughter, a voice as much Mother Isobel's as it is June's, as much June's as it is Mother Isobel's.

"On the contrary," St. Jacques says, "I'm the one who has to apologize. I'm delighted that Veronica brought you along and gave me the opportunity to make amends." They all burst out laughing and fall intertwined into the sky.

St. Jacques realizes suddenly that on awakening he will remember only the phallus, the multiple penetrations and spasming releases, that the unity and love and the way they're all five melting through one another into the infinite sky will be as beyond his own conscious mind's ability to accept as his earlier, purely sexual fantasies had been beyond Mother Isobel's comprehension.

The alarm clock goes off and he just has enough time to remind them all—June and Terri and Veronica and Mother Isobel and himself—to forget what's happened as soon as they awaken. They agree, and then all of them fall laughing out of the sky into their separate selves.

Veronica and St. Jacques wake up beside each other. They stare at each other, wide awake, more refreshed than either can remember having been in years. Neither remembers any of what passed between them in the early morning, when Veronica's symbiote had finally reached the critical point in its interaction with her nervous system and begun affecting her dreams in the same way her husband's had been affecting his—a change that had been delayed several days in her case, because she'd eaten so much less of the moldy toast than her husband had that the mold which had taken up residence in her had needed that much longer to multiply to a point where it could affect her.

They smile at each other, feeling a rare mutual sympathy and tenderness and rather surprised by it, unaware that anything has really changed. They then separate to live their separate days, St. Jacques to worry about improving his teaching methods and fantasize endless daisy chains and orgasms, though perhaps a little less obsessively than before; Veronica to work with her geology students and swim team while she daydreams about astral projection and the wonders of heaven.

It took them almost a year to realize and accept what they'd come to mean to each other, decades more to begin to fully integrate their sleeping and waking lives. Sometime during that first year they began making love to each other in the flesh again, and eventually two children were born to their union. And in those two children and their many, many descendants, the blue-green mold lived happily ever after.

My favorite short-story ideas often come to me as a sort of ironic counterpoint to something else I'm working on: usually the same general kind of idea, but skewed around so it's shooting off in an entirely different, and probably antithetical, direction. Some of "The Jamesburg Incubus" comes from ideas I was playing around with for my most recent novel, *Webs,* mixed in with reading I was doing at the time on dreams, demonology, and witchcraft, all of it finally linking up and crystalizing around St. Jacques—who, in turn, owes his existence partially to vague memories of an irritatingly pretentious French teacher I used to know, and partially to my own fears of what my life might be like if I ever end up having to teach for a living.

SCOTT BAKER

LARRY
⊙ NIVEN ⊙

MAN OF STEEL,
WOMAN OF KLEENEX

Larry Niven lives in California with his wife, Marilyn. His novel
Ringworld *won the Hugo, the Nebula, the Ditmar (Australian award
for the best International science fiction), and a Japanese award. He has
also won Hugos for his short fiction.* The Barsoom Project, *a collaboration with Steven Barnes, is his most recent novel.*

*"Man of Steel, Woman of Kleenex" is a kind of meditative essay
about Superman's sex life with Lois Lane, considering his nonhuman
powers. Have fun.*

He's faster than a speeding bullet. He's more powerful than a
locomotive. He's able to leap tall buildings at a single bound. Why
can't he get a girl?

At the ripe old age of thirty-
one,* Kal-El (alias Superman, alias Clark Kent) is still unmarried.
Almost certainly he is still a virgin. This is a serious matter. The
species itself is in danger!

An unwed Superman is a mobile Superman. Thus it has been

---

* Superman first appeared in *Action Comics*, June 1938.

alleged that those who chronicle the Man of Steel's adventures are responsible for his condition. But the cartoonists are not to blame.

Nor is Superman handicapped by psychological problems.

Granted that the poor oaf is not entirely sane. How could he be? He is an orphan, a refugee, and an alien. His homeland no longer exists in any form, save for gigatons upon gigatons of dangerous, prettily colored rocks.

As a child and young adult, Kal-El must have been hard put to find an adequate father-figure. What human could control his antisocial behavior? What human would dare try to punish him? His actual, highly social behavior during this period indicates an inhuman self-restraint.

What wonder if Superman drifted gradually into schizophrenia? Torn between his human and kryptonian identities, he chose to be both, keeping his split personalities rigidly separate. A psychotic desperation is evident in his defense of his "secret identity."

But Superman's sex problems are strictly physiological, and quite real.

The purpose of this article is to point out some medical drawbacks to being a kryptonian among human beings, and to suggest possible solutions. The kryptonian humanoid must not be allowed to go the way of the pterodactyl and the passenger pigeon.

I

What turns on a kryptonian?

Superman is an alien, an extraterrestrial. His humanoid frame is doubtless the result of parallel evolution, as the marsupials of Australia resemble their mammalian counterparts. A specific niche in the ecology calls for a certain shape, a certain size, certain capabilities, certain eating habits.

Be not deceived by appearances. Superman is no relative to homo sapiens.

What arouses Kal-El's mating urge? Did kryptonian women carry some subtle mating cue at appropriate times of the year? Whatever it is, Lois Lane probably doesn't have it. We may speculate that she smells wrong, less like a kryptonian woman than like a terrestrial monkey. A mating between Superman and Lois Lane would feel like sodomy—and would be, of course, by church and common law.

II

Assume a mating between Superman and a human woman, designated LL for convenience.

Either Superman has gone completely schizo and believes himself to be Clark Kent; or he knows what he's doing, but no longer gives a damn. Thirty-one years is a long time. For Superman it has been even longer. He has X-ray vision; he knows just what he's missing. *

The problem is this. Electroencephalograms taken of men and women during sexual intercourse show that orgasm resembles "a kind of pleasurable epileptic attack." One loses control over one's muscles.

Superman has been known to leave his fingerprints in steel and in hardened concrete, accidentally. What would he do to the woman in his arms during what amounts to an epileptic fit?

III

Consider the driving urge between a man and a woman, the monomaniacal urge to achieve greater and greater penetration. Remember also that we are dealing with kryptonian muscles.

Superman would literally crush LL's body in his arms, while simultaneously ripping her open from crotch to sternum, gutting her like a trout.

IV

Lastly, he'd blow off the top of her head.

Ejaculation of semen is entirely involuntary in the human male, and in all other forms of terrestrial life. It would be unreasonable to assume otherwise for a kryptonian. But with krypto-

---

* One should not think of Superman as a Peeping Tom. A biological ability must be used. As a child Superman may never have known that things had surfaces, until he learned to suppress his X-ray vision.

If millions of people tend shamelessly to wear clothing with no lead in the weave, that is hardly Superman's fault.

nian muscles behind it, Kal-El's semen would emerge with the muzzle velocity of a machine-gun bullet.*

In view of the foregoing, normal sex is impossible between LL and Superman.

Artificial insemination may give us better results.

V

First we must collect the semen. The globules will emerge at transsonic speeds. Superman must first ejaculate, then fly frantically after the stuff to catch it in a test tube. We assume that he is on the Moon, both for privacy and to prevent the semen from exploding into vapor on hitting air at such speeds.

He can catch the semen, of course, before it evaporates in vacuum. He's faster than a speeding bullet.

But can he keep it?

All known forms of kryptonian life have superpowers. The same must hold true of living kryptonian sperm. We may reasonably assume that kryptonian sperm are vulnerable only to starvation and to green kryptonite; that they can travel with equal ease through water, air, vacuum, glass, brick, boiling steel, solid steel, liquid helium, or the core of a star; and that they are capable of translight velocities.

What kind of a test tube will hold such beasties?

Kryptonian sperm and their unusual powers will give us further trouble. For the moment we will assume (because we must) that they tend to stay in the seminal fluid, which tends to stay in a simple glass tube. Thus Superman and LL can perform artificial insemination.

At least there will be another generation of kryptonians.

Or will there?

VI

A ripened but unfertilized egg leaves LL's ovary, begins its voyage down her Fallopian tube.

Some time later, tens of millions of sperm, released from a test tube, begin their own voyage up LL's Fallopian tube.

* One can imagine that the Kent home in Smallville was riddled with holes during Superboy's puberty. And why did Lana Lang never notice *that*?

The magic moment approaches . . .

Can human breed with kryptonian? Do we even use the same genetic code? On the face of it, LL could more easily breed with an ear of corn than with Kal-El. But coincidence does happen. If the genes match . . .

One sperm arrives before the others. It penetrates the egg, forms a lump on its surface. The cell wall now thickens to prevent other sperm from entering. Within the now-fertilized egg, changes take place. . . .

And ten million kryptonian sperm arrive slightly late.

Were they human sperm, they would be out of luck. But these tiny blind things are more powerful than a locomotive. A thickened cell wall won't stop them. They will *all* enter the egg, obliterating it entirely in an orgy of microscopic gang rape. So much for artificial insemination.

But LL's problems are just beginning.

VII

Within her body there are still tens of millions of frustrated kryptonian sperm. The single egg is now too diffuse to be a target. The sperm scatter.

They scatter without regard to what is in their path. They leave curved channels, microscopically small. Presently all will have found their way to the open air.

That leaves LL with several million microscopic perforations all leading deep into her abdomen. Most of the channels will intersect one or more loops of intestine.

Peritonitis is inevitable. LL becomes desperately ill.

Meanwhile, tens of millions of sperm swarm in the air over Metropolis.

VIII

This is more serious than it looks.

Consider: these sperm are virtually indestructible. Within days or weeks they will die for lack of nourishment. Meanwhile they cannot be affected by heat, cold, vacuum, toxins, or anything short of green kryptonite.* There they are, miniscule but dangerous; for each has supernormal powers.

Metropolis is shaken by tiny sonic booms. Wormholes, charred by meteoric heat, sprout magically in all kinds of things: plate glass, masonry, antique ceramics, electric mixers, wood, household pets, and citizens. Some of the sperm will crack lightspeed. The Metropolis night comes alive with a network of narrow, eerie blue lines of Cherenkov radiation.

And women whom Superman has never met find themselves in a delicate condition.

Consider: LL won't get pregnant because there were too many of the blind mindless beasts. But whenever one sperm approaches an unfertilized human egg in its panic flight, it will attack.

How close is close enough? A few centimeters? Are sperm attracted by chemical cues? It seems likely. Metropolis had a population of millions; and a kryptonian sperm could travel a long and crooked path, billions of miles, before it gives up and dies.

Several thousand blessed events seem not unlikely.†

Several thousand lawsuits would follow. Not that Superman can't afford to pay. There's a trick where you squeeze a lump of coal into its allotropic diamond form. . . .

IX

The above analysis gives us part of the answer. In our experiment in artificial insemination, we must use a single sperm. This presents no difficulty. Superman may use his microscopic vision and a pair of tiny tweezers to pluck a sperm from the swarm.

X

In its eagerness the single sperm may crash through LL's abdomen at transsonic speeds, wreaking havoc. Is there any way to slow it down?

---

* And other forms of kryptonite. For instance, there are chunks of red kryptonite that make giants of kryptonians. Imagine ten million earthworm-sized spermatozoa swarming over a Metropolis beach, diving to fertilize the beach balls . . . but I digress.

† If the pubescent Superboy plays with himself, we have the same problem over Smallville.

There is. We can expose it to gold kryptonite.

Gold kryptonite, we remember, robs a kryptonian of all of his supernormal powers, permanently. Were we to expose Superman himself to gold kryptonite, we would solve all his sex problems, but he would be Clark Kent forever. We may regard this solution as somewhat drastic.

But we can expose the test tube of seminal fluid to gold kryptonite, then use standard techniques for artificial insemination.

By any of these methods we can get LL pregnant, without killing her. Are we out of the woods yet?

XI

Though exposed to gold kryptonite, the sperm still carries kryptonian genes. If these are recessive, then LL carries a developing human fetus. There will be no more Supermen; but at least we need not worry about the mother's health.

But if some or all of the kryptonian genes are dominant . . .

Can the infant use his X-ray vision before birth? After all, with such a power he can probably see through his own closed eyelids. That would leave LL sterile. If the kid starts using heat vision, things get even worse.

But when he starts to kick, it's all over. He will kick his way out into the open air, killing himself and his mother.

XII

Is there a solution?

There are several. Each has drawbacks.

We can make LL wear a kryptonite* belt around her waist. But too little kryptonite may allow the child to damage her, while too much may damage or kill the child. Intermediate amounts may do both! And there is no safe way to experiment.

A better solution is to find a host-mother.

---

* For our purposes, all forms of kryptonite are available in unlimited quantities. It has been estimated, from the startling tonnage of kryptonite fallen to Earth since the explosion of Krypton, that the planet must have outweighed our entire solar system. Doubtless the "planet" Krypton was a cooling black dwarf star, one of a binary pair, the other member being a red giant.

We have not yet considered the existence of Supergirl.* She could carry the child without harm. But Supergirl has a secret identity, and her secret identity is no more married than Supergirl herself. If she turned up pregnant, she would probably be thrown out of school.

A better solution may be to implant the growing fetus in Superman himself. There are places in a man's abdomen where a fetus could draw adequate nourishment, growing as a parasite, and where it would not cause undue harm to surrounding organs. Presumably Clark Kent can take a leave of absence more easily than Supergirl's schoolgirl alter ego.

When the time comes, the child would be removed by Caesarian section. It would have to be removed early, but there would be no problem with incubators as long as it was fed. I leave the problem of cutting through Superman's invulnerable skin as an exercise for the alert reader.

The mind boggles at the image of a pregnant Superman cruising the skies of Metropolis. Batman would refuse to be seen with him; strange new jokes would circulate the prisons . . . and the race of Krypton would be safe at last.

My article on xenofertility was only party conversation until Bjo Trimble made me type it up. The years since have brought considerable feedback.

There is an underground comic that begins as Superman drops and smashes the Kandor bottle . . . and ends as The Atom implants a fertilized egg in his abdomen.

People read the article to their friends over the phone.

When the Superman movie was due, a Brit reporter videotaped some interviews at the Griffith Park Planetarium. At his behest I described some of Superman's expected problems. He held his straight face until he had what he wanted, then cracked up. A real pro.

In June 1988, Superman's fiftieth birthday sparked a convention in Cleveland, his true birthplace. Very little went as planned. A panel on crossbreeding of humans and aliens turned out to be

* She can't mate with Superman because she's his first cousin. And only a cad would suggest differently.

just me! I managed to hold the audience by reading "Man of Steel . . . ," then discussing Reed and Sue Richards (he's prehensile in every appendage!), Mr. Spock, V-for-Visitors, rishathra. . . . Sex with aliens seems to fascinate people.

LARRY NIVEN

K. W.
⊙ JETER ⊙

THE FIRST TIME

K. W. Jeter considers himself "a Los Angeles kid," despite the fact that he currently lives in Portland, Oregon. His controversial novel Dr. Adder *is considered by many to be the prototype for the "cyberpunk" subgenre of SF. It's a disturbing, raw piece of work. Since then, Jeter has published science fiction, fantasy, and horror novels, among them* Farewell Horizontal, Infernal Devices, *and* In the Land of the Dead. *"The First Time" is only his second short story, and although different from* Dr. Adder, *it has just as distressing a view of sex. Neither is for the squeamish.*

His father and his uncle decided it was about time. Time for him to come along. They went down there on a regular basis, with their buddies, all of them laughing and drinking beer right in the car, having a good time even before they got there. When they left the house, laying a patch of rubber out by the curb, he'd lie on his bed upstairs and think about them—at least for a little while, till he fell asleep—think about the car heading out on the long straight road, where there was nothing on either side except the bare rock and dirt and the dried-brown scrubby brush. With a cloud of dust rolling up behind them, his uncle Tommy could just floor it, one-handing the steering wheel, with nothing to do but keep it on the dotted line all the way down there. He lay with the side of his face pressed into the pillow, and thought of them driving, making good time, hour after hour, tossing the empties out the window, laughing and talking about mysterious things, things you only had to say the name of and everybody knew what you were talking about, without another word being said. Even with all the windows rolled down, the car would smell like beer and sweat, six guys together, one of them right off his shift at the place where they made the cinder blocks, the fine gray dust on his hands and matted in the dark black hair of his forearms. Driving and laughing all the way, until the bright lights came into view—he didn't know what happened after that. He closed his eyes and didn't see anything.

And when they got back—they always got back late at night, so even though they'd been gone nearly the whole weekend, and he'd gotten up and watched television and listened to his mom talking to her friends on the phone, and had something to eat and stuff like that, when his father and his uncle and their buddies got back, the noise of the car pulling up, with them still talking and laughing, but different now, slower and lower-pitched and satisfied—it was like it woke him up from the same sleep he'd fallen into when they'd left. All the other stuff was just what he'd been dreaming.

"You wanna come along?" His father had asked him, turning away from the TV. Just like that, no big deal, like asking him to fetch another beer from the fridge. "Me and Tommy and the guys—we're gonna go down there and see what's happening. Have a little fun."

He hadn't said anything back for a little while, but had just stared at the TV, the colors fluttering against the walls of the darkened room. His father hadn't had to say anything more than *down there*—he knew where that meant. A little knot, one he always had in his stomach, tightened and drew down something in his throat.

"Sure," he'd finally mumbled. The string with the knot in it looped down lower in his gut. His father just grunted and went on watching the TV.

He figured they'd decided it was time because he'd finally

started high school. More than that, he'd just about finished his first year and had managed to stay out of whatever trouble his older brother had gotten into back then, finally causing him to drop out and go into the army and then god knew what—nobody had heard from his brother in a long time. So maybe it was as some kind of reward, for doing good, that they were going to take him along with them.

He didn't see what was so hard about it, about school. What made it worth a reward. All you had to do was keep your head down and not draw attention to yourself. And there was stuff to do that got you through the day: he was in the band, and that was okay. He played the baritone sax—it was pretty easy because they never got any real melodies to play, you just had to fart around in the background with everybody else. Where he sat was right in front of the trombone section, which was all older guys; he could hear them talking, making bets about which of the freshman girls would be the next to start shaving her legs. Plus they had a lot of jokes about the funny way flute players made their mouths go when they were playing. Would they still look that funny way when they had something else in their mouths? It embarrassed him because the flute players were right across from the sax section, and he could see the one he'd already been dating a couple of times.

One time, when they'd been alone, she'd given him a piece of paper that she'd had folded up in the back pocket of her jeans. The paper had gotten shaped round, the same shape as her butt, and he'd felt funny taking it and unfolding it. The paper was a mimeographed diagram that her minister at her Episcopalian youth group had given her and the rest of the girls in the group. It showed what parts of their bodies they could let a boy touch, at what stage. You had to be engaged, with a ring and everything, before you could unhook her bra. He'd kept the piece of paper, tucked in one of his books at home. In a way, it'd been kind of a relief, just to know what was expected of him.

It was what worried him about going down there, with his father and his uncle and the other guys—he didn't know what he was supposed to do when they got there. He lay awake the night before, wondering. He turned on the light and got out the piece of paper the girl who played the flute had given him, and looked at the dotted lines that made a sort of zone between the diagram's throat and navel, and another zone below that, that looked like a pair of underpants or the bottom half of a girl's two-piece swimsuit. Then he folded the paper back up and stuck it in the book where he kept it. He didn't think the diagram was going to do him any good where he was going.

"All right—let's get this show on the road." His uncle Tommy leaned out of the driver's-side window and slapped the door's metal. They always went down there in Tommy's car because it was the biggest, an old Dodge that wallowed like a boat even on the straightaways. The other guys chipped in for the gas. "Come on— let's move on out." Tommy's big yellow grin was even looser; he'd already gotten into the six-pack stowed down on the floor.

For a moment, he thought they'd all forgotten about taking him along. There were already five guys in the car when it'd pulled up in front of the house, and his father would make the sixth. He stood on the porch, feeling a secret hope work at the knot in his gut.

"Aw, man—what the hell were you guys thinking of?" The voice of one of the guys in the car floated out, across the warm evening air. It was Bud, the one who worked at the cinder block factory. "There's no way you can stick seven of us in here, and then drive all the way down there."

The guy next to Bud, in the middle of the backseat, laughed. "Well, hell—maybe you can just sit on my lap, then."

"Yeah, well, you can just sit on this." Bud gave him the finger, then drained the last from a can of beer and dropped it onto the curb. Bud pushed the door open and got out. "You guys just have a fine old time without me. I got some other shit to take care of."

Tommy's grin grew wider. "Ol' Bud's feeling his age. Since that little sweetheart last time fucked up his back for him."

"Your ass."

From the porch, he watched Bud walking away, the blue glow of the streetlights making the cinder block dust on Bud's workshirt go all silver. He couldn't tell if Bud had been really mad—maybe about him coming along and taking up space in the car—or if it was just part of the joke. A lot of the time he couldn't tell whether his father and his buddies were joking or not.

"Come on—" His father had already gotten in the car, up

86

front, elbow hanging over the sill of the door. "What're you waiting for?"

He slid in the back. The seat had dust from Bud's shirt on it, higher up than his own shoulders. "Here we go," said his father, as his head rocked back into the cinder block dust. The guy next to him, his father's buddy, peeled a beer off a six-pack and handed it to him. He held it without opening it, letting the cold seep into his hands as the streets pivoted around and swung behind the car, until they were past the last streetlight and onto the straight road heading for the southern hills.

All the way down there, they talked about baseball. Or football, shouting over the radio station that Tommy had turned up loud. He didn't listen to them, but leaned his shoulder against the door, gulping breath out of the wind, his face stung red. For a long while he thought there was something running alongside the car, a dog or something, but faster than a dog could run, because his uncle Tommy had the car easily wound up to over seventy. The dog, or whatever it was, loped in the shadows at the side of the road, a big grin like Tommy's across its muzzle, its bright spark eyes looking right at him. But when another car came along, going the other way, the headlights making a quick scoop over the road, the dog wasn't there. Just the rocks and brush zooming by, falling back into the dark behind them. He pushed his face farther out into the wind, eyes squinted, the roar swallowing up the voices inside the car. The dog's yellow eyes danced like coins out there, keeping alongside and smiling at him.

"All *right*—we have uh-*rived*." His uncle Tommy beat an empty beer can against the curve of the steering wheel, then pitched it outside.

He looked up ahead, craning his neck to see around his father in the front seat. He could see a bridge, with lights strung up along it. And more lights beyond it, the town on the other side. He dropped back in his seat, combing his hair down into place with his fingers.

The lights, when they got across the bridge, were like Christmas lights, strings of little colored bulbs laced over the doorways of the buildings and even across the street, dangling up above, pushing back the night sky. There were other lights, too, the kind you'd see anywhere, blinking arrows that pointed to one thing or another, big yellow squares with the plastic strips for the black letters to stick on, covered in chicken wire to keep people's hands off.

Tommy let the car crawl along, inching through the traffic that had swallowed them up soon as they'd hit the town. So many other cars, all of them moving so slow, that people crossing the street, going from the lit-up doorways on one side to those on the other, just threaded their way through. Or if they were young guys, and the cars were bumper to bumper, they'd slap their hands down on a hood and a trunk lid and just vault over, with a little running step on the ridge of the bumpers halfway across, and just laughing and shouting to each other the whole time.

Even though it was so loud in the street—with all the car radios blaring away, with everybody's windows rolled down, and the even louder music thumping out of the doorways—he felt a little drowsy somehow. He'd drunk the beer his father's buddy had given him, and a couple more after that, and had gone on staring out at the dark rolling by the whole way down here. Now the street's noise rolled over him like the slow waves at the ocean's surface, far above him.

"Bail out, kid—let's go!" The guy beside him, in the middle of the backseat, was pushing him in the arm. His head lolled for a moment, neck limp, before he snapped awake. He looked around and saw his father and his uncle and the other guys all getting out of the car. Rubbing his eyes, he pushed the door open and stumbled out.

He followed them up the alley where they'd parked, out toward the lights and noise rolling in the street. It wasn't as bright and loud at this end; they'd left most of the action a couple of blocks back.

His father and his uncle were already down the street, laughing and swapping punches as they went, little boxing moves with feints and shuffles, like a couple of teenagers or something. His uncle Tommy was always carrying on, doing stuff like that, but he'd never seen his father so wild and happy. They had their arms around each other's shoulders, and their faces and chests lit up red as they stepped into one of the doorways, his father sweeping back a curtain with his hand. The light that had spilled out into the street blinked away as the curtain fell back into place. He broke into a run to catch up with the others.

THE FIRST TIME

Some kind of a bar—that was what it looked like and smelled like, the smell of spilled beer and cigarette smoke that had soaked into everything and made the air a thick blue haze around the lights. The others were already sitting around a table, one of the booths at the side; they'd left room for him at the end, and he slid in beside his uncle Tommy.

The man came around from behind the bar with a tray of beers, squat brown bottles sweating through the crinkly foil labels. He didn't know whether his father had already ordered, or whether the bartender already knew what they wanted, from all the times they'd been here before. He wasn't sure he'd get served, but it didn't seem to matter here how young he was; the bartender put a beer down in front of him, too. He took a pull at it as he looked around at the empty stage at one end of the room, with heavy red curtains draped around it and big PA speakers at the side. The other booths, and some of the tables in the middle, were crowded with bottles, men elbowing them aside as they leaned forward and talked, dropping the butts of their cigarettes into the empties.

Somebody poked him—it felt like a broom handle—and he looked around and saw a face grinning at him. A man short enough to look him straight in the eye where he sat; the grin split open to show brown teeth, except for two in front that were shining gold. The little man poked him again, with two metal tubes that had wires hooked to them, running back to a box that hung from a strap around the man's neck.

"Yeah, yeah—just take 'em." His father waggled a finger at the tubes, while digging with the other hand into his inside coat pocket. "Just hold on to 'em now. This is how they make you a man in these parts." His father came up with a dollar bill from a roll in the coat pocket and handed it over to the little man.

The tubes were about the size of the inside of a toilet paper roll, but shiny, and hard and cold to the touch. He looked at them sitting in his hands, then glanced up when he saw the little man turning a crank at the side of the box hanging around his neck.

An electric shock jumped out of the tubes, stinging his palms. He dropped them and jerked away. He looked around and saw his father and his buddies all roaring with laughter. Right beside him, his uncle Tommy was slapping the table with one hand, turning red and choking on a swallow of beer.

"Here—give 'em here." His father traded another dollar bill for the tubes, the wires dangling between the bottles as he took them from the little man. "Let 'er rip."

The little man turned the crank on the box, digging into it to make it go round faster and faster. His father winced with the first surge, then squeezed the tubes harder, hands going white-knuckled, teeth gritting together, lips drawn back. The crank on the box went around in a blur, until his father's hands flew open and the tubes clattered onto the table, knocking over one of the bottles. Beer foamed out and dribbled over the edge.

"Whoa! Jesus fucking Christ!" His father shook his hands, loose at the wrist. The guy sitting next over stuck out a palm and his father slapped it, grinning in triumph. The little man with the box did a kind of dance, laughing to show all the brown and gold teeth and pointing with a black-nailed finger. Then squatting down, the short legs bowing out, and cupping a hand to his crotch, acting like there was some cannonball-sized weight hanging there. The little man laughed and pointed to the man sitting in the booth again, then took another dollar bill and trotted away with the box and the tubes to another table.

He was looking at his father putting the roll of bills back into the coat pocket. His own hands still stung, and he wrapped them around the wet bottle in front of him to cool them.

"Yessir—that fucker'll sober you right up." His father signaled to the bartender. "I'm gonna need a couple more after that little bastard."

Somebody came walking over to the booth, but it wasn't the bartender. He looked up and saw one of the guys, one of his father's buddies—the guy hadn't been there the whole time they'd been messing around with the little man with the box.

"Lemme out." His uncle Tommy nudged him. "I think it's just about my turn."

He didn't know what his uncle meant, but he stood up and let Tommy slide out of the booth. The other guy took his place, sorting through the bottles on the table for the one that had been there before, that he hadn't finished.

Before he sat back down, he watched his uncle Tommy walking across the bar, squeezing past the backs of the chairs circled around the tables. There was a door in the corner with one of those wordless signs, a stick figure to indicate the men's room. But Tommy didn't head off toward that. His uncle pulled back the curtain hiding a doorway off to the side and disappeared behind it. He sat back down, but kept looking over at the curtain as he sipped at the beer that had grown warm in his hands.

Then—he didn't know how long it was—his uncle Tommy was back. Standing beside him, at the outside of the booth.

"Come on, fella—" Across the table, his father stabbed a thumb up in the air a couple of times. "Get up and let your old uncle siddown."

His uncle smelled different, sweat and something else. He got up, stepping back a little bit—the scent curled in his nostrils like something from an animal—and let his uncle slide into the booth.

He sat back down. His uncle Tommy had a big grin on his face. Around the table, he saw a couple of the other guys give a slow wink to each other, then tilt their beers up again.

Tommy glanced sidelong at him, then leaned over the table and spewed out a mouthful of blood. Enough of it to swamp across the tabletop, knocking the empty bottles over in the flood.

And he wasn't sitting in the booth then, next to his uncle. He'd jumped out of the booth, the way you would from the door of a rolling car; he stumbled and almost fell backward. Standing a couple of feet away, he listened to the men pounding the table and howling their laughter, louder than when the man with the box had shocked him.

"Tom, you shit-for-brains—" His father was red-faced, gasping for breath.

His uncle Tommy had a dribble of red going down his chin, like the finger of blood that had reached the edge of the table and dribbled over. Pretty drunk, his uncle smiled as he looked around the booth at the guys, pleased with the joke. His uncle turned and smiled at him, red seeping around the teeth in the sloppy grin.

The laughter dwindled away, the men shaking their heads and rubbing tears from the corners of their eyes. They all took long pulls at their beers. That was when he saw that there wasn't any room in the booth for him. They'd all shifted a little bit and taken up all the room; his uncle was sitting right at the end where he'd been.

They didn't say anything, but he knew what it meant. He turned around and looked across the bar, to the curtain that covered the doorway over there. It meant it was his turn now.

The woman ran her hand along the side of his neck. "You haven't been around here before, have you?" She smiled at him. Really smiled, not like she was laughing at him.

"No—" He shook his head. Her hand felt cool against the heat that had come rushing up under his skin. He pointed back over his shoulder. "I came with my dad, and his friends."

Her gaze moved past his eyes, up to where her fingers tangled around in his hair. "Uh-huh," she said. "I know your daddy."

She got up from the bed. He sat there watching her as she stood at a little shelf nailed to the wall. The shelf had a plastic-framed mirror propped up on it, and a towel and a bar of soap. She watched herself taking off her dangly earrings, gold ones, drawing the curved hooks out. She laid them down in front of the little mirror.

"Well, you don't have to worry none." She spoke to the mirror. "There's always a first time. Then it's easy after that." She rubbed a smudge away from the corner of her eye. "You'll see."

When he'd pulled aside the curtain and stepped into the dark—away from the bar's light, its noise of laughing and talking falling behind him—he hadn't even been able to see where he was, until he'd felt the woman take his hand and lead him a little farther along, back to where the doors to a lot of little rooms were lit up by a bulb hanging from the hallway's ceiling. One of the doors had opened and a man had come out and shoved past him in the narrow space, and he'd caught a whiff of the smell off the man, the same as had been on his uncle Tommy when he'd come back out to the booth.

When the woman had closed the door and come over to the bed to sit close by him, he'd held his breath for a moment, because he thought the scent would be on her too, that raw smell, like sweat, only sharper. But she smelled sweet, like something splashed on from a bottle, the kind women always had on their dressers. That made him realize that she was the first woman, the first female thing, he'd been near, for what seemed like days. All the way down here—in the car with his father and his uncle and their buddies, packed up tight with them as they'd gone barreling

92

along in the night, and then crowded around the table in the booth, the same night rolling through the street outside, until their sweat was all he could smell, right down into his throat.

"Here—you don't want to get that all mussed up." The woman had on a white slip—it shone in the dim light as she came back toward the bed. "Let's take it off." She bent down, her dark hair brushing against his face, and started unbuttoning his shirt.

He felt cold, the sweat across his arms and shoulders chilling in the room's air. The woman sat down and leaned back against the bed's pillow, dropping his shirt to the floor. "Come a little closer." She stretched out her arms toward him.

"You see . . . there's nothing to be afraid of." Her voice went down to a whisper, yet somehow it filled the little room; it ate up all the space, until there was just the bed and her on it.

"We'll go real slow, so you won't get scared." She smiled at him, her hand tracing down his rib cage. She was a lot older than him; this close to her, he could see the tiny wrinkles around her eyes, the skin that had gone soft and tissuey around the bone, dark underneath it. The sweet smell covered up something else; when he breathed her breath, it slid down his throat and stuck there.

"Look . . ." She took his hand and turned his arm around, the pale skin underneath showing. She drew a fingernail along the blue vein that ran down to the pulse ticking away in his wrist.

She dropped his hand and held out her own arm. For just a second—then she seemed to remember something. She lifted her hips to pull the slip up, then shimmied the rest of the way out of it like a quick snakeskin. She threw it on the floor with his shirt.

"Now look . . ." She traced the vein in her arm. Her fingernail left a long thin mark along it. She did it again, the mark going deeper. Then a dot of red welled up around her nail, in the middle of her forearm. She dug the nail in deeper, then peeled back the white skin, the line pulling open from the inside of her elbow to her wrist.

"Look," she whispered again. She held the arm up to his face. The room was so small now, the ceiling pressing against his neck, that he couldn't back away. "Look." She held the long slit open, her fingers pulling the skin and flesh back. The red made a net over her hand, collecting in thicker lines that coursed to the point of her elbow and trickled off. A red pool had formed between her knee and his, where their weight pressed the mattress down low.

The blue line inside her arm was brighter now, revealed. "Go on," she said. "Touch it." She leaned forward, bringing her mouth close to his ear. "You have to."

He reached out—slowly—and lay his fingertips on the blue line. For a moment he felt a shock, like the one the man in the bar had given him. But he didn't draw his hand away from the slit the woman held open to him. Under his fingertips he felt the tremble of the blood inside.

Her eyelids had drawn down, so that she looked at him through her lashes. Smiling. "Don't go . . ." He saw her tongue move across the edges of her teeth. "There's more . . ."

She had to let go of the edges, to guide him. The skin and flesh slid against his fingers, under the ridge of his knuckles. He could still see inside the opening, past her hand and his.

She teased a white strand away from the bone. "Here . . ." She looped his fingers under the tendon. As his fingers curled around it, stretching and lifting it past the glistening muscle, the hand at the end of the arm, her hand, curled also. The fingers bent, holding nothing, a soft gesture, a caress.

He could barely breathe. When the air came into his throat, it was heavy with the woman's sweet smell, and the other smell, the raw, sharper one that he'd caught off his uncle.

"See?" The woman bent her head low, looking up through her lashes into his eyes. Her breasts glowed with sweat. Her hair trailed across her open arm, the ends of the dark strands tangling in the blood. "See—it's not so bad, is it?"

She wanted him to say no, she wanted him to say it was okay. She didn't want him to be frightened. But he couldn't say anything. The smell had become a taste lying on his tongue. He finally managed to shake his head.

Her smile was a little bit sad. "Okay, then." She nodded slowly. "Come on."

The hand at the end of the arm had squeezed into a fist, a small one because her hands were so small. The blood that had trickled down into her palm seeped out from between the fingers and thumb. With her other hand, she closed his fingers around the white tendon tugged up from inside. She closed her grip around his wrist and pulled, until the tendon snapped, both ends coming free from their anchor on the bone.

She made him lift his hand up, the ends of the tendon

dangling from where it lay across his fingers. She had tilted her head back, the cords in her throat drawn tight.

"Come on . . ." She leaned back against the pillow. She pulled him toward her. One of her hands lay on the mattress, palm upward, open again, red welling up from the slit in her arm. With her other hand she guided his hand. His fingers made red smears across the curve of her rib cage. "Here . . ." She forced his finger-tips underneath. "You have to push hard." The skin parted and his fingers sank in, the thin bone of the rib sliding across the tips.

"That's right . . ." She nodded as she whispered, eyes closed. "Now you've got it. . . ."

Her hand slid down from his, down his wrist and trailing along her forearm. Not holding and guiding him any longer, but just touching him. He knew what she wanted him to do. His fingers curled around the rib, the blood streaming down to his elbow as the skin opened wider. He lifted and pulled, and the woman's rib cage came up toward him, the ones higher snapping free from her breastbone, all of them grinding softly against the hinge of her spine.

His hand moved inside, the wing of her ribs spreading back. Her skin parted in a curve running up between her breasts. He could see everything now, the shapes that hung suspended in the red space, close to each other, like soft nestled stones. The shapes trembled as his hand moved between them, the webs of sinew stretching, then peeling open, the spongy tissue easing around his hand and forearm.

He reached up higher, his body above hers now, balancing his weight on his other hand hard against the mattress, deep in the red pool along her side. Her knees pressed into the points of his hips.

He felt it then, trembling against his palm. His hand closed around it, and he saw it in her face as he squeezed it tight into his fist.

The skin parted further, the red line dividing her throat, to the hinge of her jaw. She lifted herself up from the pillow, curling around him, the opening soft against his chest. She wrapped her arm around his shoulders to hold him closer to her.

She tilted her head back, pressing her throat to his mouth. He opened his mouth, and his mouth was full, choking him until he had to swallow. The heat streaming across his face and down his own throat pulsed with the trembling inside his fist.

He swallowed again now, faster, the red heat opening inside him.

It was lying on the bed, not moving. He stood there looking at it. He couldn't even hear it breathing anymore. The only sound in the little room was a slow dripping from the edge of the mattress onto the floor.

He reached down, fingertip trembling, and touched its arm. Its hand lay open against the pillow, palm upward. Underneath the red, the flesh was white and cold. He touched the edge of the opening in its forearm. Already, the blue vein and the tendon had drawn back inside, almost hidden. The skin had started to close, the ends of the slit becoming a faint white line, that he couldn't even feel, though he left a smeared fingerprint there. He pulled back his hand, then he turned away from the bed and stumbled out into the hallway with the single light bulb hanging from the ceiling.

They looked up and saw him as he walked across the bar. He didn't push the empty chairs aside, but hit them with his legs, shoving his way past them.

His uncle Tommy scooted over, making room for him at the booth. He sat down hard, the back of his head striking the slick padding behind him.

They had all been laughing and talking just before, but they had gone quiet now. His father's buddies fumbled with the bottles in front of them, not wanting to look at him.

His father dug out a handkerchief, a blue checked one. "Here—" A quiet voice, the softest he'd ever heard his father say anything. His father held out the handkerchief across the table. "Clean yourself up a little."

He took the handkerchief. For a long time, he sat there and looked down at his hands and what was on them.

They were all laughing again, making noise to keep the dark pushed back. His father and his uncle and their buddies roared and shouted and pitched the empties out the windows. The car barreled along, cutting a straight line through the empty night.

He laid his face into the wind. Out there, the dog ran at the edge of the darkness, its teeth bared, its eyes like bright heated coins. It ran over the stones and dry brush, keeping pace with the car, never falling behind, heading for the same destination.

The wind tore the tears from his eyes. The headlights swept across the road ahead, and he thought of the piece of paper folded in the book in his bedroom. The piece of paper meant nothing now, he could tear it into a million pieces. She'd know, too, the girl who played the flute and who'd given the piece of paper to him. She'd know when she saw him again, she'd know that things were different now, and they could never be the same again. They'd be different for her now, too. She'd know.

The tears striped his face, pushed by the wind. He wept in rage and shame at what had been stolen from him. Rage and shame that the woman down there, in the little room at the end of the street with all the lights, would be dead, would get to know over and over again what it was to die. That was what she'd stolen from him, from all of them.

He wept with rage and shame that now he was like them, he was one of them. He opened his mouth and let the wind hammer into his throat, to get out the stink and taste of his own sweat, which was just like theirs now.

The dog ran beside the car, laughing as he wept with rage and shame. Rage and shame at what he knew now, rage and shame that now he knew he'd never die.

I'm a novelist; I don't write short stories. This is, in fact, my only one to date other than a short-short that Ellen Datlow commissioned for *OMNI*. The Armadillocon people in Austin wanted me to do a reading for my guest-of-honor appearance there in 1988, and I hate reading excerpts from novels, so I had to come up with something. I'd just read an article in *The Wall Street Journal* about U.S. kids getting into trouble in Mexican border towns, and combined that with some teenage memories of visits to Tijuana—dark hints from the older guys about things much worse than donkey shows. Ellen was at Armadillocon, too, so I gave her the story after I was done with the reading. Alien sex?—I thought that was the whole *point*. Is there any other kind?

K. W. JETER

PHILIP
⊙ JOSÉ FARMER ⊙

THE
JUNGLE ROT KID
ON THE NOD

Philip José Farmer's first science-fiction sale was "The Lovers," in 1952, which has become a classic of alien sex. He's won several Hugo awards. He is also the author of what may be the most shocking opening scene of a novel, that in The Image of the Beast, *which is certainly about, among other things, alien sex. "The Jungle Rot Kid on the Nod," one of the oldest stories in this volume, may shock fans of Edgar Rice Burroughs, the creator of Tarzan, but I doubt it will even surprise those familiar with the more raw fiction of* William Burroughs, *author of* Naked Lunch *and* Junky.

I f William Burroughs instead of Edgar Rice Burroughs had written the Tarzan novels . . .

Tapes cut and respliced at random by Brachiate Bruce, the old mainliner chimp, the Kid's asshole buddy, cool blue in the orgone box

from the speech in Parliament of Lord Greystoke alias The Jungle Rot Kid, a full house, SRO, the Kid really packing them in.
  —Capitalistic pricks! Don't send me no more foreign aid! You

corrupting my simple black folks, they driving around the old plantation way down on the Zambezi River in air-conditioned Cadillacs, shooting horse, flapping ubangi at me . . . Bwana him not in the cole cole ground but him sure as shit gonna be soon. Them M-16s, tanks, mortars, flamethrowers coming up the jungle trail, ole Mao Charley promised us!

Lords, Ladies, Third Sex! I tole you about apeomorphine but you dont lissen! You got too much invested in the Mafia and General Motors, I say you gotta kick the money habit too. Get them green things offen your back . . . nothing to lose but your chains that is stocks, bonds, castles, Rollses, whores, soft toilet paper, connection with The Man . . . it a long long way to the jungle but it worth it, build up your muscle and character cut/

. . . you call me here at my own expense to degrade humiliate me strip me of loincloth and ancient honored title! You hate me cause you hung up on civilization and I never been hooked. You over a barrel with smog freeways TV oily beaches taxes inflation frozen dinners time clocks carcinogens neckties all that shit. Call me noble savage . . . me tell you how it is where its at with my personal tarzanic *purusharta* . . . involves kissing off *dharma* and *artha* and getting a fix on *moksha* through *kama* . . .

Old Lord Bromley-Rimmer who wear a merkin on his bald head and got pecker and balls look like dried-up grapes on top a huge hairy cut-in fold-out thing it disgust you to see it, he grip young Lord Materfutter's crotch and say—Dearie what kinda gibberish that, Swahili, what?

Young Lord Materfutter say—Bajove, some kinda African cricket doncha know what?

. . . them fuckin Ayrabs run off with my Jane again . . . intersolar communist venusian bankers plot . . . so it back to the jungle again, hit the arboreal trail, through the middle tearass, dig Numa the lion, the lost civilizations kick, tell my troubles to Sam Tantor alias The Long Dong Kid. Old Sam always writing amendments to the protocols of the elders of mars, dipping his trunk in the blood of innocent bystanders, writing amendments in the sand with blood and no one could read what he had written there selah

Me, I'm only fuckin free man in the world . . . live in state of anarchy, up trees . . . every kid and lotsa grown-ups (so-called) dream of the Big Tree Fix, of swinging on vines, freedom, live by the knife and unwritten code of the jungle . . .

99

Ole Morphodite Lord Bromley-Rimmer say—Dearie, that Anarchy, that one a them new African nations what?

The Jungle Rot Kid bellowing in the House of Lords like he calling ole Sam Tantor to come running help him outta his mess, he really laying it on them blueblood pricks.

. . . I got *satyagraha* in the ole original Sanskrit sense of course up the ass, you fat fruits. I quit. So long. Back to the Dark Continent . . . them sheiks of the desert run off with Jane again . . . blood will flow . . .

Fadeout. Lord Materfutter's face phantom of erection wheezing paregoric breath. —Dig that leopardskin jockstrap what price glory what? cut/

This here extracted from John Clayton's diary which he write in French God only know why . . . *Sacre bleu! Nom d'un con!* Alice she dead, who gonna blow me now? The kid screaming his head off, he sure don't look like black-haired gray-eyed fine-chiseled-featured scion of noble British family which come over with Willie the Bastard and his squarehead-frog goons on the Anglo-Saxon Lark. No more milk for him no more ass for me, carry me back to old Norfolk / / double cut

The Gorilla Thing fumbling at the lock on the door of old log cabin which John Clayton built hisself. Eyes stabbing through the window. Red as two diamonds in a catamite's ass. John Clayton, he rush out with a big axe, gonna chop me some anthropoid wood.

Big hairy paws strong as hold of pusher on old junkie whirl Clayton around. Stinking breath. Must smoke banana peels. *Whoo! Whoo!* Gorilla Express dingdonging up black tunnel of my rectum. Piles burst like rotten tomatoes, sighing softly. Death come. And come. And come. Blazing bloody orgasms. Not a bad way to go . . . but you cant touch my inviolate white soul . . . too late to make a deal with the Gorilla Thing? Give him my title, Jaguar, moated castle, ole faithful family retainer he go down on you, opera box . . . *ma tante de pisse* . . . who take care of the baby, carry on family name? *Vive la bourgerie!* cut/

Twenty years later give take a couple, the Jungle Rot Kid trail the killer of Big Ape Mama what snatch him from cradle and raise him as her own with discipline security warm memory of hairy teats hot unpasteurized milk . . . the Kid swinging big on vines from tree to tree, fastern hot baboonshit through a tin horn. Ant hordes blitzkrieg him like agenbite of intwat, red insect-things which is exteriorized thoughts of the Monster Ant-Mother of the Crab Nebula in secret war to take over this small planet, this Peoria Earth.

Monkey on his back, Nkima, eat the red insect-things, wipe out trillions with flanking bowel movement, Ant-Mother close up galactic shop for the day . . .

The Kid drop his noose around the black-assed motherkiller and haul him up by the neck into the tree in front of God and local citizens which is called gomangani in ape vernacular.

—You gone too far this time the Kid say as he core out the motherkillers asshole with fathers old hunting knife and bugger him old Turkish custom while the motherkiller rockin and rollin in death agony.

Heavy metal Congo jissom ejaculate catherinewheeling all over local gomangani, they say—Looka that!

Old junkie witch doctor coughing his lungs out in sick gray African morning, shuffling through silver dust of old kraal.

—You say my son's dead, kilt by the Kid?

Jungle drums beat like aged wino's temples morning after. Get Whitey!

The Kid sometime known as Genocide John really liquidate them dumbshit gomangani. Sure is a shame to waste all that black gash the Kid say but it the code of the jungle. Noblesse obleege.

The locals say—We dont haffa put up with this shit and they split. The Kid dont have no fun nomore and this chimp ass mighty hairy not to mention chimp habit of crapping when having orgasm. Then along come Jane alias Baltimore Blondie, she on the lam from Rudolph Rassendale type snarling—You marry me Jane else I foreclose on your father's ass.

The Kid rescue Jane and they make the domestic scene big, go to Europe on The Civilized Caper but the Kid find out fast that the code of the jungle conflict with local ordinances. The fuzz say you cant go around putting a full-nelson on them criminals and breakin their necks even if they did assault you they got civil rights too. The Kid's picture hang on post office and police station walls everywhere, he known as Archetype Archie and by the Paris fuzz as *La Magnifique Merde*—50,000 francs dead or alive. With the heat moving in, the Kid and Baltimore Blondie cut out for the tree house.

Along come La sometime known as Sacrifice Sal elsewhere as

Disembowelment Daisy. She queen of Opar, ruler of hairy little men-things of the hidden colony of ancient Atlantis, the Kid always dig the lost cities kick. So the Kid split with Jane for a while to ball La.

—Along come them fuckin Ayrabs again and abduct Jane, gangbang her . . . she aint been worth a shit since . . . cost me all the jewels and golden ingots I heisted offa Opar to get rid of her clap, syph, yaws, crabs, pyorrhea, double-barreled dysentery, busted rectum, split urethra, torn nostrils, pierced eardrums, bruised kidneys, nymphomania, old hashish habit, and things too disgusting to mention . . .

Along come The Rumble to End All Rumbles 1914 style, and them fuckin Huns abduct Jane . . . they got preying-mantis eyes with insect lust. Black anti-orgone Horbigerian Weltanschauung, they take orders from green venusians who telepath through von Hindenburg.

—*Ja Wohl!* bark Leutnant Herrlipp von Dreckfinger at his Kolonel, Bombastus von Arschangst. —Ve use die Baltimore snatch to trap der gottverdammerungt Jungle Rot Kid, dot pseudo-Aryan *Oberaffenmensch,* unt ve kill him unt den all Afrika iss ours! Drei cheers for Der Kaiser unt die Krupp Familie!

The Kid balling La again but he drop her like old junkie drop pants for a shot of horse, he track down the Hun, it the code of the jungle.

Cool blue orgone bubbles sift down from evening sky, the sinking sun a bloody kotex which spread stinking scarlet gash-worms over the big dungball of Earth. Night move in like fuzz with Black Maria. Mysterious sounds of tropical wilds . . . Numa roar, wild boars grunt like they constipated, parrots with sick pukegreen feathers and yellow eyes like old goofball bum Panama 1910 cry *Rache!*

Hun blood flow, kraut necks crack like cinnamon sticks, the Kid put his foot on dead ass of slain Teuton and give the victory cry of the bull ape, it even scare the shit outta Numa King of the Beasts fadeout

The Kid and his mate live in the old tree house now . . . surohc lakcaj fo mhtyhr ot ffo kcaj* chimps, Numa roar, Sheeta

* Old Brachiate Bruce splice in tape backward here.

the panther cough like an old junkie. Jane alias The Baltimore Bitch nag, squawk, whine about them mosquitoes tsetse flies ant-things hyenas and them uppity gomangani moved into the neighborhood, they'll turn a decent jungle into slums in three days, I aint prejudiced ya unnerstand some a my best friends are Waziris, whynt ya ever take me out to dinner, Nairobi only a thousand miles away, they really swingin there for chrissakes and cut/

. . . trees chopped down for the saw mills, animals kilt off, rivers stiff stinking with dugout-sized tapewormy turds, broken gin bottles, contraceptive jelly and all them disgusting things snatches use, detergents, cigarette filters . . . and the great apes shipped off to USA zoos, they send telegram: SOUTHERN CALIFORNIA CLIMATE AND WELFARE PROGRAM SIMPLY FABULOUS STOP NO TROUBLE GETTING A FIX STOP CLOSE TO TIAJUANA STOP WHAT PRICE FREEDOM INDIVIDUALITY EXISTENTIAL PHILOSOPHY CRAP STOP

. . . Opar a tourist trap, La running the native-art made-in-Japan concession and you cant turn around without rubbing sparks off black asses.

The African drag really got the Kid down now . . . Jane's voice and the jungle noises glimmering off like a comet leaving Earth forever for the cold interstellar abysms . . .

The Kid never move a muscle staring at his big toe, thinking of nothing—wouldn't you?—not even La's diamond-studded snatch, he off the woman kick, off the everything kick, fulla horse, on the nod, lower spine ten degrees below absolute zero like he got a direct connection with The Liquid Hydrogen Man at Cape Kennedy . . .

The Kid ride with a one-way ticket on the Hegelian Express thesis antithesis synthesis, sucking in them cool blue orgone bubbles and sucking off the Eternal Absolute . . .

William Burroughs is the author of the wild classic, *The Nova Express,* from which the popular term *heavy metal* is derived. This and most of his works deal with the Nova Police, drug addiction, macho homosexuals, sodomy, terrifying alien invasions of Earth, LSD-purple prose, contempt for and disgust with women, and an absolute amorality. Whether he's a genuine or an ersatz genius, only time will determine. His apocalyptic low-life visions and inventiveness fascinate me, though their one-note repetition in his later works also weary me.

The work at hand is a pastiche-parody, my tribute, inspired while rereading William Burroughs's *Naked Lunch*. I thought, What if he, not Edgar Rice Burroughs, had written the Tarzan stories? Result: this short piece embodying the spirit of William's style and content in his peculiar mode. I had fun doing it, but may the Lord of the Jungle forgive me.

PHILIP JOSÉ FARMER

LISA
⊙ TUTTLE ⊙

HUSBANDS

Although born a Texan, Lisa Tuttle has spent most of the past decade living and writing in England. She has had two short-story collections and three novels published, most recently Gabriel *(Tor), as well as several works of nonfiction.*

One part of the triptych "Husbands" was published in the 1988 World Fantasy Convention volume Gaslight and Ghosts. *The others are original to this anthology. I think that of all the stories in this book, "Husbands" shows most vividly how humans see the "other" sex as completely alien from their own.*

I. BUFFALOED

My first husband was a dog, all snuffling, clumsy, ardent devotion. At first (to be fair to him) we were a couple of puppies, gamboling and frisking in our love for each other and collapsing in a panting heap on the bed every night. But time and puppyhood passed, as it tends to do, and as he grew into a devoted, sad-eyed, rather smelly hound, I found myself becoming a cat. It is not the dog's fault that cats and dogs fight like cats and dogs, and probably (to be fair to myself) it is not the cat's fault, either. It is simply in their nature to find everything that is most typical in the other to be the most difficult to live with. I became more and more irritable, until everything he did displeased me. Finally, even the sound of his throat-clearing sigh when I had rebuffed him once again would make my fur stand on end. I couldn't help what I was, any more than he could. It was in our nature, and there was nothing for it but to part.

My second husband was a horse. Well-bred, high-strung, with flaring nostrils and rolling eyes. He was a beauty. I watched him for a long time from a distance before I dared approach. When I touched him (open-palmed, gently but firmly on his flank, as I had been taught), a quiver rippled through the muscles beneath the smooth skin. I thought this response was fear, and I vowed I would teach him to trust and love me. We had a few years together—not all of them bad—before I understood that nervous ripple had been an involuntary expression not of fear but of distaste. Almost, before he left me, I learned to perceive myself as a slow, squat, fleshy creature he suffered to cling to his back. We both tried to change me, but it was a hopeless task. I could not become what he was; I did not even, deeply, want to be. It was not until we both realized that such a profound difference could not be resolved that he left me for one of his own kind.

I didn't intend to have a third husband; I don't believe the phrase "third time lucky" reflects a natural law. With two honorable, doomed tries behind me, and having observed the lives of my contemporaries, I concluded that the happy marriage was the oddity; in most cases, a fantasy. It was a fantasy I wanted to do without. I still liked men, but marrying one of them was not the best way to express that liking. Better to admit my allegiance to the tribe of single women: My women friends were more important to me than any man. They were my family and my emotional support. Most of them had not given up the dream of a husband, but I understood their reasons, and sympathized. Jennifer, bringing up her daughter alone, longed for a partner; Annie, single and childless and relentlessly aging, wanted a father for her child. Janice, who worked hard and lived with her invalid mother, dreamed of a handsome millionaire. Cathy was quite explicit about her sexual needs, and Doreen about her emotional ones. I had no child and didn't want one, earned a good living, seldom felt lonely, had friends for emotional sustenance, and as for sex—well, sometimes there was a lover, and when there wasn't, I tried not to think about it. Sex wasn't really what I missed, although I could interpret it that way. I yearned for something else, something more; it was an old addiction I couldn't quite conquer, a longing it seemed I had been born with.

There was a man. Now the story begins. It can't have a happy ending, but still we keep hoping. At least it's a story. There was a man where I worked. I didn't know his name, and I didn't want to ask, because to ask would reveal my interest. My interest was purely physical. How could it be anything else, when I'd never even spoken to him? What else did I know about him but how he looked? I watched how he moved through the corridors, head down, leading with his shoulders. He had broad shoulders, a short neck, a barrel chest. Such a powerful upper torso that I suspected he had built it by lifting weights. Curling black hair. An impassive face. On bad days, I thought it was noble. On good days, he looked irritatingly stupid. I did not seek him out. I tried to avoid him. But chance brought us together, even though we didn't speak. I wondered if he had noticed me. I wondered how what I felt could not be mutual, could not be real, could be, simply, a one-sided fantasy; an obsession.

Pasiphaë fell in love, they say, with a snow-white bull.

One day I went to the zoo with Jennifer and her daughter. Little Lindsay was thrilled, running from one enclosure to another, demanding to know the animals' names, herself naming the ones she recognized from her picture books.
    "Tiger."
    "Tiger! Lion!"
    "Ocelot."
    "Ocelot!"
    "Leopard."
    "Leopard!"

"Panther."

"Panther!"

I wondered what *his* name was. And what about his soul. What was his sign, his clan, his totem? What animal was he? The bull? The ox, The water buffalo. I considered the Chinese horoscope. A man born in the year of the ox was steady and trustworthy, a patient and tireless worker. Undemonstrative, traditional, dedicated. Boring, I reminded myself. And a determined materialist. He wouldn't even know what I meant if I talked about the union of souls. He was certainly married already, a husband devoted to his wife and children, never dreaming of any alternatives.

I watched Jennifer watching her daughter. I looked at the fine lines that had begun to craze the delicate fair skin of her face, and at the springy black hair compressed into an untidy bun on top of her head. The red scarf (which I had given her) swathing her neck. The set of her shoulders. Her fragile wrists. She felt me watching, and caught my hand with her thin, strong fingers; squeezed. We knew each other so well. We felt the same about so many things; we understood and trusted each other. Sometimes I knew what she was going to say before she said it. We loved each other. The love of two equals, with nothing excessive, romantic, or inexplicable about it.

"Zebra."

"Zebra!"

"Okapi."

"Okapi!"

"Giraffe."

"Giraffe!"

"Buffalo."

Buffalo. The American Bison. Order: Artiodactyla; Family: Bovidae. A powerful, migratory, gregarious horned grazing animal of the North American plains.

Thick, curly, dark-brown hair grew luxuriously on head, neck, and shoulders; a shorter, lighter-brown growth covered the rest of the body. The bull stood there, solid and motionless as a mountainside, and yet it was a warm, living mountain; there was nothing cold or hard about it. I remembered how, as a child, traveling in the back of the car on family holidays, I had gazed out at the changing landscapes and dreamed that I could stroke the distant, furry hills. Something about this creature—wild, yet tame; strange, but familiar—stirred the same, childish response. If I could touch it, I thought, if only I could touch it, something would change. I would know something, and everything would be different.

The set of his shoulders. The curve of his horns. The springy curl of his luxuriant hair. A wild, musty, grassy smell hung on the air, filled my nostrils, and I could feel a sun that wasn't there, beating down on my naked back.

"Buffalo."

Pasiphaë fell in love, they say, with a snow-white bull.

To have her desire, Pasiphaë hid inside a hollow wooden cow, and so the fearsome Minotaur was conceived.

Was that her desire? To be impregnated by a bull? I understand her passion, but not the logic of her actions. It is not Pasiphaë's story that we have been told. What we hear is the greed of Minos, the anger of Poseidon, the cunning of Daedalus. She was a tool, the conduit through which the Minotaur came to be. When her passion died did she understand what she had done, or why? Did she think, suddenly, too late, as the bull mounted her: But this isn't what I meant! This isn't what I wanted! Or was she triumphant, fulfilled? Afterward, was she satisfied? Did the desire she had felt vanish once Poseidon's will had been served, or was it waiting, nameless, incapable of fulfillment, waiting to erupt again?

We are told that Pasiphaë's love for the bull was an unnatural desire. But what is natural about any desire, for anything not necessary to sustain life? What does it mean to want a man? To want a husband?

Staring at the buffalo that cloudy day in the zoo, separated from it by distance, by time, by species, by everything that can distance one creature from another, I felt a wordless, naked desire. It was a desire that could not be named, and certainly could not be fulfilled. It was the purest lust I had ever known, unmuddied, for once, by any of the usual misinterpretations. If that had been a man staring back at me across emptiness with his round, brown,

uncomprehending eye, I would have invited him home with me. I
would have thought my feelings were sexual—sexual desire, at
least, allows satisfaction—and if they persisted beyond that, I
would have used the word *love*. I might have convinced myself that
marriage was possible; I certainly would have tried to convince
him. To have him. Forgetting that it was impossible; forgetting
that desire, by its nature, can never be satisfied.

Remember, I told myself. And then, forgetting, I wondered
what his name was.

"Buffalo?"
"Husband."

II. THIS LONGING

"Sometimes I think we made them up," I said to Rufinella. "Mythical creatures for the mythical time before Now."

We had just been to see an old movie about the relations
between men and women—husbands, single women, and wives—
a horrible story that stirred up emotions unfelt for more than
thirty years. At least in me. I don't know what Rufinella felt: she
had seemed to enjoy it. Although, given the number of times she
had had to lean over and ask me, in a loud whisper, which ones
were the men and which the women, I wondered what it was she
had enjoyed, and just how much she had understood.

Rufinella gave me a disbelieving look. "What's this? You've
joined the revisionists? You're about to confess you were a part of
the conspiracy all along? That you've been lying to your students
all these years, pretending that myth is history?"

"No conspiracy," I said. "I've always taught the truth as I've
understood it, but sometimes I wonder—what did I ever understand? How much of what I remember was true? Did they really
exist, this other . . . gender? Like us, yet so unalike? Face it, the
details are so unlikely!"

"But you said you had one."

"You can't say 'had one' like they were property—"

"People talk about them like that in the movies. And I've
heard you say it—you've always said you had a husband. What are
you telling me now—that it didn't exist?"

"He," I corrected automatically, teacher that I am. "Oh, yes,

I had a husband . . . and a father and a brother and lovers and male colleagues. . . . At least, I think I did. When I remember them, they don't seem so terribly different from the women I knew that long ago. They don't seem like strange, extinct creatures . . . they were just individuals, whom I knew. Other people, you know? I was twenty-eight years old when the men went away. That's— well, more than thirty years ago now. I've lived longer without men than I lived with them. What I remember might almost be a dream."

"If it was a dream, everybody else had it, too," said Rufinella. "And there's the evidence: there they are—or at least their shadows—on film, on video, in the newspapers, in books, in the news. . . . They were real; if you're going to judge by the evidence they left behind, they were more real than the women."

"Then maybe they woke up to reality one day, and found that the women were gone."

"Nobody dreamed *me*," said the daughter of my best friend, very firmly. Rufinella was two months old when the men disappeared. Therefore, unlike her own daughter, she had a father, but she cannot possibly remember him, or any man. Although she has tried, through hypnotic regression. According to her, she succeeded in going back before her birth, to her time in the womb. She said she could remember her mother's body. But she could not remember her father. She couldn't remember a male presence, no more than imagine how creatures called men might have differed so dramatically from creatures called women, as all history, all art, tells us they did.

Art is metaphor, and history is an art. It was *like* this. It was not like *that*. We are language-using, storytelling creatures. Trying to explain reality, we transform it. We can't travel in time and know the past that way, but only, endlessly, try to re-create it. As a teacher (I'm semiretired, now), I tried to make my students understand something they could never know for themselves. Imaginative reconstruction of a place that no longer exists. They can't go there, but neither can I. My own memories are stories I tell myself.

Maybe women did make up men, invented them the way earlier civilizations created gods, to fill a need. A group of revisionist historians—psychohistorians they call themselves—would like us all to believe that there was never any "second sex," never any "other" kind of human being except ourselves. According to them, men were a cultural invention. After all, if they were truly other than us, necessary in the same way as are male animals, how is it that we women have managed to continue to reproduce ourselves, managed to conceive and bear children, without any of the equipment or the contortions depicted in illustrated texts on human sexuality, and in a certain class of film?

I've heard many clever and convincing arguments for the revisionist view of human history, and there are times when I feel that only a native stubbornness keeps me clinging to what I "know." Yet the argument they think is the clincher for their point of view does not convince me.

Like all sane and sensible people, they still, thirty-four years after the fact, cannot come to terms with, can hardly believe, the way that men disappeared. Overnight; all at once; in the twinkling of an eye. They simply were no longer. Reality doesn't work like that; dreams do. So it makes a certain comforting sense to conclude that the whole class or gender of *men* was a dream. Nothing vanished except an illusion. There was no sudden, worldwide disappearance, but only an equally sudden change in perception. Men no longer existed because we no longer needed to pretend that they did.

Things that exist do not suddenly cease to be. They change, possibly out of all recognition, but something doesn't become nothing except through a process of transformation. This is true not only of objects, but also of needs. What happened to that need which made women invent the story of men in such convincing detail, and cling to it for so many thousands of years? Why should it be any easier to erase such a need than half the human race? How could it vanish in the blink of an eye, between one breath and the next?

I said something of this sort to Rufinella. She looked tired and sad. "Oh, yes," she said. "You're right. The need is still there, and we still don't understand it. That's why I think men are coming back."

"The same way they left?" I loved my husband very much, and grieved for him and other male friends and family when they disappeared; I had mourned for years, wanting them back. And yet, now, the thought that they might all return, be found back in place tomorrow morning, was strangely horrible.

"Oh, no. I don't think so. I don't think you're going to roll over in bed one night and find you're not alone. I think they're coming back in a different way . . . more slowly, but more surely. We've had this time, all these years, to learn to understand ourselves and to change, and we haven't done it. We've missed our chance. We've blown it, as your generation says. We still need them, and we don't know why. So men are coming back. And I think it's going to be worse for us this time; a lot worse."

Rufinella is bright and observant and cautious, not given to making rash, unprovable statements.

"Why?"

"You don't spend much time around children, do you?"

"Not much," I said. "In fact, hardly any. I suppose your Leni's birthday party was the last time."

"I spend two afternoons a week in the community nursery," Rufinella said. "And of course I live with Leni, and there's her friends, and Alice has an eight-year-old . . . since I've noticed, I've been talking to more mothers and teachers and nursery workers and . . . it's consistent. It's not isolated incidents; there's a pattern to it, and it's—"

"What?"

"I didn't mean to tell you yet—I didn't mean to tell anyone, until I was certain. Until I had more evidence. I could be wrong, I could be overreacting, imagining things. . . . I thought it was just a fad, at first. Most people who've noticed it probably think that. Because you only see a part of it, you only see what the kids in your house or your school or your neighborhood are doing, and you don't realize that they are all doing the same thing, all across the city, all across the country . . . all over the world, I suspect, although of course I don't *know* . . . yet. At first I thought . . . you know how children are; I myself remember what it was like. Making up codes, secret languages, little rituals. It's part of childhood. A children's culture. And that's what this is. They have their own culture."

I felt the way I always feel before a medical examination. I wanted to leap ahead of her, tell her before she could tell me. "And you recognize it—this culture—from the old movies."

"Not the details. The details are different. I guess they'd have to be. But, yes, I do recognize it . . . at least, I recognize one thing about it . . . you would, too, I think."

"Tell me."

"They have their own language, their own rituals. Those might differ from group to group, but the worst of it is, there are always two. Two separate classes, if you like. They've created certain differences . . . certain, consistent differences. Two types of language, two types of ritual. One group of children uses one, and one is for the other. No crossover allowed. You can't change the group you belong to, once you've picked it . . . or once it's picked *you*. I can't quite work out how the division is determined, or how early it is established, but somehow they all seem to know. A two-year-old going to nursery for the first time—it's settled before a word is spoken. They all know which group she belongs to, and there's no mistake possible, no appeal allowed. Almost as if they can see signs we can't—as if it were established at birth, the way sex used to be." Rufinella looked at me steadily, yet somehow desperately. She was pleading, I realized; hoping that I would have some advice, some wisdom from the age before hers.

"You think they're reinventing gender."

She nodded.

"What do they say about it? Have you asked them?"

"They can't explain it. They say that's just how things are. They invent new languages, they create differences, but they talk about it as if they can't help it. As if these are discoveries, not inventions."

"Maybe—"

"Don't say it! You mean that we've been blind for thirty-four years and now our children can see?"

I felt such longing, and such hope. I wished I were younger. I wanted another chance; I had always wanted another chance. I didn't understand the despair on Rufinella's face unless it was because she, too, knew she wouldn't be a part of the coming age. I said, "Maybe they'll get it right this time."

III. THE MODERN PROMETHEUS

"It was on a dreary night of November that I beheld the accomplishment of my toils."

Yes, I have been successful! I have dared to try, and managed to bring life to what to others has ever been only a dream: another race of beings, a partner-species, to end our long loneliness by being our planetary companions. Enough like us that we can communicate; yet different, so that each will have something worth communicating, bringing different visions, different experiences, to enrich the relationship of true equals.

Perhaps I shall have cause to regret my deed, but I do not think so. I think my name will go down in history as a positive example of how science can make the world a better place. I have not acted out of pride or ignorance, not for personal gain or ambition. Nor do I believe that anything that can be done should be; that scientific achievement is a valuable end in itself. No, I have thought long and hard about what I meant to do. I have considered the dangers carefully and established certain limits. And all along I have felt myself to be not an individual pursuing personal goals, but rather the representative of all womankind, acting for the greater good.

Not, of course, that everyone agrees with what I have done. Many do not see the necessity. Why create a new species? Why bring another life-form into existence? Isn't that playing god? Yes, I say, and why not? Don't we do that already, every day, as we struggle to change the world for the better? Why should we suffer the lack of something we can create? But, of course, some do not believe there *was* any such lack. Some do not even believe in the yearning that has driven me to this. Because they have never felt it, they say it is imaginary. Solid materialists, they refuse to accept the possibility that one might desire something that does not exist. Something—I hasten to qualify—that does not *yet* exist. For I believe that these unnamed longings are expressions of memory— a racial memory, if you will, whether of past or future hardly matters. Desire is timeless, but it does not deal in the imaginary. If it seems that what we want does not exist, that is true only of this time. You may be certain that you had what you desire in the past, or you may have it in the future.

I have been driven by the desire to know someone else, another being, who is not like me. Not my lover, not my child, not my mother, not any friend or stranger on this earth. And so I have created it.

What is this new creation? I thought of calling it "man" for the obvious, mythohistorical reasons. But the emotions connected to that word are mixed; and there are aspects of history better buried . . . not forgotten, but certainly not re-created. I have been careful to ensure that my "man" should not be like any man who lived before, not like any previous companion women have known. To signal this, I have given him a name that represents what many women want; I have named this, our hearts' desire, "husband."

So, now, on this not-so-dreary November night, I look through the glass side of the tank at my creation. He looks back at me, interested, intelligent, and kind, his body sleek and beautiful, his mind and spirit equal to my own. Equal, but different. I'm sure I've got it right. There will be no misunderstandings, no doomed attempts at domestication, and no struggles for power, for although we are enough alike to love each other, we will always live apart: women on dry land, husbands in the sea. Their beautiful faces and their complicated minds are like ours, but their bodies are very different. We will always live in different worlds. They must swim, having no legs to walk with, and although they breathe the same air we do, their skin needs the constant, enveloping caress of the water. We each will have our own domain, each be happy among our own kind, and yet they will find us as attractive as we find them, and so we shall seek each other out from time to time, and come together not for gain or of necessity, but from pure desire.

I look at him, the first of the new race, and when I smile, so does he. He waves a flipper; I wave a hand. I feel love bubbling up inside me, washing away the pain of the past, and I know, as he does a backflip for my admiration, that my husband feels the same. This time, it will work out for the best.

When I wrote "Husbands" I was thirty-five, had been divorced for a couple of years, and was suffering the pain of unrequited love. It was an experience I thought belonged to adolescence; I'd thought I was past it. I knew it was ridiculous. But it was also overwhelming, and quite out of my control. I thought of Fate, and of Greek myths; of the Minotaur, born because a god took vengeance on King Minos by making his wife fall in love with a mad, white bull (at least I'd had the good fortune to fall in love with another human being!); of the mystery, and the absurdity, of desire.

At the same time, I wanted to write something based on the

radical concept of Monique Wittig's "One Is Not Born a Woman" (1979), a short paper in which she declared that far from being natural categories, the division of human beings into two distinct classes of "men" and "women" is "a sophisticated and mythic construction." If our belief that human beings must be divided into two categories is a matter not of immutable fact but of learned perception, what happens if we learn to perceive differently? Particularly since there must have been a powerful reason to make us all accept that old man/woman, yin/yang way of looking at things for so long.

Two stories—one contemporary, impressionistic, set in the real world, about recognizable emotions; the other an idea, another world, another way of being, explored science fictionally. Yet I kept thinking of them as being the same story, with the same title. Then I had another idea, for a third story also dealing with the theme of desire and sexual difference, and there it was, my story: three stories, three parts of one story. That old, old story.

LISA TUTTLE

BRUCE
⊙ McALLISTER ⊙

WHEN THE
FATHERS GO

Bruce McAllister began writing science fiction and fantasy in the 1960s. His first novel, Humanity Prime, *appeared in Terry Carr's first "Ace Specials" series; his second,* Dream Baby, *appeared last year from Tor Books. His fiction appears regularly in* OMNI *and has been reprinted widely. He teaches writing at the University of Redlands, in Redlands, California.*

"When the Fathers Go" is the first story of this author I ever read. It originally appeared in Terry Carr's anthology, Universe 12. *It demonstrates perfectly McAllister's rare ability to capture the female voice in literature. And it's about the lies men and women tell each other in order to maintain rocky relationships.*

When he told me he had fa-
thered a child Out There, I felt sure he was lying. I thought of the
five years I'd been awake, the five years since his return, the five
years I'd been pleading with him for a child, and I thought of all
his lies. (They *all* come back lying.)

I was sure he was lying.

It was night in the skyroom. We were naked and wet from
another warm programmed rain, and were again pawing at each

other in good-natured frustration, laughing because the paper-thin energy field between us wouldn't let us touch.

The frustration was important.

Soon one of us would tell the room's computer to activate a stencil, a brand-new pattern for our hands to explore blindly, seeking the holes through which we might reach each other.

The frustration was so important.

Before long—if everything went right—we would be moving against the field like animals, two starved bodies no longer willing to accept the constraints so good-naturedly.

It was all a *karezza*, a game I suspected Jory liked, though I could never be sure. The only things I was sure of were the hallucinogens and the pheromas. These I knew he liked. Only these.

He might pull away suddenly from the stencil, stare at me, and walk off into the night.

And if he stayed, if he indeed stayed long enough for it to happen, it would be an event as unrelated to me as any dim nova in a distant galaxy. I would see it in his eyes: he would be somewhere else. His moment would belong to him and him alone—Out There.

I blame the hallucinogens as much as the rest. I am jealous of the Moonlight, the Starmen, Schwarzchild's Love, and Winkinblinkins. They are his real lovers.

When he spoke, I assumed it was to the room's computer. But his voice went on—the amplified stars twinkling madly through the electronic glass, the moonlight falling on our naked shoulders like a cold blue robe. He was talking to *me*.

"I'm sorry, Dorothea," he was saying. "I am, as a long-lost poet once put it, a man adrift from his duties, a man awash in his world. I should have told you long before now, but did not. Why? Because it's horrible as well as beautiful."

He paused, so emotional, so crucified by remorse, and then: "When I was Out There, Dorothea, when I had the starlocks at my back and the universe at my feet, when I'd abandoned my home world as surely as if I'd died, I took an alien lover, Dorothea, and she bore me a son. I can't believe it myself, but it is true, and the time has come."

He was histrionic. He was heroic. He was playing to some great audience I couldn't see.

And he was lying.

They say the ones who go Out There—the *diplos, greeters,* and *runners*—come back liars because of what they've seen, because of the starlock sleep, because of what they dream as they make their painful slow way through the concentric rings of sequential tokamaks, super-pinches, marriages of light-cones, and miracles of winkholes. It is a sleep (the rumors say) filled with visions of eternal parallel universes, of all possible alternative worlds—where Hitler did and didn't, where Christ was and wasn't, where the Nile never flowed, where Jory never left, or if he did, I never went to sleep for him.

They are changed by it. They come back seeing what isn't, but what might have been, what isn't but *is*—somewhere. And because they come back liars to a world fifteen years older, there will always be jobs for any man or woman willing to be a *diplo* or *greeter* or *runner*. They are the lambs. They are sacrificed in our names.

Whether Jory's lies are universes he indeed perceives, or simply the handiwork of a pathology, I do not know. I do know that there are times when I enter his lies with him and times when I do not. There are even times when I love his lies, though it embarrasses me to say so. When we lie together on the little stretch of sand below our house and make a simpler love—the roll of the waves mercifully drowning out the sucking of the great factory pipes so nearby—I want those lies, ask for them in my own way, and he gives them to me:

"Dorothea, my love, I have known women, insatiable women, women from a satyr's wildest dreams. I have known them in every port of the Empire—from Dandanek II to Miladen-Poy, from Gloster's Alley to Blackie's Hole, from the great silicon-methane bays of Torsion to the antigravity Steppes of Heart—and none of them can compare with the softest touch of your skin, with the simplest caress of your breath."

There are no ports like these. Not yet. No swashbuckling spacelanes, no pirates of the Hypervoid, no Empire. No romantic Frontier for the sowing of the human seed throughout galaxies so vast and wondrous that their glory must catch in your throat. It is, after all, a simpler, more mundane universe we inhabit.

But when he speaks to me like this, my world is suddenly grand, the ports as real as San Francisco, the women as lusty as legends, and I, a Helen of New Troy, with a strange and beautiful apple in my hand.

I could have answered him with "What was she like, Jory?" I could have entered that lie, too, and said, "Did you ever see your son, Jory?"

But this one hurt. It hurt too much.

"What do you mean, the time has come?" I asked, sighing.

He was turning away, toward the darkness of the hills behind our house.

"He is coming to live with us," he said.

I closed my eyes. "Your son?"

"Of course, Dorothea."

I hate him for it.

He knows how it hurts. He knows why.

We have encountered three races Out There. The first two—the nearest us in light-years—are indeed humanoid, offering (for some, at least) clear proof of the "seeding" theory of mankind's presence in this solar system. The third race, the mysterious Climagos, is so alien that instead of animosity and avarice we find in it a disturbing generosity—gifts like the energy fields, crystalline sleep, and the starlocks. In return, it has asked nothing but goodwill. We do not understand this. We do not understand it at all.

We have (we have decided) nothing to learn, nothing to gain, from the two humanoid species, the little Debolites and stolid Oteans. We ignore them, and are jealous of the attention the Climagos pay them. We are, it would seem, afraid of what these two humanoid species might eventually do with the Climagos' gifts. After all, we know well what it means to be "human."

"You haven't asked, but I will tell you anyway," he says.

He has followed me down to the tidepools, where I am trying to count the species of neogastropods and landlocked sculpins, to compare them against those listed in a wood-pulp book printed fifty years ago.

He seems sober, matter-of-fact. This means nothing.

Oblivious to the chugging of the factory behind him, he looks wistfully out to sea and says:

"She was Otean, of course. Her thighs like tree trunks, her

121

body a muscular fist. The sable-smooth hair that covered her glinted like gold in the sunset of their star. She was a child by their standards, but twice as old as I, and her wide dark eyes were as full of dreams as mine. That is how it happened: we both were dreamers. I'd been away too long."

It is a moving tale, in its own way convincing. Otus is indeed a heavy world, the atmosphere thick, the surface touched by less light than Earth. In turn, Otean eyes are more photosensitive, their bodies stockier, their lungs accustomed to richer oxygen. And although they are much more like us than the little Debolites are, they hate Terra; they cannot stand to be here even for a day, even in lightweight breathing gear. (Some say it is photophobia; others believe it is a peculiarity of the inner ear; still others, a vascularization vertigo.)

"I was drunk on the oxygen mix of that world," Jory is saying now, "and never did smell the lipid alienness of her. My poor blind passion never stumbled the whole long night."

I remember something else that gives credence: the marks— the dozens of tiny toothlike marks on his chest, on the inside of his arms. They've been there since I can remember, though I've never asked about them, assuming, as I did, that they'd been left by the medical instruments that prepared him for his journey.

Abruptly, somberly, Jory says, "No, I never saw the boy. I left Otus long before he was born."

It is almost convincing. But not quite.

1. Humans and Oteans are able to copulate, but fertilization is impossible; the Otean secretions are toxic. And were a sperm cell to survive, it would not penetrate the ovum; and were it to penetrate, the chromosomes would fail to align themselves on the spindle.
2. Jory was never on Otus.

One day not long after he returned and I awoke, Jory said to me: "What does a man gain by winning the universe, if by doing so he loses himself? He can never buy it back once it is bartered away." He was quoting someone, I felt sure. But I didn't ask and he didn't explain.

He was quiet for a while, and then, voice hoarse with sorrow, he whispered, "They lied to me, Dorothea, just as they lie to us all," and he began to weep. I took him in my arms and held him. I did not let go.

That was the man I knew. I have not seen him since.

I have located four species of rock shell, but it has taken nearly five hours. According to the wood-pulp book, fifty years ago I'd have found four times as many, and in half the time.

The factory has been here for thirty-five, yet it denies its pipes have ever dumped oxygen-depleting wastes into the delicate littoral zone.

The liars are so nearby, Jory.

I recall something else now, too.

Four years ago, not long after we had the addition built, Jory received a tape in the mail. He never offered an explanation; I never asked for one. That is our way. But one day I heard it, and saw it.

I was passing his new room, the one he'd built for privacy. I'd never stopped before, but this time I did because I heard a voice.

It sounded innocuous enough—mechanical and skewed to the treble like a cheap computer voice. But when I tried to understand it, I realized that it wasn't a simvoice at all, that the language I was hearing was not of Earth.

When I reached the doorway, I stepped quietly inside and stopped.

Jory was seated at the screen, his back to me, and by the way he was staring I felt sure the screen held a face, a face belonging to the voice.

I took one step and saw the screen.

There was no face. Instead, an alien landscape filled the screen, violet crags and crimson gorges bathed by an unearthly light, the entire vision quivering like a bright, solarized rag.

The voice chattered on. Jory remained hypnotized. I left quickly, shivering.

That evening I pleaded with him again. All I could think of was the gorges, the eerie light, the quivering screen. I still believed that a child, however it came, would be able to banish such strangeness from the heart and soul of the man I loved, the man I thought I knew.

* * *

Despite the Climagos' greatest gift, very few humans have traveled Out There. As our technocrats learned long ago, the exploration of space is handled best by machines, not by flesh-and-blood liabilities.

There is one matter, though, that cannot be handled by mechanical surrogates—not, that is, without risk of diplomatic insult. That matter is Business—the political and economic business between sentient races and their worlds.

The leaders of Business understand the risks, and in turn, the *diplos* of interstellar politics, the *greeters* and *runners* of interstellar trade, and the occasional *scope* of interstellar R&D are all common men and women. All contract for the money (so they claim); all are commissioned with instant diplomatic or corporate rank in the departments of state, MNCs, and global cartels that hire them; and all have little computers implanted in their skulls.

To make them what they are not.

To make them what those back on Earth so need them to be.

"She was a Debolite, Dorothea." His agony is profound, his confession sincere, tortured. "Forgive me, please. I know few women would, but I ask it of you because you, more than most, should be able to understand." The pause is a meaningful one. "I shared a meal—skinned *rodentia* of some kind and a fermented drink made from indigenous leaves—with a committee of seven provincial demipharaohs. She was their courier. Later that night, she visited me in my quarters with an urgent—and I might add, laudatory— message from the Pharaohess Herself. I was intoxicated from their infernal *tulpai,* Dorothea. Otherwise, I'd never have been able to do what I did—to touch a body like that, so small and fragile, the face a clown's, the skin like taut parchment except where the slick algae grows."

He puts his head in his hands. He slumps forward. The scar is no longer red.

He says: "I saw the boy two years later. I could barely stand the sight of him."

He seems to collapse. "Dear God," he whispers. Quietly he begins to sob.

I get up. He is probably sincere. He probably believes what he is describing. Nevertheless, I blame him and with blame comes the hate.

1. Procreation is no more likely between humans and Debolites than it is between humans and sheep.
2. Jory was never on Debole.
3. Jory does not believe in the God whose name he takes in vain.

Debole is a small planet, and does not spin. Its inhabitants— fauna and flora alike—hug the twilight zone between eternal sun and endless night, and the thermal sanity which that zone provides. The Debolites are much smaller than humans, no larger in fact than the prosimians who scampered on Earth's riverbanks forty million years ago, grist for the gullets of larger reptiles. The black algae that feeds on the secretions and excretions of their skin helps insulate them from the cold, as do the arrangements of fatty deposits around their vital organs, deposits which give them a lumpy, tumorous look. And the natural violet pigment of their dermis protects them from ultraviolet agony.

The Debolites are five thousand years away from their own natural space age. Because they are, mankind couldn't be less interested. But the Climagos are interested. This puzzles us. What do they see?

I've taken the pheroma capsules, and try not to complain.

To keep our skin's bacterial succession intact, we have not bathed. Our exertions fill the air with a nightmarish brine, and I choke on it. The copulins are fiery ants behind my eyes, I am as nauseous as I've ever been in my life. (What was the dose this time? Which series did he use? Am I developing an allergy? Is there anyone who hates them as much as I do?)

We are squirming like blood-crazed chondrichthy. Jory's breathing is stertorous from the olfactory enhancement, the steroid bombardments, and I am doing my best to emulate his passion despite the threat of peristalsis.

Suddenly, in the voice of a stranger, Jory says:

"You'll choose not to believe me, as always. That is your right, Dorothea. But I must try to prepare you."

125

I shudder, shudder again. The room is warm, sickeningly so, but Jory's body has stopped moving. What will it be this time?

"She was a Climago, Dorothea. I use the term *she* to help you—to help us both—understand what happened. Don't bother insisting that such a thing is impossible, because it *is* possible—it *indeed* happened. The Climagos are a compassionate race. They gave humanity the starlock secret; they gave humanity crystalline sleep and energy fields. And they gave one lone man—me, Jory Coryiner—another gift as well."

He pauses, mouth open, his jaw struggling.

"I don't need to tell you what they look like. You know."

I say nothing, the nausea unending.

How could I possibly know? Those who come back with descriptions are liars, and there isn't a government on Earth that appears interested in dispelling the mysteries. Even the commedia claim they can't get stills or tapes—not even of those Climagos who visit Earth. (Are they so shy? Are they so archetypally terrible to behold that the teeming masses of Terra, were they to find out, would riot, destroy their own cities, demand an instant end to diplomatic relations?)

But like everyone else, I've collected the descriptions—dozens and dozens of them. Chambered nautili with radioactive tendrils? Arachnoids cobalt-blue or fuchsia, or striped like archaic barber poles? Bifurcated flying brains? Systolic muscles with "gyroscope" metabolisms? Silicon ghosts? Colonial pelecypods looking more like death's-head skulls than clams? Which do *you* prefer, Jory?

"And you know, I'm sure," he is saying now, "how they've managed to survive on their hostile world for two hundred million years. I'm sure you know."

Perhaps I do. Perhaps I do not. I have heard the stories—and chosen to believe them—about those miracles of symbiosis, the Climagos. How their world is a litany of would-be predators, of knife-blade mandibles, deadly integuments, extruded stomachs that should have consumed every Climago on the planet a million times over—and would have were it not for the one trait that makes them not unlike us: a talent for adaptation, for cooperation, for helping and being helped.

It isn't simply cortical convolutions, though Climagos are certainly as intelligent as Terran cetaceans and pachyderms and

Homo erectus, whatever "intelligence" may mean. It is the myriad ways in which they have learned to cooperate—to co-opt and thereby to best every other species on their home planet. The apelike things (so the stories go) who for aeons lent them their prehensile hands. The great saurians who provided them with locomotion and "gross environmental-manipulation capability." The mindless coelenterates who shared their nutrient flesh with them during drought and famine. And the endless others. The helpers, and the helped.

In return, the Climagos—telepathic, patient—provided the sensory information needed to lead the day-blind lizards to new species of prey, to keep the feathery simians one step ahead of their growing enemies, to help the eternal jellyfish foresee the impending changes in the great tidal inlets of the world.

"You can understand why it happened. She was a *greeter,* too—one of theirs—and I was a lone human. As a devout student of humanity, she understood what my solitude meant; she understood that in their social needs humans are not at all like Climagos, who do not fear loneliness, but are instead like the bottle-nosed dolphins of Earth, who suffer horribly when removed from their own kind."

He pauses now, averts his eyes and sighs. I smell half-digested food. I smell my own bile. The world swims.

"There was an aeon of need within her," he is saying, "the need to help, the need to cooperate, the need to court a creature who, under other circumstances, might have been a predator. And within me, there was an aeon of need as well—the need to find kin, a creature I would recognize by the most primitive of means."

I am still on my hands and knees, unable to move, the sickness darkening with a dread. Above me, Jory's eyes are the true purple of space, and the metallic breath of nausea moves through me like a toxic tide. It is the pheromas, yes, and the sweat, the androstenol, and all the others, but it is what I see too. Whether he knows it or not, I can indeed see his Climago *greeter* clearly. It is the version most often described. The horrible consensus.

I see a man so lonely, so crazy from his years of inhuman sleep, so twisted in his pent-up libidinal soul, that he can bring himself to touch it—a worm, a slug, its rolls of fat accordioned on a cartilaginous spine, its face (do I dare call it that?) a lamprey's, the abrasive bony plates, the hundreds of tiny sucking holes pull-

127

ing the blood gently—like honey—from his chest, from the insides of his arms and thighs and—

Somehow I get up. I stumble. I rush from the room.

The footsteps behind me are heartbeats.

When I reach the bathroom, the sickness comes out. The pheromas make it the odor of death.

Behind me, a voice, disembodied:

"It wasn't like that at all," he whines. "Why can't you try to understand?"

I have started to cry.

"It was *beautiful*," he says, faithful that words can change it. "She *made* it beautiful. They are an incredibly beautiful people, Dorothea."

A moment ago, it was tears. Now, it is laughter. Here I am, kneeling in my own ambergris, as though worshiping a sunken bathtub, as though believing his most outrageous lie yet. The teeth marks, the rapture. Perhaps that, yes. But not the other.

Not a child.

I turn to him savagely. "And who carried the fetus for her? Some obliging surrogate, some Otean bound by diplomatic duty? If that strikes your fancy, Jory, just nod once and we'll tape it. But I'm puzzled, Jory. How will he reach us? The locks are far too slow. Is he coming in a taterchip can with tiny retrorockets? Or an FTL attaché case? Climagos are small, you know."

He looks at me in amazement, his eyes like a child's. I could kill him and he doesn't even know it. And I would kill him, I'm sure, were there anything near me sharper than a dryer or a toothcan. This man—this man who for five years has shown so little interest in the woman he lives with, who has heard none of my pleas—now offers me lies for a moment's absolution.

He steps toward me, takes my arm. I twist my head in a snarl, but I do not pull away.

The look is still there. He shakes his head, horribly hurt. "There's a son, yes, Dorothea, and, yes, he's very small—as you surmised. He's more Climago than human—an *alien*, yes—but he's intelligent and caring and he has the capacity to love us. Can't you at least—"

"Stop it!" I scream, hands over my ears, the smell of my own body like dung.

He goes dreamy now. He turns slowly, stares at the closed windows. I will scream again; I cannot bear what he will say.

"There's a son, yes," he begins anew. "He isn't small at all. He's a mutant, Dorothea, barely alive, and he may not make it through the starlocks. He's a pitiful thing, and he deserves our compassion. He has a human head, a nudibranch's body; he whimpers like a human child, but chokes on his own excrement if held the wrong way. Climago scientists have been studying him for years, but I want him with me now, and his mother—decent soul that she is—agrees. The child is allergic to so many things there; perhaps he will fare better here. *If* he survives the trip. *If* we can love hi—"

I hit him. I hit him on the temple, over the scar, feeling the metallic edge of the thing the corporation put there. The thing that has helped make him what he is.

The skin splits at the metal. He flinches, grabs my wrist. The blood begins to ooze.

I'm screaming something now that neither of us understands.

He says calmly, "Accept it, Dorothea. He'll be arriving soon."

He leaves me in the bathroom, where I continue to cry.

I do not see him for days.

I was a pale girl and still haven't lost it. No amount of UV—no matter how graduated—can change that, with all the Irish and English I have in my genes. I've got big bones, too—big country-girl hands, pronounced veins and tendons, and hipbones that bruise loves. "Daughter of a meatless tribe," as my father used to put it.

I wonder how I first looked to Jory.

He was the darkest man I'd ever met, as dark as an "olive" complexion can get—the curse (as he put it later) of some rather thoughtless BlackAm, Amerind, and Hmong-refugee ancestors.

His face, when he turned it to profile, was a hatchet from an ancient dream, and he frightened me at first.

I was raised on one of the last megafarms of the American Midwest. No, that's wrong. I was raised as the daughter of the senior administrator of one of the last megafarms of the American Midwest. There *is* a difference. Our house was a big plasticoated three-story Victorian in Cedar Falls, an hour's helirun from The Farm. No one ever really grew up on a farm like that.

Jory, though, was a son of the Detroit Glory Ghettos—those Recessional projects begun by a cornered liberal administration two decades before his birth. Every minute of his life had been subsidized by citizens who, at their noblest, were full of self-congratulating "concern"; at their worst, rationalized bigotry; and for 1,439 minutes of every day, apathy and indifference. He knew this. He'd grown up knowing it—1,440 minutes of every day.

For years I dreamed of a career somehow related to the magical sciences of megafarming. What I really wanted, of course, was a way never to leave home—a career to protect my narrow affections, first loves, prized childhood memories of a mother and father who worked happily for The Farm. My father, the loud, proud administrator; my mother, the taciturn gene-splicer whose love of her work showed clearly in her quiet eyes.

The last time I saw The Farm was the eve of Jory's departure. I was twenty-eight years old. The machines were still incredible—the immense nuclear combines, the computerized "octopus pickers" and "dancing diggers." The land was just as awesome—the dark pH-perfect soil stretching from horizon to horizon. But it was boring now. How could this be the world I'd romanticized for so long?

The career I finally chose to pursue—at the clear-thinking age of fourteen—was veterinary medicine. Not the anthropomorphic-pet kind (which I knew was glutted with practitioners), but the animal-husbandry kind (about which I knew absolutely nothing).

I made it as far as my fourth year of undergraduate studies, and then the world changed. I discovered people, and the dream of veterinary medicine began to fade.

One day I discovered a young man named Jory Coryiner and never dreamed the dream again.

I met him at one of the dinners my parents gave for the Huddleston Industries trainees. There were twelve this time—the usual fifty-fifty split of women and men—and Jory was impossible to miss: dark, cocky, intimidating, haloed with heroic rumors—in all, the most magnetically masculine thing I'd ever encountered in my cloistered Iowan life.

He disliked me intensely at first, I know that now. And with good reason. He knew who I was, and dreaded the inevitable patronizing. I persisted. Here was a young man all were talking about, a young man who'd won a fertboss traineeship not through federally imposed quota-tokenism but through his own impressive record, and for some reason I felt chosen, destined to understand him—his obvious need for a wall, tough carapace, calciferous shell, to hide behind.

How it happened, I can't say. After an hour's efforts, he softened. By the end of that hour, I felt I had glimpsed what few others had—the real reason for his chitinous ways: he was the son of a "welfare gloryhole" and he believed he wore that stigma for all to see in the melanin of his skin.

He was wrong, of course. To most men and women, his complexion was charismatic, magical, superior to their own. My own parents certainly never thought twice about my seeing him. But he never understood this. He still doesn't, and now, it is too late.

I should have seen it. I should have realized that the son of two mothers and two fathers—a boy shuttled back and forth from "step'nt" to "step'nt" throughout childhood—might perceive families in a different way. That a man from a Glory Ghetto who had struggled to escape the dark badge of its dependency might never stop struggling. That the moat might never dry up, the walls never crumble, the carapace never see a shedding no matter how much love fell upon it.

Were there alternative worlds in your eyes even then, Jory— places where Hiroshima never rose toward heaven, where the Jurassic Sea never dried, where the Visigoths held Italy for over five centuries?

I do not know. I lied to myself then, too.

When you told me you had contracted as a *runner* for Quanta, you took two hours to explain it. When you were through, you did not want to hear any of my questions. *Fait accompli.* You wanted no chinks, no soft underbelly through which your resolution might be undermined.

You said you were doing it because of your great boredom— and because of the money, the fortune you'd have when you returned. The fertboss position was driving you crazy, you said. Even with the antidepressants The Farm's headmeds were giving you (I knew nothing of this), your days were leaden with despair, you said.

You said, too, that you'd talked it over thoroughly with three who'd just come back. Two *greeters* and a *diplo*—three men. They were colorful talkers, yes, even a little strange at times, but they weren't crazy, not at all. And they were very happy they'd gone.

Willi, who was eight then, said the only thing he could have: he didn't want to leave. He didn't want to give up his school, his teams, his clubs, his counselor, his center, his world. I had no choice. I had to respect it. He would not be our son fifteen years later when Jory returned and I awoke, but it was Willi's life, too, and to take him with us to a future where he would have only the two of us was all wrong. I believe that still. I do.

My mother was ill. She probably would be for the rest of her life. He could not stay with them. It was Clara and Bo, our friends from Cedar Falls, who at last agreed to take him. He would live with them during the school year until he was eighteen; he would spend summers with Jory's sister in Missoula or my parents in Cedar Falls. Whichever he preferred.

That was the best I could do, and as I did it, I wept.

You signed your contract. Quanta responded, depositing fifteen years of executive salary with the Citibank trustees. While you slept in the starlocks and did your business on Climago, the capital earned. When you finally returned, you were (like the others) a millionaire and (like the others) so happy.

I slept for you, Jory, because that was my adventure, an adventure I believed was as noble as yours. All around us men and women were doing such things for their departing lovers, and I knew we would meet again—you and I—in a distant, idyllic future, to begin life anew like a modern Adam and Eve.

I slept for you, and my sad but loving parents paid for the suspension care without complaint, though they knew they were burying me.

I've seen my father only once since I awoke. Mother is dead. He had nothing to say.

I will not do that to him again.

Time marries. Time reconciles. "It is a recombiner like no other," as my mother used to say quietly. It has only been two weeks since Jory's announcement, and I have already begun to believe, to accept what I know cannot be true.

I must be prepared. I cannot afford not to be. If what Jory

claims is true, if indeed we are about to have a visitor, I must begin to prepare this house physically—and myself psychologically—for its arrival. Whatever *it* may be.

After all, the notion of a visitor is, in its own way, appealing. Anything that makes the days feel different is, in its own way, appealing.

I give it the better part of each day. I give it so much that the headaches are excruciating. But they are a small price to pay for being prepared.

1. I'm actually quite qualified to receive the creature, whatever it may be. I received a decent formal training in biology, zoology, and physiology, and I've educated myself in recent years in invertebrate and marine biology, malacology, conchology. Jory would be the first to admit this, I'm sure.
2. If the creature is indeed intelligent, I cannot afford to make it feel unwanted. Jory will insist, I am sure, that it remain with us indefinitely, and I will have to abide by that as graciously as possible.

If the creature is intelligent and feeling—*if* it is indeed from a race driven by an aeon-spanning need to help, to cooperate, to "care"—there is reason, is there not, to assume that some day I will be able to feel something resembling affection for it?

If it survives, of course.

I cannot guess his exact needs. I can only prepare for a variety of contingencies. I know, for example, that Climagos do not need daily intakes of atmosphere, that their integumentary system is "closed," that they require infusions of oxygen, nitrogen, hydrogen, and other elements only occasionally—once a week, say. And though the notion doesn't reconcile easily with hemophagia, their nutrional needs (according to the one reference tape I've been able to locate) follow a similar periodicity.

I will order the appropriate compressed gas tanks from San Francisco, and I will have a marine construction firm in Fort Bragg build a self-sterilizing, airtight room. But I need to do more homework on the nutrion. Perhaps through supplements of some kind—say, a concentrated mineral/protein mixture tailored to blood profiles on Climago—we may be able to circumvent the need for volumes and volumes of blood-bearing tissue.

I've gone ahead and phoned three exobiologists in the Bay Area and in Houston, and have extracted all the information I can without jeopardizing our secret. We just can't let people—scientists, doctors, and commedia folk—know what is about to happen here. Were the word to get out, our lives would be a hell of ruptured privacy. And if the child is as fragile as Jory claims it is, such a commotion might endanger its life.

But the exobs are willing to part with more information than either the transnational corporations or national governments seem to be, and I have unearthed the following: a Climago should be able to exist comfortably on a mixture of oxygenated, hydrogenated, and proteinized Na, K, Ca, Mg, Cl, and various iron- and copper-based transport pigments taken from Terran mammals and accessible through a durable membrane, natural or synthetic.

I haven't seen Jory in days; I have, in fact, seen him only two or three times in the past few weeks. It is as though his announcement that day—his "gift" to me—was at last able to liberate him.

Which is what he has wanted for five years.

When he visited me at the hospital just after I awoke, he said he wanted a house on this desolate coast. I thought I knew why. I imagined the harshness and solitude would be his way of bringing us together again.

I was lying to myself then.

It was the gray sea, the cold crags, the solitude itself that he wanted, not a marriage of lives. It was the inhumanity of it all that he wanted, and he wanted it more than anything else.

There are times—those rare moments when we embrace without the need to consummate—when I feel in his body the rhythms, the suckings and chuggings of the factory itself, of the great pipes that pull their material from the far seabed, of the dark engines that do to it what they do.

"Why is he coming?" I ask gently, wondering if gentleness can prevent a lie.

"His mother is dead," Jory says. "He is too human to live out the rest of his life there."

"No, Jory," I say. *"Why is he coming?"*

He looks at me sadly, cocks his head like a dog, and tries again: "Because he has a terrible congenital disorder and has very few years to live. He wants to be with his father, his cold mad feary father, before he dies."

"Please. Why is he coming?"

The smile flashes like a knife. The cruel eyes transfix me.

"Because I'm sick and tired of your nagging, your slop pails of complaint, Dorothea. I am giving you what you want and need. It's a better career than the aborted one, isn't it?"

All I can think to say is, "I see."

In a softer voice, he tells me, "Because I asked him to, Dorothea."

"Oh," I say. "And when was that?"

He looks away. "A few years ago. I've missed him so."

"Jory, a lockgram come-go takes two or three years."

"Yes, it does, but their telepathy is a very special kind. That's their survival secret, Dorothea. I can think a message to my beloved son across the whole galaxy and he can hear me. Hemispherical space is no obstacle for a love that—"

I turn. I leave him.

I am sure of it now: Jory invited his "child" to live with us before he left Climago.

Only one explanation is possible: the Climagos are immeasurably more advanced than we are in genetic engineering. They are able, through computer modeling and analog translation, to convert human genetic message into Climago genetic code. They are able to replicate human morphological and physiological capabilities in Climagoan cellular arrangements. But they made a mistake this time. The translation failed. The resulting organism: a hybrid mess, a congenitally doomed anomaly. What Jory has described.

Why they would attempt such a thing, I do not know. They are aliens, and perhaps we should not expect to understand them.

I heard voices as I came down the cedar stairs from the helipad yesterday. One was raised, almost violent, and I should have recognized it.

The other was softer, though not conciliatory.

"I can assure you," the softer voice was saying, "that we do not look sympathetically on visas for them, let alone immigration."

"And I can assure *you*"—it was Jory's voice; I recognized it now—"that if any government tries to block this, you people will know more trouble than you've ever known in your puny functionary lives. I've accommodated you and your bigoted quarantine laws; now you will accommodate me. If you do not, I can promise you I will spend what funds I have on the loudest, most public litigation this nation has ever seen. The diplomatic repercussions will not be negligible. Official prejudice is never negligible."

The softer voice said something and Jory screamed, "That's xenophobic bullshit and you know it! How in God's name can an organism that must replenish itself once a week with available equipment, that hibernates for two months of the year, that can move no faster than a walk be dangerous? A creature like that is considerably less dangerous than most federal bureaucrats, Mr. Creighton-Mark."

There was a silence. I stepped into the room.

The violence seemed to recede from Jory's eyes, which twinkled suddenly in a smile. But the violence was still there; it was there in the rippling muscle of his jaw.

"This is my spou, Mr. Creighton-Mark," he said. "Dorothea, this is the BIN—or at least a representative of it." To the official, he said, "May I assume her feelings are admissible?"

The man ignored me and said, "She knows what's at stake here?"

"Of course." The anger glowed in Jory's eyes again, the scar livid. "But why ask *me*? She's only a meter from you, and I'm sure she'd answer a question put to her. She might even thank you for the courtesy of it."

The man ignored the sarcasm. He looked at me at last, and waited.

Helpless, I looked at Jory, found eyes burning with a passion I did not recognize. If love, love for what? If hatred, toward whom?

I nodded, found myself saying, "Of course," and then repeating it. "Yes, of course."

Again the violence receded from his eyes, only to be replaced by a distance I knew all too well, as he said:

"We are childless, Mr. Creighton-Mark. I was gone for fif-

136

teen years. My spou suspended for me. Our one pre-contract child is now twenty-nine. He's a courteous young man, but he doesn't know us, and couldn't care less. Who could blame him? We abandoned him, did we not? We want to try again now—to be a family."

My face burned. I could not look at either of them. How could Jory use me like this—against this man? How could he claim feelings he'd just never had!

When I finally did look at the visitor, I could not understand what I saw. His eyes were on Jory; his expression was chaos—as though nothing Jory had said had made any sense to him, as though Jory's entire speech was the last thing he had expected to hear.

It was the look, I would realize later, of a man stunned by insanity, by the look of it, by the sound of it.

"I see," the visitor said at last, expression fading, words full of a relinquishing fatigue.

It was over. Jory had somehow won. Parting amenities were exchanged, and as he left the official offered a platitude about government's debt to those who serve its diplomatic and economic interests at great sacrifice. He stressed it—the word *great*.

The autonomous room was finished two weeks ago. The shipment of blood components arrived yesterday. I still have questions, dozens of basic ones, but there's nothing to be done about it. I've used every possible tape available through interlibrary banks and manufacturer listings, and I will not risk further exposure by contacting more "experts."

These remaining questions would worry me if Jory seemed at all anxious. But he is calm. He must feel we're prepared.

We argued today about who should copter in to SFO to get him. I insisted that both of us should, but Jory said no, that would be unfair to both "the boy" and me. I did not understand this, and I said so. Jory said only, "I need some time to prepare him."

I resent it, being excluded. Am I jealous already?

Jory took the copter to SFO this morning. I've been spending the day putting finishing touches on the special room, and on the refrigeration units with their blood substitutes and pharmaceutical stocks, all of which should allow us to control any Terran disease to which the poor thing might be susceptible. (I've done my homework. I've mustered up enough courage to phone two more exos—both at UC San Diego—to get the chemoprophylactic information we need. And I did it without making them suspicious, I am sure.)

They're here and I never heard them arrive! I've been too involved in last-minute scurrying.

I try the covered patio first, expecting Jory's voice, but I hear nothing. I start to turn, to head back toward the south patio, imagining that Jory has perhaps carried him down the cedar stairs toward our bedroom.

I see something, and stop.

A figure—it is in shadows under the patio beams. I cannot see it clearly, and what I do see makes no sense. It is too small to be Jory; it is *not* Jory. Yet I know it is too big for what he described. It is standing upright, and that is wrong too.

I walk toward it slowly, stopping at last.

My mouth opens.

I cannot speak; I cannot scream. I cannot even cry out in terror or joy.

It is a *boy*. A very real, very human boy.

He is thin, a little too thin, and he has Jory's hatchet face. He has Jory's blue-black hair.

He is, I know suddenly, more Jory than our Willi ever could have been.

I feel the tears beginning to come, and with them, the understanding. It is the kind of lie I never foresaw. There was no alien lover, no. Instead, it was a woman, an honest-to-god woman. On the lock shuttles perhaps. Or on Climago itself. A *greeter* or *diplo* or *runner* just like Jory.

This boy, this very real boy, is theirs. The truth is wonderful!

Why Jory felt he had to lie, I cannot say. I would have accepted the boy so easily, so gratefully, without it.

I take another step toward the boy, and he smiles. He is beautiful! (Don't be vain. You don't *really* care whether there's a chromosome of yours in him, do you?)

A voice intrudes suddenly, and I stop breathing.

"Amazing, isn't it, Dorothea. Can you guess how they did it?"

I turn to Jory, a plea in my eyes: *Don't ruin it. Please don't ruin it.*

"Don't worry," he says. "I've talked it over with the boy and everything is fine. He grew up with the truth and is proud of it. As he should be." He turns to the boy, winks, and smiles. "Isn't that so, August? You know a lot more about it than your dad does, right?"

The boy nods, grinning back. The grin is beautiful.

Jory is grinning too, saying, "Take a guess, Dorothea. It's nothing us human beings couldn't have done ourselves."

I look at the boy. The world is spinning. Everything I have ever known or accepted is about to become a lie.

"I don't know, Jory," I whisper.

No one says a thing, and suddenly Jory shouts:

"Cloning! Simple cloning! Nothing fancier than that. Are you surprised?"

There is nothing I can say.

"On our second night together," Jory is saying, "she put it so well. 'It's the least we can do,' she told me. 'A living symbol,' she said, 'of our refusal to accept passion's ephemeral insubstance.' "

"He's all me, Dorothea!" Jory exclaims, laughing, glowing.

I look at the boy again.

"I'm going to leave you two alone," Jory says cheerfully, "let you get to know each other better. Our copter is in dire need of a cleaning!"

The father smiles paternally. The father smiles bountifully.

I want to believe him. I so want to believe that this is, at last, the truth.

When I look into his brown eyes, I see a real boy. When I take his hand in mine, I feel one. He is human. He is Jory, and no one else. I am able, yes, to believe that no mother's chromosomes are in him; I am able to believe what Jory claims.

We start by talking about his trip through the starlocks. My voice shakes for a time, but that is all right. He, too, with his strange, halting English, is unsure of himself. We must help each other overcome the fears. We cooperate; we allow the other to help.

As we say good-night, he whispers to me, "I love you, Mother, I do," and kisses me. It catches me off guard; I laugh nervously, wondering if his father told him to say it, or if it is just the boy's own sensitivity.

He looks hurt, and I know now I shouldn't have laughed.

"I'm sorry, August." I say it as brightly as I can, taking his warm hand. "I wasn't laughing at *you;* I'd never do that. Sometimes people laugh when something surprises them, especially when it's something nice."

I squeeze his hand. He squeezes back, and I am filled with emotions I haven't felt in a long long time.

Jory is with me in bed tonight, the first time in a long time.

"August was in the starlocks?" I say, afraid to ruin the magic, but haunted by a thought.

Jory gets up on one elbow and looks at me sleepily. "Yes, he was. Why?"

"He told me he loved me, and I was wondering—"

His face lights up with a grin. "Hey, that's wonderful!"

"He's been through the starlocks," I begin again. "Would he lie to me, Jory? Would he even *know* he was lying to me?"

The cheerfulness dies. He stares at me for the longest time.

"August never lies," he says finally.

I have been awake in the darkness for hours, thinking to myself, thinking about men and boys, fathers and sons, about a man—a liar—who swears to his wife that their son is not a liar. It is a joke of sorts, a riddle. It cannot be solved.

The strange thing is, I wouldn't mind it if August did lie to me that way.

I could come to love his lies so easily.

Jory is gone again. From the house. From my life. Back to the woods, the beach, the Winkinblinkins and Starmen, the endless worlds spinning within him.

I don't mind.

I have August. I have the child who in only five days has changed my life completely. We've picnicked on the peninsula where the remaining seals sun themselves like lazy tourists. We've tramped the tidepool reefs to identify *mollusca* and to make the Kirlian photographs of their fairylike "souls." We've chartered an oceanographic trawler from Mendocino, and spent the day oohing and ahing over the dredgings. We've even found time to attend a fair in Westchester, that ugly, charming little town whose streets are lined with the slick red manzanita boles washed down by the Gualala at its meanest.

Wherever we go, I feel alive, I feel proud, I feel loved. The way people look at us can only be envy. And why not? It should be clear to anyone that August, handsome and devoted son that he is, does enjoy being with me.

It happened five hours ago. I am still shaking. I should move from this chair, but I am afraid to, afraid that if I do I will lose my mind.

August came to us a week ago.

Today he asked to use the special room.

To *use* it.

I stared at him, unable to speak, and he asked me again.

As I took him to it, I did my best not to look at him, afraid of what I might see.

At the gasketed doorway, he looked back at me tenderly and said, "I'm sorry, Mother, but I must shut the door. I think you know why."

Yes. I do.

It is not just because of the gases.

It is because of what I might see when he attends to his body, to his needs, and forgets me.

He shut the door gently, and as he did he asked me to set the food and air controls for him. He could not do this himself, he said. (Yes. I remember now. He did not hold the cameras at the tidepools. He did not remove anything from the dredgings of the trawler. He did not pay for anything with his own hand. He did not open doors. He did not prepare food. He ate little, and I never saw it enter his mouth. He was simply a vision—present and loving.)

He has been in there with his proper mix of gases and his nutritive membrane for five hours. The last thing he said to me was: "Don't worry, Mother. I used a room just like this in quarantine for sixteen months. It really wasn't so bad."

How to accept it all? How to accept it without screaming? That August is no clone, that he is not human, that he is not what I see.

That he is but a projection, the gift of illusion, a lie.

That something else entirely lives and thinks there behind the loving face.

As the truth sinks in, I begin to see what the books and tapes dared not explain, what governments must take pains not to reveal, what in my own unwillingness to expose our lives to public scrutiny I kept five experts from telling me.

I begin to understand what the word *telemanifestor* means—the word heard only once, a single tape, a passing reference buried among information I assumed was much more important. I thought I knew what "tele" meant, in all its forms.

Will I be able to live with this? When I touch his arm and feel the pulse just under the skin, what do I really touch? When he kisses me and says, "I love you, Mother, I do," what is it that really presses itself against my lips? Bony plate, accordion of fat—how can I not see them?

The scream that first rose in my throat has faded. The August-thing will soon be leaving his special room; I must try to pretend that everything is all right. It will see through the pretense, of course, but I must try anyway. As a gesture. It is intelligent, after all. It has feelings. It is a guest in my house. And I, a representative of humanity, must act accordingly. That is all I can do.

It is clear now. It is clear how the Climagos convinced the jaws and talons and eversible stomachs of their world not merely to ignore them, but to help them build a civilization on its way to the stars:

The Climagos are liars too. They have survived for two hundred million years because of the terrible beauty of their lives.

I awoke this morning to an empty, familiar bed.

It was earlier than usual. A sound had awakened me, I knew.

I listened and soon heard it again.

In the next room, on a small foam mattress, I found it. It stopped its crying as soon as I appeared, and like a fool I spent the first half hour inspecting it.

The "evidence" was there of course. Even neonatal physiognomy couldn't mute that nose. The eyes would darken, yes, but the complexion would remain the same—only slightly lighter than its father's.

I changed his Dryper and took him to the garden. Soon, he was cooing and chuckling and pulling up the flowers I'd planted only yesterday. He liked the big red zinnias most, of course, bright suns that they are, and in the end the only thing able to distract him was the sight of a cypress silhouetted against a pale morning sky. (I remember how Willi loved such things, staring for hours at a high-contrast print or a striped toy animal.)

We had played for over two hours when suddenly I remembered my appointment. August and I were going to Gualala for crabs! I'd been promising it to him for days.

What to do? (What would *August* want me to do?)

It came to me then like a breeze, a waking dream, in a voice that was indeed August's. It was *so* simple.

I rose. I took the baby to the little mattress, kissed it, and left the room without looking back. It did not cry.

Ten minutes later, just as I finished the replanting of the flowers, August appeared. *So* simple.

He was very striking in his navy-blue one-piece, hailing me from the top of the cedar stairs like a sea captain from centuries ago. I felt frumpy and told him so, but he insisted I looked beautiful, even in my earth-stained shorts.

We had a wonderful time. "Helluva season!" the erudite crabseller crowed, and we took the crabs home for a delicious salad under amplified stars.

The baby is in bed with me tonight. I know what it is, but it doesn't matter.

August is with me, too, though I cannot see him.

And Jory is wherever he wishes to be.

It has been another day of magic. Jory and I went to a mixer in Fort Bragg this evening, for the first time in years. He was all wit, wisdom, and charisma, free with his engaging tales of Climago and the exciting chases of interplanetary Business.

When we got back to the house, he stopped me and put his hands on my shoulders. I could feel their weight. "I've been insensitive as hell, Dorothea," he said. "I know that. This time, no pheromas!" He laughed, and I couldn't help but smile. "And no damned sling field or *son y lumière* either!" Face in a mocking leer, he added, "Unless, of course, you'd like to try some Everslip oil, just to keep things from being too easy."

"No, no, not the oil!" I cried in mock horror. Then, softly, I said, "I've always wanted it easy, always."

And it was. We made love—miracle of miracles!—in our very

own unadorned hoverbed, the opaque ceiling above us wonderfully boring, the unsynched music quaint, the steady lamplight charming, and no stencils to frustrate us.

The new Jory sleeps beside me, and I lie awake, happy. I can hear the sounds, yes. The footsteps, the chairs slithering, the sighs. I hear them in the den, in the distant kitchen—but they do not bother me. A faint voice within me whispers, "That is the *real* Jory; those are his sounds." But I answer: "It is only a stranger, a stranger in our house. He does not bother us, we do not bother him. He is really no more than a memory, a dim figure from a fading past, a man who once said to you, 'My son is coming to live with us,' when he didn't mean that at all, when he meant instead, 'It is my lover who is coming. . . .'"

In the morning, the tiny holes on my chest and arms will ooze for the briefest time. I will touch them lovingly. They are a small price to pay.

In a house like this one, but in a universe far far away, a stranger once said as he wept, "In the end, Dorothea, in the end all of our windows are mirrors, and we see only ourselves."

Or did he say, "In the end, Dorothea, all that matters to mankind is mankind, world without end, amen"?

Or perhaps he said nothing at all.

Perhaps I was the one who said it.

Or perhaps neither of us said a thing, and no lie was ever spoken.

Every writer knows that fiction tells its marvelous truths by *lying*, but every writer also knows that language can be used for darker lies too. "When the Fathers Go" is about the lies we tell ourselves and the lies we tell others. It also offers up Woman as the victim of the Lies that men in our culture build out of the cultural myths that bind them. In this sense, the story is a "feminist" story. In another, we're *all* Women—all victims of the Lie—and the story isn't "feminist" at all.

BRUCE McALLISTER

EDWARD
⊙ BRYANT ⊙

DANCING CHICKENS

Edward Bryant, a native of Wyoming, currently lives in a 1906 two-story brick Victorian in a very old North Denver neighborhood. He tells me that the predominant decor is simply books. As well as being an outstanding short-story writer, he also reviews books—specializing in the horror field—and, rumor has it, is an excellent creative-writing teacher. His most recent collection is a 30,000-word, 7-story contribution to Hardshell: Night Visions 4 *(Berkley), and he is currently working on the collections* Evening's Empires *and* Ed Gein's America *and the short novel* The Fetish.

"Dancing Chickens," along with one other reprint in this volume, is from the notorious, unpublished anthology of the early 1980s, New Dimensions 13, *edited by Marta Randall. Already in galleys, the book, meant to be the last in the celebrated anthology series (previously edited by Robert Silverberg), was canceled by the publisher. Neither "Dancing Chickens" nor "All My Darling Daughters," by Connie Willis, the other reprint included here from that ill-fated anthology, was ever published in a science-fiction magazine because they were considered too sexually oriented, too offensive. I turned them down at* OMNI *even though I loved them. So this is my expiation. The story was eventually published in Michael Bishop's anthology* Light Years and Dark.

Bryant started out as a science-fiction writer but, with this story, began to move away from SF and into the horror field. "Dancing Chickens" straddles both genres.

 What do aliens want?

Their burnished black ships, humming with the ominous power of a clenched fist, ghost across our cities. At first we turned our faces to the skies in the chill of every moving shadow. Now we seem to feel the disinterest bred of familiarity. It's not a sense of ease, though. The collective apprehension is still there—even if diminished. For many of us, I believe, the feeling is much like awaiting a dentist's drill.

Do aliens have expectations?

If human beings know, no one's telling. Our leaders dissemble, the news media speculate, but facts and truths alike submerge in murky communications. Extraterrestrial secrets, if they do have answers, remain quietly and tastefully enigmatic. Most of us have read about the government's beamed messages, all apparently ignored.

Do humans care?

I'm not really sure anymore. The ships have been up there for months—a year or more. People do become blasé, even about those mysterious craft and their unseen pilots. When the waiting became unendurable, most humans simply seemed to tune out the ships and thought about other things again: mortgages, spiraling inflation, Mideast turmoil, and getting laid. Yet the underlying tension remained.

Some of us in the civilian sector have retained our curiosity. Right here in the neighborhood, David told us he sat in the aloneness of the early morning hours and pumped out Morse to the silhouettes as they cruised out of the dark above the mountains and slid into the dim east. If there were replies, David couldn't interpret them. "You'd think at least they'd want to go out for a drink," David had said.

Riley used the mirror in his compact to send up heliograph signals. In great excitement he claimed to have detected a reply, messages in kind. We suggested he saw, if anything, reflections from the undersides of the dark hulls. None of that diminished his ecstasy. He believed he was noticed. I felt for him.

Hawk—both job description and name—didn't hold much with guesses. "In good time," he said, "they'll tell us what they want; tell us, then buy it, take it, use it. They'll give us the word." Hawk had plucked me, runaway and desperate young man, literally out of the gutter along the Boulevard. Since before the time of the ships, he had cared for me. He had taken me home, cleaned, fed, and warmed me. He used me, sometimes well. Sometimes he only used me.

Whether Hawk loved me was debatable.

Watching the ships gave me no answer.

I attempted to communicate every day. It was a little like what my case worker told me about what dentists did to kids' mouths before anyone had invented braces. When he was a boy with protruding teeth, my case worker was instructed to push fingers gently against those front teeth every time he thought of his mouth and how people were making fun. "Hey, Trigger! Where's Roy?" Years of gentle, insistent touches did what braces do now.

I tried to do something like that with the alien ships. Every time I fantasized smooth, alien features when I shivered in the chilly wake of an alien shadow, I gathered my mental energies, concentrated, shot an inquiring thought after the diminishing leviathan.

Ship, come to me . . . I wanted it to carry me away, to take charge, to save me from any sense of responsibility about my own actions in my own life. I knew better, but that didn't stop the temptation.

Once, only once, I thought I felt a reply, the slightest tickling just at the border of my mind. At the time it was neither pleasant nor unpleasant, more a textural thing: slick surfaces, cool, moist, one whole enclosing another. (A fist fills the glove. One hand, damp, warm: the wrist—twists.)

I tried to describe the sensation to some of the people on the street. I'm not sure who disbelieved me. I know Hawk believed. He stared at me with his dark raptor eyes and touched my arm. I danced skittishly away.

"You fit, Ricky," he said. "You really do."

"Not like that," I answer. The conversation has taken place in many variations, in many bedrooms and on many streets, and still does. "No longer. No more."

Hawk nods, almost sadly, I think. "Still going to leave?"

"I'll dance again," I say. "I'm young." Dancing was the only thing the therapists ever gave me that I loved.

"You're that," he agrees. "But you're out of shape." His voice is sad again. "At least for dancing."

"I can get back," I say helplessly, spreading my hands. "Soon." I try to ignore the fact that, as young as I am, I've abandoned my best years.

"I wish you could do it." The tone is as gentle as Hawk's voice ever gets. "It's the sticks, kiddo," he says. "You're a runaway on the skids, just off the street, in the sticks."

I don't like being reminded. He makes me remember every foster home, every set of possible parents who threw me back in the pool.

Hawk nods toward the stairs. "Come up."

I look at the darkness beyond the landing. I look at the faceted rings on the knuckles of Hawk's right hand. I stare at the floor. "No." I feel the circle tighten.

"Rick . . ." His voice shines dark and faceted.

"No." But I follow Hawk up the steps and into freezing alien shadows.

I'm planning my escape. I keep telling myself that. But that's all I do. Plan. If I left, I'd have to go someplace. There's nowhere I've ever realistically wanted to go.

Come, ships . . .

At one time I thought about hitching to Montana. I'd seen *Comes a Horseman* on late-night TV. Then I made the mistake of turning to Hawk and mentioning my plan. He raised his head from the pillow and said, "Ricky, you want to be a dancer again *and* go to Montana? You're maybe going to dance for the Great Falls Repertory Ballet?" I pretended to ignore the mockery. Someday I *would* leave. Just as soon as I made up my mind.

I gave up the Montana idea. But I still plan my escape. I've saved a few hundred dollars in tips waiting on tables at Richard's Coffee Shop. I have a dog-eared copy of *Ecotopia* and a Texaco road map of Oregon. I think Portland's probably a whole lot larger and more cosmopolitan than Great Falls. Certainly more cultural. Oregon seems familiar to me. I read a tattered paperback of *One Flew over the Cuckoo's Nest* in that fragmented past when I bounced from home to home, always waiting for them to tell my case worker I wasn't quite what they wanted.

If I really wanted to go, I'd leave. Right? Hawk jokes about it because he simply doesn't believe me. He doesn't know me. He never did find the passage to my mind.

Tonight I'm at a party at David and Lee's apartment. There are plenty of times when I wish I had the kind of relationship with someone, loving and supportive, that the two of them share.

David and Lee's apartment is on the fourteenth floor of a high-rise, rearing improbably out of a restored Victorian neighborhood. The balcony faces east and I can see all the way across the city, almost to the plains. There are maybe thirty people in the apartment, smoking, talking, drinking. Lee had laid out some lines he got at work on the big heart-shaped mirror on the coffee table, but those vanished early on. While some of the party guests watch, David is at his ham set, flashing out *dah-dit, dah-dit, dah-dah-dit* messages to the aliens.

Riley, resplendent in ermine and pearls, rushes up to my elbow. "Oh, Ricky, you've *got* to see!" I turn, look past him. People are thronging around the bar. The laughter rises and crashes uproariously. "Ricky, come *on.*" He takes my arm and propels me into the apartment.

I crane my neck to see what's going on. For once unladylike, Riley climbs onto a chair. Somebody I don't know, shiny in full leathers, is standing behind the mahogany bar. For a second I think he's wearing a white glove, but *only* for a second.

It's a chicken. The man has stuffed his fist into a plucked, pale chicken right out of a cello-wrapped package from a Safeway meat department. He wears it like a naked hand puppet. I find it hard to believe.

The man holds the chicken close to his face and talks to it like a ventriloquist crooning to his dummy. "That's a good boy, you like the party? Want to entertain the nice folks with a little dance?" I realize the headless chicken has a small black bolo tie with a dime-sized silver concho tied around its neck. Tasteful, basic black. The drumsticks are wearing doll shoes. The sheen of chicken juice on the rubbery, stippled skin starts to make me queasy.

It ought to be funny—but it's not.

The man addresses us, the audience. "And now," he says,

"the award-winning performance by a featherless biped." He nods toward David, who has come away from his radio set to watch. "Maestro, if you please." The expensive stereo cackles and we hear a tinkling piano version of "Tea for Two." The man with the chicken half crouches behind the bar top so that most of his arm is hidden. The chicken stands onstage. And starts to dance.

Evidently the joints have been cracked, because the dancer's limbs swing loose. The little shoes clatter on the Formica bar. The wings flap up and down wildly. Fluid drips to the bar.

"An *obscene* featherless biped," someone says accurately. But we all keep watching. The pimpled skin catches the light wetly. I don't think this is what the Greek philosopher who defined human beings as featherless bipeds had in mind.

The tune changes, the tempo alters—faster—"If You Knew Susie"—and the dancer is in trouble. It seems to be sliding off the manipulator's hand. The man behind the bar impatiently reaches with his free hand and screws the chicken down firmly on his fist. It makes a squelching sound like adjusting a rubber glove. Now I can smell the raw chicken. I turn suddenly and head for the balcony and the clean air that should steady my stomach.

I walk by Hawk. He lightly touches my wrist as I pass, but his eyes don't deviate from the scene on the bar. He doesn't have to look at me.

On the balcony I lean over the railing and retch. It's dark now and I have no idea who or what is fourteen stories below. Crazily I hope it will all evaporate before it hits the ground, like those immensely long and beautiful South American waterfall veils that dissolve into mist and then vanish before ever hitting the jungle floor.

Travelogs again. I want to escape.

My mind skips erratically. I also have to find a new doctor. My appointment this morning arrived at the point I've come to dread. There always comes a time when my current doctor looks at me quizzically and says, "Son, those aren't ordinary hemorrhoids." I stammer and leave.

Leave.

Good-bye, Hawk.

I'm leaving.

* * *

"But what do they want?" someone is saying as I walk across the floor. Oregon is, more or less, on the other side of that door. What do they want? Alien ships are still sliding silently between us and the stars. The watchers are out on the balcony, no longer discreet now that I've finished my purgation.

Ship, come to me . . .

Inside the apartment, the dancing chicken episode is triggering debate. I am amazed to see a confrontation between David and Lee. That they would fight is enough to make me pause.

"Sick," says Lee. "Tasteless. How could you let him spoil the party? You *helped* him."

"He's *your* friend," David says.

"*Colleague.* He stacks boxes. That's all." Lee's expression is furious. "The two of you! What sort of people think it's amusing to stick their hand inside a dead chicken?"

David says defensively, "Everyone was watching."

"And that makes it real!" Lee's amazement and anger are palpable. "Jesus! We're part of the most technologically sophisticated civilization on Earth, and yet we do this."

Riley has come up to us, looking cool and demure. "All societies are just individuals," he says reasonably. "You have to allow for a wide variation in"—he smiles sweetly—"individual tastes."

"Don't give me platitudes!" says Lee angrily. He stalks off toward the kitchen.

"Sulky, sulky," says Riley, and shrugs.

The three of us hear a chorus of *ooh*'s and *aah*'s from behind. We turn as one toward the balcony.

"I've never seen one so close," says a voice suffused with wonder. I imagine it's like sitting helplessly in a rowboat being passed by a whale. It seems as though the shining metallic skin of the alien ship is gliding past only yards from the balcony. The ship is so huge I can't accurately gauge the distance. The *whooosh* of displaced air flows through the windows. Chilly currents cocoon us.

The cold breaks the spell.

"I'm leaving," I say to the people around me. Lee and Riley seem fixed in place by the passing ship. They don't hear me. But then I don't think they ever did. "Good-bye," I say. "I'm leaving." Nobody hears me.

151

So, finally, I carry out my plans, my threat, my promise to myself.

I leave, and it feels better than I'd expected.

Someone does notice my departure, and he catches up with me at the elevator.

I try to ignore Hawk. He lounges beside the door until it slides open. Then he follows me into the car. I slap the ground-floor button with my fist.

"Stay," Hawk says.

I look at the sharpness of his eyes. "Why?"

He smiles slightly. "I haven't finished using you."

"At least that's honest."

"I've got no need to lie," he says. "I know you well enough, I can say that."

The sureness in his voice and the agreement I feel combine internally to make me feel again the sickness I felt upstairs watching the chicken dance. But now I have nothing left to purge.

The elevator brakes and I feel it all through my gut—it's the burn you get gulping ice water. The door hisses open. Hawk follows me into the apartment lobby. "Just let me go," I say without turning.

His words catch me as I reach for the outer door. "You know, Ricky, in my own way, I do love you."

I wonder if he knows the cruelty of that. I stare at him, startled. He's the first I remember saying that to me. Tears I haven't felt since childhood slide down my cheeks. I turn away.

"Stick around, kiddo," Hawk calls after me. "Please?"

"No." This time I mean it. I've made my decision. I don't look back at him. I stiff-arm the door open and lunge past a pair of aging queens; I am running as I hit the sidewalk. I barely see through the tears as a shadow deeper than the surrounding night envelops me. Rubbing eyes with wet knuckles, I look up to see an alien ship cross my vision and recede into the east. There are other ships in the sky now. Huge as they are, they still seem to dance and dart like enormous moths. What I see must be true, because others around me on the street are also gawking at the sky. Perhaps we all simply share the delusion.

"Rick!" Hawk's voice sinuously seeks me from behind.

I lower my head and bull forward.

"Ricky, look out!"

I register what my eyes must have seen all the time. The bus. The driver, wide-eyed and staring upward. The rushing chrome bumpers—

I feel no pain at first. Just the brutal physical force, the crushing motion, the slamming against the pavement. I feel— broken. Parts of me are no longer whole, that I know. When I try to move, some things don't, and those that do, don't move in the right places.

I am lying on my back. I think one leg is twisted beneath me. *Come to me, ship* . . .

One of the swooping, agitated, alien ships has parked poised, stationary above the block, above the street, above me. It masks both the city glow and the few stars penetrating that radiance. The angles are peculiar. Hawk's face enters my field of vision. I expect him to look stricken, or at least concerned. He only looks—I don't know—*possessive*, a boy whose doll has broken. Other faces now, all staring on with confusion, some with a sort of interest. I saw those faces at the party, those expressions.

As I stare past Hawk at the immobile alien ship, I know that I am dying here in the street. *And I was on the way to Oregon*. . . . Why is the alien ship above me? They'll start somewhere, Hawk had said. Sometime. With someone.

Then I feel the ice. At least I can feel something. I feel that knotted—*something*, an agency from outside me coming within, a chilly intrusion into my core.

The ship seems closer, dwarfing everything else, monopolizing my vision. They'll give us the word, Hawk had said. I had wanted the word. Now I feel very tight and unwilling.

From deep inside, spreading, flexing, tearing, ice impales me. The cold burns with a flame. I try to shrink away from it— and cannot. And then something moves. My foot. It spasms once, twice. My ankle jerks. My knee separates, cartilage wrenching apart, sliding back together, but wrong. My whole body quivers, each limb rebelling. Joints grind.

But I start to move. Slowly, horribly, without my orders, I rear up. *Stop it*, I will myself. I can't stop it.

I wonder if the aliens define featherless bipeds too?

The faces around me mirror pain as my body struggles to its

knees. No one watches the ship anymore. All eyes fix on my performance.

I am called . . . At last I am wanted.

Why aren't I dead? I'm moving and I cannot help it. My body lurches to its feet, limbs pivoting at wrong, odd angles. The fist inside me tentatively twists. I struggle to fall, to rest, but I am not allowed the luxury of ending this. Death doesn't save me. I waited too long and forfeit escape. At least I finally tried. It isn't fair, but then it never was.

The fist in me flexes, testing again.

My eyes flicker. Hawk has come to me. He watches with impassive eyes of shining black metal.

What do aliens want?

Chickens, dancing.

The path to publication for "Dancing Chickens" was odd and twisted—just as, some will say, the story itself is.

We'll start with Leigh Kennedy. Back before Leigh was a successful novelist living in Britain, she rose as a shining star in the firmament of the Northern Colorado Writers Workshop. The workshop has been around for at least a decade and a half, and has included such members as Connie Willis, Dan Simmons, Steve Rasnic Tem, Simon Hawke, John Stith, Vance Aandahl, and David Dvorkin. One day Leigh Kennedy was musing about a childhood memory: as a little girl in her mother's kitchen in Central City, high in the Colorado Rockies, Leigh had discovered the pleasures of sticking her hand inside whole uncooked chickens and making them dance like puppets. True, you had to crack the joints on the legs and wings, and the tactile sensation was pretty icky, but there was a certain Gregory Hines appeal to the whole process. This was long before similar dancing chickens appeared on the TV comedy series, "Fridays," and the image was indelibly encoded in my neurons.

Then there was the Al Pacino movie, *Cruising*. Controversial, in part, because of its depiction of gay leather bar culture, the film introduced the quaint custom of fist-fucking to mainstream audiences. My kid brother and I saw the movie in a now-shuttered movie palace in downtown Cheyenne, and noted the audience seemed something less than enthusiastic.

At some point before all this, I had been enormously impressed by Robert Silverberg's Nebula-winning "Passengers," a grimly powerful story of humans manipulated by alien forces. That emotional charge stuck with me.

Sometime early in 1981 I put fingers to typewriter keys and forced this story out. Although much of the reaction of my fellows in the writing workshop was positive, adjectives such as *repulsive, morbid,* and *depressing* were also tossed around. I felt some pessimism about the story's commercial prospects.

Then, close to Christmas, editor Marta Randall cheerfully bought the story for *New Dimensions 13.* I discovered I was in the company of such contributions as Vonda N. McIntyre's "Superluminal" and "Flying Saucer Rock and Roll" by Howard Waldrop. I was happy.

Pocket Books scheduled the anthology for its June 1982 list. Advance copies were sent out to reviewers. And then, true to the book's series number, it was canceled. The official word was that too few advance sales had been generated to warrant publication.

Marta regretfully returned the rights to the story to me.

In the meantime, Michael Bishop had been bugging me about contributing an original to his *Light Years and Dark* anthology, a project intended to be both comprehensive and daring. I sent him "Dancing Chickens." Michael didn't like the story at all and returned it with kind, but final words.

Somewhere along the line, Ellen Datlow saw the story at *OMNI* and bounced it, saying it was dynamite but entirely too raunchy for the magazine. Then, hearing of the Bishop rejection, she did me a great kindness. She took it upon herself to persuade Michael to read the piece again. He did, decided he liked the story better than before, and reversed his first decision. "Dancing Chickens" finally appeared in *Light Years and Dark* late in 1984. It hasn't been reprinted since.

Not all stories, of course, go through these Byzantine turns. But fictions are like kids, and some are more difficult than the others. I'm talking content here, too—not just marketing glitches. I hope you found "Dancing Chickens" as difficult a child to read as I did to write.

EDWARD BRYANT

PAT
⊙ CADIGAN ⊙

ROADSIDE RESCUE

Pat Cadigan's work has appeared in OMNI, Isaac Asimov's SF Magazine, *the* Magazine of Fantasy & Science Fiction, Twilight Zone, *and numerous anthologies, including* Blood Is Not Enough, Tropical Chills, Ripper!, Shadows, *and many best-of-the-year anthologies. She has been nominated for the Nebula, the Hugo, and the World Fantasy Award, and her first novel,* Mindplayers, *was a finalist for the Philip K. Dick Award. Her next novel,* Synners, *will appear in 1990, and a collection of her short fiction,* Patterns, *is currently out in hardcover from Ursus Imprints.*

Cadigan has grown into one of the most versatile writers I know. Starting with science fiction, she has branched out into fantasy and horror and can write all three with equal ease. "Roadside Rescue" is an amusing little science-fiction tale—until you think about it.

Barely fifteen minutes after he'd called Area Traffic Surveillance, Etan Carrera saw the big limousine transport coming toward him. He watched it with mild interest from his smaller and temporarily disabled vehicle. Some media celebrity or an alien—more likely an alien. All aliens

156

seemed enamored with things like limos and private SSTs, even after all these years. In any case, Etan fully expected to see the transport pass without even slowing, the navigator (not driver—limos drove themselves) hardly glancing his way, leaving him alone again in the rolling, green, empty countryside.

But the transport did slow and then stopped, cramming itself into the breakdown lane across the road. The door slid up, and the navigator jumped out, smiling as he came over to Etan. Etan blinked at the dark, full-dress uniform. People who worked for aliens had to do some odd things, he thought, and for some reason put his hand on the window control as though he were going to roll it up.

"Afternoon, sir," said the navigator, bending a little from the waist.

"Hi," Etan said.

"Trouble with your vehicle?"

"Nothing too serious, I hope. I've called Surveillance, and they say they'll be out to pick me up in two hours at most."

"That's a long time to wait." The navigator's smile widened. He was very attractive, holo-star kind of handsome. People who work for aliens, Etan thought. "Perhaps you'd care to wait in my employer's transport. For that matter, I can probably repair your vehicle, which will save you time and money. Roadside rescue fees are exorbitant."

"That's very kind," Etan said. "But I *have* called, and I don't want to impose—"

"It was my employer's idea to stop, sir. I agreed, of course. My employer is quite fond of people. In fact, my employer loves people. And I'm sure you would be rewarded in some way."

"Hey, now, I'm not asking for anything—"

"My employer is a most generous entity," said the navigator, looking down briefly. "I'll get my tool kit." He was on his way back across the road before Etan could object.

Ten minutes later the navigator closed the power plant housing of Etan's vehicle and came around to the window again, still looking formal and unruffled. "Try it now, sir."

Etan inserted his key card into the dash console and shifted the control near the steering module. The vehicle hummed to life. "Well, now," he said. "You fixed it."

That smile again. "Occasionally the connections to the motherboard are improperly fitted. Contaminants get in, throw off the fuel mixing, and the whole plant shuts down."

"Oh," Etan said, feeling stupid, incompetent, and worst of all, obligated.

"You won't be needing rescue now, sir."

"Well, I should call and tell them." Etan reached reluctantly for the console phone.

"You could call from the limo, sir. And if you'd care for a little refreshment—" The navigator opened his door for him.

Etan gave up. "Oh, sure, sure. This is all very nice of you and your, uh, employer." What the hell, he thought, getting out and following the navigator across the road. If it meant that much to the alien, he'd give the alien a thrill.

"We both appreciate this. My employer and I."

Etan smiled, bracing himself as the door to the passenger compartment of the limo slid back. Whatever awkward greeting he might have made died in his throat. There was no one inside, no one and nothing.

"Just go ahead and get in, sir."

"But, uh—"

"My employer is in there. Somewhere." Smile. "You'll find the phone by the refrigerator. Or shall I call Surveillance for you?"

"No, I'll do it. Uh, thanks." Etan climbed in and sat down on the silvery gray cushion. The door slid partially shut, and a moment later Etan heard the navigator moving around up front. Somewhere a blower went on, puffing cool, humid air at his face. He sat back tentatively. Luxury surroundings—refrigerator, bar, video, sound system. God knew what use the alien found for any of it. Hospitality. It probably wouldn't help. He and the alien would no doubt end up staring at each other with nothing to say, feeling freakish.

He was on the verge of getting up and leaving when the navigator slipped through the door. It shut silently as he sat down across from Etan and unbuttoned his uniform tunic.

"Cold drink, sir?"

Etan shook his head.

"Hope you don't mind if I do." There was a different quality to the smile now. He took an amber bottle from the refrigerator and flipped the cap off, aiming it at a disposal in the door. Etan could smell alcohol and heavy spicing. "Possibly the best spiced ale in the world, if not the known universe," the navigator said. "Sure you won't have any?"

"Yes, I—" Etan sat forward a little. "I really think I ought to say thank-you and get on. I don't want to hold you up—"

"My employer chooses where he wants to be when he wants to be there." The navigator took another drink from the bottle. "At least, I'm calling it a he. Hard to tell with a lot of these species." He ran his fingers through his dark hair; one long strand fell and brushed his temple. Etan caught a glimpse of a shaved spot near his temple. Implant; so the navigator would be mentally attuned to his employer, making speech or translation unnecessary. "With some, gender's irrelevant. Some have more than one gender. Some have more than *two*. Imagine taking *that* trip, if you can." He tilted the bottle up again. "But my present employer, here, asking him what gender he is, it's like asking you what flavor you are."

Etan took a breath. One more minute; then he'd ask this goof to let him out. "Not much you can do, I guess, except to arbitrarily assign them sex and—"

"Didn't say *that*."

"Pardon?"

The navigator killed the bottle. "Didn't say anything about sex."

"Oh." Etan paused, wondering exactly how crazy the navigator might be and how he'd managed to hide it well enough to be hired for an alien. "Sorry. I thought you said that some of them lacked sex—"

"Never said anything about sex. Gender, I said. Nothing about sex."

"But the terms can be interchangeable."

"Certainly *not*." The navigator tossed the bottle into the disposal and took another from the refrigerator. "Maybe on this planet but not out there."

Etan shrugged. "I assumed you'd need gender for sex, so if a species lacked gender, they'd uh . . ." he trailed off, making a firm resolution to shut up until he could escape. Suddenly he was very glad he hadn't canceled his rescue after all.

"Our nature isn't universal law," said the navigator. "Out there—" he broke off, staring at something to Etan's left. "Ah. My employer has decided to come out at last."

The small creature at the end of the seat seemed to have

coalesced out of the humid semidark, an off-white mound of what seemed to be fur as close and dense as a seal's. It might have repelled or disconcerted him except that it smelled so *good,* like a cross between fresh-baked bread and wildflowers. The aroma filled Etan with a sudden, intense feeling of well-being. Without thinking, he reached out to touch it, realized, and pulled his hand back.

"Going to pet it, were you? Stroke it?"

"Sorry," Etan said, half to the navigator and half to the creature.

"I forgive you," said the navigator, amused. "He'd forgive you, too, except he doesn't feel you've done anything wrong. It's the smell. Very compelling." He sniffed. "Go ahead. You won't hurt him."

Etan leaned over and gingerly touched the top of the creature. The contact made him jump. It didn't feel solid. It was like touching gelatin with a fur covering.

"Likes to stuff itself into the cushions and feel the vibrations from the ride," said the navigator. "But what it *really* loves is talk. Conversation. Sound waves created by the human voice are especially pleasing to it. And in *person,* not by holo or phone." The navigator gave a short, mirthless laugh and killed the second bottle. "So. Come on. Talk it up. That's what you're here for."

"Sorry," Etan said defensively. "I don't know exactly what to say."

"Express your goddam *gratitude* for it having me fix your vehicle."

Etan opened his mouth to make an angry response and decided not to. For all he knew, both alien and human were insane and dangerous besides. "Yes. Of course I do appreciate your help. It was so kind of you, and I'm saving a lot of money since I don't need a roadside rescue now—"

"Never called it off, did you?"

"What?"

"The rescue. You never called to tell Surveillance you didn't need help."

Etan swallowed. "Yes. I did."

"Liar."

All right, Etan thought. *Enough* was *too much.* "I don't know what transport services you work for, but I'll find out. They ought to know about you."

"Yeah? What should they know—that I make free repairs at the bidding of an alien hairball?" The navigator grinned bitterly.

"No." Etan's voice was quiet. "They should know that maybe you've been working too long and too hard for aliens." His eyes swiveled apologetically to the creature. "Not that I mean to offend—"

"Forget it. It doesn't understand a goddam word."

"Then why did you want me to talk to it?"

"Because *I* understand. We're attuned. On several frequencies, mind you, one for every glorious mood it might have. Not that it's any of your business."

Etan shook his head. "You need help."

"Fuck if I do. Now finish your thanks and start thinking up some more things to say."

The bread-and-flowers aroma intensified until Etan's nerves were standing on end. His heart pounded ferociously, and he wondered if a smell could induce cardiac arrest.

"I think I've finished thanking your employer." He looked directly at the creature. "And that's all I have to say. Under more pleasant circumstances, I might have talked my head off. Sorry." He started to get up.

The navigator moved quickly for someone who was supposed to be drunk. Etan found himself pinned against the back of the seat before he realized that the man wasn't jumping up to open the door. For a moment, he stared into the navigator's flushed face, not quite believing.

"Talk," the navigator said softly, almost gently. "Just talk. That's all you've got to do."

Etan tried heaving himself upward to throw them both off the seat and onto the floor, but the navigator had him too securely. "Help!" he bellowed. "Somebody help me!"

"Okay, yell for help. That's good, too," said the navigator, smiling. They began to slide down on the seat together with Etan on the bottom. "Go ahead. Yell all you want."

"Let me up and I won't report you."

"I'm sure I can believe *that*." The navigator laughed. "Tell us a whole fairy story now."

"Let me go or I swear to Christ I'll kill you and that furry shit you work for."

"What?" the navigator asked, leaning on him a little harder. "What was that, sir?"

"Let me go or I'll *fucking kill you!*"

Something in the air seemed to break, as though a circuit had been completed or some sort of energy discharged. Etan sniffed. The bread-and-flowers aroma had changed, more flowers, less bread, and much weaker, dissipating in the ventilation before he could get more than a whiff.

The navigator pushed himself off Etan and plumped down heavily on the seat across from him again. Etan held still, looking first at the man rubbing his face with both hands and then turning his head so he could see the creature sliding down behind the cushion. We scared it, he thought, horrified. Bad enough to make it hide under the seat.

"Sir."

Etan jumped. The navigator was holding a fistful of currency out to him. The denominations made him blink.

"It's yours, sir. Take it. You can go now."

Etan pulled himself up. "What the hell do you mean, it's mine?"

"Please, sir." The navigator pressed one hand over his left eye. "If you're going to talk anymore, please step outside."

"Step outs—" Etan slapped the man's hand away and lunged for the door.

"Wait!" called the navigator, and in spite of everything, Etan obeyed. The navigator climbed out of the transport clumsily, still covering his eye, the other hand offering the currency. "Please, sir. You haven't been hurt. You have a repaired vehicle, more than a little pocket money here—you've come out ahead if you think about it."

Etan laughed weakly. "I can't believe this."

"Just take the money, sir. My employer wants you to have it." The navigator winced and massaged his eye some more. "Purely psychosomatic," he said, as though Etan had asked. "The implant is painless and causes no damage, no matter how intense the exchange between species. But please lower your voice, sir. My employer can still feel your sound, and he's quite done with you."

"What is that supposed to mean?"

"The money is yours from my employer," the navigator said patiently. "My employer loves people. We discussed that earlier. *Loves* them. Especially their voices."

"So?" Etan crossed his arms. The navigator leaned over and stuffed the money between Etan's forearms.

"Perhaps you remember what else we were discussing. I really have no wish to remind you, sir."

"So? What's all that stuff about gender—what's that got to do with . . ." Etan's voice died away.

"Human voices," the navigator said. "No speech where they come from. And we're so new and different to them. This one's been here only a few weeks. Its preference happens to be that of a man speaking from fear and anger, something you can't fake."

Etan took a step back from the man, unfolding his arms and letting the money fall to the ground, thinking of the implant, the man feeling whatever the creature felt.

"I don't know if you could call it perversion or not," said the navigator. "Maybe there's no such thing." He looked down at the bills. "Might as well keep it. You earned it. You even did well." He pulled himself erect and made a small, formal bow. "Good day, sir," he said, with no mockery at all and climbed into the transport's front seat. Etan watched the limo roll out of the breakdown lane and lumber away from him.

After a while he looked down. The money was still there at his feet, so he picked it up.

Just as he was getting back into his own vehicle, the console phone chimed. "We've got an early opening in our patrol pattern," Surveillance told him. "So we can swing by and get you in ten minutes."

"Don't bother," Etan said.

"Repeat?"

"I said, you're too late."

"Repeat again, please."

Etan sighed. "There isn't anything to rescue me from anymore."

There was a brief silence on the other end. "Did you get your vehicle overhauled?"

"Yeah," Etan said. "That, too."

Like many people, I think about sex a lot, especially when it's too early for lunch. I was thinking about sex quite a bit when I wrote this story because I was seven months pregnant and constantly hungry. For some reason, this made me think of Robert Sheckley's fine and funny "Untouched by Human Hands," which deals with the idea of one person's meat being another's poison—that is, on an alien planet, both the aliens' meat *and* poison could be your poison, which would mean you'd have to eat something else. I don't know why this led me to remember that Robert A. Heinlein once pointed out, via his character Lazarus Long, that one person's theology was another's belly laugh, but naturally, I thought of how both these notions can be turned a little more and applied to sex—one person's happiness can be the Supreme Court's felony.

It goes further than that, as you'll know if you've ever visited an adult bookstore and paid the browsing fee. It's an educational experience. Personally, it's all right with me and I will defend to the death any consenting adult's prerogative to engage in whatever, but in terms of my own Weltanschauung, I don't call some of that stuff sex. It's a matter of personal taste for all of us and the idea of having that freedom restricted is far more repellent to my idiosyncratic sensibilities than any practices I may consider, ah, bizarre.

The key words above, I hasten to remind you, are *consenting* and *adult*.

Anyway, being at the time a very pregnant and very hungry science-fiction writer, I started thinking that we humans probably wouldn't call certain alien pleasures sex in terms of ourselves. We probably wouldn't even recognize them for what they were. But what if they wanted to do it with us anyway? What if they *did* do it and we didn't know it until it was too late? Wouldn't you just *hate* that?

PAT CADIGAN

GEOFF
⊙ RYMAN ⊙

OMNISEXUAL

Geoff Ryman is a Canadian living in Great Britain. His novella "The Unconquered Country" (Bantam) won the British Science Fiction Association Award and the World Fantasy Award. His novel The Child Garden *was recently published by Unwin Hyman in Britain and Bantam in the United States. The first part of that novel, "Love Sickness," was published separately in* Interzone *and won the British SF Association Award for best short fiction.*

"Omnisexual" is one of the few stories here about which I have nothing to say, except that it's most certainly alien.

There were birds inside of her. Was she giving birth to them? One of them fluttered its wings against the walls of her uterus. He felt the wings flutter too. He felt what she felt in a paradise of reciprocity, but she was not real. This world had given birth to her, out of memory.

A dove shrugged its way out of her. Its round white face, its surprised black eyes made him smile. It blinked, coated with juices, and then, with a final series of convulsions, pulled itself free. The woman put it on her stomach to warm it, and it lay between them, cleaning itself. Very suddenly, it flew away.

He buried his face in her, loving the taste of her.

"Stay there," she told him, holding his head, showing him where to put his tongue.

And he felt his own tongue, on a sensitive new gash that had seemed to open up along the middle of his scrotum.

She was delivered of fine milky substance that tasted of white chocolate. It sustained him through the days he spent with her.

She gave birth to a hummingbird. He knew then what was happening. DNA encodes both memory and genes. Here, in this other place and time, memory and genes were confused. She was giving birth to memories.

"Almost, almost," she warned him, and held his head again. The hummingbird passed between them, working its way out of her and down his throat. Breathing very carefully, not daring to move in case he choked, he felt a wad of warm feathers clench and gather. He felt the current of his breath pass over its back, and he swallowed, to help it.

It made a nest in his stomach. Humming with its wings, it produced a sensation of continual excitement. He knew he would digest it. The walls of its cells would break down, giving up their burden of genes. He knew they would join with his own. Life here worked in different ways.

He became pregnant. All over his skin, huge pale blisters bubbled up, yearning to be lanced. He clawed at them until they burst, with a satisfying lunging outward of fluid and new life.

He gave birth to things that looked like raw liver. He squeezed them out from under the pale loose skin of the broken blisters, and onto the ground. They pulled themselves up into knots of muscle and stretched themselves out again. In this way, they drew themselves across the ground, dust sticking to each of them like a fine suede coat.

They could speak, with tiny voices. "Home," they cried. "Home, home, home," like birds. They wanted to go back to him. They were part of him, they remembered being him, they had no form. They needed his form to act. They clustered around him for warmth at night, mewling for reentry. In the end, he ate them, to restore them. He could not face doing anything else.

Their mother ate them too. "They will be reborn as hummingbirds," she told him. She gave birth instead to bouquets of roses and things that looked like small toy trains.

He did not trust her. He knew she was collecting his memories from them. She collected people's memories. She saw his doubt.

"I am like a book," she said. "Books are spirits in the world that take an outward form of paper and words. They are the work of everyone, a collection. I am like that. I am communal. So are you."

Her directness embarrassed him. His doubts were not eased. He walked through the rustling tundra of intelligent grasses. The hairs on the barley heads turned like antennae. The grass was communal too.

When he came back to the woman who was not real, she had grown larger. She lay entwined in the grass, and hugged him; she opened up and enveloped him. Warm flesh, salmon pink with blue veins, closed over him moist and sheltering, sizzling like steak and thumping like Beethoven. He lived inside her.

Prying ribbons explored him gently, opened him up. They nestled in his ears, or crept down his nose, insinuated their way past his anus, reached needle thin down the tip of his penis. They untied his belly button, to feed him. Flesh was a smaller sea in which, for a time, he surrendered his independent being.

What conjunction could be more complete than that? When he emerged after some months, he was a different person. He had a different face. It had grown out of him, out of his old one. He looked into her eyes and saw the reflection of his new face. It was a shock. This was the face of a conqueror, a hero, older, like a head on a Roman coin.

Her eyes looked back at him, amused and affectionate. "You will go away now," she told him. "You have become bored. You should always listen to boredom or disgust. It is telling you that it is time to move."

On the other world, the world he had come from, there had been a fluorescent sign outside his window.

BUILDING TOMORROW, the sign had read, WITH THE PEOPLE OF TODAY.

It did not seem to him that this was possible.

Rain would pimple the glass of the window, breaking up the red light from the sign, glowing red light drops of blood. And he would listen to the wind outside, or fight his way along the blustery streets under clouds that were the color of pigeons.

Everything was covered over by concrete. There were no trees; the buildings had been cheaply made and were not kept clean. The people were the only things that were soft.

People lived where they worked, crawling out from under their desks in the morning, sleepy, embarrassed, polite, smelling of body processes, wearing faded robes to blanket the smells, shuffling off to the toilets to wash. Their breasts, their buttocks were wrapped and hidden. Disease was a miasma between them, like some kind of radiant ectoplasm. He would rove the blustery streets, dust in his eyes, looking at the young people. He could not believe the beauty of their faces and bodies, and he ached for them, to think that they would grow old, and he wanted to hold them and to touch them, so that the beauty would not go unacknowledged or hoarded by only one or two others. He ached to think of them losing their beauty here.

He saw them losing it. He saw what they would become. The people he worked with had tiny cookers under their desks, and they made tiny meals. Everything in the office smelled of cabbage. Their faces went lined and apologetic and pale, sagging eventually into permanent, pouchy frowns. Loss provoked a longing within him. He wanted the old. He wanted to reach out for and soothe the ghosts of their younger selves and make what was left of their bodies bloom. He wanted the young, who were doomed.

They didn't have to live this way. They could choose freedom. He did. He had a vocation, a vocation to love. To have a vocation, it is necessary to give up ambition and normality. He went to live in another place where love was allowed because life there worked differently, and disease, and procreation. Those who went there could love without risk and come back clean. He did not want to come back. He gave up his desk and the smells of cabbage. He was called a whore.

This is not a story of other planets. It is a story of being driven from within. He was driven to a different place and a different time. Visitors came there to be loved and he loved them. It was a paradise of politesse. There were the approaches, elegant, or shy; and the jokes; and the fond farewells; and the mild embarrassment of separation when it did not work, and the kindly stroking of the hair that meant—this has been nice and now it is at an end. Some of them never believed he was not doing it for money. They left, believing that.

The man began to see that he had set himself an unending task. You could not touch all human beauty, not unless you flung yourself in threads across the space between the worlds and stitched all the people and planets together in one sparkling cobweb. You could not do it, give or receive enough, unless you ceased to be human. A paradise of politesse was not quite enough.

His tastes began to change. He wanted to go in and not out, to stay with one person. He met the woman who was not real. He realized that this world had given her birth. Why she had chosen him, he did not know. Could she read his mind from his semen? First his tastes, and then his body had changed, from love and viruses.

And now he was bored with that, too.

He left the woman who was not real and walked across the austere tundra. His body had gone crazy. A steady stream of new life poured out of him, small and wet and sluglike, vomiting out of his mouth or dropping from the tip of his penis. He grew a pouch on his belly, to keep them warm. They would crawl up his stomach on batwings or hooks that looked like a scorpion's sting. Others darted about him like hummingbirds. His nipples became hard and swollen, and they exuded a thick, salty, sweaty paste. His humming children bit them to force out food. The others hung on to the hair of his chest or on to each other, mouthing him.

Berries grew on bleak and blasted shrubbery. He ate them and the fleshy protuberances that popped, like mushrooms, out of the earth. As he ate them, he knew that genetic information was being passed on to him, and through his breasts, on to his strange children. His body grew crazier.

Then autumn came and all his children dropped from him like leaves.

After the first snow, he built himself a hollow in the snow drifts. He licked the walls and his spittle froze. He lived in the hollow, naked, warming it with his body heat. He would crawl up the warm and glassy tunnel and reach out of the entrance to gather the snow. It was alive. It tasted of muesli and semen. He was reminded then of people, real and unreal.

Why had he come here at all, if it were only to huddle alone in a room made of spit? He began to yearn for company. He began to yearn for the forest, but a forest untouched by fantasy. He was a contradiction. Without simplicity, it is difficult to move. He stayed where he was.

Until he began to see things moving on the other side of the spittle wall and tried to call to them. He could see them moving, within the ice. Then he realized that they were only reflections of himself. He threw on his clothes and left the burrow in the middle of winter.

The snow was alive and it loved him. It settled over his shoulders and merged into a solid blanket of living matter that kept him warm. As he walked he turned his mouth up open to feed. Again the taste of semen.

The world was ripe with pheromones. It was the world that drew him, with constant subliminal promises of sex or something like it, of circumstance, of change. What use was an instinct when its end had no distinct form or shape? It was form or shape that he was seeking.

The snow fertilized his tongue. It grew plump and heavy. It ruptured as he was walking, spilling blood over his chin and down his throat. He knelt over the ice to see his reflection, holding out his tongue. It was covered with frantically wiggling, burrowing white tails. He sat down and wept, covering his face. It seemed that there was no way forward, no way back.

He broke off a piece of the ice and used it like a blade to scrape his tongue. The white things squealed and came free with peeling, suction-cup sounds. He wiped them onto the snow. The snow melted, absorbing them, pulling them down into itself.

He ate the ice. The ice was made of sugar. It was neutral, not alive, secreted by life, like the nuggets of sugar that had gathered along the stems of his houseplants back home. He still thought of the other world as home. He spurned the snow and survived the winter on ice.

He trudged south. Even the rays of light were sexual. They came at him a solid yellow. They shot through him, piercing him, making his flesh ache. They sent a dull yearning along the bones of forearm and thighs. His bones shifted in place with independent desire. They began to work their way loose, like teeth.

His left thigh broke free first. It tore its way out of his leg, pulling the perfect, cartilage-coated ball out of its socket with a sound like a kiss. The bone fell and was accepted by the snow, escaping. As he tried to find it, the bone above his right elbow ripped through his shoulder and followed, slipping out into the living snow. It too was lost. He was lame.

He drank his own blood, to save his strength. He walked and slept and grew new children. They were new arms, new legs, many of them, but they would not do what he wanted. They had a will of their own. They pulled back the flesh of his face while he dozed, peeling back his lips so that he gave birth to his own naked skull. His bones wanted to become a coral reef. They did not let him move. The plates of his skull blossomed out in thin calcium petals, like a flower made of salt. He waited, wistful, patient, resting, hopeless.

The spring came. The snow grew into a fleshy forest, pink and veined. There were fat, leathery flowers, and wattle-trees that lowed like cattle. Pink asparagus ran on myriad roots, chattering. His bones grew into dungeons and turrets, brain-shaped swellings, spreading fans, encrusted shrubberies. His body lurked in hidden chambers and became carnivorous again. It would lunge out of its hiding like moray eels, to seize capering scraps of flesh, dragging them in, enfolding them in shells of bone with razor edges.

Finally he became bored. Bored and disgusted and able to move.

The coral reef stirred. With its first shifting, delicate towers crumbled and fell. They smashed the fantastic calcium spirals and bridges. They broke open the translucent domes of bone. The whole mass began to articulate, bend. He pulled himself free, slithering out of its many rooms.

He no longer resembled a human being. He lay on his back, unable to right himself. It was the first night of summer, warm and still. Lying on his back, he could see the stars. He tried to sing to himself, and his many mouths sang for him. The forest swayed slightly, asleep, in the wind.

He loved the world. He finally, finally came to it. Semen prised its way out from under his thousand eyelids, scorching his eyes. It flowed from his moray mouths, from his many anuses, and from his host of genitals, a leaping chorus the color of moonlight.

The scrota burst, one after another, like poppy pods. He was no longer male. He slept in a pool of his own blood and sweat and semen.

By morning it had seeped away, given to this living world. The soil around him rippled, radiating outward. Everything was alive. Rain began to fall, washing him clean. Where he had touched the coral, he was stung and erupted in large red weals.

One of his children came to its father. It was no particular shape or gender. It had a huge mouth and was covered in lumps like acne. It was still an adolescent.

It found his real arms and legs, found the ones that were lame, and mumbled them, warming them. Deftly, with the tip of its tongue, it flicked bones out of itself, and pushed them through the old wounds back into place. Then it pruned him, biting, cutting him free from his accretion of form, into an approximation of his old shape.

"Ride me," his child whispered. Exhausted, he managed to crawl onto its back. Hedgehog spines transfixed his hands and feet, holding him on to the back of his child. The thorns fed him, pumping sugar into his veins. As he rested, growing fat, he was carried.

His desires hauled him across the world. Staring up at the changing sky, he had opportunity to reflect. He could fly apart and pull himself together. His DNA could carry memory and desire into other bodies. DNA could combine with him, to make his living flesh behave in different ways. Was it only power that pushed him? To make the world like himself? Or was it that the world was so beautiful that the impulse was to devour it and be in turn devoured?

His child set him down in a cornfield. Great thick corn leaves bent broken-backed from their stalks like giant blades of grass and moved slightly in a comfortable breeze. He had never seen a cornfield, only read about them. He and this world together had fathered one.

"You have grown too heavy," said his child. Its speech was labored, the phrases short and punctuated with gasps for air. "How long do I live?"

"I don't know," he said. It blinked at him with tiny blue eyes.

He kissed it and stroked the tuft of coarse hair on the top of its head. "Maybe I will grow wings," it said. Then it heaved its great bulk around and with sighs and shifting began its journey back.

The cornfield went on to the horizon. He reached up and broke off an ear of corn. When he bit into the cob, it bled. There was a scarecrow in the field. It waved to him. He looked away. He did not want to know if it were alive.

He walked along the ordered rows, deeper and deeper into the field. The air was warm, heavy, smelling of corn. Finally he came to a neatly cultivated border on top of the bank of a river. The bank was high and steep, the river muddy and slow moving.

He heard a whinnying. Rocking its way back and forth up the steep slope came a palomino pony. Its blond, ragged mane hung almost down to the ground.

It stopped and stared at him. They looked at each other. "Where are you from?" he asked it, gently. Wind stirred its mane. There was bracken in it, tangled. The bracken looked brown and rough and real. "Where did you get that?" he asked it.

It snorted and waved its head up and down in the air, indicating the direction of the river.

"Are you hungry?" he asked. It went still. He worked an ear of corn loose from its stalk, peeled back its outer leaves, and held it out. The pony took it with soft and feeling lips, breaking it up in its mouth like an apple. The man pulled the bracken out of its mane.

It let him walk with it along the river. It was hardly waist-high and its back legs were so deformed by rickets that the knee joints almost rubbed together when it walked. He called it Lear, for its wild white hair and crown of herbs.

They walked beside the cornfield. It ended suddenly, one last orderly row, and then there was a disorder of plants in a dry grassland: bay trees smelling of his youth, small pines decorated with lights and glass balls, feathery fennel, and mole hills with tiny smoking chimneys. Were they all his children?

They came to a plain of giant shells, empty and marble patterned. Something he had wished to become and abandoned. The air rustled in their empty sworls, the sound of wind; the sound of the sea; the sound of voices on foreign radio late at night, wavering and urgent.

All the unheard voices. The river became smaller and clearer, slapping over polished rocks on its way from the moors. The clouds were low and fast moving. The sun seemed always to be just peeking out over their edge, as if in a race with them.

They came to bracken and small twisted trees on spongy, moorland soil. There, Lear seemed to say, this is where I said I would take you. This is where you wanted to be. It waved its head up and down, and trotted away on deformed legs.

The man knelt and ate the grass. He tore up mouthfuls of it, flat inert and tasting only of chlorophyll and cellulose. It seemed to him to be as delicious as mint.

He walked into the water. It was stingingly cold, alien, clean. He gasped for breath—he always was such a coward about going into the water. He half ran, half swam across the pond and came up in the woodland on the opposite shore. Small, old oaks had moss instead of orchids. Rays of sunlight radiated from behind scurrying small clouds. The land was swept with light and shadow. Everything smelled of loam and leaf mold and whiplash hazel in shadow.

He sat down in a small clearing. There was a beech tree. Its trunk was smooth and sinuous, almost polished. The wind sighed up and down its length, and the tree moved with it. The soil moved, and out of it came his children, shapeless, formless, brushing his hand to be petted. "Home," they mewed.

Everything moved. Everything was alive in a paradise of reciprocity. The man who was real had fathered the garden that had fathered him.

The woman came and sat next to him. She was smaller, flabbier, with the beginnings of a double chin. "I'm real now," she said. They watched the trees dance until the four suns had set. All the stars began to sing.

A friend of mine nearly sold a story to *Cosmopolitan*. It was all about the usual *Cosmopolitan* subjects: sex and success. It took, however, an anti-*Cosmopolitan* line. You can't, my friend was saying, have it all. The story got all the way to the final selection stage before the editors began to get a creeping, uncomfortable feeling about it.

A few years later, I tried to do the same thing with a glossy, men-only-style magazine. It was a story about an interplanetary brothel in which the whores were nonhuman androids. It was clearly pornographic by the strict definition of the word (fiction about whores), except that it made plain the existence of such a place in any form was a tragedy. The story almost sold.

I feel friendlier toward sex now. In a way this story is a return to that brothel, except that the sexual feelings embrace the universe, and in some way transform the artificial relations into lasting, human ones. It is probably the most optimistic story I've written, and, I hope, the sexiest.

GEOFF RYMAN

CONNIE
⊙ WILLIS ⊙

ALL MY DARLING DAUGHTERS

Connie Willis lives in Colorado. She has won the Hugo and Nebula awards for her short fiction, and the John W. Campbell Memorial Award for her first solo novel Lincoln's Dreams. *Her most recent novel,* Doomsday Book (*Bantam*), *is about the plague, and her most recent collection is* The Last of the Winnebagos and Other Stories (*Bantam*).

"All My Darling Daughters" is the other reprint originally scheduled for New Dimensions 13. *Its first publication was in Connie Willis's collection* Firewatch. *It's as powerful today as it was when I first read it at* OMNI *in 1980.*

BARRETT: I'll have her dog . . . Octavius.
OCTAVIUS: Sir?
BARRETT: Her dog must be destroyed. At once.
OCTAVIUS: I really d-don't see what the p-poor little beast has
    d-done to . . .
                        —The Barretts of Wimpole Street

T͟he first thing my new room-mate did was tell me her life story. Then she tossed up all over my bunk. Welcome to Hell. I know, I know. It was my own fucked fault that I was stuck with the stupid little scut in the first place. Daddy's darling had let her grades slip till she was back in the freshman dorm and she would stay there until the admin reported she was being a good little girl again. But he didn't have to put me in the charity ward, with all the little scholarship freshmen from the front colonies—frightened virgies one and all. The richies had usually had their share of jig-jig in boarding school, even if they were mostly edge. And they were willing to learn.

Not this one. She wouldn't know a bone from a vaj, and wouldn't know what went into which either. Ugly, too. Her hair was chopped off in an old-fashioned bob I thought nobody, not even front kids, wore anymore. Her name was Zibet and she was from some godspit colony called Marylebone Weep and her mother was dead and she had three sisters and her father hadn't wanted her to come. She told me all this in a rush of what she probably thought was friendliness before she tossed her supper all over me and my nice new slickspin sheets.

The sheets were the sum total of good things about the vacation Daddy Dear had sent me on over summer break. Being stranded in a forest of slimy slicksa trees and noble natives was supposed to build my character and teach me the hazards of bad grades. But the noble natives were good at more than weaving their precious product with its near frictionless surface. Jig-jig on slick-spin is something entirely different, and I was close to being an expert on the subject. I'd bet even Brown didn't know about this one. I'd be more than glad to teach him.

"I'm so *sorry,*" she kept saying in a kind of hiccup while her face turned red and then white and then red again like a fucked alert bell, and big tears seeped down her face and dripped on the mess. "I guess I got a little sick on the shuttle."

"I guess. Don't bawl, for jig's sake, it's no big deal. Don't they have laundries in Mary Boning It?"

"Marylebone Weep. It's a natural spring."

"So are you, kid. So are you." I scooped up the wad, with the muck inside. "No big deal. The dorm mother will take care of it."

She was in no shape to take the sheets down herself, and I figured Mumsy would take one look at those big fat tears and assign me a new roommate. This one was not exactly perfect. I could see right now I couldn't expect her to do her homework and not bawl giant tears while Brown and I jig-jigged on the new sheets. But she didn't have leprosy, she didn't weigh eight hundred pounds, and she hadn't gone for my vaj when I bent over to pick up the sheets. I could do a lot worse.

I could also be doing some better. Seeing Mumsy on my first day back was not my idea of a good start. But I trotted downstairs with the scutty wad and knocked on the dorm mother's door.

She is no dumb lady. You have to stand in a little box of an entryway waiting for her to answer your knock. The box works on the same principle as a rat cage, except that she's added her own little touch. Three big mirrors that probably cost her a year's salary to cart up from earth. Never mind—as a weapon, they were a real bargain. Because, Jesus Jiggin' Mary, you stand there and sweat and the mirrors tell you your skirt isn't straight and your hair looks scutty and that bead of sweat on your upper lip is going to give it away immediately that you are scared scutless. By the time she answers the door—five minutes if she's feeling kindly—you're either edge or you're not there. No dumb lady.

I was not on the defensive, and my skirts are never straight, so the mirrors didn't have any effect on me, but the five minutes took their toll. That box didn't have any ventilation and I was way too close to those sheets. But I had my speech all ready. No need to remind her who I was. The admin had probably filled her in but good. And I'd get nowhere telling her they were my sheets. Let her think they were the virgie's.

When she opened the door I gave her a brilliant smile and said, "My roommate's had a little problem. She's a new freshman, and I think she got a little excited coming up on the shuttle and—"

I expected her to launch into the "supplies are precious, everything must be recycled, cleanliness is next to godliness" speech you get for everything you do on this godspit campus. Instead she said, "What did you do to her?"

"What did I—look, she's the one who tossed up. What do you think I did, stuck my fingers down her throat?"

"Did you give her something? Samurai? Float? Alcohol?"

"Jiggin' Jesus, she just got here. She walked in, she said she was from Mary's Prick or something, she tossed up."

"And?"

"And what? I may look depraved, but I don't think freshmen vomit at the sight of me."

From her expression, I figured Mumsy might. I stuck the smelly wad of sheets at her. "Look," I said, "I don't care what you do. It's not my problem. The kid needs clean sheets."

Her expression for the mucky mess was kinder than the one she had for me. "Recycling is not until Wednesday. She will have to sleep on her mattress until then."

Mary Masting, she could knit a sheet by Wednesday, especially with all the cotton flying around this fucked campus. I grabbed the sheets back.

"Jig you, scut," I said.

I got two months' dorm restricks and a date with the admin.

I went down to third level and did the sheets myself. It cost a fortune. They want you to have an *awareness* of the harm you are doing the delicate environment by failing to abide, etc. Total scut. The environment's about as delicate as a senior's vaj. When Old Man Moulton bought this thirdhand Hell-Five, he had some edge dream of turning it into the college he went to as a boy. Whatever possessed him to even buy the old castoff is something nobody's ever figured out. There must have been a Lagrangian point on the top of his head.

The realtor must have talked hard and fast to make him think Hell could ever look like Ames, Iowa. At least there'd been some technical advances since it was first built or we'd all be *floating* around the godspit place. But he couldn't stop at simply gravitizing the place, fixing the plumbing, and hiring a few good teachers. Oh, no, he had to build a sandstone campus, put in a football field, and plant *trees!* This all cost a fortune, of course, which put it out of the reach of everybody but richies and trust kids, except for Moulton's charity scholarship cases. But you couldn't jig-jig in a plastic bag to fulfill your fatherly instincts back then, so Moulton had to build himself a college. And here we sit, stuck out in space with a bunch of fucked cottonwood trees that are trying to take over.

Jesus Bonin' Mary, cottonwoods! I mean, so what if we're a hundred years out of date. I can take the freshman beanies and the pep rallies. Dorm curfews didn't stop anybody a hundred years ago either. And face it, pleated skirts and cardigans make for easy access. But those godspit trees!

At first they tried the nature-dupe stuff. Freeze your vaj in winter, suffocate in summer, just like good old Iowa. The trees

179

were at least bearable then. Everybody choked in cotton for a month, they baled the stuff up like Mississippi slaves and shipped it down to Earth and that was it. But finally something was too expensive even for Daddy Moulton and we went on even-clime like all the other Hell-Fives. Nobody bothered to tell the trees, of course, so now they just spit and drop leaves whenever they feel like it, which is all the time. You can hardly make it to class without choking to death.

The trees do their dirty work down under, too, rooting happily away through the plumbing and the buried cables so that nothing works. Ever. I think the whole outer shell could blow away and nobody would ever know. The fucked root system would hold us together. And the admin wonders why we call it Hell. I'd like to upset this delicate balance once and for all.

I ran the sheets through on disinfect and put them in the spin. While I was sitting there, thinking evil thoughts about freshmen and figuring how to get off restricks, Arabel came wandering in.

"Tavvy, hi! When did you get back?" She is always too sweet for words. We played lezzies as freshmen, and sometimes I think she's sorry it's over. "There's a great party," she said.

"I'm on restricks," I said. Arabel's not the world's greatest authority on parties. I mean, herself and a plastic bone would be a great party. "Where is it?"

"My room. Brown's there," she said languidly. This was calculated to make me rush out of my pants and up the stairs, no doubt. I watched my sheets spin.

"So what are you doing down here?" I said.

"I came down for some float. Our machine's out. Why don't you come on over? Restricks never stopped you before."

"I've been to your parties, Arabel. Washing my sheets might be more exciting."

"You're right," she said, "it might." She fiddled with the machine. This was not like her at all.

"What's up?"

"Nothing's up." She sounded puzzled. "It's samurai-party time without the samurai. Not a bone in sight and no hope of any. That's why I came down here."

"Brown, too?" I asked. He was into a lot of edge stuff, but I couldn't quite imagine celibacy.

"Brown, too. They all just sit there."

"They're on something, then. Something new they brought back from vacation." I couldn't see what she was so upset about.

"No," she said. "They're not on anything. This is different. Come see. Please."

Well, maybe this was all a trick to get me to one of Arabel's scutty parties and maybe not. But I didn't want Mumsy to think she'd hurt my feelings by putting me on restricks. I threw the lock on the spin so nobody'd steal the sheets and went with her.

For once Arabel hadn't exaggerated. It was a godspit party, even by her low standards. You could tell that the minute you walked in. The girls looked unhappy, the boys looked uninterested. It couldn't be all bad, though. At least Brown was back. I walked over to where he was standing.

"Tavvy," he said, smiling, "how was your summer? Learn anything new from the natives?"

"More than my fucked father intended." I smiled back at him.

"I'm sure he had your best interests at heart," he said. I started to say something clever to that, then realized he wasn't kidding. Brown was trust just like I was. He had to be kidding. Only he wasn't. He wasn't smiling anymore either.

"He just wanted to protect you, for your own good."

Jiggin' Jesus, he had to be on something. "I don't need any protecting," I said. "As you well know."

"Yeah," he said, sounding disappointed. "Yeah." He moved away.

What in the scut was going on? Brown leaned against the wall, watching Sept and Arabel. She had her sweater off and was shimmying out of her skirt, which I have seen before, sometimes even helped with. What I had never seen before was the look of absolute desperation on her face. Something was very wrong. Sept stripped, and his bone was as big as Arabel could have wanted, but the look on her face didn't change. Sept shook his head almost disapprovingly at Brown and went down on Arabel.

"I haven't had any straight-up all summer," Brown said from behind me, his hand on my vaj. "Let's get out of here."

Gladly. "We can't go to my room," I said. "I've got a virgie for a roommate. How about yours?"

"No!" he said, and then more quietly, "I've got the same problem. New guy. Just off the shuttle. I want to break him in gently."

You're lying, Brown, I thought. And you're about to back out of this, too. "I know a place," I said, and practically raced him to the laundry room so he wouldn't have time to change his mind.

I spread one of the dried slickspin sheets on the floor and went down as fast as I could get out of my clothes. Brown was in no hurry, and the frictionless sheet seemed to relax him. He smoothed his hands the full length of my body. "Tavvy," he said, brushing his lips along the line from my hips to my neck, "your skin's so soft. I'd almost forgotten." He was talking to himself.

Forgotten what, for fucked's sake, he couldn't have been without any jig-jig all summer or he'd be showing it now, and he acted like he had all the time in the world.

"Almost forgotten . . . nothing like . . ."

Like what? I thought furiously. Just what have you got in that room? And what has it got that I haven't. I spread my legs and forced him down between them. He raised his head a little, frowning, then he started that long, slow, torturing passage down my skin again. Jiggin' Jesus, how long did he think I could wait?

"Come on," I whispered, trying to maneuver him with my hips. "Put it in, Brown. I want to jig-jig. Please."

He stood up in a motion so abrupt that my head smacked against the laundry-room floor. He pulled on his clothes, looking . . . what? Guilty? Angry?

I sat up. "What in the holy scut do you think you're doing?"

"You wouldn't understand. I just keep thinking about your father."

"My *father*? What in the scut are you talking about?"

"Look, I can't explain it. I just can't . . ." And left. Like that. With me ready to go off any minute and what do I get? A cracked head.

"I don't have a father, you scutty godfucker!" I shouted after him.

I yanked my clothes on and started pulling the other sheet out of the spin with a viciousness I would have liked to have spent on Brown. Arabel was back, watching from the laundry-room door. Her face still had that strained look.

"Did you see that last charming scene?" I asked her, snagging the sheet on the spin handle and ripping a hole in one corner.

"I didn't have to. I can imagine it went pretty much the way mine did." She leaned unhappily against the door. "I think they've all gone bent over the summer."

"Maybe." I wadded the sheets together into a ball. I didn't think that was it, though. Brown wouldn't have lied about a new boy in his room in that case. And he wouldn't have kept talking about my father in that edge way. I walked past Arabel. "Don't worry, Arabel, if we have to go lezzy again, you know you're my first choice."

She didn't even look particularly happy about that.

My idiot roommate was awake, sitting bolt upright on the bunk where I'd left her. The poor brainless thing had probably been sitting there the whole time I'd been gone. I made up the bunk, stripped off my clothes for the second time tonight, and crawled in. "You can turn out the light any time," I said.

She hopped over to the wall plate, swathed in a nightgown that dated as far back as Old Man Moulton's college days, or farther. "Did you get in trouble?" she asked, her eyes wide.

"Of course not. I wasn't the one who tossed up. If anybody's in trouble, it's you," I added maliciously.

She seemed to sag against the flat wallplate as if she were clinging to it for support. "My father—will they tell my father?" Her face was flashing red and white again. And where would the vomit land this time? That would teach me to take out my frustrations on my roommate.

"Your father? Of course not. Nobody's in trouble. It was a couple of fucked sheets, that's all."

She didn't seem to hear me. "He said he'd come and get me if I got in trouble. He said he'd make me go home."

I sat up in the bunk. I'd never seen a freshman yet that wasn't dying to go home, at least not one like Zibet, with a whole loving family waiting for her instead of a trust and a couple of snotty lawyers. But Zibet here was scared scutless at the idea. Maybe the whole campus was going edge. "You didn't get in trouble," I repeated. "There's nothing to worry about."

She was still hanging onto that wallplate for dear life.

183

"Come on—" Mary Masting, she was probably having an attack of some kind, and I'd get blamed for that, too. "You're safe here. Your father doesn't even know about it."

She seemed to relax a little. "Thank you for not getting me in trouble," she said and crawled back into her own bunk. She didn't turn the light off.

Jiggin' Jesus, it wasn't worth it. I got out of bed and turned the fucked light off myself.

"You're a good person, you know that," she said softly into the darkness. Definitely edge. I settled down under the covers, planning to masty myself to sleep, since I couldn't get anything any other way, but very quietly. I didn't want any more hysterics.

A hearty voice suddenly exploded into the room. "To the young men of Moulton College, to all my strong sons, I say—"

"What's that?" Zibet whispered.

"First night in Hell," I said, and got out of bed for the thirtieth time.

"May all your noble endeavors be crowned with success," Old Man Moulton said.

I slapped my palm against the wallplate and then fumbled through my still-unpacked shuttle bag for a nail file. I stepped up on Zibet's bunk with it and started to unscrew the intercom.

"To the young women of Moulton College," he boomed again, "to all my darling daughters." He stopped. I tossed the screws and file back in the bag, smacked the plate, and flung myself back in bed.

"Who was that?" Zibet whispered.

"Our founding father," I said, and then remembering the effect the word *father* seemed to be having on everyone in this edge place, I added hastily, "That's the last time you'll have to hear him. I'll put some plast in the works tomorrow and put the screws back in so the dorm mother won't figure it out. We will live in blessed silence for the rest of the semester."

She didn't answer. She was already asleep, gently snoring. Which meant so far I had misguessed every single thing today. Great start to the semester.

The admin knew all about the party. "You *do* know the meaning of the word *restricks*, I presume?" he said.

He was an old scut, probably forty-five. Dear Daddy's age. He was fairly good-looking, probably exercising like edge to keep the old belly in for the freshman girls. He was liable to get a hernia. He probably jig-jigged into a plastic bag, too, just like Daddy, to carry on the family name. Jiggin' Jesus, there oughta be a law.

"You're a trust student, Octavia?"

"That's right." You think I'd be stuck with a fucked name like Octavia if I wasn't?

"Neither parent?"

"No. Paid mother-surr. Trust name till twenty-one." I watched his face to see what effect that had on him. I'd seen a lot of scared faces that way.

"There's no one to write to, then, except your lawyers. No way to expel you. And restricks don't seem to have any appreciable effect on you. I don't quite know what would."

I'll bet you don't. I kept watching him, and he kept watching me, maybe wondering if I was his darling daughter, if that expensive jism in the plastic bag had turned out to be what he was boning after right now.

"What exactly was it you called your dorm mother?"

"Scut," I said.

"I've longed to call her that myself a time or two."

The sympathetic buildup. I waited, pretty sure of what was coming.

"About this party. I've heard the boys have something new going. What is it?"

The question wasn't what I'd expected. "I don't know," I said and then realized I'd let my guard down. "Do you think I'd tell you if I knew?"

"No, of course not. I admire that. You're quite a young woman, you know. Outspoken, loyal, very pretty, too, if I may say so."

Um-hmm. And you just happen to have a job for me, don't you?

"My secretary's quit. She likes younger men, she says, although if what I hear is true, maybe she's better off with me. It's a good job. Lots of extras. Unless, of course, you're like my secretary and prefer boys to men."

Well, and here was the way out. No more virgie freshmen, no

more restricks. Very tempting. Only he was at least forty-five, and somehow I couldn't quite stomach the idea of jig-jig with my own father. Sorry, sir.

"If it's the trust problem that's bothering you, I assure you there are ways to check."

Liar. Nobody knows who their kids are. That's why we've got these storybook trust names, so we can't show up on Daddy's doorstep: Hi, I'm your darling daughter. The trust protects them against scenes like that. Only sometimes with a scut like the admin here, you wonder just who's being protected from whom.

"Do you remember what I told my dorm mother?" I said.

"Yes."

"Double to you."

Restricks for the rest of the year and a godspit alert band welded onto my wrist.

"I know what they've got," Arabel whispered to me in class. It was the only time I ever saw her. The godspit alert band went off if I even mastied without permission.

"What?" I asked, pretty much without caring.

"Tell you after."

I met her outside, in a blizzard of flying leaves and cotton. The circulation system had gone edge again. "Animals," she said.

"Animals?"

"Little repulsive things about as long as your arm. Tessels, they're called. Repulsive little brown animals."

"I don't believe it," I said. "It's got to be more than beasties. That's elementary school stuff. Are they bio-enhanced?"

"You mean pheromones or something?" She frowned. "I don't know. I sure didn't see anything attractive about them, but the boys—Brown brought his to a party, carrying it around on his arm, calling it Daughter Ann. They all swarmed around it, petting it, saying things like 'Come to Daddy.' It was really edge."

I shrugged. "Well, if you're right, we don't have anything to worry about. Even if they're bio-enhanced, how long can beasties hold their attention? It'll all be over by midterms."

"Can't you come over? I never see you." She sounded like she was ready to go lezzy.

I held up the banded wrist. "Can't. Listen, Arabel, I'll be late

to my next class," I said, and hurried off through the flailing
yellow and white. I didn't have a next class. I went back to the
dorm and took some float.

When I came out of it, Zibet was there, sitting on her bunk
with her knees hunched up, writing busily in a notebook. She
looked much better than the first time I saw her. Her hair had
grown out some and showed enough curl at the ends to pick up on
her features. She didn't look strained. In fact she looked almost
happy.

"What are you doing?" I hoped I said. The first couple of
sentences out of float it's anybody's guess what's going to come out.

"Recopying my notes," she said. Jiggin', the things that make
some people happy. I wondered if she'd found a boyfriend and that
was what had given her that pretty pink color. If she had, she was
doing better than Arabel. Or me.

"For who?"

"What?" she looked blank.

"What boy are you copying your notes for?"

"Boy?" Now there was an edge to her voice. She looked
frightened.

I said carefully, "I figure you've got to have a boyfriend." And
watched her go edge again. Mary doing Jesus, that must not have
come out right at all. I wondered what I'd really said to send her off
like that.

She backed up against the bunk wall like I was after her with
something and held her notebook flat against her chest. "Why do
you think that?"

Think what? Holy scut, I should have told her about float
before I went off on it. I'd have to answer her now like it was still a
real conversation instead of a caged rat being poked with a stick,
and hope I could explain later. "I don't know why I think that. You
just looked—"

"It's true, then," she said, and the strain was right back,
blinking red and white.

"What is?" I said, still wondering what it was the float had
garbled my innocent comment into.

"I had braids like you before I came here. You probably
wondered about that." Holy scut, I'd said something mean about
her choppy hair.

"My father—" she clutched the notebook like she had

187

clutched the wallplate that night, hanging on for dear life. "My father cut them off." She was admitting some awful thing to me and I had no idea what.

"Why did he do that?"

"He said I tempted . . . men with it. He said I was a—that I made men think wicked thoughts about me. He said it was my fault that it happened. He cut off all my hair."

It was coming to me finally that I had asked her just what I thought I had: whether she had a boyfriend.

"Do you think I—do that?" she asked me pleadingly.

Are you kidding? She couldn't have tempted Brown in one of his bone-a-virgin moods. I couldn't say that to her, though, and on the other hand, I knew if I said yes it was going to be toss-up time in dormland again. I felt sorry for her, poor kid, her braids chopped off and her scut of a father scaring the hell out of her with a bunch of lies. No wonder she'd been so edge when she first got here.

"Do you?" she persisted.

"You want to know what I think," I said, standing up a little unsteadily. "I think fathers are a pile of scut." I thought of Arabel's story. Little brown animals as long as your arm and Brown saying Your father only wants to protect you. "Worse than a pile of scut," I said. "All of them."

She looked at me, backed up against the wall, as if she would like to believe me.

"You want to know what my father did to me?" I said. "He didn't cut my braids off. Oh, no, this is lots better. You know about trust kids?"

She shook her head.

"Okay. My father wants to carry on his precious name and his precious jig-juice, but he doesn't want any of the trouble. So he sets up a trust. He pays a lot of money, he goes jig-jig in a plastic bag, and presto, he's a father, and the lawyers are left with all the dirty work. Like taking care of me and sending me someplace for summer break and paying my tuition at this godspit school. Like putting one of these on me." I held up my wrist with the ugly alert band on it. "He never even saw me. He doesn't even know who I am. Trust me. I know about scutty fathers."

"I wish . . ." Zibet said. She opened her book and started copying her notes again. I eased down onto my bunk, starting to feel the post-float headache. When I looked at her again, she was dripping tears all over her precious notes. Jiggin' Jesus, everything I said was wrong. The most I could hope for in this edge place was that the boys would be done playing beasties by midterms and I could get my grades up.

By midterms the circulation system had broken down completely. The campus was knee-deep in leaves and cotton. You could hardly walk. I trudged through the leaves to class, head down. I didn't even see Brown until it was too late.

He had the animal on his arm. "This is Daughter Ann," Brown said. "Daughter Ann, meet Tavvy."

"Go jig yourself," I said, brushing by him.

He grabbed my wrist, holding on hard and pressing his fingers against the alert band until it hurt. "That's not polite, Tavvy. Daughter Ann wants to meet you. Don't you sweetheart?" He held the animal out to me. Arabel had been right. Hideous little things. I had never gotten a close look at one before. It had a sharp little brown face, with dull eyes and a tiny pink mouth. Its fur was coarse and brown, and its body hung limply off Brown's arm. He had put a ribbon around its neck.

"Just your type," I said. "Ugly as mud and a hole big enough for even you to find."

His grip tightened. "You can't talk that way to my . . ."

"Hi," Zibet said behind me. I whirled around. This was all I needed.

"Hi," I said, and yanked my wrist free. "Brown, this is my roommate. My *freshman* roommate. Zibet, Brown."

"And this is Daughter Ann," he said, holding the animal up so that its tender pink mouth gaped stupidly at us. Its tail was up. I could see tender pink at the other end, too. And Arabel wonders what the attraction is?

"Nice to meet you, freshman roommate," Brown muttered and pulled the animal back close to him. "Come to Papa," he said, and stalked off through the leaves.

I rubbed my poor wrist. Please, please let her not ask me what a tessel's for? I have had about all I can take for one day. I'm not about to explain Brown's nasty habits to a virgie.

I had underestimated her. She shuddered a little and pulled her notebooks against her chest. "Poor little beast," she said.

* * *

"What do you know about sin?" she asked me suddenly that night. At least she had turned off the light. That was some improvement.

"A lot," I said. "How do you think I got this charming bracelet?"

"I mean really doing something wrong. To somebody else. To save yourself." She stopped. I didn't answer her, and she didn't say anything more for a long time. "I know about the admin," she said finally.

I couldn't have been more surprised if Old Scut Moulton had suddenly shouted, "Bless you, my daughter," over the intercom.

"You're a good person, I can tell that." There was a dreamy quality to her voice. If it had been anybody but her I'd have thought she was masting. "There are things you wouldn't do, not even to save yourself."

"And you're a hardened criminal, I suppose?"

"There are things you wouldn't do," she repeated sleepily, and then said quite clearly and irrelevantly, "My sister's coming for Christmas."

Jiggin', she was full of surprises tonight. "I thought you were going home for Christmas," I said.

"I'm never going home," she said.

"Tavvy!" Arabel shouted halfway across campus. "Hello!"

The boys are over it, I thought, and how in the scut am I going to get rid of this alert band? I felt so relieved I could have cried.

"Tavvy," she said again. "I haven't seen you in weeks!"

"What's going on?" I asked her, wondering why she didn't just blurt it out about the boys in her usual breakneck fashion.

"What do you mean?" she said, wide-eyed, and I knew it wasn't the boys. They still had the tessels, Brown and Sept and all the rest of them. They still had the tessels. It's only beasties, I told myself fiercely, it's only beasties and why are you so edge about it? Your father has your best interests at heart. Come to Daddy.

"The admin's secretary quit," Arabel said. "I got put on restricks for a samurai party in my room." She shrugged. "It was the best offer I'd had all fall."

Oh, but you're trust, Arabel. You're trust. He could be your father. Come to Papa.

"You look terrible," Arabel said. "Are you doing too much float?"

I shook my head. "Do you know what it is the boys do with them?"

"Tavvy, sweetheart, if you can't figure out what that big pink hole is for—"

"My roommate's father cut her hair off," I said. "She's a virgie. She's never done anything. He cut off all her hair."

"Hey," Arabel said, "you are really edging it. Listen, how long have you been without jig-jig? I can set you up, younger guys than the admin, nothing to worry about. Guaranteed no trusters. I could set you up."

I shook my head. "I don't want any."

"Listen, I'm worried about you. I don't want you to go edge on me. Let me ask the admin about your alert band at least."

"No," I said clearly. "I'm all right, Arabel. I've got to get to class."

"Don't let this tessel thing get to you, Tavvy. It's only beasties."

"Yeah." I walked steadily away from her across the spitting, leaf-littered campus. As soon as I was out of her line of sight, I slumped against one of the giant cottonwoods and hung on to it like Zibet had clung to that wallplate. For dear life.

Zibet didn't say another thing about her sister until right before Christmas break. Her hair, which I had thought was growing out, looked choppier than ever. The old look of strain was back and getting worse every day. She looked like a radiation victim.

I wasn't looking that good myself. I couldn't sleep, and float gave me headaches that lasted a week. The alert band started a rash that had worked its way halfway up my arm. And Arabel was right. I was going edge. I couldn't get the tessels off my mind. If you'd asked me last summer what I thought of beasties, I'd have said it was great fun for everyone, especially the animals. Now the thought of Brown with that hideous little brown and pink thing on his arm was enough to make me toss up. I keep thinking about your father. If it's the trust thing you're worried about, I can find out for you. He has your best interests at heart. Come to Papa.

My lawyers hadn't succeeded in convincing the admin to let me go to Aspen for Christmas, or anywhere else. They'd managed to wangle full privileges as soon as everybody was gone, but not to get the alert band off. I figured if my dorm mother got a good look at what it was doing to my arm, though, she'd let me have it off for a few days and give it a chance to heal. The circulation system was working again, blowing winds of hurricane force all across Hell. Merry Christmas, everybody.

On the last day of class, I walked into our dark room, hit the wallplate, and froze. There sat Zibet in the dark. On my bed. With a tessel in her lap.

"Where did you get that?" I whispered.

"I stole it," she said.

I locked the door behind me and pushed one of the desk chairs against it. "How?"

"They were all at a party in somebody else's room."

"You went in the boys' dorm?"

She didn't answer.

"You're a freshman. They could send you home for that," I said, disbelieving. This was the girl who had gone quite literally up the wall over the sheets, who had said, "I'm never going home again."

"Nobody saw me," she said calmly. "They were all at a party."

"You're edge," I said. "Whose is it, do you know?"

"It's Daughter Ann."

I grabbed the top sheet off my bunk and started lining my shuttle bag with it. Holy scut, this would be the first place Brown would look. I rifled through my desk drawer for a pair of scissors to cut some air slits with. Zibet still sat petting the horrid thing.

"We've got to hide it," I said. "This time I'm not kidding. You really are in trouble."

She didn't hear me. "My sister Henra's pretty. She has long braids like you. She's good like you, too," and then in an almost pleading voice, "she's only fifteen."

Brown demanded and got a room check that started, you guessed it, with our room. The tessel wasn't there. I'd put it in the shuttle bag and hidden it in one of the spins down in the laundry room. I'd wadded the other slickspin sheet in front of it, which I felt was a fitting irony for Brown, only he was too enraged to see it.

"I want another check," he said after the dorm mother had

given him the grand tour. "I know it's here." He turned to me. "I know you've got it."

"The last shuttle's in ten minutes," the dorm mother said. "There isn't time for another check."

"She's got it. I can tell by the look on her face. She's hidden it somewhere. Somewhere in this dorm."

The dorm mother looked like she'd like to have him in her Skinner box for about an hour. She shook her head.

"You lose, Brown," I said. "You stay and you'll miss your shuttle and be stuck in Hell over Christmas. You leave and you lose your darling Daughter Ann. You lose either way, Brown."

He grabbed my wrist. The rash was almost unbearable under the band. My wrist had started to swell, puffing out purplish-red over the metal. I tried to free myself with my other hand, but his grip was as hard and vengeful as his face. "Octavia here was at a samurai party in the boys' dorm last week," he said to the dorm mother.

"That's not true," I said. I could hardly talk. The pain from his grip was making me so nauseated I felt faint.

"I find that difficult to believe," the dorm mother said, "since she is confined by an alert band."

"This?" Brown said, and yanked my arm up. I cried out. "This thing?" He twisted it around my wrist. "She can take it off any time she wants. Didn't you know that?" He dropped my wrist and looked at me contemptuously. "Tavvy's too smart to let a little thing like an alert band stop her, aren't you, Tavvy?"

I cradled my throbbing wrist against my body and tried not to black out. It isn't beasties, I thought frantically. He would never do this to me just for beasties. It's something worse. Worse. He must never, never get it back.

"There's the call for the shuttle," the dorm mother said. "Octavia, your break privileges are canceled."

Brown shot a triumphant glance at me and followed her out. It took every bit of strength I had to wait till the last shuttle was gone before I went to get the tessel. I carried it back to the room with my good hand. The restricks hardly mattered. There was no place to go anyway. And the tessel was safe. "Everything will be all right," I said to the tessel.

Only everything wasn't all right. Henra, the pretty sister,

wasn't pretty. Her hair had been cut off, as short as scissors could make it. She was flushed bright red and crying. Zibet's face had gone stony white and stayed that way. I didn't think from the looks of her that she'd ever cry again. Isn't it wonderful what a semester of college can do for you?

Restricks or no, I had to get out of there. I took my books and camped down in the laundry room. I wrote two term papers, read three textbooks, and like Zibet, recopied all my notes. He cut off my hair. He said I tempted men and that was why it happened. Your father was only trying to protect you. Come to Papa. I turned on all the spins at once so I couldn't hear myself think and typed the term papers.

I made it to the last day of break, gritting my teeth to keep from thinking about Brown, about tessels, about everything. Zibet and her sister came down to the laundry room to tell me Henra was going back on the first shuttle. I said good-bye. "I hope you can come back," I said, knowing I sounded stupid, knowing there was nothing in the world that could make me go back to Marylebone Weep if I were Henra.

"I am coming back. As soon as I graduate."

"It's only two years," Zibet said. Two years ago Zibet had the same sweet face as her sister. Two years from now, Henra too would look like death warmed over. What fun to grow up in Marylebone Weep, where you're a wreck at seventeen.

"Come back with me, Zibet," Henra said.

"I can't."

Toss-up time. I went back to the room, propped myself on my bunk with a stack of books, and started reading. The tessel had been asleep on the foot of the bunk, its gaping pink vaj sticking up. It crawled onto my lap and lay there. I picked it up. It didn't resist. Even with it living in the room, I'd never really looked at it closely. I saw now that it couldn't resist if it tried. It had tiny little paws with soft pink underpads and no claws. It had no teeth, either, just the soft little rosebud mouth, only a quarter of the size of the opening at the other end. If it had been enhanced with pheromones, I sure couldn't tell it. Maybe its attraction was simply that it had no defenses, that it couldn't fight even if it wanted to.

I laid it over my lap and stuck an exploratory finger a little way into the vaj. I'd done enough lezzing when I was a freshman to know what a good vaj should feel like. I eased the finger farther in.

It screamed.

I yanked the hand free, balled it into a fist, and crammed it against my mouth hard to keep from screaming myself. Horrible, awful, pitiful sound. Helpless. Hopeless. The sound a woman must make when she's being raped. No. Worse. The sound a child must make. I thought, I have never heard a sound like that in my whole life, and at the same instant, this is the sound I have been hearing all semester. Pheromones. Oh, no, a far greater attraction than some chemical. Or is fear a chemical, too?

I put the poor little beast onto the bed, went into the bathroom, and washed my hands for about an hour. I thought Zibet hadn't known what the tessels were for, that she hadn't had more than the vaguest idea what the boys were doing to them. But she had known. Known and tried to keep it from me. Known and gone into the boys' dorm all by herself to steal one. We should have stolen them all, all of them, gotten them away from those scutting godfucking . . . I had thought of a lot of names for my father over the years. None of them was bad enough for this. Scutting Jesus-jiggers. Fucking piles of scut.

Zibet was standing in the door of the bathroom.

"Oh, Zibet," I said, and stopped.

"My sister's going home this afternoon," she said.

"No," I said, "Oh, no," and ran past her out of the room.

I guess I had kind of a little breakdown. Anyway, I can't account very well for the time. Which is edge, because the thing I remember most vividly is the feeling that I needed to hurry, that something awful would happen if I didn't hurry.

I know I broke restricks because I remember sitting out under the cottonwoods and thinking what a wonderful sense of humor Old Man Moulton had. He sent up Christmas lights for the bare cottonwoods, and the cotton and the brittle yellow leaves blew against them and caught fire. The smell of burning was everywhere. I remember thinking clearly, smokes and fires, how appropriate for Christmas in Hell.

But when I tried to think about the tessels, about what to do, the thoughts got all muddy and confused, like I'd taken too much float. Sometimes it was what Zibet Brown wanted and not Daughter Ann at all, and I would say, "You cut off her hair. I'll never give her back to you. Never." And she would struggle and struggle against him. But she had no claws, no teeth. Sometimes it was the admin, and he would say, "If it's the trust thing you're worried about, I can find out for you," and I would say, "You only want the tessels for yourself." And sometimes Zibet's father said, "I am only trying to protect you. Come to Papa." And I would climb up on the bunk to unscrew the intercom but I couldn't shut him up. "I don't need protecting," I would say to him. Zibet would struggle and struggle.

A dangling bit of cotton had stuck to one of the Christmas lights. It caught fire and dropped into the brown broken leaves. The smell of smoke was everywhere. Somebody should report that. Hell could burn down, or was it burn up, with nobody here over Christmas break. I should tell somebody. That was it, I had to tell somebody. But there was nobody to tell. I wanted my father. And he wasn't there. He had never been there. He had paid his money, spilled his juice, and thrown me to the wolves. But at least he wasn't one of them. He wasn't one of them.

There was nobody to tell. "What did you do to it?" Arabel said. "Did you give it something? Samurai? Float? Alcohol?"

"I didn't . . ."

"Consider yourself on restricks."

"It isn't beasties," I said. "They call them Baby Dear and Daughter Ann. And they're the fathers. They're the fathers. But the tessels don't have any claws. They don't have any teeth. They don't even know what jig-jig is."

"He has her best interests at heart," Arabel said.

"What are you talking about? He cut off all her hair. You should have seen her, hanging on to the wallplate for dear life! She struggled and struggled, but it didn't do any good. She doesn't have any claws. She doesn't have any teeth. She's only fifteen. We have to hurry."

"It'll all be over by midterms," Arabel said. "I can fix you up. Guaranteed no trusters."

I was standing in the dorm mother's Skinner box, pounding on her door. I did not know how I had gotten there. My face looked back at me from the dorm mother's mirrors. Arabel's face: strained and desperate. Flashing red and white and red again like an alert band: my roommate's face. She would not believe me. She would put me on restricks. She would have me expelled. It didn't matter. When she answered the door, I could not run. I had to tell somebody before the whole place caught on fire.

"Oh, my dear," she said, and put her arms around me.

I knew before I opened the door that Zibet was sitting on my bunk in the dark. I pressed the wallplate and kept my bandaged hand on it, as if I might need it for support. "Zibet," I said. "Everything's going to be all right. The dorm mother's going to confiscate the tessels. They're going to outlaw animals on campus. Everything will be all right."

She looked up at me. "I sent it home with her," she said.

"What?" I said blankly.

"He won't . . . leave us alone. He—I sent Daughter Ann home with her."

No. Oh, no.

"Henra's good like you. She won't save herself. She'll never last the two years." She looked steadily at me. "I have two other sisters. The youngest is only ten."

"You sent the tessel home?" I said. "To your *father*?"

"Yes."

"It can't protect itself," I said. "It doesn't have any claws. It can't protect itself."

"I told you you didn't know anything about sin," she said, and turned away.

I never asked the dorm mother what they did with the tessels they took away from the boys. I hope, for their own sakes, that somebody put them out of their misery.

———————————————————

ARABEL: Is it necessary always to use the ugliest word?
HENRIETTA: Yes, Arabel—when you're describing the ugliest
     thing.

> from *The Barretts of Wimpole Street*
> by Rudolf Besier

Edward Moulton Barrett would have been shocked and outraged by this story. So, I suppose, would his poetic daughter, Elizabeth. They were, after all, Victorians, and members of that most staid and shockable Victorian society, the respectable middle class.

And Edward Barrett was certainly respectable. A widower and father of ten children, he was a model of parental devotion. He was especially protective of his invalided daughter, Elizabeth, who had not been out of her room for years. He knelt and prayed with her every night.

And if he insisted that his children obey him in everything, he was only demanding the honor the Scripture said was due a parent. If he forbade them to marry or even to have friends, he was only trying to protect them from the worldliness and evil he saw everywhere. He had only their best interests at heart.

None of which explains why Robert Browning, who had befriended the invalided daughter, wrote her, "You are in what I should wonder at as the veriest slavery," and "I truly wish that you may never feel what I have to bear in looking on, quite powerless and silent while you are subjected to this treatment."

"Don't think too hardly of poor Papa," Elizabeth wrote Robert, and described her father as "upright and honorable."

None of which explains why she fled her father's house, telling no one, not even her sisters, because "whoever helps me, will suffer through me," and taking her dog Flush with her because she didn't dare leave him behind.

I may be wrong about her reaction to this story. Her easily embarrassed Victorian soul would have been shocked by the language, of course, but she would have recognized the story. And the characters.

CONNIE WILLIS

RICHARD CHRISTIAN
⊙ MATHESON ⊙

AROUSAL

Richard Christian Matheson writes short stories, screenplays, teleplays, and novels. He also creates and executive produces half-hour comedy and one-hour dramatic television series and writes and produces feature films. His first novel, Created By, *will be published in 1990 by Doubleday. A collection of his short stories,* Scars and Other Distinguishing Marks, *was published by SCREAM/PRESS and Tor in 1988. He has written and sold five original screenplays, all of which have been produced, two with his father, Richard Matheson. Along with Matheson senior he is starting his own production company. Obviously, he never sleeps.*

"Arousal" was originally commissioned by me for a group of horror shorts to appear in OMNI *but was pulled by our managing editor (male) at the last minute because of its sexual content. Naturally, I snapped it up for this anthology. It's a quite contemporary interpretation of the demon lover theme, long a staple of literature.*

She stared.

Trying to be sure. Trying to hide it.

He was somehow perfect, somehow virulent; handsome in a way that slit her restraint open. Drew her in. He was about thirty.

By himself in the bar. The town, asleep ten stories below, was flat and black. Streetlights stared up, inspecting the hotel bar with orange eyes, and occasionally a sleepy police car would pass, roving pointlessly.

She stared more, wiping long nails with a napkin.

She was becoming sure. *It was in his eyes.*

The *thing.*

Maybe even more than the ones before.

She ordered another kamikaze and walked to the pay phone, passing him. He stared out the window, chewing on a match, and she noticed the way his index finger traced the edge of his beer as if touching a woman's body.

The look.

Every location, she found it.

When the company was done filming and she'd finished going over the next day's setups with whichever director she was currently working under, she'd grab the location van back to the hotel the studio had booked the production team into, pick up mail and messages at the front desk, and go to her room. Always exhausted, always hating being an assistant director. Hating not being the one to set the vision. Run the set.

Be in control.

Then she'd strip; shower. Let the water scratch fingernails down her body as she closed tired eyes. Try to let the sensations take over. Try to feel something. But she never did.

She couldn't.

The sensual voyage her girlfriends felt when they were alone and naked, touching their bodies, allowing their skin to respond, no longer interested her. Her body searched for greater responses. Searched for the one who could hold her the right way, touch her with the exact touch. Make her respond; transcend. Stare into her eyes when she came.

Stare with that look.

She stood at the phone and called collect. Her husband was asleep and when he answered told her he loved her. She said it back but kept watching the man. He was pressing his lips against the matchstick, gently sucking it in and out as she stared in unprotected fascination.

Her husband offered to wake the kids so they could tell her good-night.

"They miss Mommy," he told her, in a sweet voice she hated.

She didn't hear what he'd said then, and he told her again, asking if she were all right; she sounded tired, distracted. She laughed a little, making him go away by calming him. He told her again he loved her and wanted to be with her. To make love. She was silent, watching the man across the barroom, catching his glance as he tried to get the waitress's attention.

"Do you miss me?" her husband asked.

The man was looking at her. Her husband asked her if she was looking forward to making love when she got back into town. She kept staring at the man. Her husband asked again.

"Yes, darling. Of course I am. . . ."

But it was a lie. It never stopped being one. He did nothing for her. She wanted something that would make her forget who she was, what her life was. Something real.

Something unreal.

Her husband had gone to get the kids though she told him not to. He wouldn't listen, and when she lifted cold fingers from her closed eyes, head bowed in private irritation, the man was standing next to her, buying cigarettes from a machine.

"Say hello to Mommy, kids."

The kids spoke sleepily over the phone while the man stared at her, lighting his cigarette, eyes unblinking. She told them to go to sleep, and that she loved them. But she was watching the man's eyes moving down her face, slowly to her neck, her breasts. Further. He quickly looked back at her and she allowed the look to do whatever it wanted.

They went to his room.

Nothing was said. They made love all night and she clutched at the sheets on either side of her sweating stomach with both hands, bunching up the starched cotton, screaming. He touched her so faintly at one point, it felt like nothing more than a thought; a wish. Her body arched and tensed, the pillow beneath her head soaked.

He tied her to the bedposts with silk scarves and blew softly onto her salty mouth, gently kissed her eyelids. He circled his tongue around her ears and whispered rapist demands that made her come. He massaged her until her skin effervesced, until her fingers pulled wildly at the scarves that held her wrists to the bed.

Until she moaned with such pleasure, she thought she was in someone else's body.

Or had left her own.

Everything he did aroused her like she'd never been and when he finally untied her, she slept against his chest, held in his soothing arms. She murmured over and over how incredible it had been, stunned by what he'd made her feel. What he was still making her feel.

He said the only thing he would.

"You won't forget tonight."

When she awakened at dawn, he was gone. No note, no sign. There was a knock on the door and she answered, wrapping a towel around herself. Room service rolled in a large breakfast, complete with omelet, café au lait, and a newspaper.

He'd taken care of everything.

She sat in bed and ate, untying the newspaper, aching sweetly from the evening, covered with tender welts and bite marks. The food tasted delicious and the flavors on her tongue made her want to make love. She smiled, listened to the birds outside her window. Their soft opera gave her goose bumps, and as she opened the newspaper, the sound of its crisp folds made her nipples tingle. She laughed a little, remembering the incredible way he'd licked and sucked them last night. They were still sensitive.

As she read, she sipped at her coffee and the creamy heat of it made her part her legs slightly as it spread over her tongue and ran down her throat, warm like sperm.

She began to breathe harder, sipping more, twisting her shoulders as a tingle ran delicate electricity across her shoulders; up her spine.

As she read the front page, she allowed her fingers to drift on the inky surface and could feel the words; their shape and length. The curve of the individual letters. The sound the sentences created in her mind.

She felt herself getting wet.

It was *fantastic;* her body responsive to every detail of the morning; its sounds, colors. Even the feel of the blanket, the scraping texture of the wool making her think about him, the hair on his chest and face. God, why hadn't she asked his name? He was the greatest lover she'd probably ever have and she knew it.

She laughed out loud, feeling a strange, new woman inside coming forth; emerging.

The ice in the orange juice was melting and when it rubbed against the glass, the sound made her softly, involuntarily moan. She smiled and lit a cigarette, sensing an unfamiliar fulfillment in her cells and nerves. A happiness.

Lost control.

The cigarette flame gave off a heat she could actually feel and she began to perspire. She shook a bit, grinning, and blew the match out, watching the tiny curls of smoke that peeled from its blackened tip and smelled like the man's scent. She couldn't stop herself from sliding a trembling hand onto a breast. Her skin was hot and as the sounds of the birds got louder outside her window and the hotel began to wake up below her, making faraway morning sounds, she listened and began to groan pleasurably from the noise.

The smell of the unfinished food and the warm air from the heating vent felt like a caress, and her nipples got harder, her pubic hair more wet. Her eyes wandered lazily, sexually around the room and noticed the furniture; the way the fabric on the couch fit its plaid shapes together so perfectly, each cushion like the next. It made her shut her eyes in exquisite torture. She opened them and caught a glimpse of the ballpoint pen which the hotel provided on the bedside table. Its red color pleased her and she groaned happily. Her eyes drifted on. The ashtray on the floor, filled with crippled cigarettes and gum wrappers excited her, its smells and patterns making her think of making love, of the man entering her and . . .

She suddenly realized what was happening and noticed an article on the front page section of the paper about a grotesque murder that had occurred the night before. A family had been gunned down by two men in ski masks and as she imagined it, her fingers moved over her body, searching wildly, uncontrollably. Scratching, squeezing. Shivering. She didn't understand the sexual storm her body felt as her mind filled with images of bullets shredding skin, faces twisting in horror, bodies slumping.

The tensing percussion.

The shudder.

She began to come again.

She couldn't stop the orgasm and it drenched her like a toxic wave that rose high and fainted; collapsing, then rising again.

Her body was wet with sweat and her teeth bit into her bottom lip, making it bleed. She squeezed herself so hard she began to bruise, more bluish ponds growing under her skin. Her arms drew back to the bedposts and grabbed tightly to either as if crucified, fingers white; desperate. She screamed louder and louder, flailing, coming again and again, not able to stop the flood of sights, sounds; tactile impressions.

She saw her children and began to cry.

Then, in her mind, she could see the man's face. His easy smile. The way he touched her.

The *look*.

She passed out for a few moments but the sound of maids beginning to vacuum and cars honking outside awoke her and she couldn't stop her body from starting to respond again.

Enabling.
The smile that watches.
The hand that reassures.
The enabler passes no judgment.
Doesn't deal in permission or sanction.
Only indulgence; assistance.
Yet in taking no position, it is a criminal,
    however unbloodied.
It poisons with a helping gesture.
And it becomes the pallbearer before we are gone.
It stands by and watches a houseful of screaming
    frailties burn to death.
This is a story about enabling.
About dreams bringing crucifixion.
And about those who allow us to dream.

RICHARD CHRISTIAN MATHESON

LEWIS
⊙ SHINER ⊙

SCALES

Lewis Shiner's latest novel, Deserted Cities of the Heart *(Bantam) was nominated for the Nebula Award. His upcoming mainstream novel* Slam *(Doubleday) is about skateboarding, anarchy, and parole. Also upcoming is an original anthology benefiting Greenpeace called* When the Music's Over *(Bantam), which he is editing. Shiner's early short stories were mostly science fiction. More recently, he has been writing mainstream and horror. His story "Love in Vain," originally published in* Ripper!, *has been reprinted in* The Year's Best Science Fiction *and* The Year's Best Fantasy *(St. Martin's) and is most definitely horror. So is "Scales."*

There's a standard rat behavior they call the Coolidge Effect. Back when I was a psych major, before I met Richard, before we got married, long before I had Emily, I worked in the lab fifteen hours a week. I cleaned rat cages and typed data into the computer. The Coolidge Effect was one of those experiments that everybody had heard of but nobody had actually performed.

It seems if you put a new female in a male's cage, they mate a few times and go on with their business. If you keep replacing the female, though, it's a different story. The male will literally screw himself to death.

Someone supposedly told all this to Mrs. Calvin Coolidge. She said, "Sounds just like my husband."

It started in June, a few days after Emily's first birthday. I remember it was a Sunday night; Richard had to teach in the morning. I woke up to Richard moaning. It was a kind of humming sound, up and down the scale. It was a noise he made during sex.

I sat up in bed. As usual all the blankets were piled on my side. Richard was naked under a single sheet, despite the air-conditioning. We'd fought about something that afternoon. I was still angry enough that I could find satisfaction in watching his nightmare.

He moved his hips up and down. I could see the little tent his penis made in the sheet. Clearly he was not squirming from fear. Just as I realized what was happening he arched his back and the sheet turned translucent. I'd never watched it before, not clinically like that. It wasn't especially interesting and certainly not erotic. All I could think of was the mess. I could smell it now, like water left standing in an orange juice jar.

I lay down, facing away from him. The bed jolted as he woke up. "Jesus," he whispered. I pretended to be asleep while he mopped up the bed with some Kleenex. In a minute or two he was asleep again.

I got up to check on Emily. She was face down in her crib, arms and legs stretched out like a tiny pink bearskin rug. I touched her hair, bent over to smell her neck. One tiny, perfect hand clutched at the blanket under her.

"You missed it, Tater," I whispered. "You could have seen what you've got to look forward to."

I might have forgotten about it if Sally Keeler hadn't called that Friday. Her husband had the office next to Richard's in the English department.

"Listen," Sally said. "It's probably nothing at all."

"Pardon?"

"I thought somebody should let you know."

"Know what?"

"Has Richard been, I don't know, acting a little weird lately?"

For some reason I remembered his wet dream. "What do you mean weird?"

Sally sighed dramatically. "It's just something Tony said last night. Now Ann, I know you and Richard are having a few problems—that's okay, you don't have to say anything—and I thought, well, a real friend would come to you with this."

Sally was not a friend. Sally was someone who had been over to dinner two or three times. I hadn't realized my marital problems were such common knowledge. "Sally, will you get to the point?"

"Richard's been talking to Tony about this new grad student. She's supposed to be from Israel or something."

"So?"

"So Richard was apparently just drooling over this girl. That doesn't sound like him. I mean Richard doesn't even *flirt*."

"Is that all?"

"Well, no. Tony asked him what was the big deal and *Richard* said, 'Tony, you wouldn't believe it. You wouldn't believe it if I told you.' Those are like his exact words."

"Does this mystery woman have a name?"

"Lili, I think he said it was."

I tried to picture Richard, with his thinning hair and stubby little mustache, with his glasses and pot belly, sweeping some foreign sexpot off her feet.

Sally said, "It may not be anything at all."

One new associate professorship would open up next year. Richard and Tony were both in the running. Richard was generally thought to have the edge. "I'm sure you're right," I said. "I'm sure it's nothing at all."

"Hey, I wouldn't want to cause any problems."

"No," I said, "I'm sure you wouldn't."

The next Wednesday Richard called to say he'd be home late. There was a visiting poet on campus for a reading. I looked it up in the paper. The reading was scheduled for eight.

At 8:30 I put Emily in the station wagon and we drove over to the Fine Arts Center. We didn't find his car.

"Well, Tater," I said. "What do you think? Do we go across Central and check the hot sheet motels?"

She stared at me with huge, colorless eyes.

207

"You're right," I said. "We have too much pride for that. We'll just go home."

There was a cookout that weekend at Dr. Taylor's. He was department chairman largely on the strength of having edited a Major American Writer in his youth. Now he had a drinking problem. His wife had learned that having parties at home meant keeping him off the roads.

The morning of the party I told Richard I wanted to go. By now he was used to my staying home from these things. I watched for signs of disappointment. He only shrugged.

"You'd better start trying to find a sitter," he said.

After dinner we began the slow, seemingly random movements that would inevitably end with the women in one part of the house and the men in another. Already most of the wives were downstairs, clearing up the soggy paper plates and empty beer bottles. I was upstairs with Jane Lang, the medievalist, and most of the husbands. Taylor had made a pejorative remark about women writers and everyone had jumped on him for it. Then Tony said, "Okay, I want to see everybody come up with a sexist remark they believe is true."

Taylor said, a little drunkenly, "Men have bigger penises than women."

Jane said, "Usually." Everyone laughed.

Robbie Shappard, who was believed to sleep with his students, said, "I read something the other day. There's this lizard in South America that's extinct now. What happened was another species of lizard came along that could perform the mating rituals better than the real females. The males all fucked the impostors. The chromosomes didn't match, of course, so no baby lizards. The whole species went toes up."

"Is that true?"

"I read it in the *Weekly World News*," Robbie said. "It has to be true. What I want to know is, what does it mean?"

"That's easy," Jane said. "When it comes to sex, men don't know what's good for them."

"I think men and women are different species," Tony said.

"Too easy," Robbie said. "They've just got conflicting programs. When we were living in caves we had these drives designed

208

to produce the maximum number of kids from the widest range of partners. The problem is we've still got those drives and they're not useful anymore. That's what did in those poor lizards."

Tony said, "Okay, Ann. Your turn. Be serious, now."

"I don't know," I said. "I guess I subscribe to the old business about how women are more emotional."

"Emotional how?" Tony said. "Be specific."

"Right," Robbie said. "Be brief and specific. It's fifty percent of your grade riding on this."

I looked at Richard. He seemed distracted rather than contentious. "Well, men always seem concerned with exactitude, being able to measure things." There was some laughter, and I blushed. "You know. Like they don't want to say 'I'll love you forever.' They want to say, 'At current rates our relationship could reasonably be expected to continue at least another six months.' Whereas I would appreciate the gesture. Of saying 'forever.' "

Tony nodded. "Good one. Rich?"

"You want one? Okay. Here's what Robbie was trying to say earlier, only without the bullshit. Men want women and women want babies."

Everyone went quiet; it wasn't just me overreacting. The first thing I thought of was Emily. What did Richard mean? Did he not want her anymore? Had he never wanted her? I'd heard that people felt this way when they were shot. No pain, only a sense of shock and loss, the knowledge that pain would surely follow.

"Speaking of babies," I said into the silence, "I should call home. Excuse me." I walked out of the room, looking for a phone, wanting most of all to be away from Richard.

I found a bathroom instead. I washed my face, put on fresh lipstick, and wandered downstairs. Sally found me there and raised an eyebrow. "Well?"

"Well what?"

"I assume you're here for a look at her."

"Who?"

"Lili. The mystery woman. All the men in the department are in love with her. Haven't you heard?"

"Is she here?"

Sally glanced around the room. I knew most of the women in the den with us. "I don't see her now. She was here a minute ago."

"What does she look like?"

"Oh, short, dark . . . sexy, I suppose. If you like eyeliner and armpit hair."

"What's she wearing?"

"Is that more than idle curiosity I hear in your voice? A tank top, a red tank top. And blue jeans. Very tight."

"Excuse me," I said, finally seeing the phone. "I have to call home."

The sitter answered on the second ring. Emily was asleep. There were no problems. "Okay," I said. I wanted to be home with her, to blow raspberries on her belly and feel her fingers in my hair. The silence had gone on too long. I said thank-you and hung up.

I couldn't face going back upstairs. It would be a boy's club up there by now anyway. Fart jokes and cigars. A sliding glass door opened up to the backyard. I walked into the darkness, smelling summer in the cut grass and the lingering smoke from the grill.

Richard found me there when the party broke up. I was sitting in a lawn chair, watching the Dallas sky, which glows red all summer long. Something about all the lights and the polluted air.

"Nice move," Richard said. "Just walk right out on me, let the entire fucking party know our marriage is on the rocks."

"Is it?"

"What?"

"On the rocks. Our marriage. Are we splitting up?"

"Hell, I don't know. This isn't the time to ask, that's for sure. Oh no. Don't start. How are we supposed to walk out with you crying like that?"

"We'll go around the side of the house. Taylor's too drunk to know if we said good-night or not. Answer my question."

"I said I don't know."

"Maybe we ought to find out."

"What does *that* mean?"

"Let's do whatever it is people do. See a counselor or something."

"Okay."

"Okay? That's all? Just 'okay'?"

"You're the one pushing for this, not me."

"Fine," I said, suddenly giddy. It was like standing on the edge of a cliff. Would I actually do something irreversible? Only

Emily held me back. Then I looked at Richard again and thought, do I really want this man as her father?

"Fine," I said again. "Let's get out of here."

My best friend Darla had been divorced twice. She recommended a Mrs. McNabb.

"Oh, God," I said. "It's going to be so expensive. Is it really going to help?"

"What do you care about help?" Darla said. "This is step one in getting rid of the creep. The rest gets easier. Believe me, it gets easier. My second divorce was no worse than, oh, say, being in a body cast for six months."

I sat in front of the phone for a long time Monday. I was weighing the good and bad in our marriage, and I was throwing anything I could find onto the scales. Everything on the good side had to do with money—the house, Richard's insurance, financial security. It wasn't enough.

I got us an appointment for the next morning. When I told Richard about it Monday night he looked surprised, as if he'd forgotten the whole wretched scene. Then he shrugged and said, "Okay, whatever."

We left Emily at the sitter's house. It was hard to let go of her. Richard kept looking at his watch. Finally we got away and drove downtown, to a remodeled prairie-style house off of East Grand.

Mrs. McNabb was five-eleven, heavy in the chest and hips, fifty years old with short hair in various shades of gray. No makeup, natural fiber clothes, neutral-colored furniture. A single, ominous box of Kleenex on the table by the couch.

When we were both settled she said, "Now. Are either of you involved with anyone outside the marriage."

I said, "You mean, like, romantically?"

Richard was already shaking his head.

"That's right," Mrs. McNabb said.

"No," Richard said.

"No," I said.

She looked at Richard for a long time, as if she didn't believe him. I didn't believe him either. "What?" he said. His arms had been folded across his chest from the moment he sat down. "I said *no*, there's nobody else."

After a few minutes she split us up. Richard waited in reception while she asked me questions. Whenever I said anything about Richard she made me preface it with "I think" or "it seems to me." I didn't mention Lili or my suspicions. Then I sat outside for half an hour, reading the same page of *Newsweek* over and over again, not able to make any sense of it.

Finally Richard came out. He was pale. "We're done," he said. "I paid her and everything."

We got in the car. Richard sat behind the wheel without starting the engine. "She asked about my parents," he said. He looked out the windshield, not at me. "I told her about how my father always made my mother bring him the mail, and then he would open it up and throw what he didn't want on the floor. And then my mother would have to get down on her knees and pick it up."

He looked so lost and childlike. I suddenly realized that the only other person who could understood what we were both going through was Richard. It was hard not to reach out for him.

"She asked me were they happy," he said. "I said no. And then the weirdest thing happened. I found myself explaining all this stuff to her. Stuff I didn't know I knew. How I'd always believed it would be so easy for my father to make my mother happy. That a marriage should work if you just didn't throw your trash on the floor for the other person to pick up. I don't remember Mrs. McNabb saying anything, it was just suddenly I had this flash of understanding. How I'd spent my life looking for an unhappy woman like my mother, to prove how easily I could make her happy. Only I was wrong. I couldn't make you happy after all."

That wonderful, brief moment of intimacy was gone. I was now an "unhappy woman." I didn't much like it.

"I feel all wrung out," he said, and started to cry. I couldn't remember the last time I'd seen him cry. "I don't know if I can go through this again."

"This was just the start," I said. "We haven't gotten *anywhere* yet."

He shook his head and started the car. "I don't know," he said. "I don't know if I can go on."

And that was the end of counseling. The next time I brought it up Richard shook his head and refused to talk about it.

By that point he "worked late" at least two nights a week. It embarrassed me to hear the shopworn excuse. I pictured him in his office, his corduroys around his ankles, some exotic olive-skinned wanton sprawled on her back across his desk, her ankles locked behind his waist, her mouth open in an ecstatic scream, the rest of the department shaking their heads in shame as they passed his door.

I couldn't stop thinking about it. I lay awake at night and tortured myself. One morning in August I was so far out of my head I called Sally. "This woman Richard is supposed to be seeing. Lili or whatever her name is. Describe her."

"Can you spell slut, dear? What more do you need to know?"

"I want the details. Like you were doing it for the police."

"Oh, five-six I guess. Wavy brown hair, just to her shoulders. Deep tan. Makeup, of course. *Lots* of makeup. Did I mention armpit hair?"

"Yes," I said, "you did."

During summer sessions Richard taught a two-hour class from one to three every afternoon. Assuming he was not so far gone that he'd given up teaching entirely. At 1:15 I climbed the marble stairs to the second floor of Dallas Hall, looking for the woman Sally had described.

There was nobody in the common room. I got a cup of coffee and found Robbie in his office. "Hi," I said awkwardly. "I'm looking for one of Richard's students? Her name is Lili something? He had this paper he needed to give her and he forgot it this morning."

He didn't buy my story for a second, of course. "Ah, yes. The redoubtable Lili. She was around a while ago. I could give it to her if you wanted."

"No, that's okay. I should try to find her myself."

"Well, you can't miss her. She's only about five-one, with olive skin, blond hair to her waist, and . . . well, you know."

"And great tits," I said bitterly. "Right?"

Robbie shrugged, embarrassed. "You said it. Not me."

The descriptions didn't exactly match. I suspected Robbie was not seeing her with much objectivity. For that matter, neither was Sally.

The offices faced out into a central room that was divided into a maze of cubicles. I wandered through them for a while with no luck. On my way out I stopped at Taylor's secretary's office. "I'm looking for a student named Lili? She's short, with . . ."

"I know, the most gorgeous black hair in the world. I would hardly call her short, though—oh. There she goes right now."

I turned, hearing heels click on the polished floor. "Thanks," I said, and ran into the hall.

And froze.

She looked at me for no more than a second or two. Afterward I couldn't say how tall she was, or describe the color of her hair. All I saw were her eyes, huge and black, like the eyes of a snake. It must have been some chemical in her sweat or her breath that I reacted to on such a blind, instinctive level. I could do nothing but stare at her with loathing and horror. When her eyes finally let me go I turned and ran all the way back to my car.

I picked Emily up at the sitter's and took her home and held her for the rest of the afternoon, until Richard arrived, rocking silently on the edge of the couch, remembering the blackness of those eyes, thinking, not one of us. She's not one of us.

That Friday Richard came home at four. He was a half hour late, no more than that. Emily was crawling furiously around the living room and I watched her with all the attention I could manage. The rest of my mind was simply numb.

Richard nodded at us and walked toward the back of the house. I heard the bathroom door close. I put Emily in her playpen and followed him. I could hear water running behind the bathroom door. Some wild bravado pushed me past my fear. I opened the door and walked in.

He stood at the sink. He had his penis in one hand and a bar of soap in the other. I could smell the sex he'd had with her, still clinging to him. The smell brought back the same revulsion I'd felt at the sight of her.

We looked at each other a long time. Finally he turned off the water and zipped himself up again. "Wash your hands," I said. "For God's sake. I don't want you touching anything in this house until you at least wash your hands."

He washed his hands and then his face. He dried himself on a hand towel and carefully put it back on the rack. He sat on the closed lid of the toilet, looked up at me, then back at the floor.

SCALES

"She was lonely," he said. "I just . . . I couldn't help myself. I can't explain it to you any better than that."

"Lili," I said. "Why don't you say her name? Do you think I don't know?"

"Lili," he said. He got too much pleasure out of the sound of it. "At least it's out in the open now. It's almost a relief. I can talk to you about it."

"Talk to me? You *bastard!* What gives you the idea that I want to hear anything . . . *anything* about your cheap little slut?"

It was like he hadn't heard me. "Every time I see her she's different. She seduces me all over again. And there's this loneliness, this need in her—"

"Shut up! I don't want to hear it! Don't you care what you've done? Doesn't this marriage mean anything to you? Are you just a penis with legs? Maybe you're sick of me, but don't you care about Emily? At all?"

"I can't . . . I'm helpless. . . ."

He wouldn't even offer me the dignity of putting it in past tense. "You're not helpless. You're just selfish. A selfish, irresponsible little prick." I saw myself standing there, shouting at him. It wasn't like me. It was like a fever dream. I felt weightless and terribly cold. I slammed the bathroom door on my way out. I packed a suitcase and put Emily in her carseat and carried her outside. It wasn't until we were actually moving that she started to cry.

For me it took even longer.

Darla knew everything to do. She told me to finish the story while she drove me to my bank. I took all but a hundred dollars out of the checking account, and half the savings. Then she called her lawyer and set up an appointment for Monday morning. By midnight I had a one-bedroom apartment around the corner from hers. She even loaned me some Valium so I could sleep.

Even with the Valium, the first few days were hard. I would wake up every morning at five and lie there for an hour or more while my brain wandered in circles. Richard had said, "Every time I see her she's different." And everyone I asked about her had a different description.

Helpless. He said he was helpless.

After a week of this I saw it wasn't going to go away. I left Emily with Darla and spent the evening at the library.

Back when I was a lab assistant, back when I first met Richard, I took English courses too. Richard was a first-year teaching assistant and I was a love-struck senior. We read Yeats and Milton and Blake and Tennyson together. And Keats, Richard's favorite.

I found the quote from Burton's *Anatomy of Melancholy* in Keats's *Selected Poetry*. "Apollonius . . . by some probable conjectures, found her out to be a serpent, a lamia; and that all her furniture was, like Tantalus' gold . . . no substance, but mere illusions." The lamia had the head and breasts of a woman and the body of a snake. She could change her appearance at will to charm any man. Like Lilith, her spiritual ancestor, she fed off the men she ensnared.

> I saw pale kings and princes too,
> Pale warriors, death pale were they all;
> They cried—"La Belle Dame sans Merci
> Hath thee in thrall!"

I drove back toward my apartment. The night was hot and still. Suppose, I thought. Suppose it's true. Suppose there *are* lamias out there. And one of them has hold of Richard.

Then, I thought, she's welcome to him.

I brought Emily home and went to bed.

By the second week it was time to look for work. With luck, and child support, I hoped to get by with a part-time job. I hated the idea of Emily in day care even half days, but there was no alternative.

I left her at the sitter's at nine o'clock. I came back a few minutes after noon. The sitter met me at the door. She was red-faced, had been crying.

"Oh, God," she said. "I didn't know where to find you."

I would stay calm, I told myself, until I found out what was wrong. "What happened?"

"I only left her alone for five minutes. We were out here in the yard. The phone rang and I went inside, and—"

"Is she hurt?" I said. I had grabbed the sitter's arms. "Is she alive? What *happened?*"

"I don't know."

"Where *is* she?"

"I don't know!" she wailed. "She just . . . disappeared!"

"How long ago?"

"Half an hour? Maybe less."

I turned away.

"Wait!" she said. "I called the police. They're on their way. They have to ask you some questions . . ."

I was already running for the car.

Subconsciously I must have made the connection. Lamia. Lilith. The legends of stolen children, bled dry, turned into vampires.

I knew exactly where Emily was.

My tires screamed as I came around the corner and again as I hit the brakes. I slammed the car door as I ran for the house. A fragment of my consciousness noticed how dead and dry the lawn looked, saw the yellowing newspapers still in their plastic wrappers. The rest of my mind could only say Emily's name over and over again.

I didn't bother with the doorbell. Richard hadn't changed the locks and the chain wasn't on the door. There were no lights inside. I smelled the faint odor of spoiled milk.

I went straight to the bedroom. The door was open.

All three of them were in there. None of them had any clothes on. Richard lay on his back. Lili crouched over him, holding Emily. The smell of spoiled milk was stronger, and the smell of sperm, and the alien sex smell, Lili's smell. There was something else, something my eyes couldn't quite make out in the darkness, something like cobwebs over the three of them.

Lili turned her head toward me. I saw the black eyes again, staring at me without fear or regret. I couldn't help but notice her body—the thick waist, the small drooping breasts.

I said, "Let go of my baby."

She pulled Emily toward her. Emily looked at me and whimpered.

I was shaking with rage. There was a gooseneck table lamp by

217

the bed and I grabbed it, knocking over the end table and spilling books across the floor. I swung it at Lili's head and screamed, "Let her go!"

Lili put her arms up to protect herself, dropping Emily. I swung the lamp again and she scrambled off the bed, crouched like an animal, making no effort to cover herself.

Emily had started to cry. I snatched her up and brushed the dust or whatever it was away from her face.

"Take the child," Lili said. I had never heard her voice before. It was hoarse and whispery, but musical, like pan pipes. "But Richard is mine."

I looked at him. He seemed drugged, barely aware of what was going on around him. He hadn't shaved in days, and his eyes seemed to have sunken deep into his head. "You can have him," I said.

I backed out of the room and then turned and ran. I drove to my apartment with Emily in my arms, made myself slow down, watch the road, stop for red lights. No one followed us. "You're safe now, Tater," I told her. "Everything's going to be okay."

I bathed her and fed her and wrapped her in her blanket and held her. Eventually her crying stopped.

The police found no sign of Richard at the house. The place was deserted. I changed the locks and put it up for sale. Lili was gone too, of course. The police shook their heads when her descriptions failed to add up. Untrained observers, they said. It happened all the time. Richard and Lili would turn up, they assured me, probably at some resort hotel in Mexico. I shouldn't worry.

One night last week the phone woke me up. There was breathing on the other end. It sounded like someone fighting for air. I told myself it wasn't Richard. It was only breathing. Only a stranger, only a run-of-the-mill obscene phone call.

Some days I still wake up at five in the morning. If lamias are serpents, they can't interbreed with humans. Like vampires, they must somehow turn human children into their successors. I have no doubt that was what Lili was doing with Emily when I found her.

I can't say anything, not even to Darla. They would tell me about the stress I've been under. They would put me in a hospital somewhere. They would take Emily away from me.

She seems happy enough, most of the time. The only changes in her appearance are the normal ones for a healthy, growing baby girl. She's going to be beautiful when she grows up, a real heart-breaker. But puberty is a long way away. And I won't know until then whether or not she is still my daughter.

Time is already moving much too fast.

In college back in the early seventies I took a course called "The Bible as Literature." This was great fun and something our current climate of religious extremism would no longer permit. We dared treat Christianity like any other myth, as a source for allusions, metaphors, and plots. We also talked about the Bible as a piece of literature unto itself—asking who wrote the various sections and when, what earlier works were swiped to create it, why various pieces of writing were included or left out. I added several words to my vocabulary, like "pseudepigraphal" (which friends have hounded me for using in conversation). I also got interested—even a little obsessed—with Lilith.

Lilith, you all remember, was Adam's first wife, who was kicked out of the Garden for fornicating with demons, and so on. She is the dark, sexy underbelly of the Judeo-Christian myth. She is Keats's Belle Dame sans Merci, horror's succubus, Greece's Lamia. She is the first vamp and the first vampire. She is the Kind Men Like.

I'd wanted to write a Lilith story for years. I'd also toyed with the idea of writing a companion piece to "Love in Vain," a story that used a serial killer to talk about men's ideas about women. I wanted to tackle the same subject from the woman's perspective, a literary "answer record" if you will, like "Dance with Me Henry." I would have written something like the present story eventually, but I have to give Ellen credit for pushing me to it.

I should also mention that, in struggling desperately for a title during the final draft, I hit upon "Scales" without remembering where I'd first seen it. I later realized I had stolen it from a brilliant, but unpublished, mermaid story by fellow Austinite Nancy Sterling. My thanks to her for being generous enough to let me keep it.

LEWIS SHINER

ROBERTA
⊙ LANNES ⊙

SAVING THE WORLD AT THE NEW MOON MOTEL

Roberta Lannes is a native Southern Californian. She has been teaching junior high school English, art, and assorted related courses for nineteen years and until recently maintained a commercial and fine art business on the side. She began selling stories to literary reviews in college but in the past few years has been making a name for herself with powerful, dark, psychological horror stories in such notable anthologies as Cutting Edge *and* Lord John Ten. *She is currently working on a novel of supernatural fiction,* Glass Tomb. *"Saving the World at the New Moon Motel" is science fiction and one of her lighter pieces.*

The brass bell clanged over the screen door of the New Moon Café. Terri turned, once again, to see if it might be Earl come to beg her forgiveness and haul her butt home. It was a trucker. She sighed heavily and held out her cup for a warm-up.

"Go home Terri. That's your eleventh cup of coffee. I wouldn't be surprised if you're still up in a couple of days and can't, for the life of you, remember what coulda kept you from sleepin'."

"Please, Mary Ann, I want to be wide awake when Earl gets here."

The coffee sloshed over the top and into the saucer. Terri giggled, giddy with caffeine. "Thanks."

"He ain't gonna come, Terri. He's a stubborn man. And he ain't in the prettiest spot, either, with you knowin' about his affair with Florence and all . . ."

Acid bit her stomach. A twist of pain in her heart made her gasp. She didn't need to hear anyone speak of it again. She just wanted him to say he was sorry. Grovel a little. Then maybe they could go on with their lives and not be hurting each other like that anymore. Hell, it wasn't the first time, and she'd done her share of messing around, but this was different.

She drank down half the cup of coffee, filled it back up with cream, and added five teaspoons of sugar. She opened the menu then let it slap closed. She ordered her third piece of apple pie à la mode. Or was it her fourth and she'd had three brownies? She couldn't remember.

The bell. She looked over her shoulder.

A man. Short, maybe five feet tall, but thickly built. And handsome in an exotic way. His round dark eyes reminded Terri of a snake's. He wore a smart-looking leather jumpsuit. He moved smoothly, gracefully, like someone with a foot more height and the agility of a dancer.

She turned back to her coffee. The bars closed at two. Much of their clientele trickled into the café, nearly filling the place. But Terri sat alone at the counter. He sat down beside her.

She shifted uneasily on her stool. She hadn't had a man interested in her since before she'd had little Earl and put on sixty pounds. Maybe this one was one of those guys she read about in *Real Romance* that like their women large. She needed this. Badly.

Mary Ann noticed the man's obvious interest and gave Terri a wink. Terri smiled at the man as she picked up her fork to dig into her pie.

The man smiled back. He reached for a food-stained menu wedged behind the napkin dispenser.

Terri cleared her throat. "If you're looking for dessert, they have the best apple pie. . . ." She pointed to hers.

"Thank-you." He looked up at Mary Ann. "I want same."

"You won't be sorry. Hi. My name is Terri Sipes." She held

out a hand. He looked at it curiously, took it in his, and turned it over, examining it. She pulled it away.

His eyes met hers. "Thank-you. My name." He paused, took a gulp of air. "Name is Pauldor."

His voice was strange. Deep, brittle, emotionless. It was like Earl's when she'd asked for an explanation of his behavior with Florence. He'd droned on and on in that same tone, not making much sense. Her stomach churned.

"Paul Door? A nice name. Where are you from?"

He looked blankly at her, then smiled. He gulped air again and whistled. "Thank-you. I am from the other side of the world." He made a giggling noise at some private joke. "And you are from here?"

Terri looked to Mary Ann and back to Paul. He seemed nervous, she thought. A foreigner.

"Here? Yes, I live in town. Up the highway a few miles." She slipped her wedding ring off under her napkin and put it in her coat pocket. "What are you doing so far from home?"

"I am in travel." He smiled, licked his lips. A long pale tongue. Terri shivered.

"Travel? Oh, how wonderful. I would love to travel. I haven't been but a state away in my whole life. What do you do, work for a travel agency?"

He brightened and his voice took on some expression. "I do. I do advance work. I go ahead. I seek new places to take tour. People. Visit. Is this good place?"

Terri shrugged. She didn't know. "I bet you could take a tour through Olympia. They make great beer there. Then you could sort of slide through Budd. Canada's just a bit aways up north. It's supposed to be incredible."

"People are easygoing, friendly like you?"

This was getting good. He leaned closer. Now if Earl would just walk in . . .

"Yes, oh, yes. Very friendly. At least the women. Like me."

"You. You are special? Women?"

Terri puffed. "Well, *I* think so. Not all women are . . ." She thought hard. "Not all women are as warm and giving as I am."

He beamed, clapped his hands together. "Special. Good. Very good."

She got the feeling they weren't quite communicating, but he was from a foreign country and she didn't speak any language but English. And the universal language. Love. An idea was beginning to grow in her. She would just have to take advantage of this situation and seek retribution for Earl's infidelity. Definitely. The Bible came to mind. An eye for an eye. A screw for a screw.

Terri swallowed the last piece of pie and purred.

"Would you be interested in seeing the accommodations in the motel here? They are quite nice. . . ." She smoothed her sweater.

"This is proposition, yes?"

This guy was blunt. She'd never been picked up by a foreigner before. Maybe they just got right to it.

"Maybe . . ."

He grabbed their checks and presented Mary Ann with a roll of twenties. Both women's eyes went wide. Mary Ann took two twenties and handed him back the rest. Terri slipped behind the counter and pulled her friend close.

"Pay dirt!" She whispered.

"What if Earl comes while . . ."

"You said yourself he won't show. Look. I need this. I deserve to make myself feel better any ol' way I want. I'll see Earl in the morning with a smile on my face and forgiveness in my heart. It will be worth it."

"Well, good luck. But, I dunno. I heard those little guys have little you-know-whatses. I wanna hear all the details. . . ."

Terri looked smug. "I'm not worried. You should have seen his . . ."

Paul took her arm and steered her out of the café and into the motel office. She marveled at his ease of movement, his style. If he moved like this out of bed, heavens, she could hardly stand the thrill she felt at the possibilities.

As many times as she'd eaten at the café, Terri had never seen the inside of the motel. Their room was off the highway. Paul opened the door and followed her in. The walls were faded puce cinder block. Over the chenille-covered double bed was a large velveteen tapestry depicting a group of dogs playing poker. That seemed to fascinate Paul. He murmured something about animals and humans while Terri flicked on the TV.

"Damn, it's scrambled. Got a quarter?"

Paul was sitting on the bed, feeling the texture of the wall.

223

The light from the New Moon Motel sign outside cast a reddish glow over him. He blinked and looked at her.

"What, thank-you?"

"The TV is on cable. If we put money in it, we can watch it."

"I do not want TV. I come for you Terrisipes."

"Hm, maybe we could get cozy first. I'm not into quickies."

"Cozy. Is that good?"

She went to the bed and sat down beside him. She tried to reach into his leather jacket, but he pulled away. His smile faded.

"What, thank-you, is this?"

Terri put her lips to his and let her tongue slide out. His mouth hung agape. He pushed her away and stood.

"Hey, I thought you wanted me? This is too weird. First you're in a hurry, then you're cold. Maybe you need to be inspired."

She stood and slowly peeled off her sweater, then her stretch jeans. Paul seemed mesmerized. She was on to something. She took her boots off slowly, then pulled down her knee socks and flung them over her shoulder. Paul was drooling. She reached behind her back and unhooked her bra. Her breasts came tumbling out over her stomach. Paul began gasping for air. She pinched the sides of her briefs and drew them down over her hips. She turned so he could see her huge backside and bent over to lower the panties to the floor.

Paul was speechless and paralyzed with passion. He sat on the bed, his erection tenting his leather pantsuit. In fact, there were many lumps beneath the textured gray skin.

Terri waited. Nothing. Well, there was one more thing she could try.

"I'll be in the shower when you're ready, sweetie. . . ." She swung her hips as she walked into the bathroom. She could hear him gurgling behind her.

The anticipation fired her adrenaline. With all the sugar and caffeine in her system, she felt like a rocket about to take off. She also felt anger at Earl. She could kill the bastard. Kill him and move to Sedona where an old boyfriend ran a convenience store. But no. She wanted to use this energy to give herself the best lay she'd had in years. . . .

She turned on the water, adjusting the temperature. She tucked her permed hair into a skimpy plastic cap the motel

224

thoughtfully provided and got in. The water felt great. The tension began to melt slightly. And she could take as long a shower as she pleased. At home, Earl got homicidal if she used up the hot water on her body, for chrissakes.

She rubbed the lilac-scented soap over her plump expanse of flesh until the lather was as thick as whipped cream. She let the warmth wash over her, the energy flow through her.

The shower door opened and Pauldor stood naked, sort of, his gray leather suit hanging off his back, his pinkish underskin glistening with sweat. Terri's eyes went to his groin. Her face brightened. He was not only well-hung, but he had almost a dozen more erections over his chest and stomach. Each one just as red and rigid as the one in his groin.

He got in and embraced her. The projections attached themselves to her with squishing suction pops. The last one slid gingerly in where it should. Terri yelped with pleasure and pain as the suction grew. Then she moved like she'd never done before. She gave it all she had. Take this Earl Sipes.

Pauldor gurgled loudly, his eyes rolling up into his head, leaving pale orbs, his hands kneading her, clawing her backside.

She was there. She howled, thankful she was not at home where Earl said everyone in the surrounding trailers could hear her. Paul gave an equally loud, but more pained sound, and the erections popped off. He stared down at his groin for a moment, seeming not to believe what he saw, then collapsed onto the shower floor.

Terri stared down at where once there had been a penis. She felt a slight burning and a cramp when the blackened flesh fell to the metal drain and washed between the slats. She put her hand to her mouth, then began to laugh. It was like she'd been stung by a bee and . . . no, she shook her head. This was something else. She knew foreigners had to be different in some way.

She checked to see if he was breathing and turned off the water. She decided he just needed to rest and tiptoed out.

As she dressed she noticed the marks the suction left. They were raw, sensitive to the touch. She carefully pulled her sweater back on. The scratches on her backside hurt too. For all the pain, she felt more satisfied than she could remember. Foreigners. She'll have to tell Mary Ann about this one. Whew!

She shut the door quietly behind her and walked a little awkwardly back to the café.

Mary Ann was surprised to see her.

"You're back so soon. Musta been a bust."

"It was . . . incredible." She sighed, radiant.

"No kidding. Well, I hope so. Earl called. He wants your ass home. *Now.*"

"Really? Oh, this is perfect. I feel great and Earl's gonna be terrible jealous when he sees all the hickies I got. I'll see ya!"

Terri was almost outside, stopped, then turned back and grinned.

"Take good care of my friend Paul if he comes in for breakfast. He should have a hearty appetite. And by the way, not all small guys are . . . you know. Some of 'em have more than you could imagine."

She winked at Mary Ann and was gone.

Mary Ann shrugged and looked at her watch. She had a break coming in twenty minutes. Maybe he would be rested by then. She would just have to go find his room. Yup. She would.

Memories serve in the genesis of most writers' stories, and this story is no different. At the age of nineteen, I hitchhiked up to Washington from Los Angeles to escape my parents' divorce. I found myself with an entire evening to kill and no place to stay. The all-night diner I stopped in to eat seemed as good a place as any to hang out until dawn, so I slipped into a booth. The drama that unfolded that night was not unlike the tale just told. This gal's name was Dandy, her runaround husband's, Bob. Her friend behind the counter, Priscilla, came around from time to time to give me unsolicited updates on the woeful condition of Dandy's marriage and state of mind. It wasn't an alien who came in and took the edge off Dandy's anger, but he was plenty strange. It was Priscilla's comment about this man that stuck in my mind and spawned this story. She said, "That guy's got to be from another planet to get involved with Dandy and her problems." Who knows? Neither one of them ever came back in that night. . . .

ROBERTA LANNES

226

JAMES
⊙ TIPTREE, JR. ⊙

AND I AWOKE
AND FOUND ME
HERE ON THE
COLD HILL'S SIDE

When "And I Awoke and Found Me Here on the Cold Hill's Side" was published in 1971, it was commonly assumed that the author was male. When James Tiptree, Jr.'s, first collection Ten Thousand Light-Years from Home *was published in 1973, this was still the assumption. Not until 1977 did Alice Sheldon admit that she was Tiptree, that she was born in Chicago, was the daughter of a well-known geographer and travel writer, was an experimental psychologist, and that she worked for the American government, and for some of that time in the Pentagon. Tiptree and her husband died tragically in 1987, but she left a legacy of fiction that ranged from anthropological SF to space opera and some of the most astute perceptions on male/female relationships that have been written about, including the classic reprinted here.*

He was standing absolutely still by a service port, staring out at the belly of the Orion docking above us. He had on a gray uniform and his rusty hair was cut short. I took him for a station engineer.

That was bad for me. Newsmen strictly don't belong in the bowels of Big Junction. But in my first twenty hours I hadn't found anyplace to get a shot of an alien ship.

227

I turned my holocam to show its big World Media insigne and started my bit about What It Meant to the People Back Home who were paying for it all.

"—it may be routine work to you, sir, but we owe it to them to share—"

His face came around slow and tight, and his gaze passed over me from a peculiar distance.

"The wonders, the drama," he repeated dispassionately. His eyes focused on me. "You consummated fool."

"Could you tell me what races are coming in, sir? If I could even get a view—"

He waved me to the port. Greedily I angled my lenses up at the long blue hull blocking out the starfield. Beyond her I could see the bulge of a black-and-gold ship.

"That's a Foramen," he said. "There's a freighter from Belye on the other side, you'd call it Arcturus. Not much traffic right now."

"You're the first person who's said two sentences to me since I've been here, sir. What are those colorful little craft?"

"Procya," he shrugged. "They're always around. Like us."

I squashed my face on the vitrite, peering. The walls clanked. Somewhere overhead aliens were off-loading into their private sector of Big Junction. The man glanced at his wrist.

"Are you waiting to go out, sir?"

His grunt could have meant anything.

"Where are you from on Earth?" he asked me in his hard tone.

I started to tell him and suddenly saw that he had forgotten my existence. His eyes were on nowhere, and his head was slowly bowing forward onto the port frame.

"Go home," he said thickly. I caught a strong smell of tallow.

"Hey, sir!" I grabbed his arm; he was in rigid tremor. "Steady, man."

"I'm waiting . . . waiting for my wife. My loving wife." He gave a short ugly laugh. "Where are you from?"

I told him again.

"Go home," he mumbled. "Go home and make babies. While you still can."

One of the early GR casualties, I thought.

"Is that all you know?" His voice rose stridently. "Fools.

Dressing in their styles. Gnivo suits, Aoleelee music. Oh, I see your newscasts," he sneered. "Nixi parties. A year's salary for a floater. Gamma radiation? Go home, read history. *Ballpoint pens and bicycles*—"

He started a slow slide downward in the half gee. My only informant. We struggled confusedly; he wouldn't take one of my sobertabs but I finally got him along the service corridor to a bench in an empty loading bay. He fumbled out a little vacuum cartridge. As I was helping him unscrew it, a figure in starched whites put his head in the bay.

"I can be of assistance, yes?" His eyes popped, his face was covered with brindled fur. An alien, a Procya! I started to thank him but the red-haired man cut me off.

"Get lost. Out."

The creature withdrew, its big eyes moist. The man stuck his pinky in the cartridge and then put it up his nose, gasping deep in his diaphragm. He looked toward his wrist.

"What time is it?"

I told him.

"News," he said. "A message for the eager, hopeful human race. A word about those lovely, lovable aliens we all love so much." He looked at me. "Shocked, aren't you, newsboy?"

I had him figured now. A xenophobe. Aliens plot to take over Earth.

"Ah Christ, they couldn't care less." He took another deep gasp, shuddered and straightened. "The hell with generalities. What time d'you say it was? All right, I'll tell you how I learned it. The hard way. While we wait for my loving wife. You can bring that little recorder out of your sleeve, too. Play it over to yourself some time . . . when it's too late." He chuckled. His tone had become chatty—an educated voice. "You ever hear of supernormal stimuli?"

"No," I said. "Wait a minute. White sugar?"

"Near enough. Y'know Little Junction Bar in D.C.? No, you're an Aussie, you said. Well, I'm from Burned Barn, Nebraska."

He took a breath, consulting some vast disarray of the soul.

"I accidentally drifted into Little Junction Bar when I was eighteen. No. Correct that. You don't go into Little Junction by accident, any more than you first shoot skag by accident.

"You go into Little Junction because you've been craving it, dreaming about it, feeding on every hint and clue about it, back there in Burned Barn, since before you had hair in your pants. Whether you know it or not. Once you're out of Burned Barn, you can no more help going into Little Junction than a sea-worm can help rising to the moon.

"I had a brand-new liquor I.D. in my pocket. It was early; there was an empty spot beside some humans at the bar. Little Junction isn't an embassy bar, y'know. I found out later where the high-caste aliens go—when they go out. The New Rive, the Curtain by the Georgetown Marina.

"And they go by themselves. Oh, once in a while they do the cultural exchange bit with a few frosty couples of other aliens and some stuffed humans. Galactic Amity with a ten-foot pole.

"Little Junction was the place where the lower orders went, the clerks and drivers out for kicks. Including, my friend, the perverts. The ones who can take humans. Into their beds, that is."

He chuckled and sniffed his finger again, not looking at me.

"Ah, yes. Little Junction is Galactic Amity night, every night. I ordered . . . what? A margarita. I didn't have the nerve to ask the snotty spade bartender for one of the alien liquors behind the bar. It was dim. I was trying to stare everywhere at once without showing it. I remember those white boneheads—Lyrans, that is. And a mess of green veiling I decided was a multiple being from someplace. I caught a couple of human glances in the bar mirror. Hostile flicks. I didn't get the message, then.

"Suddenly an alien pushed right in beside me. Before I could get over my paralysis, I heard this blurry voice:

" 'You air a futeball enthushiash?'

"An alien had spoken to me. An *alien*, a being from the stars. Had spoken. To me.

"Oh, god, I had no time for football, but I would have claimed a passion for paper-folding, for dumb crambo—anything to keep him talking. I asked him about his home-planet sports, I insisted on buying his drinks. I listened raptly while he spluttered out a play-by-play account of a game I wouldn't have turned a dial for. The 'Grain Bay Pashkers.' Yeah. And I was dimly aware of trouble among the humans on my other side.

"Suddenly this woman—I'd call her a girl now—this girl said

something in a high nasty voice and swung her stool into the arm I was holding my drink with. We both turned around together.

"Christ, I can see her now. The first thing that hit me was *discrepancy*. She was a nothing—but terrific. Transfigured. Oozing it, radiating it.

"The next thing was I had a horrifying hard-on just looking at her.

"I scrooched over so my tunic hid it, and my spilled drink trickled down, making everything worse. She pawed vaguely at the spill, muttering.

"I just stared at her trying to figure out what had hit me. An ordinary figure, a soft avidness in the face. Eyes heavy, satiated-looking. She was totally sexualized. I remembered her throat pulsed. She had one hand up touching her scarf, which had slipped off her shoulder. I saw angry bruises there. That really tore it, I understood at once those bruises had some sexual meaning.

"She was looking past my head with her face like a radar dish. Then she made an 'ahhhh' sound that had nothing to do with me and grabbed my forearm as if it were a railing. One of the men behind her laughed. The woman said, 'Excuse me,' in a ridiculous voice and slipped out behind me. I wheeled around after her, nearly upsetting my futeball friend, and saw that some Sirians had come in.

"That was my first look at Sirians in the flesh, if that's the word. God knows I'd memorized every news shot, but I wasn't prepared. That tallness, that cruel thinness. That appalling alien arrogance. Ivory-blue, these were. Two males in immaculate me-tallic gear. Then I saw there was a female with them. An ivory-indigo exquisite with a permanent faint smile on those bone-hard lips.

"The girl who'd left me was ushering them to a table. She reminded me of a goddamn dog that wants you to follow it. Just as the crowd hid them, I saw a man join them, too. A big man, expensively dressed, with something wrecked about his face.

"Then the music started and I had to apologize to my furry friend. And the Sellice dancer came out and my personal introduc-tion to hell began."

The red-haired man fell silent for a minute, enduring self-pity. Something wrecked about the face, I thought; it fit.

He pulled his face together.

"First I'll give you the only coherent observation of my entire evening. You can see it here at Big Junction, always the same. Outside of the Procya, it's humans with aliens, right? Very seldom aliens with other aliens. Never aliens with humans. It's the humans who want in."

I nodded, but he wasn't talking to me. His voice had a druggy fluency.

"Ah, yes, my Sellice. My first Sellice."

"They aren't really well-built, y'know, under those cloaks. No waist to speak of and short-legged. But they flow when they walk.

"This one flowed out into the spotlight, cloaked to the ground in violet silk. You could only see a fall of black hair and tassels over a narrow face like a vole. She was a mole-gray. They come in all colors, their fur is like a flexible velvet all over; only the color changes startlingly around their eyes and lips and other places. Erogenous zones? Ah, man, with them it's not zones.

"She began to do what we'd call a dance, but it's no dance, it's their natural movement. Like smiling, say, with us. The music built up, and her arms undulated toward me, letting the cloak fall apart little by little. She was naked under it. The spotlight started to pick up her body markings moving in the slit of the cloak. Her arms floated apart and I saw more and more.

"She was fantastically marked and the markings were writhing. Not like body paint—alive. Smiling, that's a good word for it. As if her whole body was smiling sexually, beckoning, winking, urging, pouting, speaking to me. You've seen a classic Egyptian belly dance? Forget it—a sorry stiff thing compared to what any Sellice can do. This one was ripe, near term.

"Her arms went up and those blazing lemon-colored curves pulsed, waved, everted, contracted, throbbed, evolved unbelievably welcoming, inciting permutations. *Come do it to me, do it, do it here and here and here and now.* You couldn't see the rest of her, only a wicked flash of mouth. Every human male in the room was aching to ram himself into that incredible body. I mean it was *pain*. Even the other aliens were quiet, except one of the Sirians who was chewing out a waiter.

"I was a basket case before she was halfway through. . . . I won't bore you with what happened next; before it was over there

were several fights and I got out. My money ran out on the third
night. She was gone next day.

"I didn't have time to find out about the Sellice cycle then,
mercifully. That came after I went back to campus and discovered
you had to have a degree in solid-state electronics to apply for off-
planet work. I was a pre-med but I got that degree. It only took me
as far as First Junction then.

"Oh, god, First Junction. I thought I was in heaven—the
alien ships coming in and our freighters going out. I saw them all,
all but the real exotics, the tankies. You only see a few of those a
cycle, even here. And the Yyeire. You've never seen that.

"Go home, boy. Go home to your version of Burned Barn. . . .

"The first Yyeir I saw I dropped everything and started walking after it like a starving hound, just breathing. You've seen the
pix of course. Like lost dreams. *Man is in love and loves what
vanishes.* . . . It's the scent, you can't guess that. I followed until I
ran into a slammed port. I spent half a cycle's credits sending the
creature the wine they call stars' tears. . . . Later I found out it was
a male. That made no difference at all.

"You can't have sex with them, y'know. No way. They breed
by light or something, no one knows exactly. There's a story about
a man who got hold of a Yyeir woman and tried. They had him
skinned. Stories—"

He was starting to wander.

"What about that girl in the bar, did you see her again?"

He came back from somewhere.

"Oh, yes. I saw her. She'd been making it with the two
Sirians, y'know. The males do it in pairs. Said to be the total sexual
thing for a woman, if she can stand the damage from those beaks. I
wouldn't know. She talked to me a couple of times after they
finished with her. No use for men whatever. She drove off the P
Street bridge. . . . The man, poor bastard, he was trying to keep
that Sirian bitch happy single-handed. Money helps, for a while. I
don't know where he ended."

He glanced at his wrist again. I saw the pale bare place where
a watch had been and told him the time.

"Is that the message you want to give Earth? Never love an
alien?"

"Never love an alien—" He shrugged. "Yeah. No. Ah, Jesus,
don't you see? Everything going out, nothing coming back. Like

the poor damned Polynesians. We're gutting Earth, to begin with. Swapping raw resources for junk. Alien status symbols. Tape decks, Coca-Cola, and Mickey Mouse watches."

"Well, there is concern over the balance of trade. Is that your message?"

"The balance of trade." He rolled it sardonically. "Did the Polynesians have a word for it, I wonder? You don't see, do you? All right, why are you here? I mean *you*, personally. How many guys did you climb over—"

He went rigid, hearing footsteps outside. The Procya's hopeful face appeared around the corner. The red-haired man snarled at him and he backed out. I started to protest.

"Ah, the silly reamer loves it. It's the only pleasure we have left. . . . Can't you see, man? That's *us*. That's the way we look to them, to the real ones."

"But—"

"And now we're getting the cheap C-drive, we'll be all over just like the Procya. For the pleasure of serving as freight monkeys and junction crews. Oh, they appreciate our ingenious little service stations, the beautiful star folk. They don't *need* them, y'know. Just an amusing convenience. D'you know what I do here with my two degrees? What I did at First Junction. Tube cleaning. A swab. Sometimes I get to replace a fitting."

I muttered something; the self-pity was getting heavy.

"Bitter? Man, it's a *good* job. Sometimes I get to talk to one of them." His face twisted. "My wife works as a—oh, hell, you wouldn't know. I'd trade—correction, I have traded—everything Earth offered me for just that chance. To see them. To speak to them. Once in a while to touch one. Once in a great while to find one low enough, perverted enough to want to touch me—"

His voice trailed off and suddenly came back strong.

"And so will you!" He glared at me. "Go home! Go home and tell them to quit it. Close the ports. Burn every god-lost alien thing before it's too late! That's what the Polynesians didn't do."

"But surely—"

"But surely be damned! Balance of trade—balance of *life*, man. I don't know if our birthrate is going, that's not the point. Our soul is leaking out. We're bleeding to death!"

He took a breath and lowered his tone.

"What I'm trying to tell you, this is a trap. We've hit the supernormal stimulus. Man is exogamous—all our history is one long drive to find and impregnate the stranger. Or get impregnated by him, it works for women too. Anything different-colored, different nose, ass, anything, man *has* to fuck it or die trying. That's a drive, y'know, it's built in. Because it works fine as long as the stranger is human. For millions of years that kept the genes circulating. But now we've met aliens we can't screw, and we're about to die trying. . . . Do you think I can touch my wife?"

"But—"

"Look. Y'know, if you give a bird a fake egg like its own but bigger and brighter-marked, it'll roll its own egg out of the nest and sit on the fake? That's what we're doing."

"You've only been talking about sex." I was trying to conceal my impatience. "Which is great, but the kind of story I'd hoped—"

"Sex? No, it's deeper." He rubbed his head, trying to clear the drug. "Sex is only part of it, there's more. I've seen Earth missionaries, teachers, sexless people. Teachers—they end cycling waste or pushing floaters, but they're hooked. They stay. I saw one fine-looking old woman, she was servant to a Cu'ushbar kid. A defective—his own people would have let him die. That wretch was swabbing up its vomit as if it was holy water. Man, it's deep . . . some cargo-cult of the soul. We're built to dream outward. They laugh at us. They don't have it."

There were sounds of movement in the next corridor. The dinner crowd was starting. I had to get rid of him and get there; maybe I could find the Procya. A side door opened and a figure started toward us. At first I thought it was an alien and then I saw it was a woman wearing an awkward body-shell. She seemed to be limping slightly. Behind her I could glimpse the dinner-bound throng passing the open door.

The man got up as she turned into the bay. They didn't greet each other.

"The station employs only happily wedded couples," he told me with that ugly laugh. "We give each other . . . comfort."

He took one of her hands. She flinched as he drew it over his arm and let him turn her passively, not looking at me. "Forgive me if I don't introduce you. My wife appears fatigued."

I saw that one of her shoulders was grotesquely scarred.

"Tell them," he said, turning to go. "Go home and tell them."
Then his head snapped back toward me and he added quietly, "And
stay away from the Syrtis desk or I'll kill you."

They went away up the corridor.

I changed tapes hurriedly with one eye on the figures passing
that open door. Suddenly among the humans I caught a glimpse of
two sleek scarlet shapes. My first real aliens! I snapped the recorder shut and ran to squeeze in behind them.

MICHAELA
⊙ ROESSNER ⊙

PICTURE PLANES

Michaela Roessner was born in San Francisco and raised on the East Coast, the West Coast, and Southeast Asia. She graduated from college with a B.F.A. in ceramics and an M.F.A. in painting and keeps her hand in by making mixed media masks. Her first novel Walkabout Woman, *a powerful, moving story about the aboriginal dream-time, won the William Crawford award for first fantasy novel. She is also winner of The John W. Campbell Award for Best New Writer of 1987/88. Her most recent novel is set in San Jose, California. "Picture Planes," the sole poem in this volume, uses evocative imagery to describe a mutually destructive relationship between an alien and human.*

The doorway makes a picture—
Within the room she stands framed,
Leaning over slightly.
He draws his tongue along her backbone,
Wetly caressing each vertebra.
Moving upwards he reaches her wing spurs.
He licks them hard.
She whimpers with pleasure.
Then holding her tightly
He bites them off.

She snarls in pain.
He strokes her front, along the two long rows of nipples
To comfort her,
And tells himself that now she cannot leave him.
The sun shines through the window
Warming her back
Where two streams of blood
Course from her shoulder blades
Down her back
To his groin.
He mounts her from behind.

The door is open again.
The composition has changed.
She has given birth three times now
To brightly colored geometric objects
That lie heaped in one corner
Gathering dust.
He sits in the chair,
The only furniture in the room
Watching her stand at the window.
Arms stretched like a cross to the sun,
She hums.
He calls her to him.
She comes and stands before him.
He draws his hand up between her legs
Until she parts them.
He's ready,
So with no preliminaries
He pulls her onto him.
Once inside,
To make it up to her,
He nuzzles her face and ears
Till she softens and hums
As if he, too, was the sun,
Hot and molten within her.
She strokes his hair
As he pivots beneath her.
But when she is aroused

He doesn't dare let her mouth
Too near his throat.

The door doesn't shut easily.
She asks for clothing,
Hoping to hide the sharp buds
On wrists and ankles.
He got her when she was young.
She's grown
And now stands eye to eye with him.
He should give her up
But can't.
One day
While he strokes and nibbles her sex,
She pulls her feet up fast
And tries to gut him.
When he next returns
He brings a knife.
Pinning her down,
He cuts the new spurs off.
After that she's passive.
He can pull himself up onto her
Without fear.
Finally
Wrapping himself around her,
Rubbing himself against her bright sleek skin,
Pouring his hips into her as quickly or slowly
As he wants to.

The room is lit with sunlight
Except where the shattered window
Raggedly reveals the trueness of the forever night outside.
She lies broken below,
The pavement already absorbing her.
He has to admit to himself
That he knew all along
She would find a way to escape him.

This nasty little bit of work started innocently enough with an internal image like a painting by Vermeer—looking through a doorway into a room filled with buttery, creamy, golden light. No one was more surprised than I with the way it took off from there.

MICHAELA ROESSNER

PAT
⊙ MURPHY ⊙

LOVE AND SEX AMONG THE INVERTEBRATES

Pat Murphy won the Nebula Award twice in 1987—for her second novel The Falling Woman *and for her novelette "Rachel in Love." Her most recent novel is* The City, Not Long After (*Doubleday*), *and Bantam will be publishing her short-story collection* Points of Departure.

"Love and Sex Among the Invertebrates" seems like the perfect way to end an anthology of alien sex—it's just the next evolutionary step. . . .

This is not science. This has nothing to do with science. Yesterday, when the bombs fell and the world ended, I gave up scientific thinking. At this distance from the blast site of the bomb that took out San Jose, I figure I received a medium-size dose of radiation. Not enough for instant death, but too much for survival. I have only a few days left, and I've decided to spend this time constructing the future. Someone must do it.

It's what I was trained for, really. My undergraduate studies were in biology—structural anatomy, the construction of body and bone. My graduate studies were in engineering. For the past five years, I have been designing and constructing robots for use in industrial processing. The need for such industrial creations is over now. But it seems a pity to waste the equipment and materials that remain in the lab that my colleagues have abandoned.

I will put robots together and make them work. But I will not try to understand them. I will not take them apart and consider their inner workings and poke and pry and analyze. The time for science is over.

The pseudoscorpion, Lasiochernes pilosus, *is a secretive scorpionlike insect that makes its home in the nests of moles. Before pseudoscorpions mate, they dance—a private underground minuet—observed only by moles and voyeuristic entomologists. When a male finds a receptive female, he grasps her claws in his and pulls her toward him. If she resists, he circles, clinging to her claws and pulling her after him, refusing to take no for an answer. He tries again, stepping forward and pulling the female toward him with trembling claws. If she continues to resist, he steps back and continues the dance: circling, pausing to tug on his reluctant partner, then circling again.*

After an hour or more of dancing, the female inevitably succumbs, convinced by the dance steps that her companion's species matches her own. The male deposits a packet of sperm on the ground that has been cleared of debris by their dancing feet. His claws quiver as he draws her forward, positioning her over the package of sperm. Willing at last, she presses her genital pore to the ground and takes the sperm into her body.

Biology texts note that the male scorpion's claws tremble as he dances, but they do not say why. They do not speculate on his emotions, his motives, his desires. That would not be scientific.

I theorize that the male pseudoscorpion is eager. Among the everyday aromas of mole shit and rotting vegetation, he smells the female, and the perfume of her fills him with lust. But he is fearful and confused: a solitary insect, unaccustomed to socializing, he is disturbed by the presence of another of his kind. He is caught by conflicting emotions: his all-encompassing need, his fear, and the strangeness of the social situation.

I have given up the pretense of science. I speculate about the motives of the pseudoscorpion, the conflict and desire embodied in his dance.

I put the penis on my first robot as a kind of joke, a private joke, a joke about evolution. I suppose I don't really need to say it was a private joke—all my jokes are private now. I am the last one left, near as I can tell. My colleagues fled—to find their families, to seek refuge in the hills, to spend their last days running around, here and there. I don't expect to see anyone else around anytime soon. And if I do, they probably won't be interested in my jokes. I'm sure that most people think the time for joking is past. They don't see that the bomb and the war are the biggest jokes of all. Death is the biggest joke. Evolution is the biggest joke.

I remember learning about Darwin's theory of evolution in high school biology. Even back then, I thought it was kind of strange, the way people talked about it. The teacher presented evolution as a *fait accompli*, over and done with. She muddled her way through the complex speculations regarding human evolution, talking about *Ramapithecus, Australopithecus, Homo erectus, Homo sapiens*, and *Homo sapiens neanderthalensis*. At *Homo sapiens* she stopped, and that was it. The way the teacher looked at the situation, we were the last word, the top of the heap, the end of the line.

I'm sure the dinosaurs thought the same, if they thought at all. How could anything get better than armor plating and a spiked tail. Who could ask for more?

Thinking about the dinosaurs, I build my first creation on a reptilian model, a lizardlike creature constructed from bits and pieces that I scavenge from the industrial prototypes that fill the lab and the storeroom. I give my creature a stocky body, as long as I am tall; four legs, extending to the side of the body then bending at the knee to reach the ground; a tail as long as the body, spiked with decorative metal studs; a crocodilian mouth with great curving teeth.

The mouth is only for decoration and protection; this creature will not eat. I equip him with an array of solar panels, fixed to a sail-like crest on his back. The warmth of sunlight will cause the creature to extend his sail and gather electrical energy to recharge his batteries. In the cool of the night, he will fold his sail close to his back, becoming sleek and streamlined.

I decorate my creature with stuff from around the lab. From the trash beside the soda machine, I salvage aluminum cans. I cut them into a colorful fringe that I attach beneath the creature's chin, like the dewlap of an iguana. When I am done, the words on the soda cans have been sliced to nonsense: Coke, Fanta, Sprite, and Dr. Pepper mingle in a collision of bright colors. At the very end, when the rest of the creature is complete and functional, I make a cock of copper tubing and pipe fittings. It dangles beneath his belly, copper bright and obscene looking. Around the bright copper, I weave a rat's nest of my own hair, which is falling out by the handful. I like the look of that: bright copper peeking from a clump of wiry black curls.

Sometimes, the sickness overwhelms me. I spend part of one day in the ladies' room off the lab, lying on the cool tile floor and rousing myself only to vomit into the toilet. The sickness is nothing that I didn't expect. I'm dying, after all. I lie on the floor and think about the peculiarities of biology.

For the male spider, mating is a dangerous process. This is especially true in the spider species that weave intricate orb-shaped webs, the kind that catch the morning dew and sparkle so nicely for nature photographers. In these species, the female is larger than the male. She is, I must confess, rather a bitch; she'll attack anything that touches her web.

At mating time, the male proceeds cautiously. He lingers at the edge of the web, gently tugging on a thread of spider silk to get her attention. He plucks in a very specific rhythm, signaling to his would-be lover, whispering softly with his tugs: "I love you. I love you."

After a time, he believes that she has received his message. He feels confident that he has been understood. Still proceeding with caution, he attaches a mating line to the female's web. He plucks the mating line to encourage the female to move onto it. "Only you, baby," he signals. "You are the only one."

She climbs onto the mating line—fierce and passionate, but temporarily soothed by his promises. In that moment, he rushes to her, delivers his sperm, then quickly, before she can change her mind, takes a hike. A dangerous business, making love.

Before the world went away, I was a cautious person. I took great care in my choice of friends. I fled at the first sign of a misunderstanding. At the time, it seemed the right course.

I was a smart woman, a dangerous mate. (Odd—I find myself writing and thinking of myself in the past tense. So close to death that I consider myself already dead.) Men would approach with caution, delicately signaling from a distance: "I'm interested. Are you?" I didn't respond. I didn't really know how.

An only child, I was always wary of others. My mother and I lived together. When I was just a child, my father had left to pick up a pack of cigarettes and never returned. My mother, protective and cautious by nature, warned me that men could not be trusted. People could not be trusted. She could trust me and I could trust her, and that was all.

When I was in college, my mother died of cancer. She had known of the tumor for more than a year; she had endured surgery and chemotherapy, while writing me cheery letters about her gardening. Her minister told me that my mother was a saint—she hadn't told me because she hadn't wanted to disturb my studies. I realized then that she had been wrong. I couldn't really trust her after all.

I think perhaps I missed some narrow window of opportunity. If, at some point along the way, I had had a friend or a lover who had made the effort to coax me from hiding, I could have been a different person. But it never happened. In high school, I sought the safety of my books. In college, I studied alone on Friday nights. By the time I reached graduate school, I was, like the pseudoscorpion, accustomed to a solitary life.

I work alone in the laboratory, building the female. She is larger than the male. Her teeth are longer and more numerous. I am welding the hip joints into place when my mother comes to visit me in the laboratory.

"Katie," she says, "why didn't you ever fall in love? Why didn't you ever have children?"

I keep on welding, despite the trembling of my hands. I know she isn't there. Delirium is one symptom of radiation poisoning. But she keeps watching me as I work.

"You're not really here," I tell her, and realize immediately that talking to her is a mistake. I have acknowledged her presence and given her more power.

"Answer my questions, Katie," she says. "Why didn't you?"

I do not answer. I am busy and it will take too long to tell her about betrayal, to explain the confusion of a solitary insect confronted with a social situation, to describe the balance between fear and love. I ignore her just as I ignore the trembling of my hands and the pain in my belly, and I keep on working. Eventually, she goes away.

I use the rest of the soda cans to give the female brightly

colored scales: Coca-Cola red, Sprite green, Fanta orange. From soda cans, I make an oviduct, lined with metal. It is just large enough to accommodate the male's cock.

The male bowerbird attracts a mate by constructing a sort of art piece. From sticks and grasses, he builds two close-set parallel walls that join together to make an arch. He decorates this structure and the area around it with gaudy trinkets: bits of bone, green leaves, flowers, bright stones, and feathers cast off by gaudier birds. In areas where people have left their trash, he uses bottle caps and coins and fragments of broken glass.

He sits in his bower and sings, proclaiming his love for any and all females in the vicinity. At last, a female admires his bower, accepts his invitation, and they mate.

The bowerbird uses discrimination in decorating his bower. He chooses his trinkets with care—selecting a bit of glass for its glitter, a shiny leaf for its natural elegance, a cobalt-blue feather for a touch of color. What does he think about as he builds and decorates? What passes through his mind as he sits and sings, advertising his availability to the world?

I have released the male and I am working on the female when I hear rattling and crashing outside the building. Something is happening in the alley between the laboratory and the nearby office building. I go down to investigate. From the mouth of the alley, I peer inside, and the male creature runs at me, startling me so that I step back. He shakes his head and rattles his teeth threateningly.

I retreat to the far side of the street and watch him from there. He ventures from the alley, scuttling along the street, then pauses by a BMW that is parked at the curb. I hear his claws rattling against metal. A hubcap clangs as it hits the pavement. The creature carries the shiny piece of metal to the mouth of the alley and then returns for the other three, removing them one by one. When I move, he rushes toward the alley, blocking any attempt to invade his territory. When I stand still, he returns to his work, collecting the hubcaps, carrying them to the alley, and arranging them so that they catch the light of the sun.

As I watch, he scavenges in the gutter and collects things he finds appealing: a beer bottle, some colorful plastic wrappers from candy bars, a length of bright yellow plastic rope. He takes each find and disappears into the alley with it.

I wait, watching. When he has exhausted the gutter near the mouth of the alley, he ventures around the corner and I make my move, running to the alley entrance and looking inside. The alley floor is covered with colored bits of paper and plastic; I can see wrappers from candy bars and paper bags from Burger King and McDonald's. The yellow plastic rope is tied to a pipe running up one wall and a protruding hook on the other. Dangling from it, like clean clothes on the clothesline, are colorful pieces of fabric: a burgundy-colored bath towel, a paisley print bedspread, a blue satin bedsheet.

I see all this in a glance. Before I can examine the bower further, I hear the rattle of claws on pavement. The creature is running at me, furious at my intrusion. I turn and flee into the laboratory, slamming the door behind me. But once I am away from the alley, the creature does not pursue me.

From the second-story window, I watch him return to the alley and I suspect that he is checking to see if I have tampered with anything. After a time, he reappears in the alley mouth and crouches there, the sunlight glittering on his metal carapace.

In the laboratory, I build the future. Oh, maybe not, but there's no one here to contradict me, so I will say that it is so. I complete the female and release her.

The sickness takes over then. While I still have the strength, I drag a cot from a back room and position it by the window, where I can look out and watch my creations.

What is it that I want from them? I don't know exactly.

I want to know that I have left something behind. I want to be sure that the world does not end with me. I want the feeling, the understanding, the certainty that the world will go on.

I wonder if the dying dinosaurs were glad to see the mammals, tiny ratlike creatures that rustled secretively in the underbrush.

When I was in seventh grade, all the girls had to watch a special presentation during gym class one spring afternoon. We dressed in our gym clothes, then sat in the auditorium and watched a film called *Becoming a Woman*. The film talked about puberty and menstruation. The accompanying pictures showed the outline of a young girl. As the film progressed, she changed into a woman, developing breasts. The animation showed her uterus as it grew a lining, then shed it, then grew another. I remember watching with awe as the pictures showed the ovaries releasing an egg that united with a sperm, and then lodged in the uterus and grew into a baby.

The film must have delicately skirted any discussion of the source of the sperm, because I remember asking my mother where the sperm came from and how it got inside the woman. The question made her very uncomfortable. She muttered something about a man and woman being in love—as if love were somehow all that was needed for the sperm to find its way into the woman's body.

After that discussion, it seems to me that I was always a little confused about love and sex—even after I learned about the mechanics of sex and what goes where. The penis slips neatly into the vagina—but where does the love come in? Where does biology leave off and the higher emotions begin?

Does the female pseudoscorpion love the male when their dance is done? Does the male spider love his mate as he scurries away, running for his life? Is there love among the bowerbirds as they copulate in their bower? The textbooks fail to say. I speculate, but I have no way to get the answers.

My creatures engage in a long, slow courtship. I am getting sicker. Sometimes, my mother comes to ask me questions that I will not answer. Sometimes, men sit by my bed—but they are less real than my mother. These are men I cared about—men I thought I might love, though I never got beyond the thought. Through their translucent bodies, I can see the laboratory walls. They never were real, I think now.

Sometimes, in my delirium, I remember things. A dance back at college; I was slow-dancing, with someone's body pressed close to mine. The room was hot and stuffy and we went outside for some air. I remember he kissed me, while one hand stroked my breast and the other fumbled with the buttons of my blouse. I kept wondering if this was love—this fumbling in the shadows.

In my delirium, things change. I remember dancing in a circle with someone's hands clasping mine. My feet ache, and I try to stop, but my partner pulls me along, refusing to release me. My feet move instinctively in time with my partner's, though there is no music to help us keep the beat. The air smells of dampness and mold; I have lived my life underground and I am accustomed to these smells.

Is this love?

I spend my days lying by the window, watching through the dirty glass. From the mouth of the alley, he calls to her. I did not give him a voice, but he calls in his own way, rubbing his two front legs together so that metal rasps against metal, creaking like a cricket the size of a Buick.

She strolls past the alley mouth, ignoring him as he charges toward her, rattling his teeth. He backs away, as if inviting her to follow. She walks by. But then, a moment later, she strolls past again and the scene repeats itself. I understand that she is not really oblivious to his attention. She is simply taking her time, considering her situation. The male intensifies his efforts, tossing his head as he backs away, doing his best to call attention to the fine home he has created.

I listen to them at night. I cannot see them—the electricity failed two days ago and the streetlights are out. So I listen in the darkness, imagining. Metal legs rub together to make a high creaking noise. The sail on the male's back rattles as he unfolds it, then folds it, then unfolds it again, in what must be a sexual display. I hear a spiked tail rasping over a spiny back in a kind of caress. Teeth chatter against metal—love bites, perhaps. (The lion bites the lioness on the neck when they mate, an act of aggression that she accepts as affection.) Claws scrape against metal hide, clatter over metal scales. This, I think, is love. My creatures understand love.

I imagine a cock made of copper tubing and pipe fittings sliding into a canal lined with sheet metal from a soda can. I hear metal sliding over metal. And then my imagination fails. My construction made no provision for the stuff of reproduction: the sperm, the egg. Science failed me there. That part is up to the creatures themselves.

My body is giving out on me. I do not sleep at night; pain keeps me awake. I hurt everywhere, in my belly, in my breasts, in my bones. I have given up food. When I eat, the pains increase for a while, and then I vomit. I cannot keep anything down, and so I have stopped trying.

When the morning light comes, it is gray, filtering through the haze that covers the sky. I stare out the window, but I can't see the male. He has abandoned his post at the mouth of the alley. I watch for an hour or so, but the female does not stroll by. Have they finished with each other?

I watch from my bed for a few hours, the blanket wrapped around my shoulders. Sometimes, fever comes and I soak the blanket with my sweat. Sometimes, chills come, and I shiver under the blankets. Still, there is no movement in the alley.

It takes me more than an hour to make my way down the stairs. I can't trust my legs to support me, so I crawl on my knees, making my way across the room like a baby too young to stand upright. I carry the blanket with me, wrapped around my shoulders like a cape. At the top of the stairs, I rest, then I go down slowly, one step at a time.

The alley is deserted. The array of hubcaps glitters in the dim sunlight. The litter of bright papers looks forlorn and abandoned. I step cautiously into the entrance. If the male were to rush me now, I would not be able to run away. I have used all my reserves to travel this far.

The alley is quiet. I manage to get to my feet and shuffle forward through the papers. My eyes are clouded, and I can just make out the dangling bedspread halfway down the alley. I make my way to it. I don't know why I've come here. I suppose I want to see. I want to know what has happened. That's all.

I duck beneath the dangling bedspread. In the dim light, I can see a doorway in the brick wall. Something is hanging from the lintel of the door.

I approach cautiously. The object is gray, like the door behind it. It has a peculiar, spiraling shape. When I touch it, I can feel a faint vibration inside, like the humming of distant equipment. I lay my cheek against it and I can hear a low-pitched song, steady and even.

When I was a child, my family visited the beach and I spent hours exploring the tidepools. Among the clumps of blue-black mussels and the black turban snails, I found the egg casing of a horn shark in a tidepool. It was spiral-shaped, like this egg, and when I held it to the light, I could see a tiny embryo inside. As I watched, the embryo twitched, moving even though it was not yet truly alive.

LOVE AND SEX AMONG THE INVERTEBRATES

* * *

I crouch at the back of the alley with my blanket wrapped around me. I see no reason to move—I can die here as well as I can die anywhere. I am watching over the egg, keeping it safe.

Sometimes, I dream of my past life. Perhaps I should have handled it differently. Perhaps I should have been less cautious, hurried out on the mating line, answered the song when a male called from his bower. But it doesn't matter now. All that is gone, behind us now.

My time is over. The dinosaurs and the humans—our time is over. New times are coming. New types of love. I dream of the future, and my dreams are filled with the rattle of metal claws.

This is a story about sex and love and death and evolution. I'm struck sometimes by the limited view that many people seem to take of evolution. Many people seem to regard *Homo sapiens* as the final word, the obvious end point of millennia of evolutionary change. When speculating about future changes in our species, people often predict changes that push us farther down the path we have already taken. The man of the future characteristically has an enormous forehead to accommodate his tremendous brain. Unfortunately, looking at the past provides no clues about the shape of the future. Dinosaurs, looking back on their past successes, might have predicted that their descendants would sport better armor and larger bodies.

Years ago, the essays of Loren Eisley, noted anthropologist and naturalist, made me aware of how foolish and limiting such a view of evolution really is. The forces that brought about the opposable thumb and the upright stance are with us still; the changes haven't stopped. The future is coming and we really don't know what it will look like.

PAT MURPHY